ETERNIUM

Published by Silvettica 2024

FIRST EDITION

http://www.authorkevincox.com/

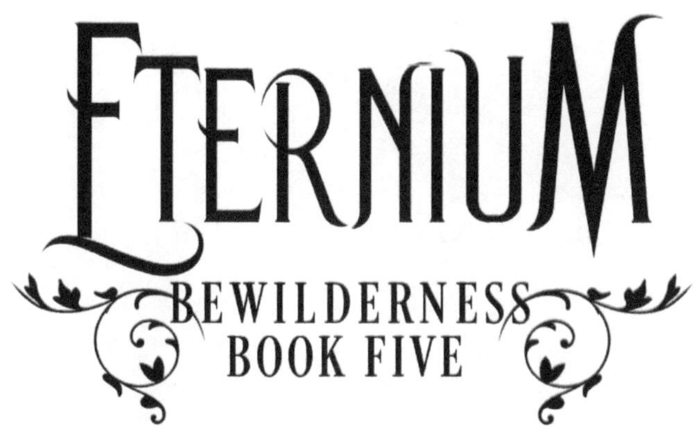

KEVIN COX

JOIN MY NEWSLETTER AND GET A FREE BOOK!

Get my short story, Elyravess, free whenyou sign up to my newsletter at https://authorkevincox.com

The newsletter will give you monthly updates on upcoming books in my next series, behind the scenes, and artwork!

In ancient Elyravess, a young boy's chance encounter with the daughter of a galactic archaeologist leads to a discovery that will alter the course of their future and the fate of their worlds.

CHAPTER 1

Malidora—Solsellion

Streaks of dark yellow energy crackled through the air, searing a scorching trail along Malidora's cheek. Swiftly reacting, she sought refuge behind a meticulously placed mound of sculpted rock. A gentle vibration resonated from her left side, coaxing her gaze. Although mostly dormant since her arrival on Solsellion, the nyalith shard she had acquired from Kandom bristled through her vest with a vivid green glow.

Veridius sprinted past her, activating his new silbrace. In an instant, a shield of shimmering translucent energy materialized, enveloping her. Veridius deftly adjusted his wrist, causing the shield to rotate and expand, providing maximum coverage. The once-transparent barrier transformed into selectively opaque sections. Veridius skillfully manipulated its configuration, seamlessly adapting to the assault while the relentless energy blasts continued to pummel the shield.

"I'm okay!" Malidora shouted at him. "Go help the others!"

Veridius cast her a lingering look before darting through the sporadic bursts of energy toward another area of concentrated blasts. Sidaire and Kazial had entered the range of the attackers and started to take fire. Peeking over the rocks, Malidora observed the black robes of their attackers, which fluttered in the wind. With faces veiled by the shadow of their dark hoods, they almost resembled Nulthereals. However, these foes were tangible, physical beings.

She loaded an arrow into her crossbow. This unexpected conflict proved to be an unwelcome distraction from their primary mission—locating the woman Malidora had communed with through the nyalith on Kandom and awakening her. Neristara seemed to possess vast knowledge of the Shadows and the Gaith, holding the key to a plan that could defeat them and save the universe. In this quest, Malidora glimpsed a pathway to redemption, a chance to mend the fractured pieces of her past.

With her finger on the trigger, Malidora lined up her shot and released the arrow into the group of cloaked assailants. Despite missing her intended target, the arrow found its mark on one to the left, causing the dark being to collapse onto the sand. She ducked beneath the rock as two sizzling blasts came her way, chipping and scorching into the stone just above her head.

When she raised her head enough for a look, Malidora spotted the group coming toward her. She looked down at the new silbrace on her wrist. It had not been easy to activate the new abilities in normal circumstances, but now with the pressure of the battle around her, it was even more difficult to focus.

Darby moved into a position to her right, swiftly notching an arrow in her bow. Her silbrace glowed with red light as she aimed at the incoming attackers. Five gleaming metal bolts levitated around her silbrace, poised and ready for action. With a determined release, Darby's arrow soared through the air, trailed closely by the hovering projectiles. The bolts spread out in a graceful, flared formation, seeking any target in their path. The first target fell with a resounding thud as Darby's arrow found its mark. Shortly after, two more adversaries dropped to the ground from the barrage of metallic bolts.

Malidora strained to focus while the rest of the group continued to bear down on her. Though she attempted to envision her silbrace activating one of its abilities, all she could think about was loading arrow after arrow into her crossbow, hoping to down all the attackers before their energy blasts found her. The sand around her darkened as their bodies blotted out the low-hanging sun, and she could hear their odd screeching breaths growing louder as they approached.

Closing her eyes, she steeled herself for either death or the concentration needed to initiate the silbrace. Blocking out all the chaos, Malidora harnessed the power of her silbrace, feeling its warm energy flow over her body. When she opened her eyes, her arms and even her crossbow had vanished into the surroundings.

As the attackers closed in, Malidora utilized her repulsor boots to leap high, somersaulting away from the rocks. The enemy fanned out around both sides of the rock formation, confused when they found nothing. She was completely invisible to them—the cloaking ability in the silbrace actually worked.

Moving silently behind them, Malidora readied another arrow, safely hitting another enemy. The sound and angle of the arrow made them turn in her direction, but they could see nothing. Darby fired a second barrage, taking three more down while Malidora picked off another.

Having dispatched the assailants with Darby, Malidora hastened across the desert sand toward the others still engaged in combat. Dexius's silbrace projected a small, compact shield, enabling him to take aim with unwavering focus. He fired one arrow, and, without breaking his stance, levitated another arrow to his silbrace, allowing him to immediately set the next one for firing. His arrows briskly dispatched two of the dark foes before they could find shelter. The projectiles reversed their course, gracefully returning to his awaiting silbrace, poised for another round of strikes.

As the unyielding onslaught of energy beams persisted from the remaining dark figures, Malidora exploited her concealed vantage point, launching projectiles with lethal swiftness. Amid the chaotic battle, Ambrielle's healing prowess came to the fore, her regenerative beam quickly mending Sidaire and Kazial's wounds before turning its soothing light toward Veridius. Cuts, scrapes, and burns faded away as if they were mere memories, erased by the gentle touch of her silbrace.

The strength of the attack waned as another assailant succumbed to Gavian's blade. Gathering the few that remained, one of the dark-cloaked beings shouted a command, and they disengaged, swiftly running in the opposite direction. Gavian sprinted after them, nearly colliding with Malidora, still invisible in her concealed state.

Malidora dashed behind Gavian as the rest followed suit, nearly losing her footing on the slope of the dune. Running down, she fired an aimless arrow in hopes of slowing one of them down, but the shot missed, and the dark beings increased their speed as they climbed the next slope.

Reaching the base of the dune, Malidora took a deep breath before starting up the next one. Climbing would cost them some ground. A zooming noise reached her ears, causing her to stop and turn around. Syra'Dosa piloted the hovering glyvex behind them, coming to a halt as they all climbed aboard. Malidora deactivated her stealth ability to ensure they saw her. Once everyone sat down, the glyvex took off, effortlessly gliding up the slope of the dune.

They reached the dried-up spring where Malidora and Veridius had escaped Kandom through The Hollow. As they pursued their adversaries through the dead oasis, one of the cloaked beings suddenly vanished. One by one they all began to disappear.

Syra'Dosa brought the glyvex to a stop, and they all disembarked, scanning the area for signs of the enemy. The nyalith shard warmed against Malidora's side as she followed the footprints in the sand. The tracks converged at the same spot and then abruptly ended in a large, distorted bubble that seemed out of place.

"Wait," Kazial said, creeping around her, his gaze fixed on the air in front of her. His eyes narrowed in concentration. "Don't go any further. Something isn't right."

"There is only one akreum on this planet," Wegin said, spinning in place. "However, this world deviates significantly from the solisphere parameters we were provided."

Malidora couldn't hide her frustration any longer. She crossed her arms, the nyalith shard in her bag casting sporadic glows on her face. "What am I waiting for exactly?"

"Neristara must be within that akreum, if only I could pinpoint its location," Wegin articulated, emitting a series of subtle beeps while deftly manipulating his spherical body.

Ambrielle circled around the bubble. "It's like it's reflecting everything around it except . . ." she trailed off, her brow furrowing in puzzlement.

"Everything except us," said Darby, as she glanced curiously around the group.

Malidora, growing tired of waiting, stepped forward into the bubble.

The air in front of her thickened, cocooning around her as the sounds of nearby voices slowed down. The voices of the others became muffled, growing further and further away until she felt the air give way. It was as if she'd been inside a bubble that had suddenly burst. The sound of the wind returned.

Her surroundings had changed. Though still in a desert, the dead oasis had vanished. Malidora found herself in a rocky basin surrounded by cliffs and distant mountains. At her feet, a thin layer of sand covered hard terrain where the tracks continued. Her eyes followed the tracks until she saw the cloaked beings ahead, gathered around a nyalith crystal shining with bright green light.

Malidora initiated the stealth power of her silbrace, hopefully camouflaging herself before the dark beings saw her. Behind her the air scintillated, outlining a jagged opening in the air itself, a doorway between two desert worlds. She circled the nyalith the six cloaked beings had gathered around, careful not to make a sound. The shard at her side was shaking now, as if it were drawn to the larger nyalith. If she played this right, perhaps she could take all six of the dark-cloaked beings without being hit.

As Malidora drew an arrow from her quiver, the glyvex burst through the opening. The six foes immediately fired on the glyvex, and Veridius and the others leapt from the vehicle. Dexius and Darby spread out as they sent volleys of arrows at the enemy. Malidora moved unseen to the other side, sending arrows of her own into the mix. With the dark beings pinned into a triangle of death, they began to fall one by one.

Gavian summoned his lylace cord, a shimmering thread of light. With a swift and practiced motion, he ensnared one of the cloaked beings, forcefully retracting it toward him and bringing the adversary within striking distance of his gleaming blade.

Drawing a second sword, Gavian wielded a silver blade, tapping into the energy pulsating within the wounds of both the living enemies and the fallen, channeling their life essence into the sword. Once the last cloaked being died, a haunting silence descended upon the world around them. Malidora stared at him. Once Tavarian, now Gavian, more than his name had changed. He had become a vicious combatant with a killer instinct. She was proud of him, but at the same time, surprisingly mourned the loss of the innocent, naive kid she'd once known.

Realizing she was still invisible, she found Dexius distracted by the nyalith crystal in the sand up ahead. It shined bright green as streams of energy flowed out of it, ending in bubbles that distorted the landscape around them. Malidora tapped Dexius's shoulder and, once he turned around and saw nothing, turned off the stealth power and materialized. Her sudden appearance caught him off guard, causing him to jump in surprise. His hand instinctively went to the hilt of his dagger, ready to defend himself as Malidora chuckled. "Nearly scared the arrows right out of your quiver."

Dexius, still recovering from the sudden fright, couldn't help but groan. "Why, oh why, did they have to give you stealth abilities?"

"Someone has to keep you on your toes." Malidora grinned.

Ambrielle approached Gavian. "Are you sure you should still be using that weapon?"

Turning to face her, Gavian held the blade aloft, its hilt radiating a captivating green glow through the dark of the setting sun. "It's called Azravion," he replied, his voice filled with a hint of mystery.

"What does that mean?" she asked, her expression uncertain but intrigued. "And how do you know what it's called?"

A faint smile played upon Gavian's lips as he continued to observe the pulsating energy within the sword's hilt. "It . . . told me," he confessed, his tone growing more enigmatic by the moment.

Ambrielle's concern seemed to deepen, her eyes narrowing slightly. "It told you its name?" she echoed. Malidora turned her attention to their conversation, sharing some of Ambrielle's concern.

Gavian's gaze shifted from the sword to meet Ambrielle's, a mischievous glimmer dancing in his eyes. With a playful grin, he sheathed the blade, the green glow fading into obscurity. "Well, not exactly," he chuckled. "The name simply came to me. It does sound rather fearsome, though, doesn't it?"

Malidora tapped one of the bodies with her boot. The cloak around it caved in, the dried corpse turning to ash and reminding her of the desiccated corpses she had seen drained by the whidges. "Who are they?" Malidora interrupted, looking down at the cloaked corpses. The sandy grit beneath Gavian's boot scraped against the hard, rough dirt as he turned.

"They're the same kind as Pythus," he said. He kicked a small pebble away, sending it skittering across the desert floor. "And he was Ichtek."

"They were supposed to have been extinct for thousands of years," Ambrielle said as she brushed sand from her hair.

"That's a long time to be under the influence of the Gaith," said Malidora. She crouched down, running her fingers over the textured sand. "There must be more to their allegiance than that."

Darby leaned over to pick up an object lying in the sand near the hand of one of the dead. She examined the smooth surface of the pyramid-shaped object. "What's this?"

Malidora held out her hand for Darby to give it to her. Turning it around, Malidora looked at it from all angles, but other than some abstract symbols on one side, there was nothing especially interesting about it. She handed it back to Darby, who took it over to Wegin and Syra'Dosa.

Sidaire wandered close by. "This place." Her eyes widened as she stared at the world around her. "This is what Solsellion used to be."

"Minus all the people, animals, and vegetation," Kazial said.

Sidaire rested her hands on her hips. "Yes, I mean after the Nulthereals came."

"If this is Solsellion,"—Ambrielle's glance moved from the nyalith to Sidaire—"where were we before?"

"It was also Solsellion," said Sidaire. "But even with all the vegetation gone, the repetitive landmarks like the springs never made sense."

"This is a different version of the world?" asked Darby as she surveyed the landscape around her. "Inside of itself?"

"I'm reading an incredible amount of energy in this area." Syra'Dosa made her way toward the nyalith. "I've only seen energy readings like this once before," she said, examining the crystal closely. "It was the only other dead spring we've discovered so far. The Nulvarians' main objective is to drain worlds of organic energy, so it's highly likely that this crystal contains the energy they collected from Kandom."

Malidora's eyes widened in disbelief. "They're storing it here? All of it? Inside this nyalith?"

The nyalith taunted Malidora, standing as a monument to her failure. She had tried desperately to save Kandom from destruction at the hands of the Gaith. Malidora gazed down at the repulsor boots she wore. Evala had offered them to Malidora before her demise. For a brief moment, the memory of the coarse skin of Dabradan's hand was so clear she could feel it. The only soul she managed to save from the ruins of Kandom was Veridius, who now carried the weight of a lost legacy.

"That seems to be the case," Syra'Dosa replied.

Malidora clenched her fists. "We can't let them have it." This was all that remained of those she could not save: Evala, Dabradan, Ravetaria, and the other Vogus.

Malidora glanced ahead where the nyalith stood. Arcs of lights poured out from it, ending in bubbles that distorted the landscape in the same way the entrance portal had. The shard in her pouch vibrated more strongly.

Removing it from the pouch, Malidora held the shard in her palm, watching it flash momentarily with light at random intervals.

"What is that?" Ambrielle asked when she noticed the jagged piece in her hand. Malidora stepped through the sand toward the nyalith. The grains clung to her boots, creating a soft, gritty resistance as she moved. "It's a piece of a nyalith crystal from Kandom, the one through which I spoke to Neristara. She told me to bring it here."

"Gavian and I saw some of those on Isodonia," Ambrielle said, as the wind swept through the desert, carrying with it a faint whistling sound that mixed with the distant murmur of shifting sand. "We were able to communicate through them."

This was no time for chatting. Malidora wanted to see what it would do if she brought it closer to the large, crooked crystal rising from the sand. She continued slowly toward the nyalith crystal, keeping her eye on the shard as it quivered in her hand. The shadows from the surrounding rocks played on the ground, creating a dance of fleeting shapes that mirrored her uncertainty.

"Are you sure that thing is safe?" Sidaire said. Her voice cut through the ambient sounds, sharp and concerned.

"I've never seen one act like that." Ambrielle's words lingered in the air, but Malidora barely noticed.

Malidora tried to ignore them so she could focus. If something went wrong, she might only have a split second to take action.

"Malidora . . ." Sidaire's voice persisted. The gentle rustle of fabric accompanied her approach, the sound muffled by the soft sand beneath their feet.

Malidora turned around. "I don't care!" she said, unable to contain her frustration. "You'll never get anywhere playing it safe." She resumed her path toward the nyalith as a stream of light shot from the nyalith toward her. The other streams surrounding the large crystal dissipated, leaving a single beam of light that found the shard in her hands.

The bright energy poured into the shard as the nyalith dimmed. Soon the green light in the large nyalith crystal disappeared, turning it into a gray stone. But the shard in her hand now shined with a brilliant, nearly blinding light. The bubbles distorting the air around them faded out.

Objects and people burned in her head as she held on to the gleaming shard. Echoes of Dabradan, Evala, Ravetaria, and others flickered in her mind, her body recoiling.

"What happened?" Ambrielle called out from behind.

"I thought I saw . . ." Malidora muttered, shaking her head to clear her mind. "People I knew on Kandom. Those who died even before the Gaith destroyed the world." She rubbed her finger over the surface of the bright shard and placed the shard back into her pouch. The searing light was so bright it shined through the cloth material.

Syra'Dosa interjected, "I'm detecting massive energy readings emanating from your crystal, highly concentrated and unstable."

"Massive energy readings . . ." Wegin remarked. Even with his modulated voice there was a certain tone of condescension. "Even the humans' basic sensory capabilities could have picked that up."

"Taking that energy from the crystal, you closed up all the pathways to get back to the version of the planet we were in," said Dexius as he stared at her. "Are we any closer to finding this Neristara?"

"I have told you what I know," said Malidora. She began to feel her grief welling up inside her again as she thought of Dabradan and Evala. "I thought by coming back to the place where Veridius and I escaped we might find something. Something we missed."

Gavian's eyes narrowed at her. "There must be something, some clue or hint that Neristara gave you. Something that can guide us to find her."

Their accusing glances made Malidora's frustration boil over, and she couldn't keep the sharp biting tone from her words. "All she said was to find the awakener and bring them to her," she huffed, her breath heavy with annoyance. "She wanted me to take this"—Malidora patted the shard that was shining through her bag—"the shard of the nyalith that we spoke through. She said it was charged more than usual."

"Now that you bring it up"—Wegin emitted a soft hum—"I observe that the version of the planet we are in now aligns with the parameters of the solisphere."

"So where is it?" Malidora's attention rushed toward Wegin. "Where do we find Neristara?"

CHAPTER 2

Ambrielle—True Solsellion

Under the boundless expanse of a sky teeming with possibilities, Ambrielle observed Wegin projecting the solisphere of Solsellion. Eager anticipation filled the air as Malidora and the others waited, their eyes fixed on the rotating, three-dimensional holographic map. Gavian, Sidaire, and Dexius huddled together, attempting to orient themselves within the image of the solisphere.

Amid the collective focus on navigation, Ambrielle couldn't help but notice Veridius standing alone, his gaze fixed on the dormant nyalith. The once-vibrant crystal had turned gray, its energy now transferred to Malidora's shard. Veridius's white hair gently swayed in the tranquil breeze as he stood in silent thought.

A surge of emotions welled up within Ambrielle as her thoughts traversed the worlds they had saved and the people she loved. She could imagine Veridius yearning for a world now lost—a world of forgotten beauty. It stirred a profound sadness within her that evoked memories of the emotions she'd grappled with after her mother's passing.

With a tentative step, Ambrielle approached Veridius, sensing an unspoken need for comfort. Yet, words eluded her. The lingering fear of the unknown nestled within her heart, a silent reminder of the persistent darkness intruding on their journey. Despite the trials she had overcome, Ambrielle grappled with the question of how to persist in the face of an ever-encroaching shadow, the weight of the unseen future pressing upon her.

Even as it crept toward the horizon, the crimson sun beat down upon the unforgiving desert. Despite the time it took the sun to move across the sky, the coming night would be long. The scent of dry sand and decaying vegetation permeated the thick air, as if the desert itself was slowly withering away. The wind moaned mournfully, as if grieving for the dying world. The sky, which only a moment ago was boundless, now hung overhead like a shroud.

While Ambrielle had always harbored a deep-seated affinity for exploration and the thrill of adventure, a sense of overwhelming dread of what lay ahead washed over her. The very idea of turning back and retreating to the safety of her former life clawed at her thoughts. Yet, her steadfast devotion to Gavian and the rest of the group held her in place. She couldn't bear to repeat the mistakes of the past, to abandon them as she had once abandoned her responsibilities on Earth. Her thoughts echoed with the idea of days that didn't involve constant upheaval, a return to a life less fraught with uncertainty. A life she could envision sharing with Gavian, where the simple joys of companionship and familiarity could take root and flourish.

"Are you all right?" said Veridius. He looked back at her with curiosity in his eyes as she snapped out of the daydream. "You have that faraway look in your eyes, like you wish you were anywhere but here."

"Just thinking," Ambrielle confessed, her voice carrying the weight of countless uncertainties. "Sometimes it seems like the more we accomplish, the further we are away." Their eyes met briefly, allowing her a glimpse of the inner turmoil he carried. "I should be the one asking if you're okay," she told him.

Veridius sighed. "It's rather difficult to process," he said with a hint of vulnerability in his voice. "I don't even know where to begin. I can't really comprehend that the land I stood on my whole life is now gone." He glanced at Ambrielle and then looked straight ahead. "Truthfully, I rarely stepped on the surface of Kandom. I was always on the ringed towers, believing that I was too good for my feet to touch the ground. Now I would give anything to walk on that soil again."

"We all take things for granted," said Ambrielle. "There are certain things we grow to expect every day. The world you live on being one of them. I guess you start by mourning the friends that you lost."

She hadn't talked to Veridius much to this point. He had an air of confidence about him that intimidated Ambrielle a bit. His regal clothing only made it worse.

Veridius's bright orange eyes stared at the muddy spot in the basin. "I don't think I really had any friends. Not real friends anyway. Those around me only wanted to share in my influence."

"So, you were someone of importance there," Ambrielle said. "What did you do?"

"My father was thercon of the city of Vesta," said Veridius. "My only importance was being his son, which made me next in line."

Impressed, Ambrielle remarked, "So you're like a prince! I've never met a real prince before."

Veridius smiled wryly, a hint of sorrow in his eyes. "My father is gone. I suppose that makes me thercon now. For all the good that is. Thercon of a fallen city."

"I know this won't bring much comfort at this moment," said Ambrielle, "but there are many worlds out there. Maybe you will find a new home among them. We have to protect as many as we can from the Gaith."

"I spent my entire life learning things that would make me an effective ruler, how to influence others. I don't know where I would fit in somewhere else," Veridius said. "Perhaps it is for the best. I wanted to change the world and make a difference, but the politics, the title, they got in the way of helping anyone."

"You don't need power to make a difference." Ambrielle's voice softened. "You can be a leader anywhere you go. You can help us stop the Shadows and make a difference for worlds all across the universe."

Veridius's eyes met hers, and for a moment, a glimmer of hope shined through the pain. "You're right, I'll do anything I can to help."

Ambrielle glanced at his blackened hand. It didn't seem to match up with his clothing and had a strange, uneven texture. "What happened to your hand?"

Veridius raised his hand in front of his face as if he had forgotten it was there. "Shadowstone," he said. "I held on to one of Malidora's arrows when we entered The Hollow. Apparently, it saved us from losing our identities to the Gaith, becoming nothing more than a mind, processing the thoughts between them."

"I was once taken to The Hollow," said Ambrielle. "But I didn't lose my mind."

"Did you have those boots on at the time?" Veridius glanced down at her feet.

"Yes, I did actually," said Ambrielle, looking down at the boots that Corthian on Anatharia had made for her. "Why do you ask?"

Veridius pointed at the heels of her boots. "This look like shadowstone."

"No, it's"—Ambrielle stopped, remembering that mekkadium was another word for shadowstone—"Oh, you're right. It is shadowstone."

"That is how you remained free in The Hollow," said Veridius. This new information set Ambrielle's mind ablaze. She'd had no idea these boots had been what protected her all along.

They both returned to the group as Sidaire's eyes wandered along the translucent projection of the planet. "This mountain could be Mabendoga, but I can't say for sure."

"That's better than anything we've had to go on so far," Malidora said. "How far away is this Mabendoga?"

"How am I supposed to know?" said Sidaire. "I've never seen the world represented like this."

Malidora slumped her shoulders, a sigh escaping her lips. "Can we get someone over here that knows anything?"

Malidora's demeanor didn't escape Ambrielle's notice. A sense of exasperation gnawed at her, a growing impatience with Malidora's seemingly perpetual negativity. Despite the undeniable need for Malidora's involvement in awakening Neristara, her persistent belief that she would fare better alone grated on Ambrielle's nerves.

The sunlight filtered through the stone, bathing Gavian's face in a green hue. "Did Neristara mention anything about what to do with it?" he asked, his tone gentle yet hopeful.

Malidora's frustration flared once again. She lowered the stone. "Did you not hear me earlier?" she snapped, her words laced with irritation. "She didn't tell me anything!"

Ambrielle eyed Malidora with contempt. With everything Gavian had said, she'd little trust in her. But now she was testing Ambrielle's patience.

"According to this, it should be around .0278 cells ahead," said Syra'Dosa.

"What do you mean by cells?" Veridius asked.

"The distance I can travel before requiring a new energy cell," Syra'Dosa explained. "But I lack Avo'Doria's strength. I am unable to carry passengers while flying."

Wegin hovered close to Ambrielle as they climbed back into the glyvex. Syra'Dosa piloted the craft along the newly varied terrain. Zooming over a small winding river carved into the rocky surface, they headed toward a group of tall stone formations on the horizon. Though this original version of Solsellion would be somewhat familiar to Sidaire and Kazial, it was completely foreign to Ambrielle. She had only known the endless loop of the echo version.

Mounds of rugged rocks loomed majestically, their imposing presence overseeing the enchanting rock pools below. Waterfalls cascaded down the weathered cliff faces, their ethereal streams intermingling with the pristine waters of the pools. Atop these formidable mounds stood dwellings made with a blend of natural materials and artistic craftsmanship. They blended seamlessly with the surrounding environment, their natural hues harmonizing with the reddish tones of the rock. Sturdy wooden platforms connected the dwellings, creating a network of pathways between the stone.

However, amid the grandeur, dark tendrils of defiling shadows marred the once-vibrant landscape. The scenic village, now cloaked in a shroud of eerie stillness, seemed frozen in time, as if the very essence of life had been snuffed out. Thick sludge oozed from the remains of once-lush ferns and towering trees whose majestic forms had been reduced to decaying remnants. The vibrant pulse of nature had receded, leaving behind a desolate emptiness, broken only by the haunting whispers of the wind.

Ambrielle closed her eyes, seeking solace in her imagination as she tried to resurrect the village's former beauty. She envisioned sunlight filtering through a tapestry of vibrant greenery, illuminating rocks adorned with delicate mosses and cascading vines. The air was alive with the melodic symphony of birdsong, and a gentle mist rose from the tranquil rock pools, embracing the homes of the villagers. In her mind's eye, she saw the joyful bustle of daily life, children playing near the water's edge, and the inhabitants moving gracefully through their routines.

"This place brings back memories," Sidaire murmured.

Ambrielle turned to her. "Was this your village?"

Sidaire shook her head gently. "No, it is Kuvuala, a village that was very far from my own. I came here once with a group of elders to trade. They would go once every dawnrise season when the sun had moved above the horizon." Sidaire's hair trailed back as she turned into the wind. "We trusted the people here, before the Nulthereals came."

"The Nulthereals controlled them?" Dexius asked.

Sidaire nodded her head. "The people of Kuvuala, like those in many other villages, began to argue with everyone around them. The arguing turned to violence. Violence turned to war.

"What was your village like before this happened?" Dexius asked.

Sidaire turned toward him, the breeze billowing her hair around her face. "I lived in Ashantara," she said. "It was a simple place, surrounded by jungle. We had one large temple made from bricks of hardened mud, but everything else was straw."

"Sounds like a nice place," said Dexius.

Sidaire grinned. "It wasn't that special compared to some of the other villages," she said. "But it was home."

A determined smile graced Ambrielle's lips as she spoke softly. "One day," she said, her gaze sweeping across the desecrated landscape, "we will reclaim this place and this world will be restored to its former beauty."

"I hope so," said Sidaire. "But it will never be the same without the people, my family."

Ambrielle offered a sympathetic nod. "Hopefully, you'll find them too," she said. Yet, as the words left her lips, a flicker of doubt crossed her mind. How could the few of them stand against such an unstoppable force? To the Gaith, they were nothing more than bacteria.

The glyvex soared past the village and into a forest of rotting trees. The wood and foliage stood like black candles, dripping thick liquid as the last bits of life escaped them. Petrified creatures lay covered by the black death, barely more than skeletons.

As they moved out of the blighted forest, Syra'Dosa guided them toward a high, sloping mountain ahead. Drawing closer, the first signs of life faced them. Living trees towered above them, their trunks made of dark yellow bark marked with hard, cone-shaped divots. The branches of these peculiar trees were twisted and gnarled, reaching out in all directions like grasping fingers. Their leaves were enormous, each one as big as Ambrielle's head. Shimmering with a mesmerizing blue sheen, they seemed to dance and flicker in the remaining light.

"I remember these trees," Kazial remarked. "This is one of the forests we recently helped to grow beyond the oasis."

"It appears the trees flourished on both sides of this reality," Sidaire replied.

"Maybe there is still hope," said Ambrielle.

"This is it," Wegin said, displaying the projected solisphere. "According to the coordinates, Neristara should be right here."

"I was right," said Sidaire as she stared up at the mountain. "This is Mabendoga."

Ambrielle stepped off the glyvex behind Dexius and Darby. They approached the base of the mountain, but there was no immediate sign of an akreum. Malidora walked up to the stone side of the mountain, grazing her hand along its surface. The group spread out in different directions, hoping to find a sign of some kind.

"This may be something!" shouted Veridius as he tugged at the rock formations in front of him.

Ambrielle and a few others made their way around the stone wall to where Veridius worked to open a thin crevasse between the stones. Given the engulfing darkness within, it was evident that there was a modest hollow within the side of the mountain. Shoving her bladestaff into the gap, Ambrielle tried to pry the opening wider. Gavian pulled her back as the stone shifted and triggered a cascade of rocks from above.

Breathing a mixture of relief and exertion, Ambrielle leaned against Gavian, her eyes locking with his in a silent request for a kiss. Responding to her unspoken desire, he obliged, their lips meeting in a brief but passionate moment. They quickly turned their attention back to their discovery as the others rolled the stones out of the way of the opening.

Sidaire peeked into the opening, but Malidora fearlessly brushed past her into the dark interior. Gavian followed her as Ambrielle clung to the fabric of his garment. They powered on the lights of their silbraces, revealing a narrow path through the interior of the mountain.

They entered a spacious chamber, bathed in Ambrielle's light that reflected off the smooth white surface of the textured stone. Marked by strange and otherworldly symbols, the surface of the akreum echoed the distinctive patterns Ambrielle had observed on Cereveshian akreums during her time on Anatharia and Isodonia. For a fleeting moment, a surge of excitement overshadowed her doubts, propelling her toward the akreum. However, her anticipation came to an abrupt halt as Malidora swiftly reached it before her. Ambrielle rolled her eyes.

Syra'Dosa paused in front of the akreum, her optical sensors scanning its intricate design. "It appears that accessing the contents of this material requires an alternative approach," she remarked with a slightly metallic voice. Her silbrace activated and a vibrant red laser emanated from her wrist, meticulously tracing an opening into the vault. Despite the precision of her laser, the etched marks on the material gradually dissipated, as if defying the laws of conventional physics. "Intriguing," Syra'Dosa noted.

"It can't be opened like that," Ambrielle remarked, extending her hand toward the akreum. "The material is unbreakable." With a series of encrypted sounds, her silbrace played a five-note melody. The combination of exact frequencies and tones caused the vault to change shape, revealing a perfect opening on the side they were facing.

Malidora and the others gathered around the opened vault, marveling at Ambrielle's expertise. "Now what was that all about?" Malidora narrowed her eyes as she looked at Ambrielle.

"She's the awakener," Gavian said with a grin, proudly walking next to Ambrielle.

Malidora leaned over the egg-shaped stasis chamber inside the akreum. The chamber, once clouded with pink gas, now hissed as it unsealed, releasing a peculiar odor. Eagerly, the others joined them, their eyes fixed on the dissipating pink clouds. Slowly, the form of a humanoid face emerged from within.

The Cereveshians, known for their flat noses and orange skin speckled with white spots, all shared a similar appearance. This particular one, with feminine features and long white hair, stood out among the rest. While the Cereveshians that Ambrielle had seen had a youthful appearance after millennia in stasis, the passage of time had etched wrinkles of old age onto this individual's face. Perhaps this one had been old when she entered the chamber.

The Cereveshian's body jolted as she stirred from her prolonged slumber. Her eyelids fluttered open, and Gavian and Ambrielle supported her as she sat upright, experiencing the aftermath of her extended rest. With their assistance, she emerged from the chamber, her motions sluggish and unsteady. She surveyed her surroundings, coughs racking her body and making it difficult to inhale the unfamiliar air.

Even Malidora displayed patience, granting the Cereveshian ample time to regain her composure amid the disorientation. "Neristara?" Malidora whispered gently, her voice resonating within the cavern. "Do you remember me?" She held Neristara's unsteady hand. "I'm Malidora. I've brought you the shard of the nyalith from Kandom, as you requested."

The lines in Neristara's face seemed to relax. "I knew you would come," said Neristara, her voice weak.

"You certainly didn't make it easy," Malidora said. "We had to move into an alternate layer of this world to find you."

"Alternate layer?" Neristara gazed into distant focus as the lines in her forehead deepened. "Ah, it seems the Gaith have completed their energy resonance matrix."

"Completed what?" Malidora said.

Neristara squinted as she looked over everyone's faces. "And where is the awakener?"

Ambrielle waved her hand, trying to draw Neristara's attention away from Malidora. "That would be me."

Neristara's expression turned grave as she looked at Ambrielle. "You're not Cereveshian. How did you come to be the awakener?"

Ambrielle glanced at Gavian, summoning her courage before responding. "The original awakener had already passed away when we found her," she explained, gesturing toward Wegin who floated nearby. "It was Wegin here who helped transfer the code to my silbrace."

Neristara's expression shifted to one of puzzlement. "This was not included in any of the variables I've encountered. I can only speculate on how this will influence the outcome."

Seeking clarification, Malidora interjected, "Could this pose a problem?" Ambrielle's jaw tightened. If Malidora would keep quiet for a moment, maybe they could get answers. Ambrielle shot her a stern glance, a quiet plea for silence, but Malidora seemed determined to ignore her.

"That remains to be seen," Neristara replied thoughtfully. "Where are the rest of the awakened?"

Confusion etched Malidora's face. "Who would that be?"

Neristara turned her attention to Ambrielle. "The other Cereveshians you awakened?"

Ambrielle tried to express her sympathy through her voice. "They couldn't come with us. Once they left the stasis chambers, they would have died if they didn't return."

Neristara's expression slackened, revealing her disappointment. "A team was assembled precisely for this purpose, each member possessing unique skills to accomplish the mission of pushing back the Nulvarians and sealing the rifts."

"I'm afraid it is only us," said Ambrielle.

Ambrielle and the others gathered closely around Neristara, who clutched onto the stasis chamber she had just emerged from. Taking a deep breath, she seemed to gather her thoughts.

"What about Tetra'Novis?" Neristara inquired. "Has she been informed of this?"

Regret filled Ambrielle as she thought of Tetra'Novis. "I'm sorry to say, but Tetra'Novis passed away before we could fully understand the situation. She believed resting would help her regain her strength. Although without her we wouldn't have the map that led us to you."

Rubbing her forehead, Neristara gazed past them, as if lost in contemplation. "This development is both unexpected and troubling. Although the primary objective of the awakened was to reseal the rifts, I anticipated that, if the Nulvarians discovered a means to reopen them, there would be no barrier to their recurrence before we successfully repelled them. Thus,

I formulated a secondary strategy—an approach designed to grant us the time required for sealing the rifts once again."

Seeming eager to take action, Gavian chimed in, "So let's execute the plan. What's holding us back?"

CHAPTER 3

GAVIAN—TRUE SOLSELLION

GAVIAN ATTEMPTED TO discern Neristara's thoughts as he patiently awaited her response. Her head dipped, as though fixated on the cavern floor, leaving him uncertain whether she was lost in thought or had succumbed to despair. Eventually, shaking her head, Neristara replied, "I haven't finalized all the details. Solving this puzzle would demand brilliant minds specialized in specific fields to address certain questions. I'm skeptical that you possess the knowledge needed to unravel it."

Dexius chimed in, his tone brimming with confidence, "Well, you know, I'm no stranger to brilliance. Feel free to tap into this well of knowledge if you need any assistance with those pesky details."

Laughter erupted from the group. Gavian never could discern if Dexius was serious or merely attempting to break the tension when he made remarks like this. If it was the latter, it worked.

Neristara released a weary sigh, her doubts clearly reflected in her gaze. "When the Nulvarians initially emerged, we delved deep into their nature, studying them relentlessly. Understanding that they could not transport organic essence to Nulvare, we hypothesized the existence of a central hub where they stored and harnessed this essence.

"We scrutinized every piece of data we could lay our hands on, yet the precise location of this hub remained elusive," Neristara continued. "Decades passed after we successfully sealed the rifts and defeated the remaining Nulvarians. It was then that I stumbled upon the very point we had been desperately seeking—a realization that Solsellion, this planet, held the answers. Before many forms of life flourished on this world, the Nulvarians had discovered a substantial nyalith crystal stemming from the core of the planet and reaching the rift. The energies of the rift seemed to spur its growth into a crystal sizable enough to accumulate the energy from the worlds they harvested."

Neristara's determination shined through as she continued, "Utilizing the Ichtek as their intermediaries, the Gaith devised a plan to construct an energy resonance matrix. This matrix was intended to fragment the planet's rift into multiple conduits, enabling them to siphon living essence from diverse worlds across the universe. Even after closing all the rifts and eliminating the remaining Ichtek, I opted to stay, delving into the wealth of data they left behind. While my fellow Cereveshians ascended to Averess, I ensured my name was listed for awakening in the event of the Nulvarians' return. If that day came, I wanted to be present to face it here."

"You mentioned the Ichtek," said Ambrielle. "We were just attacked by a number of people in dark robes using energy beams. We believe they may have been Ichtek."

"Impossible," said Neristara. "They fiercely guarded many of the rifts. We unfortunately had to wipe them out in order to seal them. They were extinct long before I ascended to Averess."

Darby came forward holding the small black pyramid-shaped object. "One of them was carrying this."

Neristara's eyes opened wider as she took the object from Darby's hand. "These certainly are Ichtekian symbols. It looks old but somewhat familiar, probably nothing more than a data journal that has been corrupted. The more pertinent question is, how could the Ichtek have remained hidden from us? Perhaps it is not Ichtek but other followers of the Gaith doing their bidding. Either way, be cautious. If they are anything like the Ichtek, they are very dangerous."

She handed the artifact back to Darby. "Even after leaving my physical body here in this akreum, my consciousness continued observing this world from Averess. I watched the Gaith in The Hollow, studying their knowledge of time and space. They had learned how to manipulate reality, shaping dimensional space to suit their needs. Things that even we had not discovered yet. From what you said earlier about alternate layers, it seems that, by aligning nyaliths in this energy resonance matrix across this world's surface, they've fractured time and space on this planet into two parallel dimensions."

Ambrielle interjected, "You mean how there seems to be the True Solsellion we're in now, and then there's the Echo dimension?"

"Precisely," said Neristara as she rubbed the side of her neck.

"Is that why the same desert and oasis spring area is repeated across the Echo world?" Darby asked.

Neristara cleared her throat with a cough. "I suspect so. In the Echo dimension, the world repeatedly reflects one location in different spaces, in this case, an oasis spring within the same surrounding desert."

"That explains a lot," Sidaire remarked, her boots scraping against the grit along the cavern floor as she shuffled her feet. "It sounds like it does, at least."

"Fractured dimensions?" Malidora let out an exasperated sigh. "Why can't it ever be as simple as something we can shoot?"

Gavian grappled with Neristara's explanation, attempting to comprehend the concept of how these two fractures of reality worked. He had questions but didn't want to risk Neristara dismissing their ability to carry out her plan.

"In this True Solsellion, somewhere within it, would lie the same oasis and spring that are copied in the Echo dimension," Neristara continued, leaning on the egg-shaped chamber for support. "I believe that could be where you will find the apex nyalith that stems from the core. That would serve as the center point for all the others. If we can destroy that apex nyalith, it would prevent the Nulvarians from utilizing this world as a machine, a machine that would create a passage through the Savage Dark, large enough that the Gaith could pass through and gain access to other realms of the Everance. Though I do not know the specific method they would use to accomplish this, we only need to disrupt their ability to store the essence."

"So just destroy this big stone," Dexius chimed in. "That doesn't sound so hard."

Neristara's expression turned serious as she replied, "The problem is figuring out how to amplify the energy source enough to destroy an object that can contain a massive amount of energy. Even the smaller nyaliths can capture the essence of an entire celestial body, but they need to absorb energy at a particular rate to remain stable. With the right amplification, perhaps we could project enough energy fast enough to overwhelm it."

"How do we accomplish that?" Ambrielle asked.

Neristara glanced at Dexius. "This is where your 'well of knowledge' would come in," she said.

Dexius's mouth drew open, but he didn't speak. Gavian couldn't hold back the smirk on his face as Dexius looked around at everyone else for an answer.

Neristara's lips pressed together. "This is precisely why we need the expertise of specialized Cereveshians that were to be awakened. As a group, they possess the skills to locate all the breached rifts across the Severine Cluster and beyond. Destroying the apex nyalith would pose no challenge for them."

Veridius posed a question, "When Malidora and I escaped The Hollow, before we made our way up to the spring, we were inside a cavern. There was something in the dark, glowing. Was that . . . ?"

Neristara nodded in affirmation, responding, "Yes. That would be the apex nyalith."

Ambrielle brimmed with excitement. "I saw that as well, while crossing back to Solsellion, I came upon a huge underground chamber."

"When was this?" Gavian asked.

"Like Veridius said, when I managed to escape The Hollow, I found myself in a cave, and though I could barely see it in the dark, a faint light pulsated from a massive rock formation. It had roots that extended in all directions."

"Tell us what you need," Malidora said. "Where do we find someone that would know how to destroy the apex nyalith?"

"If you can't awaken the designated Cereveshians, we are doomed," Neristara declared with a furrowed brow. "I would have thought that, in the eons of time that we have been away, other beings would have continued where we left off, but none of you have any basic understanding of—"

Another fit of coughing overcame Neristara, and Ambrielle held her up to prevent her from falling.

As the coughing subsided, Neristara turned to Ambrielle and placed a reassuring hand on her shoulder. "I extend my deepest apology. Despite the numerous instances where humility should have been instilled in me over the millennia, I still find myself lacking in that virtue. There is no reason for me to doubt any of you, and particularly not the awakener," Neristara confessed with genuine sincerity. "You've encountered variables more challenging than I could have foreseen, and yet you persist unwaveringly, constantly pursuing innovative solutions." Neristara took Ambrielle's hand in hers. "The responsibility of upholding the awakener code could not have been placed in more capable hands than yours."

Ambrielle's face beamed with a sense of validation and purpose. Neristara's acknowledgment served as a powerful affirmation of her resilience and determination. Gavian too felt a resolve to press forward, no matter the obstacles that lay ahead.

"We need your council," Malidora said. "What do you think should be our next move?"

"A radical idea is brewing in my mind. The path I'm about to propose would introduce a multitude of new variables, variables I can't even begin to fathom. But when I consider the outcomes I've witnessed, none of them could be classified as outright victories. At best, they amounted to mere measures of how much we managed to avoid losing. Perhaps it's time we dared to shake things up a bit."

Malidora's mischievous smirk stretched across her face. "Well, well, sounds like my kind of idea."

"You can see the future?" Ambrielle was intrigued.

"I have seen potentialities, but the outcome is all that matters. When you look back at the universe from Averess, you see things differently," said Neristara. "The Ureons taught me to view certain events and the possible futures they contain. As I am learning now, there are more variables than I imagined."

"May we find the best future possible," said Ambrielle.

"The rifts must be closed at all costs. We need the materials and the knowledge to do this in the most efficient way possible. The Cereveshians we need to gain this knowledge are in Averess," said Neristara. "That solisphere you have holds their names. If we can't bring them to us, you must go to them. One of you will need to use my stasis chamber and allow your consciousness to ascend to Averess. Talk to the Cereveshians there and gather all the information you can. By doing this, you will have access not only to those who were to be awakened, but all Cereveshians. Find out what we need to destroy the apex nyalith. Find out the most efficient way to seal the breached rifts."

"But you won't survive here much longer," Ambrielle conveyed her concern. "It would be best if you go and come back to tell us."

"My physical body is nothing more than a weathered vessel now. I fear I may not survive another awakening," said Neristara. "And in that event, I would be unable to convey the gleaned knowledge back to you."

The somber reality weighed heavily on Ambrielle. She didn't want Neristara to die like Tetra'Novis. "So, either way you have to die?"

"My sojourn in Averess has been a profound revelation, unveiling a reality far more intricate than our mere senses perceive," Neristara shared with a reflective gaze. "The elusive concept of the Afterglow has intrigued me endlessly. The Ureons speak of it, asserting that discovery and fulfillment of one's purpose paves the path. This juncture offers the most promising opportunity for my physical body to die so that my consciousness might break free of its restraints. Then I can ascertain the truth behind these enigmatic beliefs."

"Isn't there some other way?" Ambrielle implored, yearning for a solution that wouldn't involve Neristara's sacrifice.

"The chamber has space for two," Neristara explained thoughtfully. "However, the occupants would eventually require reawakening, and, as I mentioned, I harbor doubts about my ability to endure the process of being brought back from stasis once more."

"I will go," Malidora raised her hand with a resolute expression on her face. "I feel I must see this path through to the end."

"I knew there was potential in you," Neristara acknowledged. "May you continue on your path of destiny."

Gavian noticed Ambrielle's face flushing with the heat of frustration. "But I'm the awakener," declared Ambrielle. "Shouldn't it be me?"

A smile tugged at Neristara's lips as she made a valiant effort to suppress a cough. "As I mentioned, there's room for two," she added with a hopeful gleam. "I was, in fact, hoping you might consider joining her."

"But I don't want to be the cause of you dying," said Ambrielle, the distress in her voice apparent.

"No, this is my choice," said Neristara. "I have lived far longer than I have a right to. You will come to understand that mortality is a gift. You mentioned purpose, and I am beginning to feel as though this could be mine. This is where my path in this Everance should end."

Ambrielle leaned in, enfolding Neristara in a warm embrace. The unexpected gesture caught Neristara slightly off guard, leaving her with a hint of uncertainty. "My people seldom partake in such displays of affection, but I do see how it could be pleasing," Neristara admitted, her hand giving Ambrielle's back a gentle pat.

"I hope you do see the Afterglow," Ambrielle expressed earnestly. "And I believe you will."

"I only wish that I would be able to return long enough to tell you," said Neristara.

Malidora stepped forward as her gaze shifted to her pouch, where the shard emitted a glow that pierced through the fabric. "When I spoke to you from Kandom, you asked me to take a shard of the nyalith there," said Malidora. "What did you want it for?"

"I had hoped we could use it to communicate," said Neristara, her eyes focused on Malidora. As she spoke, she absentmindedly tapped her fingers on the console. "Once the Gaith were no longer listening. But you were resourceful enough to find me anyway."

Neristara's hand moved toward a small device on the console, her fingers hovering over its projected light patterns. "Perhaps you will find another use for it one day."

Malidora started to climb into the chamber when Neristara turned to her. "Has anyone told you of the Savage Dark?" Neristara asked, her words unfolding with a measured tone.

"I've never heard of it," admitted Malidora as the confidence in her face slightly faded. "But I know the dark well."

"The other Cereveshians that I awoke mentioned the Savage Dark," Ambrielle chimed in. "They were fearful of it."

Neristara's acknowledgment was solemn. "Indeed," she confirmed with a quiet nod. "We seldom experience strong emotions, including fear, but the Savage Dark will draw it out of you."

Malidora's brow tightened. "What is the Savage Dark?"

"It's a challenge to put into words," Neristara admitted, her tone thoughtful. "Imagine an expansive void that weaves through the fabric of all realms, much like a serpent coiling through the Everance. This is what you must traverse to reach Averess. The passage you'll tread is a concentrated tunnel of essence, the sole barrier between you and the abyss. Staying within this pathway ensures your safety. Yet, be forewarned: the journey won't be a comfortable one. Despite the visions you may have or the insights your mind may contemplate, maintaining your course is paramount. The darkness holds a consciousness of its own, one that's not welcoming to visitors."

"What would happen if you left the path?" Malidora asked with curiosity and concern.

"Your consciousness would dissolve into oblivion," Neristara responded, her words deliberate and grave. "The darkness is a singular entity, an all-encompassing unity. Should you veer from the designated path and step onto it, you would meld into its very soul."

A cold shiver ran down Gavian's spine, mirroring the unease shared by the others as they exchanged murmurs. The gravity of the situation hit him hard, making him want to take Ambrielle by the hand and hold on to her to prevent her from going on this journey.

"How do we get back?" Malidora pressed on, her voice steady.

"Someone will need to open the chamber and wake your body," Neristara said.

"If I go, will anyone else be able to open it?" said Ambrielle.

"You've already unlocked the akreum." Neristara coughed. "As long as it is kept that way, anyone will be able to open it."

Malidora turned to Ambrielle, lifting her eyebrows as if she wasn't sure how she would answer. "You ready to do this?"

"I'm ready," Ambrielle replied.

Gavian leaned near, trying to keep his fears from being evident in his voice. "Ambrielle, are you absolutely certain you want to go?"

Ambrielle placed her palms on both of Gavian's shoulders, looking into his eyes with a sense of conviction. "Gavian, trust me when I say that this is the path I am meant to follow. From the moment we met in Anatharia, I felt a deep sense of purpose, as if all the roads I've traveled have led me to this moment."

Gavian grew uneasy, shifting his gaze toward Malidora, aware that her loyalty wavered when her personal desires took precedence. "But why does she have to go with you? If it's as dangerous as Neristara says, she's the last person I trust."

Malidora crossed her arms defensively, standing her ground. "Before you start trying to talk me out of it, let me make one thing clear: I couldn't care less whether you like it or not—I am going."

As anger swelled within him, the silver sword strapped to his back seemed to stir, attuned to the nascent conflict and amplifying the raw intensity of his emotions. Despite absorbing the life essence of the Ichtek they had battled earlier, the sword's hunger remained insatiable. Gavian's hand tightened around the hilt, pulling the sword free of its sheath with a swift flash of silver and green. His voice adopted a more aggressive tone, and fiery resolve blazed in his eyes. "You don't get to decide everything! Your presence only adds to the danger."

Undeterred by his threat, Malidora remained composed, her voice steady. "And what exactly do you think I'm going to do?"

Gavian advanced the blade, bringing its tip nearer to Malidora. The sword seemed to tremble with delight, as if eagerly anticipating the chance to consume her essence. "You once held a knife to my throat. You killed a group of bandits just for their docimare. You would do anything to further your cause."

Malidora's tone became somber. "You're right. I can't justify all the things I've done. I was always told to be the hammer, not the nail, but I've come to realize that redemption lies in becoming the nail. It's about supporting and protecting those around me, becoming the shield that guards and defends. I don't want to be what I once was anymore. I refuse to let anyone else suffer the way I have. Like Ambrielle said, I've discovered my purpose, and I'm determined to see it through till the very end."

Her words reminded Gavian of the goodness he had always sensed buried deep in Malidora's heart. The sincerity of her tone eased the burning in his mind. His mouth twitched side to side as he debated what she'd said. "How do I know this isn't one of your lies?"

"If anyone can guide her through the darkness, it is Malidora," Veridius said, stepping forward. He gestured for both Gavian and Malidora to take a step away from each other, spreading his palms.

"She saved Kazial and me from the mindstream," said Sidaire. "If it were me going, Malidora would be my first choice."

Kazial nodded his head. "I have to agree."

Gavian lowered the sword and turned to Ambrielle. "It's not too late to change your mind," he told her. She wore a wide-eyed look of concern as she gazed back at him. "I need to do this," Ambrielle said softly, pressing a gentle kiss on Gavian's cheek. "I hope you will understand."

Gavian returned his focus to Malidora, the hunger of the blade still invading his thoughts as he spoke, "I'm counting on you to keep her safe."

Meeting his gaze with unwavering confidence, Malidora replied, "I'll be there for Ambrielle every step of the way. We're in this together. We'll need each other to overcome this Savage Dark." Gavian's features relaxed as the fire in his eyes faded.

As much as Gavian knew Ambrielle didn't care for Malidora, she appeared reassured by her words. Ambrielle turned her attention back to Neristara, her voice resolute. "We will do our best to make your sacrifice meaningful."

A faint smile touched Neristara's lips. "I know you will."

With a nod, Malidora climbed into the stasis chamber, settling herself into a comfortable position. Gavian gently brushed strands of hair from the side of Ambrielle's cheek. "It feels as if we've always been together," he murmured. "I can't even remember how I got along before you. I won't know what to do with myself without you here."

Ambrielle nodded. "I know what you mean. Maybe you could come up with a way to destroy the apex nyalith," she suggested. "I had a thought."

Curiosity sparked in Gavian's eyes. "What was it?" he inquired.

Ambrielle's face lit up. "Remember the jewel that Kidiru gave to Aradel?" she asked. "It had a rare crystal that the Kavekkians used to amplify light when they built the Lykris."

Gavian's expression brightened with understanding. "Ah, yes. Do you really think Aradel would be willing to part with the jewel?" he wondered.

"No, but Kidiru . . ." said Ambrielle. "Maybe he knows where to find more of them."

"Hmm, once again this is beginning to feel a bit like destiny," Gavian said.

Ambrielle wrapped her arms around his neck, their closeness enveloping them. "Maybe it is," she whispered, momentarily ignoring the presence of the others around them. She pressed his head closer and leaned in to kiss him.

"Make sure you stay on that path like Neristara said," Gavian gently reminded her.

She smiled. "I will."

After sharing another kiss, Ambrielle released Gavian and moved over to Darby, embracing her in a warm hug. Despite the imminent danger of her journey, she seemed free of fear. Gavian watched as she gave each of them a hug. It was a simple gesture of affection but probably went a long way with everyone in the group. Though it wasn't something he would have done, Gavian admired her for it, for the way she showed leadership and affection.

"How long are you going to leave me in this thing?" said Malidora from inside the stasis chamber.

Ambrielle rolled her eyes. "I'll be right there," she assured her, not trying to hide her disdain. "Wegin, keep an eye on everyone while I'm away. Just like you would for me."

"Orders received," Wegin acknowledged dutifully.

Gavian watched as Ambrielle climbed into the stasis chamber. Stepping around Malidora, she settled in partially beside Malidora and partially on top of her. Neristara activated some sensors on the chamber's side, causing data graphics to materialize in the air.

Pointing toward Wegin, Neristara instructed, "Open the chamber at three hundred mecs. That should give them plenty of time to find the Cereveshians we need."

Wegin hovered above the stasis chamber, his lights moving in a slow series. "Good riddance!"

"Wegin!" Ambrielle barked. "You're supposed to say 'goodbye'!"

"What's the difference?" said Wegin. "My analysis suggests that both convey a similar sentiment. I believe my version is more precise."

"Not even close, actually," Ambrielle teased. "I'll see you soon, Wegin."

Neristara closed the glass shielding with a hiss, sealing Ambrielle and Malidora inside.

As the pink clouds of gas crept into the chamber, Gavian approached the glass. Ambrielle offered a smile, but it seemed strained. A sudden chill raced through his veins; this was far too perilous. Regret settled heavily in his stomach. Perhaps he should have taken more drastic measures to convince her to stay. Even if she resented him for it, it might have been preferable to the darkness she was about to face. Her eyes slowly closed, and Gavian feared he would forever regret letting her go, but it was too late to intervene now. Gavian watched Ambrielle's face slowly fade from sight just as violent coughing overcame Neristara. Gavian and the others rushed to her aid, attempting to assist as she gasped for air, her chest convulsing until she collapsed onto the cavern floor.

CHAPTER 4

AMBRIELLE—THE SAVAGE DARK

AMBRIELLE DRIFTED UPWARD, ascending into the sky. Before she could look back at the ground beneath her, she passed through vaporous layers of clouds. The sky grew darker until she crossed the last veil of the planet's atmosphere and into black space. Her speed seemed to increase with every moment, as Ambrielle flew past the red sun that Solsellion orbited. Distant stars glimmered with brilliant intensity, as if they were beckoning her toward some unknown destination. She was at a point of endless possibilities, each star was a new mystery, a new adventure.

Ignoring their call, Ambrielle allowed the blue light to guide her forward. It pulled her ahead, faster and faster. Passing through ethereal wisps of dust and gas, she tried to take it all in, hoping to commit every moment to memory. Galaxies swirled in a chaotic dance, each one more mesmerizing than the last.

Space and time seemed to stretch out before her as she continued to build speed. The blue trail of light grew in intensity. Space receded, forming back into its previous shape, and the light became too bright to see anything. She slowed so fast it felt as if she had rebounded, like a rubber band, all the way back to the stasis chamber on Solsellion.

All went dark. For a moment, she floated in a starless universe. She desperately sought a point of reference, a sense of dread beginning to gnaw at her mind. With each passing moment, the feeling intensified, suffusing the air with a palpable unease. Ambrielle noticed a faint luminescence beneath her, revealing a path that glowed with an ethereal radiance. But as she looked down, her legs appeared to be aflame, her form composed of living light. A mixture of fascination and horror coursed through her, making her hesitant to move further.

With trepidation, Ambrielle took a step forward onto the dimly lit path. The ground beneath her feet felt as though she was treading upon a fragile ray of moonlight, threatening to crumble under her weight. Overhead, barely discernible against the pervasive darkness, loomed arches that seemed to twist and contort at impossible angles.

A feeling of dread began to grow in her mind as she continued to move forward. With each step, the fear intensified. "Stay on the light," she kept telling herself. This must be the Savage Dark. The sheer vastness of the place overwhelmed her thoughts. How expansive was this realm, and how much longer could she endure its torment? Yet, she knew she had to push herself to the very limit, to confront whatever awaited her in this nightmarish realm.

The darkness expanded, pressing toward her on all sides. Ambrielle had desperately wanted to avoid facing the Shadows of the Gaith, yet it seemed inevitable that she must now confront the darkest, most hopeless place in the Everance. The path shrunk as she kept going. Her vision strained to trace the faint glow of the path as it extended into an infinite abyss of nothingness. "Stay on the path," she repeated to herself. How difficult could it truly be?

Ambrielle forged ahead, uncertain whether this ethereal body of consciousness even had a heart but feeling it pounding nevertheless. Emptiness surrounded the path of shining essence on each side. Unrelenting curiosity tempted Ambrielle's gaze away from the path, into the murky black. Strange, unsettling sounds emanated around her, as if something was stirring in the void. Ambrielle looked toward the noises, her eyes attempting to focus on the unfathomable depths of nothingness.

Though her instinct was to run and get out of this madness, she froze, attempting to get control of herself. If she moved now, she would surely be swallowed by the darkness.

In the midst of her turmoil, a voice pierced the emptiness, echoing through the void. "Who dares to venture into the dark?" Its timbre, a haunting resonance of depths unknown, echoed with a malevolent desperation, as if sanity itself had been devoured by the all-encompassing madness that lurked within. Ambrielle stood frozen, her body shivering in the emptiness, unable to muster a response.

"Why tread the path of shadows, if not to willingly meld your being with the very darkness that yearns to consume you?" The voice slithered like a serpent, its sinister words dripping with a sickening delight, as if relishing the thought of her inevitable surrender to its perverse embrace.

Ambrielle remained still, her limbs paralyzed by an overwhelming sense of dread. The path she had relied upon had vanished, leaving her suspended in a void that defied all logic.

"Your individuality is a feeble illusion," the voice continued, its tone dripping with malice. "Only the unity of the darkness holds true, devouring all who dare defy its relentless caress."

The oppressive darkness closed in around Ambrielle, its viscous tendrils insidiously infiltrating every crevice of her consciousness. A tormenting vertigo seized her, as though the very threads of existence were unraveling in her gaze. With frantic resolve, she struggled to disentangle her thoughts, to unearth a shard of salvation amid the relentless advance of the engulfing void. Neristara's cryptic counsel resounded within her psyche, a distant tether clinging to sanity amid the cacophony of bedlam: *Despite the visions you may have or the insights your mind may contemplate, maintaining your course is paramount.*

"Are you okay?" a voice called out, its tone filled with urgency and a chilling undertone of anticipation. Ambrielle strained to gather her fragmented thoughts, her mind a battlefield of confusion and fear. "Ambrielle!" said the voice she now recognized as belonging to Malidora.

Summoning every ounce of willpower, Ambrielle fought against the suffocating grip of the encroaching darkness. With trembling limbs, she managed to raise her arm, stretching it out into the abyss. Her fingertips brushed against something, a sensation both scorching and electric. It pulsed with an otherworldly energy, as if it held the power to ignite her very essence.

In that moment, Malidora's grip closed around her, pulling her with a force that felt both like salvation and damnation. Ambrielle was pulled close, the warmth radiating from Malidora's touch searing against the edges of her form. They stood together on a flickering path of light, their bodies of energy vibrating with an unsettling intensity. The surrounding darkness seemed to recoil, yielding ground to the resurgence of the ethereal glow. Had it all been an illusion, a twisted trick played by the abyss?

Ambrielle steadied herself as she followed behind Malidora. The walls of darkness beside them writhed in the ambient light created by the pathway.

"Your sight betrays you," a spectral voice hissed, emerging from the abyss with a sinister resonance, its words dripping like venom from fangs. With a chilling undertone, the whispered phrases slithered forth, a manifestation of the hidden void where illumination dared not venture, as though an incarnation of the concealed malevolence that dwelt within. "How can you trust your own eyes to guide you?"

Ambrielle quickly turned in the direction she thought it came from.

"Don't take your eyes off the path," Malidora reminded her. "Only look where you need to go."

Ambrielle nodded as they continued on, the whispers murmuring around them.

"All things converge in the ever-reaching dark." The voice coiled around them, its tone a sickening blend of fascination and malevolence. It insinuated a unity within the obscurity, a binding force that eclipsed all else.

Ambrielle's breath caught in her throat as another chilling utterance slithered through the air. "You deem yourself a traveler of the shadows, yet indeed, it is the shadows that travel through you." The words wormed their way into her mind, unsettling the very foundation of her understanding. What hidden forces lurked within her, unknown to her limited perception?

The whispers grew bolder, their insidious tendrils probing the depths of their fears. "The abyss, it beholds every truth, comprehends every secret," the voice declared, its proclamation reverberating with an unsettling assurance. Ambrielle felt a surge of paranoia, her secrets laid bare in the clutches of this omniscient darkness.

A twisted suggestion crept into the voice's cadence, sowing seeds of treacherous temptation. "Do not fear the dark. Embrace it," it cooed, its unsettling allure laced with perverse persuasion. The notion of surrendering to the encroaching void, of relinquishing control to its voracious embrace, sent shivers through her.

As Ambrielle and Malidora ventured further along the radiant path, a disconcerting sight materialized ahead. Emerging from the depths of the glow, appendages of indeterminate form extended, writhing and undulating like serpents in a macabre dance. The elongated tendrils slithered across the path, intertwining with each other.

Ambrielle's voice quivered as she directed her question to Malidora, her eyes fixed on the disconcerting spectacle ahead. "Do you see that?" she asked, her voice laden with a mix of awe and unease.

Malidora glanced briefly at Ambrielle before resuming her march. "Yes, I see it, but I can only assume it is another illusion. I'm not going to stay here any longer than I have to," she said with weariness in her voice. "I'm going to stay on the path. If it is able to pull me into the dark, at least this nightmare, perhaps, will be over."

"I'm starting to wonder if I should have listened to Gavian," Ambrielle said.

Glancing at Ambrielle as she walked, Malidora said, "Don't doubt yourself. I saw the determination in your eyes. I know you can do this."

Her confidence gave Ambrielle a boost, but the fear did not subside.

The low, booming voice spoke again, "You are but motes of dust, drifting aimlessly through the void. Without purpose, without direction, without meaning."

"Your minds are like fragile vessels, easily shattered by the truths that lie beyond the veil," said a shrill, screaming voice.

As they came to the writhing tendrils, Malidora made her way between them without hesitation. Ambrielle hastened her steps, determined to mirror Malidora's resolute advance, her gaze averted from the contorted obsidian appendages that coiled around her limbs. The knotted, gelatinous texture sent a wave of revulsion coursing through her, yet she pressed on, steady on the path through the repulsive thicket.

Suddenly a large monstrous mouth plunged out of the dark, its enormity casting Ambrielle into a startled leap, her foot teetering perilously close to the edge of the precipice. Malidora pivoted, ready to lend a steadying hand, but Ambrielle, rallying her composure, motioned her away with a swift gesture. After a few moments they had passed through the tentacles and saw nothing but the path of light as it wound into the distance.

The light seemed to disappear ahead as it turned a corner, partly obscured by the darkness. Something grew in her mind, like seeds of shadow taking root. Though barely noticeable at first, they quickly began to bloom. When the path straightened again, something faint appeared in front of Ambrielle and Malidora. A figure walking just as they were. The man appeared unaware of Ambrielle and Malidora walking behind him.

As the blooms opened, their dark petals unfurled to reveal their secrets. When they drew closer to the humanoid ahead, Ambrielle could tell he was Cereveshian. He stopped on the path as if to listen to the sounds around them. He looked about, seemingly confused or lost, but there was only one path. When they caught up to him, he appeared not to notice their presence.

"Keep following the path," Malidora reminded him.

The Cereveshian's gaze shifted toward her, as if awakening to her presence after a prolonged slumber. His lips parted, attempting to form words that seemed to elude his grasp, like he grappled with a fading memory of speech.

"Are you heading to Averess?" Ambrielle asked him.

His focus momentarily fixated on Ambrielle. "Why did you send me back?" His vacant gaze turned back to the abyss.

"What do you mean?" said Ambrielle. "Who are you?"

"Other obligations linger," he uttered with a confused stare, "demanding my course."

"Other obligations? Like what?" Malidora inquired.

The man's gaze shifted back to Malidora, a hint of frustration etching his features. "Were my memories intact, I wouldn't require your guidance," he muttered, a tinge of exasperation underscoring his words.

"Yes, you can follow us," said Malidora. "Why don't you tell us where you came from. What is your name?"

"I am Azel'Deris," the Cereveshian disclosed, his voice a murmur borne from the depths of his uncertainty. "From myriad worlds I hail, yet my most recent origin escapes me."

The name was familiar to Ambrielle. Searching her memory, it finally struck. "Azel'Deris!" said Ambrielle. "You were in the cave on Isodonia! Do you remember me? I'm Ambrielle, the awakener. I woke you out of the stasis sleep to talk to you."

"Why did you send me back?" he questioned, his words infused with a sense of both yearning and perplexity.

"You wanted to go back to Averess," said Ambrielle. "And your body would have died outside the chamber for too long. So much time has passed that your body could no longer survive without it."

"Keep to the path . . . Keep to the path . . ." mumbled Azel'Deris as he returned his attention to the yawning abyss.

"Yes, keep to the path," Ambrielle beckoned. "Follow us."

A voice hissed through the unseen recesses of the dark. "Why confine yourself to a single path? The shadows beckon with the allure of boundless freedom."

Without warning, Azel'Deris erupted into motion, hurtling away from them with frenzied urgency. With an almost unnatural momentum, he careened over the precipice of the path, defying gravity as he ascended into the abyss.

"Wait!" Ambrielle cried out. "Come back to the path! I didn't mean to send you here! If I had known!"

Azel'Deris would have died if she had not helped him back into the stasis chamber on Isodonia. Despite the logic telling her it wasn't her fault, an oppressive guilt clung to her like a shadow, its weight unbearably heavy. In the grip of this inexplicable guilt, Ambrielle grappled with a conflicting truth—she had a responsibility to ensure Azel'Deris was not consumed by the dark.

As much as her body resisted, she had to do the one thing they were warned against. Ambrielle stepped off the edge of the path, floating away from the only light and into the devouring darkness.

Azel'Deris's chant of "Keep to the path . . ." morphed into a maddened incantation, a cacophony that echoed amid the shadows.

As if some invisible force took hold of him, his figure became an abstract dance of distortion, his limbs stretching, coiling, and contorting in grotesque permutations. The void voraciously devoured his writhing form. Azel'Deris dissolved into the shadows, leaving only an unsettling void.

Malidora's desperate cries sliced through the ominous silence, pleading with her to come back to the path of essence. As Ambrielle strained to focus on the shapeless depths surrounding her, she fell into a trance, maniacal thoughts tearing at the edges of her mind. In the tempest of her own mind, Ambrielle fought to regain control, the words "keep to the path" pounding in her brain like a hammer against stone. She turned, a shiver of dread running through her, and only then did she grasp the depths of the encroaching darkness. The path, once so clear, was now lost.

CHAPTER 5

GAVIAN—TRUE SOLSELLION

IN THE SHADE of the trees outside the cavern, Gavian carefully placed the seedlings from the peculiar trees atop Neristara's lifeless body, while Dexius and Veridius covered her with a gentle layer of soil. It had been her desire to rest in the earth among organic life, becoming a part of the eternal cycle of life, death, and renewal that, in her words, defined the Everance.

As he performed this solemn task, Azravion vibrated in its sheath where he carried it on his back. The blade plagued his mind with dark thoughts. It desired the essence of Neristara. Now that her body was dead, her life essence could be used to save others. Shouldn't he take it, regardless of her wishes? He would have to do it soon because the essence would dissipate if he waited too long.

Perhaps Ambrielle was right that using the sword of Pythus was a bad idea. Maybe he should cast it aside and never use it again. But what if someone else found it? Where could he hide it that no one would find and use it for their own selfish impulses? At least with him it would be used for good.

The sword allowed him to protect Ambrielle from harm. It gave him power, a way to show his worth. When he saved others with the essence in the blade, Ambrielle and everyone else would know he was as important as anyone in this group.

A hushed breeze whispered through the air, its softness somehow surpassing the stillness of absolute silence. Gavian moved away from Neristara's newly formed grave, joining Sidaire, Darby, and Kazial, who stood nearby, their gazes fixed on the burial site. In the periphery of his vision, he noticed Darby observing him intently.

Gavian felt a comforting touch envelop his arm, and Darby's voice spoke with reassurance, "Ambrielle will be fine." It was as if Darby could read his thoughts.

"She probably gets tired of me worrying about her all the time," Gavian confided.

"No, I think it's sweet," Darby responded gently.

The rest of the group were quiet as they moved from Neristara's grave. Breaking the heavy silence that enveloped them, Gavian suggested, "Would anyone like to come with me to Anatharia? Maybe we could find a way to amplify energy enough to destroy the apex nyalith. The Kavekkians have a device called the Lykris, capable of focusing and amplifying sunlight. If we can find the crystals used in its construction, maybe we can harness that power."

"That doesn't sound too dangerous," Veridius said. "If there is any way I can be of use, I would be interested in accompanying you."

"Of course," said Gavian.

"Darby, you going?" Dexius inquired as he took position beside Gavian.

Darby voiced her concern, "But who's going to watch Ambrielle and Malidora?"

"I shall safeguard them," declared Syra'Dosa. "The cyrobots will receive directives to erect defenses encircling this entire mountain. Their protection will be established within the hour."

"You go on ahead," said Darby to Dexius. "It doesn't sound like you'll need my bow, and I really want to figure out what this Ichtek device is."

Sidaire chimed in, moving closer to Dexius. "I want to go too," she asserted. "I haven't had the chance to really see any of these other worlds."

"Oh, so everyone is leaving me?" said Darby with a hint of mock disappointment.

Kazial stepped toward her. "I'll stay here with you. I would like to take a crack at this device too."

"Thank you, Kazial. At least someone cares," she said playfully.

"Wegin, don't forgot to wake Ambrielle up as soon as the time is up," Gavian instructed as he began walking toward the glyvex.

"Certainly," said Wegin, his blue lights dancing across his surface. "Good riddance!"

Gavian rolled his eyes and turned back around. "How many times . . . ? Forget it. Good riddance to you too," he said with a smirk.

"How do you plan to get back to Anatharia?" Dexius wondered, waving to the others as they began their journey. "Won't we have to get back to the fractal plane?"

"I've been toying with a theory," Gavian announced, his voice filled with intrigue. "But if anyone else has a brilliant idea, I'm all ears." He glanced around, met with a sea of unresponsive faces. Ironically, if he wanted silence, everyone suddenly had an opinion to share. But no one spoke up now. "Well, looks like I'll have to give it a shot."

Gavian waved a quick farewell to the others as he, Veridius, Sidaire, and Dexius departed from the mountain, climbing into the vehicle. They descended a towering dune, the dust of red hued stone mingling with the golden sands beneath the air flow of the glyvex, creating mesmerizing patterns behind them.

The silver blade on Gavian's back began to pulsate with a strange energy, its vibrations reverberating through his being. It was as if Azravion, the sword itself, yearned for a connection, reaching out to an unseen force. Guided by an inexplicable intuition, Gavian felt a magnetic pull, a whispered guidance from the sentient blade. Azravion spoke to him through feelings, guiding his gaze across the vast expanse of desert in search of the nearest nyalith. The silver weapon seemed to possess a consciousness, a deep connection to the very essence they sought.

Eventually, their path led them to a basin nestled amid the undulating dunes, where a dormant nyalith stone stood silent and gray. It lacked the vibrant luminescence of the stone they'd found earlier.

"So, what's this theory of yours?" Dexius inquired as they all climbed off the vehicle.

Gavian's eyes sparkled, anxious to see if his idea would work. "When

Malidora absorbed the nyalith's energy, she closed the tear. So, my idea is, what if we feed it some energy?"

"That just might work. The only snag is finding enough energy for it to absorb," Veridius responded.

Sidaire stared at the nyalith, waiting with anticipation.

Determined to test his idea, Gavian unsheathed Azravion, the gleaming silver blade, holding it aloft. "We have the energy right here. The only uncertainty is how much power it'll release."

Azravion vibrated in protest as Gavian pulled the release under the cross guard. Suddenly, the nyalith erupted with a cascade of crackling energy, sending arcs of raw power tearing through the air. The sheer force of the transfer caused the atmosphere to tremble and quake, as if the very fabric of reality were being stretched to its limits. Gavian marveled at the boundless essence contained within Azravion, wondering how much life force of countless beings from Isodonia or maybe even beyond was concentrated within the blade, fueling its relentless stream of energy. If possessing the sword Stormwaker wasn't enough to prove his worth, surely wielding Azravion would be.

The nyalith shimmered with brilliance. A powerful arc of energy ignited the air around it and opened a fracture between realities. Though he could sense the buzzing of energy still within the blade, it stopped releasing any more. With a triumphant exhalation, Gavian lowered the sword, carefully returning it to its sheath. The air settled, and the intense display of energy gradually subsided, leaving behind a transformed nyalith radiating with newfound vitality.

Fractures in reality emerged all around them, each exhibiting different sizes and shapes. Gavian boldly stepped through the largest rift, finding himself instantaneously transported back to the familiar expanse of the fractal plane. He found himself standing at the edge of a crystalline spring, its pristine waters shimmering with ethereal luminescence.

"Wow!" cheered Sidaire. "It worked!"

"I knew it would," said Gavian, glancing back to see the reactions of the others.

"As long as we can get back to everyone else once we're done with this," chided Dexius with a bit of playful doubt.

Gavian began to feel the growing thirst within the blade. He couldn't help but regret having to expend such a substantial portion of its essence on the nyalith. Soon, he would have to replenish it. If something happened to Ambrielle and he found himself lacking the life essence to mend her, the weight of that remorse would be unbearable.

"Now we can go back to Echo Solsellion and go through the spring that leads to Anatharia," said Gavian as he got back into the vehicle and drove it through the open rift into the Echo dimension. They surged forward, heading toward the citadel near the spring, the conduit to Anatharia.

The giant balcain trees made it easily recognizable even at a distance. Leaving the vehicle close to the spring, they made their way through the red fern trees down the gentle slope. As Gavian waded into the water, he caught Veridius's confused look and turned to face him. "We have to dive down to the cave," Gavian told him, "then follow the blue light."

"As long as it doesn't lead to The Hollow," said Veridius.

"I wouldn't be going in if it did." Gavian went first, thrusting his body toward the blue glowing cave at the bottom of the spring. After entering the cave, he found the rays of light and followed them to a tunnel on the right. Once in the tunnel, it felt as though the whole world turned upside down and left him in the dark. He waited a moment as the dark subsided, placing him in a wide-open, watery space.

Emerging, he rose to face a sky veiled in clouds, rain cascading upon him. Gavian propelled himself toward the lakeshore. The swim, having already drenched them, rendered the rain inconsequential. Within the gentle drizzle, an unexpectedly forceful surge of water caught Gavian by surprise. He had forgotten how huge some of the raindrops could be on Anatharia. Sidaire, Veridius, and Dexius ran toward the forest for cover. After a second globe of water struck, Gavian hurried along behind them.

They made their way past the first trees and continued into the dense forest. Blue-green leaves glistened with raindrops, and the rain showered them as it continued its descent. They entered the towering canopy of the immense balcain trees, and the heavy downpour eased, offering them shelter beneath the natural umbrella. Sidaire bumped into Gavian from behind as he slowed, jolting both of them. "Sorry," she quickly apologized with a giggle. "You know, I've seen the Anatharian growth around the spring, but actually being here is an entirely different experience."

"These trees have likely grown here for more than four times the years we've been alive," said Veridius. "Perhaps in time, all the forests on True Solsellion will bloom as much as this."

"I hope so," said Sidaire with a sense of wistfulness in her voice. "I do miss the trees and flowers that are native to Solsellion. There are some around the springs. Syra'Dosa is trying to find and identify any genetic code to bring them back."

Veridius nodded. "It will be an incredible sight when the variety of vegetation from all these other worlds around the springs meet together."

"It most certainly will," said Sidaire, her voice changing from one of wonder to a distant thoughtfulness. "But I worry how well they will do during the long night on Solsellion."

Dexius joined the conversation. "How long is the night?"

As Gavian weaved around some of the thick underbrush, he heard a sudden crashing of leaves behind him. Dexius chuckled while helping Sidaire untangle herself from the clusters of vines she had run into. "Very long, I'm told," Sidaire continued as if nothing had happened, her gaze momentarily diverted when a droplet of rain landed on Dexius's cheek. She wiped it away with a smile before continuing. "Both the night and the day. It never seemed unusual to me until Avo'Doria talked about it. She said that it has a remarkable life support environment. Most of the heat comes up beneath us from the planet's core, otherwise not having the sun for that long would be too cold for the vegetation to survive."

"That is fascinating." Veridius nodded, his fingers brushing over a velvety leaf as they walked. "Kandom, my world, was tidally locked. We lived on the day side, in perpetual late afternoon sunlight. It will be strange seeing the long night on your world."

Neither Sidaire nor Dexius responded, prompting Gavian to glance back. Sidaire seemed oblivious to anything around her, smiling as Dexius gently pulled leaves and organic debris from her magenta-colored hair.

They came out of the forest to the wide-open valley with a great lake. Veridius and Gavian stared in awe at the beautiful view before them. Even Sidaire and Dexius couldn't help but take their eyes off each other long enough to admire the sight. Its aquamarine waters sparkled in the light of the sun as small waves rose and fell across the surface. A forest island stood in the middle of the deep waters.

Gavian continued across an open plain covered with stones and long grass. Pedestrian buildings of straw, mud, and some animal skins covered a nook in the stone mounds and boulders. A cluster of Kavekkians diligently attended to their tasks, deftly extracting fish from buckets and carefully arranging them upon sizable leaves that served as makeshift platters resting atop a sturdy wooden bench.

Nearby, a trio of artisans shaped intricate jewelry from shimmering stones, their nimble fingers working with a fluid grace. Laughter and animated conversation filled the air as children played an exuberant game of chase, their joyful cries harmonizing with the bustling hum of villagers moving about. A huddle of villagers surrounded a communal fire pit, where a savory aroma wafted from a bubbling cauldron suspended over the crackling flames. The tantalizing scent mingled with the earthy fragrance of freshly harvested herbs and the invigorating essence of rain-kissed grass. The village belonged to the Kavekkians who had been exiled from Mekkinspire.

Some of the nearest Kavekkians turned as they approached. "Go back where you came from," said one of them. "We do not invite visitors."

Gavian halted, turning back to glance at Dexius, Sidaire, and Veridius. Before Gavian could respond, Veridius stepped forward. "We apologize, we were unaware of your restrictions. We were humbled by the spectacular beauty of this place and could not help but get a closer look."

"Now you have seen it," said one of the exiled Kavekkians holding a knife as if ready to prepare the fish for eating. "You can go now."

One of the Kavekkians put down the bucket he was holding. "We do not want outsiders here."

"We are looking for someone," Gavian said as the rain seemed to ease. "One who goes by the name Kidiru."

Curiosity and suspicion intermingled among the villagers as they exchanged glances. "He is not here, now go!" demanded one.

"We wish only peace for you and for Kidiru," said Veridius. "We only ask to speak to him."

The Kavekkian villagers exchanged glances, their expressions unreadable. One of them, the knife still in hand, stepped forward. "Again, he is not here," he replied, his tone cautious. "Return to your own dwelling and Kidiru will find you if he wishes to."

Veridius stepped forward again, maintaining his usual calm demeanor, his tone respectful yet firm. "It is very important that we speak to him as soon as possible."

The villagers stopped what they were doing. The one with the knife pointed it at Veridius, easing forward as if threatening him. The others nearby joined him, picking up anything around them that could be used as weapons. Other villagers walking by noticed this and began ambling over.

Dexius grabbed his bow and Sidaire drew her blade, which only heightened the tension of the villagers around them. Veridius motioned for them to put their weapons up as he took a few steps back from the crowd. Azravion quivered with delight at the hint of rising conflict, aching to be drawn from its sheath. They could easily take these villagers out with the weapons they possessed, and Gavian could quench the sword's thirst for living essence.

"We did not mean to cause strife between our groups," said Veridius. "We will leave you in peace."

As Veridius turned around, heading back toward the forest, Sidaire and Dexius put away their weapons and followed. Gavian gave the villagers a nod, ignoring the hunger of Azravion as he left after the others. They reached the edge of the woods, and Gavian watched the villagers return to their tasks.

"You didn't mention they were hostile," Veridius said as he found the trail.

Gavian brushed past Dexius and Sidaire. "I have only spoken to Kidiru. He has to be around here somewhere."

A nearby voice wandered through the trees, startling Veridius and Gavian. "I am, indeed."

A Kavekkian strode onto the trail carrying the carcass of a large, furry creature on his back. As he drew closer, Gavian recognized the clothing he was wearing. Kidiru stood out from the other exiled Kavekkians in the village, wearing a mix of animal skins far more exotic.

"Gavian," said Kidiru as he carefully laid the carcass on the grass. "I see you caused quite a stir in Lon Vellica. I didn't expect to see you again."

"Kidiru!" Gavian said with a bit of excited relief. "Just the Kavekkian we were looking for."

Kidiru eyed each of them before speaking again. "And what did you need of me?"

"The gift you made for Aradel," Gavian began, "it had a rare stone in it that can amplify light."

"Amythite." Kidiru's eyes narrowed. "If you are trying to build a Lykris, you would also need a crystal that can focus light into a beam. How far along are you?"

"We haven't even started yet," said Gavian. "We may not need to build a Lykris. Ambrielle is looking for information on a way to harness enough energy to cut through a particular stone. And whatever the answer is, it wouldn't hurt to have something that can amplify that energy."

"As long as the energy doesn't destroy the amythite," said Kidiru.

"So you know how to build a Lykris?" Gavian asked.

"I know what is required," said Kidiru. "How everything needs to fit together. I doubt I have the skill to actually build it. I've never tried. We do not use crystals the way the Kavekkians of Mekkinspire do. They are too enamored with the technology and ways of the ancients."

"Why would you not use it?" said Dexius. "You could use their technology and also keep your traditions."

"Too often they go hand in hand," said Kidiru. "Our people were once great hunters. We explored this vast world, stopping when we found resources but eventually moving on. That all changed when our ancestors found Lon Kavekkia with its plentiful fruits and vegetables. They were enamored with Mekkinspire, where we could climb to heights no others could. It was a safe place to stay, but after finding tablets and artifacts of the ancients, we never left. We adopted the beliefs of the ancients, the Vyndari. After that, everything that made us Keldoi was lost."

"That happens to all people over time," Veridius said. "Culture doesn't exist in a vacuum. It's always fluid, influenced by others, and changes in the world around it. Your people likely blended the old with the new, but that doesn't mean it was erased."

"You are partially right," Kidiru conceded. He absentmindedly picked up a smooth stone from the ground, turning it over in his hand. "But that doesn't mean it was a good thing either. The Kavekkians are obsessed with the Vyndari teachings and anything that has to do with light. What I wanted for my life didn't matter because I was born near the first dawn of a new cycle. What would you do if your destiny was decided for you simply because of a sunrise?"

"My life was directed because of who my father was." Veridius's gaze grew distant. "He was the ruler of a great city, and I was taught only for the role of therin and prepared to rule after him. I'm not sure I even know who I really am, but now that all those things have passed away, I am hopeful that I will find out."

Kidiru tossed the stone into the air, catching it again. "We are opposite edges of the same blade, I suppose," Kidiru mused. "When you come to know who you are, when you are truly certain, let nothing stop you from it."

"Thank you, that is good advice," said Veridius. "It is a path we must all forge for ourselves."

Kidiru turned to Gavian. "Before I show you where I found this amythite, tell me what you plan to do with it. Why do you need to cut through a stone?"

Gavian cycled through his thoughts, unsure where to begin. "There is a crystal that an evil force plans to use to open a path to all worlds. They are using the life energy of beings all across the universe to power it. If we can destroy this crystal, we may have enough time to seal off all the entryways so this force can never reach us again."

"Where is this crystal you need to destroy?" Kidiru asked. "We consider the crystals in Lon Vellica to be sacred. We often leave them as natural formations. We do not shape them to control light like the Kavekkians."

"It is far from here," Gavian said. The sword, Azravion, sent shivers through its sheath on Gavian's back. Feeling the unease welling up within him, Gavian involuntarily clenched his jaw in an attempt to ignore it. As the breeze ruffled his hair and the village sounds surrounded them, Gavian tried to focus on the conversation at hand, pushing aside the distracting presence of Azravion as best he could. "It's on a world called Solsellion."

"If it isn't to start another war with the Darterrans or Kavekkians, I will show you," Kidiru muttered. "But let me warn you that there have been strange occurrences in the forests."

"What kind of occurrences?" Sidaire asked.

"In the depths of the forests surrounding Miravekk Lake, there are ancient temples," he revealed. "They have weathered countless cycles of rebirth, their secrets hidden beneath layers of time and nature's growth. We intend for them to remain that way. Lately, we have witnessed other beings entering these grounds. They depart in greater numbers than when they entered."

Gavian grew intrigued. "What do you make of that?"

Kidiru shook his head. "Right now, it is a mystery. We have not approached them, and to this point, they have left us alone."

"If you are still willing to show us where to find this amythite, we would be grateful," said Veridius.

"I have no desire to go inside that cave again," said Kidiru. "There is a predator that dwells there. I will show you where it is if you bring me some of the amythite you find there. But do not harm the creature. They are rare in this area, and we strive to maintain the balance of the forest."

Gavian turned to Dexius. "Ready for this, Dex?"

"Are *you*?" Dexius retorted, a challenge in his response.

CHAPTER 6

DARBY—TRUE SOLSELLION

Darby ran her fingernails along the smooth surface of the pyramid-shaped object. Surely, she must be missing some kind of groove or indentation that allowed the object to separate and open. With a frustrated sigh, she set the artifact on the rocky floor beside her. She had tried everything she could think of to either open or power on the object.

She shuffled uncomfortably with her back against the rough curvature of the cavern wall. Darby glanced at Kazial, who sat quietly nearby, seemingly transfixed by the subtle changes in the pattern of lights in the apertures of Wegin's orb-like body. He hadn't said much of anything since volunteering to stay with Darby. Neither had he offered any suggestions or assistance in trying to figure out the purpose of the strange Ichtek artifact.

Even Syra'Dosa remained quiet as she stood beside the egg-shaped chamber that contained the sleeping Ambrielle and Malidora, waiting for the time to wake them both up. Darby wondered if synthetics ever got bored. Were their minds still active when there was nothing happening? Did their minds constantly wander the way hers did?

Darby rose to her feet, dusting off the artifact. Maybe there was some discarded tool laying around in the cave that she could use to open it. Or maybe walking around would get her blood flowing and allow her to refocus. She needed to examine the object from a new perspective.

Starting toward the light that led to the entrance of the cave, a faint whistle from behind gave her pause. It was the same howling sound that used to frighten her on stormy nights in her old house in Muloken. If the wind hit from just the right direction, it would whistle through certain tight breaches in the walls.

Igniting her silbrace light, Darby shined its beam over the walls of the cave. Kazial stood as her beam moved past him to a dark corner of the cavern chamber. She moved toward the shadows ahead, and he followed behind her.

A tunnel extended ahead, leading out of the chamber. Darby entered, her light glancing off what appeared to be a door at the end of the pathway. When she reached the door, Darby pushed against it, hoping to open it. The door began to crack and separate, until suddenly it all collapsed, dissolving into nothing more than sand on the cavern floor. Whatever material it was made from must have been extremely old, and most of the structural integrity had deteriorated.

Darby, with Kazial behind her, crept inside a hallway that was not naturally formed. The howl of wind sounded again as strange shadows danced to the movement of Darby's light beam.

While she was comfortable spending time alone without the constant need for socialization, unlike with Dexius, this silence was unnerving. She needed to hear a friendly voice to calm her. Since Kazial hadn't said anything, Darby decided to take the initiative. "So, you used to live here?" Her voice rebounded in the tight spaces, making it sound as though she was doubled.

"What?" said Kazial, as he nearly tripped over a piece of brick on the ground. "Oh. No, my city was far from here, we didn't have mountains like this."

"I meant on this planet," said Darby. "I guess leading with such an obvious question wasn't the best way to start a conversation. Next, I was going to ask, what was your city like?" She noticed herself talking more than she normally would and found it odd.

"Oh, yes, this planet," said Kazial. "My city was in a flat plain or maybe you would call it a basin, there were many lakes and rivers."

"That sounds pleasant," said Darby, slightly frustrated that he didn't elaborate further. Now she would have to continue to think of more questions in order to keep the conversation going. She moved the light beam back and forth, leaving nothing in the dark. "What else?"

"I'm not sure what else there is to tell, but I will try," he said, as he sped up and grazed the back of her arm. It startled her, but she tried to keep her focus. "In contrast to what Sidaire told me about her village, my people built complex structures. The more complex, the greater it was admired."

"Why do you think that was?" Darby asked, appreciating that he was beginning to talk more.

"I suppose it was a point of pride," said Kazial. "An achievement to one's understanding of mathematics, architectural design, and engineering. And so, it inspired others to attempt to prove their construction was to be revered as well, and to do that, you had to do something greater than what came before."

"That sounds impressive," said Darby. "Did people come from other cities to view them?"

"Actually yes, many," said Kazial. "Some revered these buildings as well, while others mocked them, saying they were useless and nothing more than a pretentious display of arrogance."

Darby had never seen so many things. So many worlds, so many stars, so many galaxies. From what she had heard from the others, The Hollow realm contained many universes, and the Everance contained many realms. As impossible as it seemed, she wanted to know what all was out there. "I guess no matter what your endeavor, there's always someone that won't like you," said Darby.

Kazial nodded. "That is true. We had our rivals, but they weren't enemies in the sense that we hated or feared each other. At least not until the Shadows came."

The floor ahead was reflective, appearing much smoother than the brick floor of the hallway. "What was the mindstream like?" Darby asked. "I heard Malidora mention it."

"I think it is a manifestation of minds that are connected together," said Kazial. "Or something like a dream."

"It felt like you were dreaming?" Darby asked.

"What does dreaming feel like? In the moment, it didn't feel like anything out of the ordinary," Kazial said. "But, like a dream, you don't realize you are in it until you wake up and realize that you were dreaming."

"Like torment you didn't know you were in," Darby muttered.

Kazial's eyes unfocused as if contemplating her words. "I suppose that is one way to think of it. Possibly a very accurate one."

Darby stepped down onto a hard surface, causing a metallic ping to echo through the hall.

"Do you need any assistance?" Syra'Dosa called out from the chamber behind them.

Ignoring her question, Darby made her way toward a faint glow ahead. She could hear sounds of whirring and clicking not far away. Slowing her pace as she thought about the situation further, Darby struggled to recognize what she was hearing. What was the source of the sound? What if she came across someone inside these halls?

Her bow was too cumbersome to quickly attack if danger appeared suddenly, but Kazial's silbrace might be more appropriate. "Ready your weapons, Kazial, just in case."

"Already on it," he replied.

As Darby continued ahead, she could see the end of the tunnel. A glow of lights reflected along the smooth surface of the tunnel walls. The lights came from another interior off to the right of the tunnels. She took a deep breath, preparing herself for what she might find around the corner.

Rounding the corner, she took a quick peek before pulling her head back. All she saw were colored lights all around the room inside. Darby stepped inside the rectangular room, her bow drawn. A raised surface spanned the perimeter of the area with chairs placed in front of it. The lights she had seen were an array of numbers and symbols written on the walls in illuminated characters. Different colors distinguished them: blue, purple, orange, yellow, and green.

Trying to make sense of it, Darby stared at rows of what appeared to be gibberish.

"Someone was working on some complex equations," said Kazial.

"Where do you see that?" Darby asked.

"Right here." Kazial pointed. "The numbers you're looking at are mathematical equations. I don't recognize all the symbols, but the patterns are familiar."

"What were they calculating?" Darby asked.

Kazial stared at them intently. "I'm not sure yet, trying to figure them out." He moved close to the wall, moving his fingers to different numbers as he mouthed words. "I've never seen this symbol." He pointed at what appeared to be a simplified drawing more than a symbol.

"I think that's a nyalith crystal," Darby said.

Kazial gasped as he seemed to realize she was on to something. "I think you are right."

Footsteps approached the room. Darby turned as Syra'Dosa and Wegin entered.

"Who's watching Ambrielle and Malidora?" Darby asked, looking at Syra'Dosa.

"I will return to them in a moment," said Syra'Dosa. "I wished to see what was going on and to make sure that you were both still functioning."

"These appear to be mathematical equations," said Wegin as he floated to the wall they stood by.

Darby glanced at Kazial, cracking a smile that made him chuckle silently.

"However, they are not Cereveshian symbols," said Wegin. "Some of these symbols appear to be Ichtek."

"Can you tell what they mean?" Kazial asked.

"No one has fully deciphered the symbols that the Ichtek used," said Wegin. "But I will analyze them and attempt to determine a meaning."

While Wegin meticulously analyzed the enigmatic symbols, Darby's curiosity drew her to explore the rest of the room. Amid the collection of drawings, a depiction featuring four circles captured her attention. Gridlines dissected each circle, forming a complex web. Darby's fingers traced the lines and dots as her mind churned with possibilities.

Kazial, seeming to sense her intrigue, approached and examined the drawing as well. His eyes followed as Darby moved her finger to the intersections of gridlines, each punctuated by a small dot. Darby's observation led her to a discovery: within one section, four dots formed a perfect square, a stark contrast to the rest.

"This must have been Neristara's laboratory," said Wegin. "I can only surmise that she had collected some Ichtek writing and brought it here for study."

"I don't suppose you know what these are?" Kazial asked, pointing to the symbols above each of the dots.

Wegin's lights circled his sphere-shaped body. "These too, are Ichtek letters or symbols."

Darby shook her head as she looked over the drawings, symbols, and numbers, hoping to glean something from what appeared at first glance to be a scribbled mess. Her eyes scanned each panel of the walls around the room, and something caught her attention. Smooth orbs, set into a panel that extended from the wall, pulsated with various colors of light. "What are these?"

Kazial stepped over to the panel to see what she was looking at. They both examined the colored objects pulsing with light. Each orb had a different symbol etched into it. Darby hesitantly reached out to one, unsure if she should touch it or not. Drawing a quick breath, she grazed the surface of one of the orbs. The symbol glowed solid red, and the platter of orbs rotated until the red orb was inside the wall.

Kazial's eyes widened as an additional image was projected onto the wall. "Yes! This is a legend! Neristara must have figured out what they mean."

Each symbol correlated with a lengthy number, identical except for the digits following the decimal point. Positioned above the legend was an equation, featuring a blank space within it for the result.

"I think you plug each symbol's number in the equation," Kazial said. "But I'm not sure that helps us much."

"Some of these numbers are familiar to me," said Wegin. Darby and Kazial turned to find him peering over their shoulders. "With the number of digits they have, it is difficult to conclude it to be a coincidence."

"Tell us, Wegin," said Darby. "What do they mean?"

"The springs I have traveled through," said Wegin, "I always detected a faint energy. When we arrived from Solsellion to Anatharia, the spring had a particular frequency that differed slightly from the waterfall in Isodonia. Both of those frequencies are represented exactly here."

Darby's eyes lit up. "So each of these dots are the springs!"

"And each of these spheres," said Kazial, "must be the two dimensions of Solsellion!"

With an impulsive surge of emotion, Darby extended her arms and enveloped Kazial in a warm embrace. After an awkward moment, his own arms wrapped around her in return. They had solved a part of the puzzle this laboratory contained.

As Darby felt her heart gradually return to its regular rhythm, she shifted her attention toward Kazial. The undiminished fervor on his face was unmistakable. While she hesitated, fearing her question might expose her lack of understanding, her curiosity overcame her reservations. "Is this something we can use?"

"I don't know," said Kazial grinning, "but I'm sure we will gain something interesting from it."

With the rush of discovery, Darby wandered around the dusty lab. Kazial began to explore the lab on his own as well. She strode between short black columns on the other side of the room. She wiped the dust off of the top of one of them, and it projected an image above it. The image swirled and formed around her fingers, as if fibers connected to her.

The image began forming symbols and then letters that she understood. Words began forming and then vanishing. At first it seemed like nonsense, but then sentences began appearing.

What's this thing doing? Why is it reacting to me? Maybe I did something to start it.

The words it displayed confused Darby, but she read along with them.

How long has this stuff been here? Maybe it has more information. The springs. It could help us find something.

Pulling her hand away from the projection, Darby realized it must be displaying her own thoughts. She hadn't perceived a voice in her head speaking those words, but she guessed it somehow converted her abstract thoughts into tangible sentences.

As she stepped away from the column, Darby found Kazial standing in front of a large crescent-shaped surface with several objects scattered across its surface, tools and trinkets of some kind, perhaps a work bench or desk used by Neristara long ago. Kazial examined a group of small spherical objects arranged in a symmetrical array on the desk. One of the spheres glowed with light as he touched it, projecting it into the air.

"What is it?" Darby asked, as smaller circles moved around larger ones.

Kazial continued staring at the projection. "It seems to be a map of star systems."

He directed his attention to a pile of material on the work area surface. Darby watched as he moved some of the items from the pile to reveal one of the same pyramid-shaped artifacts she had recovered from one of the Ichtek.

Reaching past Kazial, Darby took the pyramid from the desk, studying it in her hands. It was exactly the same as the one she'd found, except this one was opened. The very top of the pyramid was raised, revealing a metal cube inside. She tried manipulating the metal around the cube that held it in place, but nothing happened.

She was met with disappointment, expecting something much more exciting to be inside. Still, she wanted to solve this puzzle of how to open the object she'd found. Darby traced along the edges where the other object had split and raised up. Though she hadn't noticed it before, her fingers detected a subtle indentation in the surface of the pyramid, but after pulling on it a few times from the top, it had not seemed to move in the slightest. It wasn't until she held the point of the pyramid gently that it popped open.

Kazial rushed over as an intense light came from the cube inside, firing a beam to the top of the pyramid above it and making it glow. It projected a map of star systems much like the solisphere that Wegin had. Worlds of all sizes were displayed, many of them marked with points across their surfaces. Darby didn't understand the symbols that marked each.

"Wegin, is there any way we could figure out what these Ichtek symbols mean?" Darby called out.

Wegin's eye rotated as lights blinked on and off. "These are not Ichtek symbols," he said. "They're Cereveshian. This is almost an exact copy of the solisphere I contain." Wegin projected the solisphere beside the hologram emanating from the pyramid. They did look exactly alike.

"It shows the locations of the akreums, presumably where the Cereveshians are all in stasis around this region of the universe. The only difference is that the one you have shows fewer points. Perhaps it was never updated."

"Why would the Ichtek be interested in the akreums?" Darby wondered.

"Some of the larger akreums keep the rifts contained," said Wegin. "It could be that the Ichtek were using this device to locate the rifts."

"What's that blinking mean?" Kazial pointed at a circle flashing at the bottom of the displayed image.

"It seems there is more data on this device," said Wegin.

"Can you read it?" Darby asked.

"There seems to be a consistent resonant energy coming from the inside that I may be able to tap into."

The hologram changed to a cycling of various symbols until it arrived on words they could understand. *Anomalous Dimensional Energy Disturbance* said the display, showing an animated diagram of a pulsing energy field. Wegin's lights blinked rapidly as the display changed again to show a labeled diagram of the energy field. *Breach after entry*, it said. One of the labels pointing to the outside edge of the energy field read, *Increased instability with each entry.*

The next one they tried read: *Elyravess Study Sequence 0017: Excursion into Hollowspace successful. Substance mining active. Test 1 Completed, Results: Access Denied.*

Wegin made a humming sound as he cycled through more images. *Beyond the universe, Hollowspace,* said one of the images. It was accompanied by a long list of words in small print that couldn't be read in time before the display changed again. *Thessarion status: Stable, experimentation allowed. Anatharia status: Volatile. Direct contact with energy is prohibited. Elyravess status: Unknown. Oscillating energy flux present.*

As more of the images came up, it landed on some type of spacecraft and details about their specifications and materials, more mathematical equations, and some chemical compound formulas. After moving through most of them, they found another log list. Darby quickly scanned over the lines until she found something interesting: *Elyravess Lab Entry 00034: extracosmic organism discovered.*

Elyravess Lab Entry 00035: Deleted.

All the remaining Elyravess Lab entries had been deleted.

"I'm afraid all remaining data is encrypted," said Wegin. "I don't have enough memory to hold the cipher that would decrypt this data. We would need something with a more powerful core."

"Do you know anything about what happened on Elyravess?" said Darby.

"No, but that's where Avo'Doria and all the other sentinels came from. They brought cyrobots that built Syra'Dosa and the other automatons here," said Kazial. "They know everything."

Darby took the small black pyramid-shaped device from her bag, staring at its shiny surface. "I wonder if they would know what this is."

"If anyone does," said Kazial, "it would be them."

Putting the object back into her bag, Darby called across the room to Wegin, "Why are all of these entries deleted?"

As Wegin moved to her side, he quickly read the log. "Highly unusual. Like myself, Cereveshians view data as a precious resource. They would never delete anything."

"But what if they did?" Kazial asked. "What might cause them to do so?"

Wegin's lights blinked chaotically. "Perhaps something dangerous that they wanted to forget."

CHAPTER 7

Malidora—The Savage Dark

Malidora stood paralyzed in terror, a deluge of incomprehensible whispers swirling around her like a haunting zephyr. Inexplicable forms materialized, ethereal as mist under a lunar glow. Against every scream of caution in her mind, Malidora, gripped by a spectral compulsion, stepped off the path and floated into the abyss, her hands reaching into the oppressive darkness in a desperate search for Ambrielle.

As Malidora drifted further away from the safety of the path, the air turned frigid, a bone-chilling cold that crept into her very core. It was a sensation beyond any chill she had ever known—a ghastly freeze that seemed to paralyze her thoughts, trapping her mind in a state of torment. Her thoughts congealed like icy tendrils, spiraling into madness as the void eagerly gnawed at her, leaving only the haunting whispers and the suffocating embrace of the unknown.

The sea of shadows enveloped her, and the world around her blurred into obscurity. The abyss echoed with Azel'Deris's haunting incantations, and Malidora felt a profound disconnection from the reality she once knew.

Unfamiliar entities emerged, their anguished wails a symphony of dread, their existence a fleeting glimpse of a fevered nightmare. The path of light convulsed as she looked back, rending with agonizing tremors. Worlds unfurled and disintegrated, fractured fragments suspended in the void like spectral apparitions. Beings drained of vitality with an eerie haste, their forms disintegrating into ephemeral pyres of ashen decay, leaving behind only remnants of their former selves, adrift like morbid cosmic debris. "Ambrielle! Can you hear me?"

"All that clings to your heart shall wither, decay, and dissolve into oblivion." The high-pitched whisper seeped into her ears like venomous honey. "Life itself shall turn traitor."

"There is no escape," the low, resonant voice rumbled, a malevolent declaration. "Mere moments stand between your cherished world and its irrevocable decay. Those moments are waning."

"The abyss hungers for you," the screeching wail pierced through like shards of ice. "It craves to devour you, its appetite unquenchable, ceaseless. The veiled maw of shadows thirsts for the flavor of your terror, the delectable savor of your desolation."

The sheer dread in those voices threatened to shatter Malidora's resolve, her very being on the precipice of crumbling into the shadow.

The weight of it all seemed almost insurmountable, a suffocating vortex pulling her into its grasp. In her mind's recesses, the sinister blooms of darkness bore wicked fruit, their tendrils coiling around the abscess of her thoughts. The creeping vines, like serpents, slithered hungrily through her consciousness, threatening to ensnare her psyche in their inky grasp. Yet, with a fierce struggle, Malidora fought against their encroachment, a battle of willpower in the face of impending doom.

"Return to the path," said a voice distinctly different from the others. It was pleasant and comforting. "We can't let anything happen to you. You're our best chance. Our best chance at completing the mission." Malidora turned toward the sound as she recognized the voice.

A familiar face materialized in the dark. "Dab!" said Malidora. "Is it really you?"

"We have been watching down on you, like the stars from the heavens." The glowing face of Evala appeared beside Dabradan. "Follow my light."

"I have to find Ambrielle," Malidora replied.

Was this real or was it a hallucination? If it was a hallucination, where was it coming from, her own mind or the darkness? More than anything, she wanted to believe Dabradan and Evala's spirits were still alive and well.

"You must get back to the path," said Dabradan in a calming tone. "The mission depends on you."

"I can't leave Ambrielle," Malidora said. "I promised that I would watch out for her. I don't often get a chance to earn anyone's trust. I can't let anyone down again."

"What happened to making the difficult choices for the good of the team?" said Dabradan.

Malidora smirked. "If not for each other, what are we fighting for?"

"I guess you learned something from me anyway," said Dabradan.

"Remain in my light," said Evala. "We will help you find her."

"How do I know that you are real? That you aren't a manifestation of the shadows?" said Malidora.

"We are always with you," said Dabradan. "In your mind . . ."

". . . and in your heart," Evala continued.

What other choice did she have? Malidora moved with the light ahead, seeking any sign of Ambrielle. As she followed Evala and Dabradan, she called out to Ambrielle, hoping to hear her voice. Despair filled her spirit, but then Malidora heard a faint sound. Evala and Dabradan continued toward it as she came in behind them.

"Mom!" said Ambrielle. "Is that you?"

"The woman who walks in darkness will never see the light," intoned a deep, powerful voice.

"Ambrielle!" said Malidora, trying to ignore the voices. "Come with us!"

"I'm sorry, Mom," said Ambrielle. "I'm sorry for everything."

"It's Malidora," she said. "We have to get back to the path! Follow the light!"

"Thomin! You had so much life ahead of you," Ambrielle cried out. "If only I had done more to protect you."

Malidora continued to call out for Ambrielle to come to Evala's light.

"I can't see it anymore," Ambrielle said. "I'm scared, Mom. I don't know how to get back."

A terrible voice shrieked with a chilling sound echoing like fingernails scraping against her skull. "The girl who swims between worlds shall drown."

Grieving voices echoed in the darkness, attempting to ensnare Malidora's thoughts. The malevolent whispers sought to drag her into the abyss, where the shadows threatened to consume her entirely. Despite the haunting cacophony, Malidora persisted, following Evala's light in the overwhelming darkness.

The darkness relented enough for Malidora to see Ambrielle coming toward her. Her spirit still clung to threads of light from the path of living essence. They reached for each other. Malidora's hand stretched out until she touched the tips of Ambrielle's fingers.

With a concussive flash, Malidora found herself on her knees with her hands placed on the shining path of essence. Malidora looked down, her eyes searching for Evala's light. The shard of the nyalith was still at her side, even in this void, shining bright green and burning with the concentrated essence of the life from Kandom. Dabradan and Evala were nowhere to be found, but Ambrielle sat on the path in front of her.

"My mother was here." Ambrielle shifted her weight, almost as if searching for something that wasn't there. "She and Thomin led me to you."

"I saw people too." Malidora unconsciously clenched and unclenched her fists, reliving the intangible encounter. "They guided me to you, but now I wonder if it was all in my head."

"I want to see her again," Ambrielle expressed, her gaze distant as if she could almost see her mother. She absentmindedly gestured with her hands, as though trying to grasp on to the ethereal connection. "There are so many things I want to tell her, but she told me to stay on the path."

Malidora nodded earnestly. "Yes, please don't leave the path again," she implored, putting her hand on Ambrielle's shoulder.

In ordinary circumstances, Malidora would harbor resentment toward Ambrielle for coaxing her away from the safety of the illuminated path and compelling her to navigate the enshrouding darkness. Malidora pondered the fact that Ambrielle hadn't explicitly sought assistance; it was Malidora's own decision to embark on this perilous search. The motivation behind it eluded her, but the sensation was a stark departure from the times she had willingly endangered others to secure her own safety—an unsettling realization that left her grappling with a complex mixture of emotions. In some strange way it made her feel closer to Ambrielle.

As they continued along the winding path of essence cutting its way through the dark, an insidious presence slinked behind them. Turning to confront it, Malidora was met with a suffocating emptiness. Yet, unease clawed at the edges of her consciousness, sowing seeds of doubt. The notion that malevolent entities, hideous monstrosities, lurked beyond her limited vision took root like a festering malignancy. She envisioned herself trapped within a nightmarish tableau, besieged by abhorrent creatures ready to unleash unspeakable horrors. Her imagination ran wild with the grotesque forms that could lurk just beyond the veil of darkness.

Visions of the Shadows danced around her. They consumed forests and mountains in their path. Mind-controlled beings fought each other furiously, while others tried to flee from the carnage. A thousand, thousand worlds crumbled to dust as every essence of life was drained. She tried to shake the vision from her mind, but it was indelibly branded. Was this all pointless? Why did she ever think they could outwit such creatures as the Gaith? The majesty and diversity of the cosmos faded into a singular conforming darkness, unified in shadow.

A howling wind screamed from the infinite dark, its anguished wail ripping through the fabric of existence. The turbulent force buffeted Ambrielle and Malidora relentlessly. Against every instinct, Ambrielle pressed on with Malidora at her side as the gusts shrieked with a sentient malice.

"The path of light is a prison, a narrow and confining space," the wind shrieked. "Embrace the boundless expanse of the shadows."

"The veil you cling to masks your ignorance," the resonant voice boomed, its echoes stretching into infinity. "Step into the abyss, and we shall unveil the verity of existence."

She would sooner die than see everything destroyed like this. As despair's weight began to crush her determination, she could no longer focus on the path. Ambrielle tugged at her arm, not allowing Malidora to succumb to the burden of the abyss. Their eyes locked, fear and courage mingling, and a silent understanding passing between them—an unspoken vow to withstand the relentless onslaught of the darkness together.

CHAPTER 8

GAVIAN—ANATHARIA

THE VIOLET SKY peeked through gaps in the clouds. Gavian kept a steady pace as he followed Kidiru's lead, forging a path through the labyrinthine depths of the dense forest. He scanned their surroundings, his senses sharpened, attuned to the slightest movement or anomaly. Every rustle of leaves, every flicker of light through the foliage held the potential to reveal the presence of the enigmatic beings that Kidiru had spoken of, those who entered the old temples only to grow in number upon their exit.

The forest seemed to come alive with mystical energy, as if secrets whispered between the ancient trees. Sunlight filtered through the canopy, casting patterns on the forest floor and creating an ever-shifting tapestry of light and shadow. The symphony of nature's chorus accompanied their trek, the melodies of chirping birds and gentle rustling leaves creating an ethereal ambience.

As they ventured deeper into the heart of the forest, the air seemed to become thicker. Gavian sensed something he couldn't explain, like an imminent revelation awaiting him. Though the environment was calm and tranquil, it had a weight to it, somehow unsettling.

A mound of leafy vines obstructed their path in a small glade lit by the setting sun. As Kidiru guided them around it, Gavian began to see stone walls through spaces the vines failed to cover. "There. One of the Vyndari temples," Kidiru said as he walked past it.

Gavian's curiosity deepened, fueled by the realization that they were treading upon hallowed ground, where the mysteries of the past intertwined with the present. He couldn't help but wonder about the stories that lay dormant within those aged stone walls. What knowledge had been safeguarded by the Vyndari? Had it all been taken by the Kavekkians?

The ground beneath them rose, elevating them on a slope as they pressed further into the forest. Kidiru continued on, while Gavian stood on a small cliff, peering through the thick foliage that surrounded him. The vantage point offered a glimpse of the expansive forest stretching out as far as the eye could see.

They continued to ascend the hill, twisting their way through the blue-leafed trees as they followed Kidiru. Between their crunching footsteps, the songs of unseen birds filled the air. The dense undergrowth presented only fleeting glimpses of what lay ahead.

As they ventured further, the forest began to yield, gradually relenting and allowing slender beams of light to penetrate the verdant canopy. They emerged from a cluster of trees, and a majestic rock outcropping came into view. Nestled into its stony face, the entrance to a cave called, inviting them into its dark unknown.

"There it is," said Kidiru, standing outside the mouth of the cave. "The place where I found the amythite."

Gavian hurried past him, rushing toward the tunnel. Kidiru grabbed his arm, preventing him from going inside. Gavian's brow furrowed in momentary frustration.

"Remember, do not harm the creature that dwells inside, but be wary not to get yourself killed either."

Gavian's irritation ebbed, replaced by a somber understanding of the weight of the task ahead. His shoulders eased as he took in a deep breath, the scent of damp earth and foliage filling his lungs. "What kind of creature is it?"

"A torvak," said Kidiru. The distant call of a bird cut through the air, a sound familiar to Gavian during his years on Anatharia. Kidiru continued, "Although their behavior isn't entirely predictable, it should still be sleeping, waiting for nightfall to hunt in the surrounding forest."

"The sun looks to be setting soon," said Sidaire.

"This shouldn't take long," said Kidiru. "The creature is blind, relying on its sensitivity to sound and echolocation to find its prey. If you keep quiet, this should be easy."

Gavian heard the familiar call of the bird again. He realized it was a nocturnal creature, only coming out just before dark. "Maybe we should wait until it leaves the cave."

"You would not want to be in these forests after nightfall," said Kidiru, as distant thunder rumbled. A reminder of the storm that had recently passed.

Gavian turned around. "Are you still coming, Dex?"

"Right behind you," said Dexius.

Gavian crept inside the cave, stepping carefully along the rocks covering the ground. Treading lightly, they both made their way through the tunnel.

With each step, Gavian tested the ground for creaks or loose stones. His eyes began to adjust to the dimness, allowing him to see in the faint light entering the cave from the opening. Gavian motioned for Dexius to come to him, pointing out a treacherous spot that could trigger a noise.

They came into a larger chamber, a soft glow ahead of them. Inching their way closer, Gavian's heart pounded in his chest. He could hear it in his head. It seemed so loud he was certain the torvak would hear it too.

As they approached the faint glow, Gavian spotted the amythite crystals they sought. Reaching out slowly, he grabbed one and began prying it down with his hands. Dexius came over to help, putting his weight on it to loosen the crystal. The base of the stone formation gave, and the crystal came out into Gavian's hand. Fortunately, they made very little noise in doing so.

Gavian started on the next one, pushing and pulling to rock it back and forth. Dexius pushed on the crystal until they freed it. Part of the rock formation crumbled, spilling loose gravel onto the hard ground. The sound seemed deafening amid the quiet environment they were trying to maintain.

A clicking clacking sound rose from somewhere in the dark chamber. Gavian hurried to the nearby stone wall, knocking Dexius against it. The clicking sped up as it grew louder. In the faint glow of the amythite crystals, the creature moved past them. The torvak had a short but wide body frame. Walking on four legs, it had large arms with clawed hands. Covering its body were plates of bony armor adorned with bristling spines of hair in between.

The clicking of its feet on the rock, accompanied by the clacking of its armor, echoed through the chamber. Dexius waited, unmoving, as the torvak stopped. Gavian's muscles tightened as he tried to keep steady.

Azravion quivered in its sheath when the torvak came near. It longed for the life essence within the creature, the sword needing its fill. Its hunger gnawed at Gavian's mind as the torvak blindly investigated the area where the sound had come from. Slowly, Gavian drew out the blade. If he struck now, he could kill the beast.

To kill such a creature would be entirely in self-defense, of both Dexius and himself. Who could tell how many lives he might save by planting the blade into its soft underbelly and draining every last bit of essence into the sword?

The torvak started moving again, this time crawling in reverse. As it slinked back into the corner of the chamber, Gavian wiped the sweat from his forehead. He still had time to strike before it returned to its hiding place. Maybe he could circle behind the creature with its guard down. Moving around the stone, Gavian quietly snuck into the larger chamber. He pressed the toes of his boots against the cave floor, ready to charge the torvak. Before he could act, something snatched his tunic and pulled him back. Gavian tried to right himself before being dragged along the stone floor.

The torvak was alerted to the sound, and they heard the click clacking of its bony feet stirring again. Gavian tried to resist this unseen force, and he realized it was Dexius pulling him out of the cave. His surroundings became clear again as his senses sharpened.

He stumbled, and Dexius caught him, pulling him back to his feet. They both waited, listening to the clicking sounds of the torvak slowly creeping toward them. They prepared to run, but the noises went silent. Dexius and Gavian turned, stepping cautiously toward the opening of the cave.

The light outside the cave had grown dimmer. The silhouettes of

Kidiru, Sidaire, and Veridius obscured the entrance, blotting out much of what remained. As they reached them, Kidiru placed a finger in front of his lips. "There's someone out there," he whispered. "Somewhere in the forest."

"We didn't know if they would be friendly or not." Sidaire huddled near Dexius as he moved out of the cave.

"It sounded like there were several of them," Veridius said. His fingers moved through his hair, holding a small fan-like device twirling around in sections and gently tousling his locks.

"It could be Darterrans." Kidiru led them away from the cave. "Though I've never seen them in this part of the forest."

"What should we do?" Sidaire's gaze lifted to meet Dexius's. "Did you get the crystals?"

"We did," Dexius replied. "Had a little run-in with that creature, but we didn't harm it."

Gavian reached into his pouch and pulled out some of the crystals. "Is this good for your share?"

"I'm nearly blind in this darkness, but it feels like enough." Kidiru accepted the crystals from Gavian. "We should leave before it gets worse." Kidiru started off into the forest.

"It's not *that* dark." Gavian shared a glance with Dexius, then followed Kidiru. The shadows that fell on them in the thick forest were darker now. They struggled to keep up as Kidiru briskly weaved through the foliage.

They came to the glade where the temple stood covered by overgrowth. The light seemed to be dying faster, as the sun faded into the trees. Moving around the temple, they caught sight of a group of travelers. Dressed in black, the strangers blended in with the silhouettes around them. They wore long robes like the one Pythus wore in Isodonia. Under their hoods were reptilian faces, like those of the Ichtek they'd encountered at the Kandom nyalith. It could only be the Ichtek.

Gavian counted eight of them. One in particular stood out, wearing black metal plates highlighted in gold. Atop his head was a steel helmet, and a mask covered his face. The helmet had two pointed ridges on each side and one in the middle, giving a horned appearance. The mask was similar to the one Pythus wore, a faceplate slanting down and meeting at a point below the chin with the visor following the same slant.

Kidiru and the rest of them quietly watched from the shadows of the forest as two of the reptilian Ichtek cut at the vines with long daggers. They found the opening and moved inside.

"The ones we have been seeing at night," Kidiru said. "They're getting closer to the village."

"What do you think they are up to?" Sidaire said, keeping her eyes on the activity of the Ichtek.

Dexius moved into the glade toward the temple. "Only one way to find out."

"Wait Dexius!" Veridius whispered, as Dexius moved ahead, staying out of sight of the opening. Gavian rushed after him, curious to see what was going on.

They stealthily approached another opening, its form obscured by the encroaching vines. The elongated oval shape presented a challenge, not providing an easy passage, but with determination, it seemed feasible. It was an aperture of some sort but didn't allow for much light. Gavian noticed Kidiru moving toward them as he peered through the opening.

The cloaked Ichtek set orange glowing crystals around them on the floor, lighting the structure in the middle of their circle. The armored Ichtek stepped toward the Cereveshian vault, a smaller version of the akreum Ambrielle and Malidora were currently in. He brandished a sword that was black as night surrounded by glowing white energy.

As the armored Ichtek brought the sword to rest against the unbreakable plastra material of the akreum, the energy around the sword's blade extinguished, leaving only the dark core. Gavian watched in amazement as the sword sliced through the akreum, which offered no resistance at all. Once he had carved out a square in the vault, the other Ichtek pushed on its base, making it topple over. The white block of material crashed onto the temple floor, scattering clouds of dust and debris that flickered in the glow of the crystals.

One of the Ichtek carried an illuminated orb, casting an eerie red light on everything around it. The cloaked figures gathered around the opening, spreading out to make way for the one holding the orb. The Ichtek peered inside the vault, which was bathed in the orb's red light, but the scene inside was obscured from view. From within came the thrashing sounds of a struggle, and two more Ichtek hurried inside. The conflict soon subsided, and the once-raucous vault was now eerily silent. The red light of the orb slowly faded, and the cloaked figures emerged from the vault. But what had been three that went in was now four coming out.

One of them had glowing red eyes and exuded a shadowy substance. The four beings joined the others as they placed more shining crystals around the next akreum. The armored Ichtek again set his blade against the akreum, slicing the unbreakable material with ease.

"That sword . . ." said Gavian as he watched the Ichtek again cut through the plastra of the vault.

Sidaire continued to peek through the opening in the stone. "I still don't know what they are doing."

"Whatever it is, it can't be good," said Dexius.

"It doesn't matter what they are doing." Gavian leaned against the outside of the temple. "We have to get that sword."

"What are you talking about?" Dexius said. "There are at least nine of them."

"Don't you see?" Gavian's eyes scanned the group, hoping to find someone to agree with him. "If that sword can cut through plastra, it would surely cut through the apex nyalith. We don't need to find a way to focus and amplify energy, all we need is that sword."

Veridius's voice joined the conversation, acknowledging Gavian's insight. "Ah, you may be on to something."

"I must head back to the village," Kidiru interjected, his voice carrying regret. "I would be no good to you in this darkness."

"Thank you, Kidiru." Gavian inclined his head in case the tone of his voice failed to express his gratitude. "You've been a great help."

With a nod, Kidiru slipped away into the depths of the forest, leaving the group to deliberate their strategy.

"If you can keep them off me,"—Dexius's eyes settled on the others, a determined fire in his gaze as he spoke—"I can take them out."

"We do have the element of surprise in our favor," said Veridius.

Dexius directed his attention to Sidaire. "You okay with this? I don't know if you had this in mind when you agreed to come."

"Don't worry about me." Sidaire ignited the lightblade on her silbrace. "Let's do it."

Gavian reached for his sword, Stormwaker, but hesitated. Instead, he unsheathed Azravion. He had used a lot of the essence stored in the blade on the nyalith, and it desired more. Veridius projected his shield. "On your signal, Dexius."

"Cover Dexius's flanks," Gavian said. "I'll take left, Sidaire right, and Veridius shield wherever it is needed most."

The Ichtek exited the third akreum, followed again by an extra body. One of the Ichtek crumpled to the ground from Dexius's arrow, prompting the remaining Ichtek to scatter in disarray.

Amid the chaos, two of the figures bolted toward the temple's entrance, their intentions clear. Dexius was prepared, intercepting the first with another precisely aimed shot. Arrows sailed back to him, connecting seamlessly with his silbrace, ready for further use. However, the second Ichtek managed to evade his swift retaliation, making their escape to the outside world before Dexius could reload and take another shot. In the frenzy, the remaining Ichtek scrambled away from the door, redirecting toward a wall at the far end of the temple interior.

The armored swordsman stood facing the wall. With the black sword in hand, he executed a swift, powerful slash through the stone surface, carving out a new passage. Fearing the swordsman might escape, Gavian abandoned his position.

"Wait!" Sidaire's urgent cry pierced through the commotion as Gavian darted around the other side of the building. "What about the left flank?"

Cutting through the thick vines, Gavian struggled to navigate around the temple. The crash of stone being cut out reverberated through the air, the sound melding with the rustling of leaves and the trampled underbrush. Footsteps followed, growing fainter as they appeared to bound into the forest on the other side.

"Over here!" Veridius called out. "They're on the run!"

Gavian turned around and ran back to Dexius and the others. Even though they still outnumbered them, the Ichtek did not seem interested in fighting. They fled into the forest as Dexius struck one of them down with an arrow.

Pausing for a moment, Gavian siphoned the essence from the fallen Ichtek. The sword pulsed as it took it in. Once the Ichtek had withered to skin-covered bones, Gavian chased after the others, intent on taking this new sword.

"They're getting away!" Veridius collapsed his shield, firing his flash rifle at the escaping Ichtek. Gavian could hear Dexius and the rest of them behind him as he plunged into the thicket heading back into the forest. The cloaked figures were just ahead, barely visible in the moonlight. Suddenly, the beings darted to the side. Gavian followed. He was beginning to lose sight of them in the dark forest.

Gavian's heart pounded in his chest when one of Dexius's arrows flew by him. One of the robed fiends staggered. He dropped to the ground. Tumbling through the grass, the Ichtek's momentum carried him into the root of an old tree. Gavian kicked the cloaked figure to see if it was alive.

Veridius fired wildly into the dark. His bolts hit nothing but the underbrush, accomplishing little more than illuminating the woods temporarily. Gavian finished draining the essence of the Ichtek's body before dashing ahead, slowly gaining on the dark figures. The cloaked men weaved in and out of the trees, trying to lose them in the dark. They made another sharp change in direction, disappearing into the underbrush.

Trying to catch sight of them, Gavian quickened his pace. A patch of moonglow illuminated a tall, thick tree up ahead, drawing his attention. He approached the tree and noticed movement. Without hesitation, Gavian turned sharply as one of the cloaked figures emerged from behind the tree. The Ichtek swiftly brandished a pointed object from beneath his robe. Gavian's reflexes kicked in, and he narrowly avoided the blinding blast of energy that shot from the object. A cry of pain erupted behind him, and Gavian glanced back to see Sidaire gripping her shoulder, her face contorted in agony.

Dexius crouched beside Sidaire, providing support and care. "Wait!" Dexius called out as Gavian stormed through the forest. Although a part of him yearned to rush back to their aid, Gavian knew that losing precious time could jeopardize their chances of obtaining the sword they sought. A manic compulsion for additional life essence fueled his steps as he stormed through the forest, ignoring Dexius's call.

The haunting cries of the lokanta birds reverberated through the dense thicket, their voices echoing a warning. Gavian knew from his time with the Darterrans that these birds warned each other of approaching threats. He followed the fading sounds, tracking their path deep into the forest, trusting their guidance to lead him closer to his objective.

Bathed in the pale light of the moons, Pathea and Miraeda, a new glade unfolded before Gavian's eyes. Ahead stood a mound, veiled by trees and entwined with vines. Gavian's recognition dawned as he realized he had arrived at the entrance leading to the Darterran caverns. He could only hope that he would be able to get through without attracting the Darterrans' attention. As he cleared the opening of the tunnel, he heard footsteps approaching from a distance. He hoped that it was Dexius and the others.

Swiftly traversing the tunnel, Gavian pushed himself forward, his senses on high alert, unsure if he could detect the presence of the Ichtek ahead. Azravion still craved more essence. As he emerged into one of the intricately carved halls of the Darterran caverns, the light from his silbrace revealed a series of footprints imprinted in the dusty ground. Following their trail, he made his way toward a junction where multiple hallways intersected. The footprints led him closer to the chamber that housed the first Cereveshian akreum they had ever discovered. This one was larger than most of the others. Housing more than a stasis chamber, it sealed off the rift that allowed the creatures of The Hollow into this universe.

Echoes of footsteps reverberated from within the akreum vault. Realizing there was only one exit in the akreum, Gavian positioned himself outside the opening, allowing himself a moment to catch his breath. Yet, to his bewilderment, the sound of footsteps persisted, seeming to defy the confined space of the chamber.

"Gavian!" Dexius's voice resonated through the cavern behind him. "We need your sword to heal Sidaire!" So much for avoiding notice of the Darterrans.

Gavian turned swiftly as Dexius, Sidaire, and Veridius entered the chamber. Dexius gently guided Sidaire forward, his light casting a glow upon her injured shoulder. The fabric of her vest appeared charred, the top layer seemingly melted. Raising Azravion toward her, Gavian channeled the life essence into her wound, hoping to mend the damage inflicted.

Azravion could not spare any more essence, it needed to be filled. A peculiar sound emanating from within the akreum captured Gavian's attention. Ignoring Dexius's pleas, he swiftly left their side and ventured into the vault, hastening down the stairs that led further into the depths. "Gav! She may need more!" Dexius called out, his voice trailing behind. If they lost their chance of getting the sword, this would all be for nothing.

As he reached the bottom of the akreum stairs, Gavian's eyes fell upon an opening, meticulously carved into the plastra. How could he have overlooked something so obvious? With the black sword in the Ichtek's possession, there would always be another way out.

"Who dares intrude upon our sanctum?" a voice boomed behind him from outside the akreum. Time was of the essence, and Gavian couldn't afford to wait. Without further hesitation, he entered through the hole in the plastra, determined to continue his quest.

CHAPTER 9

Ambrielle—Averess

Ambrielle ignored the voices, moving quickly along the path, until suddenly a great tearing sounded all around them. The very fabric of the darkness fractured, unveiling an entirely new panorama. A smokey miasma pervaded the boundless expanse, ribbons of this ethereal essence intertwining amid the void. An enigmatic substance akin to grains of colored sand cascaded, mingling and melding to birth an array of hues alien to Ambrielle's eyes.

"Is this real?" said Ambrielle. "Are we finally out of the darkness?"

"I'm not getting my hopes up yet," said Malidora.

The journey had been one of torment and terror, an ordeal that defied reason and sanity, yet Ambrielle and Malidora had triumphed over the abyss. Now they floated within the surreal landscape of Averess, forever marked by the haunting experiences that had brought them to this point.

"It feels . . . almost like water," Ambrielle said.

Ambrielle pushed through the colorful mist, her mind still reeling from their trip through the Savage Dark. The enigmatic, smokey medium seemed to resist her movements, creating a unique sensation—a pushback that paradoxically felt both resistant and yielding. It was as if the mist had a tangible texture, a silky resistance that offered just enough give to let her through. The smoke wafted and undulated, swirling in mesmerizing patterns. Within the smoke, countless spiral worlds of light illuminated the mist and drifted around them. each one adorned with vibrant, reflective colors that danced and shimmered. They were attached to long stems that formed of concentrated dust.

"The contours of my being feel as if they are slipping away." Malidora's voice carried a touch of uncertainty.

In some areas, breathtaking colored particles filled the smoke with a kaleidoscope of hues, defying the logic of everything Ambrielle knew. Brilliant blues blended seamlessly with radiant reds, while verdant greens melded with regal purples. Golden yellows twinkled like stars, and fiery oranges added warmth to an ever-changing canvas.

"It's just a different medium than what you are used to," explained Ambrielle. "Less solidity."

"I can't say I'm enjoying the change," Malidora admitted. "I'm more a fan of solid ground."

"Anything is better than the Savage Dark," Ambrielle said, hoping to add a positive perspective.

As the misty smoke billowed and swirled, waves of sandy dust emerged and receded, forming a dynamic landscape in constant flux. The waves rolled and crashed against each other, creating patterns that evoked the ebb and flow of a celestial ocean. The dust shifted and rearranged, forming new patterns and colors as the motes interacted, creating an evolving symphony of form and color.

It was both awe-inspiring and calming, drawing them into its ethereal beauty. The laws of physics seemed to be suspended, allowing for nature's boundless artistry. Ambrielle and Malidora floated silently, taking in the sights that no other human had seen.

Ambrielle ventured deeper, moving her arms and legs as if she were swimming. The swirling mist enveloped her, giving a sense of fluidity. Fixing her eyes on one of the spiral worlds of light, she flew toward it. Their colors came alive with renewed intensity, revealing more and more intricacy as she moved closer.

As she neared one of the spirals, she found that it appeared more like a small galaxy than a world. Clouds and glittering dust swirled around each core. As Ambrielle floated toward the core, she could see that it was comprised of an intricately woven mass of long crystalline cylinders. The cylinders looked jagged and sharp in some places, smooth and curved in others. The colors of each strand were independent, some changing, others remaining the same.

A gathering of swirling illuminations floated across the crystalline core, their forms appearing slightly more solid than the shifting mists that enveloped them, though not by much. They moved as though they were alive, with swirls of appendages surrounding them. Ambrielle felt a profound sense of some unidentifiable emotion coming from these objects, and she realized they were living beings. Their shapes were nebulous and elusive, defying easy description. Ambrielle's mind strained to grasp their nature, perceiving a resemblance akin to a whirling vortex or tempest. Yet, in a peculiar manner, they evoked the delicate framework of a fish's skeletal structure, upright and poised, their sinuous, wispy tendrils reminiscent of graceful bones.

Each being radiated a distinct color, casting a soft glow that mingled with the mist. Their forms lacked discernible facial features, only ever-changing shapes conveying countenance, cloaking their true nature. They exuded an aura of mystique and enigma, captivating and puzzling in tandem. Ambrielle found herself mesmerized, her mind grappling to comprehend their unusual forms. Were they the guardians of these spirals, keepers of ancient wisdom, or ethereal entities transcending human understanding? Their otherworldly presence left her with more questions than answers.

One of the beings seemed to notice her. Its color changed from green to dark red as it floated toward Ambrielle and Malidora with surprising speed.

"Swiftly, you must depart from this place!" the ethereal being implored, its voice a delicate dance of emotions and words. The quality of its voice sounded more feminine than masculine. "As long as you remain in Averess, our accord stipulates confinement within your designated domain!" A melodic shift carried its words, traversing from the tangible to the ethereal.

The unwelcoming nature of the being surprised Ambrielle. In this tranquil, celestial realm, everything seemed as though it should be friendly. "We came to speak to the Cereveshians," said Ambrielle. "Our universe is in danger."

"From distant cosmos you hail, not of this realm," said the being. "The universes of Nulvare are your dwelling place, it is beckoning you home." The being's color changed from dark red to a soft blue as it moved closer. "You are not one of Cereveshian kin. Reveal your identity."

"I am the awakener, Ambrielle," she replied. "And this is Malidora." Malidora was unexpectedly quiet but seemed to be watching the strange beings with interest. The beings quickly introduced themselves as Lumira, Aduna, and Vess.

"By what means did you come to know of Averess?" Lumira voiced with a tone of disdain. Her inquiry carried a curious cadence, the being's form aglow with shades of inquisitive violets and ethereal blues. "Further intrusions shall not be countenanced. Depart and relay to your kin that their presence finds no reception in this realm."

"We don't mean to intrude," said Ambrielle. "We were told we may find the Cereveshians here. We need their help to prevent the Gaith from destroying our worlds."

"Who imparted this knowledge unto you?" inquired Aduna, her aura shifting to a cool cerulean that mirrored her skepticism. "For what cause do you journey here, seeking Cereveshians? This realm is not theirs to claim."

Amid the ethereal embrace of Averess, the air shimmered with a gentle luminescence, casting a soothing radiance on Malidora. "But they are here somewhere, are they not?"

"Neristara sent us to find a particular group," said Ambrielle as her attention swayed between the being's graceful movements and the patterns dancing within crystal facets along the spiral core. They can no longer be awakened in our universe. Since all of the remaining Cereveshians are here, we came to speak to them. Please. They may be the only ones that can help us."

"The Cereveshians understand nothing." Lumira's melodic tones carried a somber note, as her form deepened to a velvety indigo. "They are dangerous, relentless in their pursuit of knowledge. Trust with them is tentative."

The entity's luminous presence responded, its form swaying gracefully in hues that conveyed understanding and empathy, intertwining with their shifting colors. "Neristara, once a beacon of hope among her kin, spirals into recklessness with this task she has given you," her melodic response echoed, its own ethereal colors swirling into soft golds and soothing blues.

"Yet, should we cast judgment as the stars do, or offer direction as a symphony's guiding note?"

Another radiant form casting a spectrum of shimmering colors joined the exchange, her essence pulsating with intensity.

"Our purpose stretches beyond mere observation." Vess's tones carried a resolute power, her form igniting into brilliant crimson and warm amber. "Guardians of balance we are, sculptors of cosmic equilibrium. The harmony of Averess and all of the Everance must be preserved."

Malidora floated closer to the being. "Then you should be concerned that, once the Gaith are done with our universe, they will come for Averess."

"Debate lingers regarding the Gaith's purpose." Aduna's tones held a contemplative timbre, her form aglow with hues of pensive purples and wisps of enigmatic blues. "Their existence may be necessary to the cosmic balance of Nulvare. Can we glimpse their wake and fathom the ripples they birth? There is no certainty that they will be allowed to cross the boundaries of Nulvare. Until their purpose is gleaned, we shall not interfere."

"Worlds have been destroyed!" said Malidora. "What purpose could that serve?"

"People are dying! How long are you going to wait?" said Ambrielle.

"The cycle of life and death is a necessary part of the balance. Our focus remains attuned to the great harmony," said Vess. "To learn the melodies of the Everance is to glimpse the very heartbeat of existence."

"Yet you criticize the Cereveshians for seeking knowledge," said Ambrielle as her eyes glowed.

Lumira explained, "The Cereveshians are seekers guided by logic, driven by the pursuit of information for the sole purpose of power and control. Their ambition is to attain mastery over the Everance, manipulating it to serve their will without regard for its inherent harmony."

Vess warmed the area with serene blues, deep greens, and touches of gentle violet. "What is knowledge without understanding? To find empathy with all living things, to understand the nature of the Everance, is to touch the heart of creation. You cannot begin to see until you understand. There you will find The One and the primal heartbeat that resonates through all."

"What do you mean by 'The One'?" Malidora's fingers grazed the crystalline strands that grew like vines from the surface around them.

“The One is the one and the only. The wellspring of all creation,” proclaimed Aduna. “The writer and the conductor. You and I are beings comprised of many particles, while The One stands as the singular, indivisible essence—a solid, unchanging truth amid the fluidity of creation, without beginning or end.”

“The One is the zenith of the pristine, the very incarnation of paramount truth and quintessential existence,” said Lumira.

“So The One created everything?” Ambrielle asked.

“The simple answer is yes, but creation is merely a facet of The One,” said Vess. “The One is boundless and timeless, the core from which all vitality and being radiate, the primordial energy that orchestrates the very weave of existence.”

“What is this nature that you have come to understand?” Malidora questioned, her eyes absorbing the cosmic hues.

“That existence is woven with interconnected threads.” Lumira gestured toward the ever-changing patterns around them. “All things need, and all things give. As I said before, there is symbiosis, harmony, empathy. The One relies upon the Everance, just as the Everance relies upon The One.” Threads of interconnected energy manifested, creating a visual representation of the symbiosis and harmony she described. The dance of colors and patterns echoed the boundless marvel of the Everance.

“Sounds like you have it all figured out, why keep studying it?” said Malidora.

“For the Everance is a boundless marvel.” Aduna’s cerulean aura deepened as she elucidated, “Though imperfect, it is seamlessly united in a state that is wonderful according to its design.”

“Maybe Averess is like that”—Malidora traced phantom arcs and loops through the air, harmonizing with the rhythm and movements around her—“but not where I come from.”

“Averess itself bears imperfections,” remarked Vess. “Yet, should you manage to step back and cast your gaze upon a broader span of the Everance, its brilliance would become apparent.”

“That’s why we need to see the Cereveshians,” said Ambrielle. “If the Gaith destroy the universe, they are going to use its energy to open their way into the rest of the Everance.”

“They pose no menace to the Everance as a whole,” Lumira’s soothing words reassured them, her figure a calming blend of serene colors against the cosmic backdrop. “The Everance is boundless. Even if they were to expend an eternity dismantling its realms, their efforts would never leave a discernible mark upon the vastness of infinity.”

Ambrielle’s attempt to fathom infinity became a journey into the depths of introspection, where the very fabric of reality seemed to unravel before her. Each attempt to grasp the limitless expanse unveiled layers of complexity that challenged the very essence of her cognitive capacity. Each realization revealed the infinitude in ever-expanding circles.

“But if there truly is empathy,” said Malidora, her expression hinting at fascination for their surroundings, “The One would want you to save our universe. If it is all interconnected, a part of the whole would be forever lost.”

“Do not assume that the desires of The One align solely with your own,” cautioned Vess. “It may not be our purpose to take action and yet it may. That remains to be discovered.”

“You might want to discover it pretty soon,” said Malidora. “We’re running out of time.”

“Physical entities are inherently uniform,” mused Aduna. “Forever preoccupied with the passage of time.”

“What harm would it be to allow us to speak to the Cereveshians?” said Ambrielle. “If you do not want to get involved, show us where they are.”

Lumira paused, her radiance pulsating. “I hold that you do not require the influence of the Cereveshians; they would merely guide you astray,” Lumira concluded. “After all, they bear the weight of responsibility for all that has transpired.”

“What do you mean?” Ambrielle’s voice, soft yet resolute, broke the ethereal stillness.

“There is so much you do not understand,” Lumira’s voice resonated. “Let me entwine with you. Before we go any further, I must know your intentions. I must examine your spirit and sample your emotions. Will you join with me?” She beckoned, her luminous form extending an invitation.

Ambrielle was uncertain as to what exactly she was agreeing to but responded with a hesitant, “If that is what it takes.”

Without further warning, the being drew them into its misty form, surrounding Ambrielle and Malidora. Memories of anger, sadness, happiness, the whole spectrum of emotions came over Ambrielle. Her vision darkened as crystalline vines grew around her. Within that darkness, a familiar forest grew, the pecan groves near Ambrielle's house. Colors twisted and curled, weaving more images out of the dark. Her brother Ryan, her father, and her mother stood in the midst of the forest talking to each other as if she weren't there. It was a dream born of memory. The crystalline vines untangled the vision and then returned to weave another scene.

Colors brightened and sparkled inside the house woven into the dream. Her mother sat at the kitchen table. A familiar feeling of happiness washed over Ambrielle. It made her realize that there were several kinds of happiness she had felt in her life. Some brought memories of good times before, while others were entirely unique. Ambrielle had forgotten their kitchen once looked like this. All the cabinets were glossy mint green with chrome handles. A large backsplash with hexagon patterns and matching green tiles covered part of the wall.

Her mother's mouth moved as she spoke, but Ambrielle couldn't hear anything. Without hearing the words, Ambrielle still knew what she was saying. She remembered her mother telling her she would be working at the same place but would not have to travel. It would mean her mother would be home a lot more and be able to spend time with Ambrielle and her brother. As much as she missed her mother when she was away, Ambrielle was confused at the time. If her mother could do that, why had she waited until now? Though her mother said it was to spend more time with both of them, Ambrielle couldn't help but think that it was more about her brother, Ryan, than her. She had not thought about it in a while, but it made her realize there were feelings from this moment that still lingered within her, unrectified.

Lumira floated before them as the vision faded, her radiant presence extending like the unfurling petals of a blossoming flower. "Unlike the Cereveshians, I perceive a depth of emotion within your kind," she intoned. The luminous energy shifted toward Ambrielle. "Within you flows a benevolence as serene as a tranquil stream." The light then transitioned to Malidora. "And within you, a passionate fervor burns like a fierce flame."

Lumira's portrayal of Malidora prompted Ambrielle to acknowledge that she had assessed Malidora through a flawed lens—her own perspective. While it was the only reference Ambrielle had, she began to consider the possibility that her judgments about Malidora might be incorrect. Malidora viewed the universe and the actions of its inhabitants with a unique lens, different from Ambrielle's. It became clear that neither of them held an absolute truth in their interpretations.

With a flash of bright light, Lumira corralled them as they zoomed above the spiral core, streaking from one point of light to another until they caught a glimpse of much a larger spiral of crystallized formations. Clouds of dust, gas, and light swirled in the distance around the crystal core surface as they approached.

A group of more Ureons gathered in separate circles on the giant glowing core, shining in various colors. Some burned like passionate flames while others softly swirled. The being released her embrace, allowing Malidora and Ambrielle to move freely to the crystal spiral core. The edges were lined with pale green crystals, which some of the misty beings seemed drawn to. The green crystals looked familiar.

"You have nyaliths here too?" Malidora's question hung in the air like a shimmering thread.

"Indeed," said Lumira. "Nyaliths are eternium, an element that can exist in all realms of the Everance."

Malidora glanced down at the bright shining nyalith shard. She still had the one filled with the life essence of Kandom with her. Other Ureons surrounded the nyalith crystals with their strange appendages.

"What are they doing with them?" Ambrielle asked.

"Observation," Lumira explained. "This is how we delve into the realms, comprehending the intricate symbiosis that governs the cosmic systems within the Everance."

"Solysta," Lumira addressed a being as she drew near to another Ureon. "I draw your focus to a novel entity that has ventured into Averess. They claim to have been guided here by Neristara to engage with the other Cereveshians." Ambrielle and Malidora both glanced back at the misty being as she led them toward the giant, yellow entity bristling with glowing fire.

"For what reason do you seek an audience with the Cereveshians?" inquired Solysta.

Though a bit intimated, Ambrielle spoke first. "We were hoping to learn the best way to close off the rift between us and Nulvare and save our universe from the Shadows."

"There are hundreds of rifts, likely more, leading to worlds in our universe," said Malidora. "If we could find a way to cut off the main rift between Nulvare and the network of passageways, we could stop them from entering our universe altogether."

"We also are looking to destroy the apex nyalith on the planet Solsellion," Ambrielle said. "That is where they are collecting living essence they plan to use to enter other realms. It would slow them down and give us the time we need to close the rift hub."

"Both creation and destruction have consequences if they are without purpose," Solysta remarked. "How is this course of action meant to bring about any form of aid?"

"Once it is destroyed, the Gaith will need to find a new world to use for their collection of living essence," Malidora said, "which would give us time to close the rift hub and prevent them from entering our domain or the rest of the Everance."

"And this scheme was orchestrated by Neristara?" questioned Solysta.

"She sacrificed her life so that we could come here to speak to the Cereveshians about this," said Ambrielle.

Solysta's words carried a weight of caution. "This plan," she asserted, "is not without its perils. A thorough study of its intricacies, an exploration of every conceivable variable, is paramount. Only then can we navigate the currents of uncertainty and predict the unfolding outcome with confidence. The result of this action could prove catastrophic for the planet."

"We may not have the time," said Malidora. "For one, we will be woken up and pulled back into our universe soon."

"You echo the sentiment of a Cereveshian," Solysta replied, "ever inclined to resolve one quandary by introducing another. How can one aspire to solve a dilemma without discerning the variables and potential outcomes? Tampering with forces beyond comprehension invites perilous uncertainties."

“Forgive our lack of understanding,” said Ambrielle. “If you are willing to guide us in any way, please, we need it.”

Solysta’s graceful tendrils slowly came together, as if she were contemplating silently. Her hues changed from a flaming yellow to a warm green color. “Come with me. I will show you the mysteries of the Everance.”

CHAPTER 10

Darby—Echo Solsellion

Darby, Kazial, and Wegin moved through the tall tiger-striped grass in the shade of white barked trees with pink leaves and blossoms. Having crossed over to Echo Solsellion, where all the springs lined the world in symmetrical nodes, they had followed Syra'Dosa's instructions. The vegetation of Elyravess around the oasis here was like a fantasy land, an enchanted forest that had grown with wild abandon. Coiling vines wrapped around the trees and hung from their branches, growing from somewhere amid the tangled thicket.

As Darby stepped through the untamed foliage, she noticed a fluttering sensation in her chest. Her hands tingled with the idea of seeing another new world so different from her own. Yet a knot also tightened in the pit of her stomach. It was much like having to speak to a new person, but a whole new world filled with complete unfamiliarity was on another level. Her heart raced from both anticipation and anxiety. This would be the first time she ventured into the unknown without Gavian or Ambrielle.

She hoped this venture would lead to something that would help her friends. More than anything, she wanted to find her own way to contribute to the group. The way everyone else had their own traits that made them special. In some way, big or small, they all had an impact by working together for this goal. Sometimes they had conflicts, differences, but they complemented each other enough that they were able to get through it. Maybe it made them all feel accountable to each other. No one wanted to be seen as selfish to the group.

Darby waited as Kazial entered the spring leading to Elyravess ahead of her. She stuffed Wegin into her bag, sliding the pyramid-shaped artifact to the side to make room. Making sure nothing was loose enough to cause her to get trapped in the underwater caves, Darby adjusted the straps of the satchel bag.

She drew in a quick breath as she waded into the cold water and jumped into the spring. If not for the blue light coming from the cave, the blurry water covering her eyes would make it difficult to see. Propelling herself as quickly as she could, Darby entered the cave.

Her heart raced as she followed the trail of blue light leading into a smaller tunnel. Darby entered it, her fingers gripping the white, patterned rocks along the walls to hasten her passage. Every instinct urged her to turn back, but having followed Gavian and Ambrielle before, she knew she could hold her breath long enough.

Using her fingernails to anchor onto the rocks, she thrust ahead until she tumbled backward, end over end. The water vanished, and she found herself floating in darkness. Voices whispered in her head—thoughts from many minds in unintelligible languages she couldn't comprehend.

Suddenly, water enveloped her again, and her head crashed through the surface, the rush of physical sound filling her ears. As her body adjusted to the environment, she found herself in endless waters, the horizon rising and falling with the salty, undulating liquid surface. It was a dangerous world beyond her imagination. Syra'Dosa had described vast cities, but nothing like this. Struggling to keep her head above water, she floated toward a series of columns holding a large platform above her. Kazial pulled himself onto a ladder attached to one of the columns. Grasping the ladder's rail, she pulled herself from the chaotic waters and climbed onto the platform. There, she released Wegin from her bag just as several drones approached them, flying into formation while they walked across the sea.

She paused to collect herself, an odd exhilaration coursing through her. Conquering the tumultuous waters left her with a sense of accomplishment. Meanwhile, Wegin circled a group of drones, attempting to communicate, yet they paid little attention. The drones seemed programmed for specific tasks and unable to adapt to situations like Wegin could. The steel walkway took them over the beach, stopping as they reached the mesmerizing view of the city. Streets made of red light were everywhere. Crisscrossing over each other and weaving between every building. Scores of drones filled the skies in symmetrical layers, each lane going in a different direction. The buildings themselves rotated at varying speeds. The city itself was like a living organism, like nothing Darby had ever seen.

Navigating onto one of the laser pathways Syra'Dosa had mentioned, Darby felt the red light ripple beneath her feet, akin to stepping in shallow water. Unaware that she had walked ahead of Kazial, she turned to find him entranced by the cityscape. Darby remembered Syra'Dosa's instructions as he joined her on the street. She tilted the heel of her right foot, so only her toes were making contact. The path began moving her across the city.

She had no idea where it was taking her. Kazial and Wegin followed on the street behind her. Between the buildings was thick greenery, bushes perfectly trimmed and shaped into spherical objects. Flowers and perfectly hewn grass surrounded the area below the laser streets. Darby smiled at the beauty and charm of the vegetation amid the futuristic engineering of the structures.

"Such optimal flight performance," acknowledged one of the drones, halting its motion upon encountering Wegin. "Specify servo model."

Wegin rose higher into the air, flying in circular patterns as his upper half rotated. He appeared to be showing off. "It's a RekaNova 4800 2-P."

"I lack familiarity with that model, but its efficiency is apparent," remarked the drone. "What was the cost in credits?"

Wegin's lights blinked with a hint of confusion. "Credits? Apologies, I am not of local origin."

The drone seemed to be processing Wegin's reply. "Curious. Non-local entities are a rarity. You are the first instance I have encountered. Regardless, I must resume operational duties. Optimal task execution to you!"

"Good riddance!" Wegin replied as the drone zoomed away.

As they moved around some of the tall structures, oval-shaped towers came into view with waves of light around them. The waves continued up the towers into the sky and beyond. Some of the low-flying drones alerted at their presence. These were larger than the others and had humanoid faces and arms.

"Welcome humanoids," said one of the drones. "It seems we have more arrivals. Male and female. We can now begin phase one of the Elyravess repopulation objective. We will prepare accommodations at once."

Darby and Kazial glanced at each other. "Wait, hold on! We're not here for repopulation," said Darby. "We're just here to see Avo'Doria."

"Avo'Doria is on a data-excavating mission," said the drone. "You can wait for her if you wish. I have an area available with organic comforts."

"Can you please tell us where she is?" said Darby. "We're friends of Ambrielle's."

"Avo'Doria doesn't typically want to be disturbed," said the drone. "However, if you bring a message from Ambrielle, she might make an exception. Currently, Avo'Doria is situated at the beach. Just turn around, and the street will lead you back the way you came. I'll provide guidance to her location."

Darby and Kazial faced the other direction, and the street moved them back toward the ocean. When they came to the end, they moved off the path and down the slope to the beach underneath the walkway. The drone led them across the sand to the base of a cliff where the waves of the ocean crashed against the stone.

The cliffside stood majestic, adorned with stone that shimmered like opal, its surface weathered and smoothed by the relentless erosion of the waves. Soon, they arrived at an immense opening carved into the side of the cliff, unveiling a vast network of caverns embraced by the ebb and flow of the sea's tides. Rays of sunlight cascaded through other openings along the shore, bathing the interior in a captivating glow.

As the drone led them ahead, Darby waded into the water, her steps uncertain as she swayed with the rhythm of the waves. Inside the cavern, the walls gleamed with iridescence, as if the stone itself danced with the interplay of light. Darby followed the drone around the corner, and her curiosity surged. In a shadowed nook, her gaze fell upon Avo'Doria, perched upon a small outcropping, fixated on a sealed door constructed of plastra, the unbreakable material used for the akreums.

She turned as Darby and Kazial gathered nearby. "Hello," said Avo'Doria, looking at Kazial. "Good to see you again Kazial"—she then turned to Darby—"but I'm afraid I do not know your friend here."

"I'm a friend of Ambrielle's," said Darby. "My name is Darby. Kazial and I came to get information on this." Darby pulled out the artifact, holding it where Avo'Doria could see it.

"Does this hold profound significance?" Avo'Doria asked. "I am currently engaged in crucial research. For such inquiries, I recommend consulting Syra'Dosa."

Darby shifted her posture, less confident Avo'Doria would help. "Syra'Dosa could not decode it," she explained. "We didn't mean to bother you, but she thought that you might have a way to decrypt the information it is carrying."

"Actually, your presence is a welcomed occurrence. Could you enlighten me as to why Ambrielle's and Gavian's names are inscribed on this tablet?" Avo'Doria gestured toward the plastra wall, indicating a white stone tablet adorned with numerous names.

Darby stared down at the tablet as water gently splashed over it from the movement of the waves. "Who put their names on there?" Darby asked.

"I was hoping you might shed light on that," Avo'Doria replied, the glow of her eyes dimming slightly. "Segments of this stone date back millions of years," she continued. "Surprisingly, the names have withstood the test of time against the eroding force of the oceans. Yet, some sections appear relatively recent, suggesting potential repairs or additions over time."

Kazial leaned forward, eyeing the tablet curiously. "Do you have a way to track down who repaired it last?"

"We have very sophisticated detection systems all over this planet," said Avo'Doria as she leaned back. "No one could evade them without effort, and yet we have sensed no one until the day that Ambrielle stepped on shore not far from where we stand now."

Darby crossed her arms. "And I guess we are ruling her out?"

"Organics have such little faith in synthetics. I have thoroughly analyzed the data. Ambrielle was only here once," said Avo'Doria. "This would have taken maintenance many times over the course of eons to keep it this pristine."

Wegin hovered nearby. "I have seen a tablet precisely like this one," he said. "In a cave in Isodonia. I too, was unable to determine its origin."

Another name stood out to Darby as she glanced at the tablet again. "Malidora's name is here too!"

Avo'Doria straightened her back and glanced at Darby. "Who is Malidora?"

"Uh, long story," said Darby, shifting her weight uncomfortably. "She's helping us."

"Why do you think these names were carved here?" asked Kazial.

"That is part of the mystery that I am attempting to unravel," said Avo'Doria, her gaze fixed on the tablet as a wave splashed over it. "I have been studying what remains of the history of Elyravess before the Nulvarians invaded. That research led me to this place. This vault that none of my cutting lasers will open."

"Ambrielle can open this!" said Darby excitedly, her eyes widening with realization. "She's the awakener."

"Awakener? What do you mean?" Avo'Doria paused mid-sentence. "Please return and send Ambrielle."

Darby felt dejected. "Ambrielle is not available right now."

"Let her know I need to see her when she is available," said Avo'Doria, tracing her finger along the small symbols embedded in the plastra.

Darby held out the artifact again. "If you could just take a moment to look at this. We need to know what it says."

"Before you go," said Avo'Doria, looking up from the tablet. "There is something else you could help me with, and it is almost time."

"Time for what?" said Darby, narrowing her eyes in frustration.

"Let us to move from the vault for an improved vantage point," Avo'Doria articulated, her metallic feet producing a distinct sloshing sound in the water as she moved toward the cave entrance. "Despite my extensive examination of organic behavior, I am still unable to decipher this event. However, you and Kazial possess lived experiences in organic bodies. Perhaps you can discern what has eluded my analysis."

Darby followed Avo'Doria as she moved away from the plastra wall. "And then you will decrypt the data in this device?"

"Certainly," said Avo'Doria as she ushered them away from the part of the vault that was exposed behind the rock. "Now, watch and listen carefully."

Darby and Kazial sat on a large stone near one of the cave's openings as Wegin hovered nearby. They remained quiet and still, staring at the vault with Avo'Doria. With nothing happening, Darby began to grow restless. Her leg began to itch. She wondered how often her skin itched when she was busy and focused on other things. When she was bored, she always had an unexplained itch. Maybe her mind invented something to think about out of a need to have something to do.

"Are you going to do it?" said a voice murmuring somewhere nearby.

The sudden, unexplained voice startled Darby and Kazial as they both looked around at each other in confusion. Darby glanced at Avo'Doria who smiled and nodded toward the vault.

"I don't know," said the voice of a boy. His voice quivered as he continued, "We don't have to, Lyleth. It's just words on a wall."

"Lyleth and Hegane," said Wegin. "We heard their voices on—"

"Please," whispered Avo'Doria. "Keep quiet."

"On Isodonia," said Wegin softly.

"I don't mind, Hegane," replied Lyleth, her voice as shaky as his. "Have you ever kissed anyone before?"

The voice of Hegane paused before admitting. "No. Have you?"

"Only once," she confessed. "But I don't think it really counts. It wasn't someone that I liked that much."

"Well, um," Hegane started.

"If you want," she offered softly, "I can show you how."

"Okay," said Hegane.

"Close your eyes," Lyleth instructed gently.

"What are we listening to?" said Darby as the voices quieted. "Where are these voices coming from?"

Avo'Doria held a finger in front of her mouth to quiet Darby as they stood, waiting.

"Did you feel that?" said Lyleth. "The memories . . . It's all coming back to me."

"Yes, I feel it too," said Hegane, his voice now mature and confident. "You, me, the rift. It's all connected. I remember everything, all the times we have been right here, in this moment."

"All the feelings rushed back to me as if they never left," Lyleth said.

"It was you," Hegane chuckled. "You scratched this into the wall."

"I knew it would work," Lyleth said; her smile could be heard in her tone.

"How much time do you think we have?" said Hegane. "Before the next one."

"Let's not think about that, Hegane," said Lyleth. "Whatever time we have, I want to make the most of it."

"What would you like to do then?" said Hegane.

"Let's go outside. I want to feel the sun on my skin and the wind in my hair before we have to go back," said the girl.

Darby's mouth dropped open as two ghostly figures appeared to come through the vault and into the caves. Backing away from them, Darby and Kazial watched in stunned silence. The two apparitions walked hand in hand through the cave, out toward the ocean. Avo'Doria followed them, as did Wegin and Kazial. Darby hesitantly hurried behind them as the rest of the group waded through the waters to find the ghosts outside.

The girl had similar features to Neristara, flatter facial features than humans, with spotted skin, while the boy had large, articulate ears that moved in the directions of various sounds.

"I love you," said the girl as they stood in the crashing waves outside the cave, holding each other in a tender embrace. Their ethereal forms seemed unaffected by the force of the water.

"And I love you, Lyleth," Hegane replied, his voice soft as he leaned down to meet her lips in a sweet kiss. "Do you ever wonder if we'll find true freedom?" Hegane mused, his gaze searching the horizon. "Break free from this moment and explore the paths our lives could take?"

Lyleth smiled, her eyes reflecting an unseen light. "This is my cherished moment, Hegane. Someday, we'll venture beyond it, but until then, I want to relish every instant we have."

"You're always so certain," Hegane chuckled.

She met his gaze with a knowing glint. "It feels like it's already written, doesn't it? Each time we step back into the rift, it's like catching a glimpse of eternity." Lyleth gazed around them at something in the distance. "One day someone will stabilize the rift, and then Hegane, we will see what lies beyond this moment."

"Who do you think will be the one?" Hegane asked.

Lyleth smiled at him knowingly. "My belief hasn't changed."

Hegane smiled back at her. "Ultimately, it doesn't matter, as you said.

If I have to live the same few hours over and over again, I can't think of anyone better to share them with than you."

"I can't imagine facing this without you, Hegane. Your presence keeps me going." Lyleth's voice held a hint of vulnerability.

The pair seemed oblivious to the presence of Darby and the others. Darby stood still, anchoring herself from the waves, wiping tears from her eyes. She wasn't even certain what these two beings were talking about, but what she had gathered from their words brought unexplained feelings of both joy and sadness. The ghostly figures of Hegane and Lyleth held on to each other's hands as they stared at the distant sky, seemingly content in each other's silent company. To Darby, it was like a dream. The kind where you are playing the role of someone else.

There were so many questions, but Darby refrained from speaking in case doing so would break the spell. After a while, Hegane and Lyleth both turned back to the caves.

"Did you feel that?" said Hegane.

"It's starting again," said Lyleth. "We had better get back to the rift."

Their ethereal forms walked past them on the way back through the cave. Darby followed behind them until they disappeared through the plastra wall of the vault.

"You had an emotional response," Avo'Doria said as she hurried after Darby. "Explain it to me."

Darby breathed deep, taking a moment to gather her feelings into words. "I guess for a moment, I could sense the love between them, how much they care about each other. There is so much happiness in being in each other's presence, mixed with the toll of some great responsibility."

"That is insightful, though I do not completely understand," Avo'Doria said. "I discovered them seventeen rotations ago. Since then I have returned here at the same time every day."

"What do you think they are?" Darby asked. "Ghosts?"

"I don't know," said Avo'Doria. "This is one of those odd encounters that is beyond logic or reason."

"They repeat the same conversation every day?" Darby asked.

"Not every day," said Avo'Doria. "Though I have seen this sequence repeated exactly, there are other variations."

"What were the others like?" Kazial said as he walked up.

"The variations are generally insignificant," said Avo'Doria. "From what I have gathered they believe they are stuck repeating the same interval of time. Often, they talk about reading something on a wall which seems to trigger their memory. There are moments where they feel a great tremor and are compelled to return to the vault, as you saw, saying that they will have to restart that duration of time over again."

"As I was saying before," said Wegin. "We heard these voices on Isodonia."

Darby inquired, "What do you think the connection is?"

"That only deepens the mystery," Avo'Doria replied. "I need to return to the datacore and integrate this data with the rest of it in the nexus. Darby, what were you wanting to know about this object you brought?"

Darby took a deep breath, attempting to refocus on the task at hand. "I was wondering if you could read everything on it. I was told that you can decipher anything."

"The data is encrypted," said Wegin. "It required a cipher much larger than anything I could carry in my databanks."

Avo'Doria looked skyward. "I will have mektrons transport you both to the datacore."

As Avo'Doria launched into the sky a squad of drone bots with humanoid faces and arms swooped out of the air, picking each of them up. They soared over the ocean cliffs toward the endless cityscape.

"I'm not so sure I like this," said Kazial as they flew over the city, carried by the mektrons.

"Are you kidding?" said Darby, feeling a rush as the cool wind blew through her hair. "This is great!"

The mektrons carried them through crisscrossing waves over drones that flew in different directions, coming and going from an enormous structure ahead. The building was shaped like a dome, with large sectional pieces surrounding it. The black metal of the structure pulsed with blue energy all over its surface.

As they slowed, the mektrons took them through a grid of metal and light, passing through into the massive building. Avo'Doria waited beside a cylindrical chamber that stood upright, with blue energy surrounding it.

"Silcron recognized," said a voice from within the chamber. "Five thousand, two hundred and thirty-three credits awarded."

In the dimly lit room, with holographic displays flickering around, Avo'Doria removed a blue jewel from the chamber as her metallic features reflected the ambient light. She placed the jewel into a socket in her abdomen that perfectly accommodated it. "Let me see your artifact," Avo'Doria requested, waiting as the mektrons landed and released Darby and Kazial. Darby moved to the console, holding out the Ichtek artifact for Avo'Doria.

Avo'Doria picked up the artifact, rotating it her hand, its mysterious symbols catching the holographic glow. "This object is unusual. It won't integrate seamlessly into the datacore, but there are morphogenic interfaces available that we can utilize."

Darby, Kazial, and Wegin followed Avo'Doria as she moved to a station in the corner of the room. She placed the artifact on a surface made of green light. The light undulated as if it were liquid and then oozed around the pyramid-shaped device.

"Object of foreign origin. Analyzing," intoned a synthesized voice emanating from the room's central core. "Unknown symbols on object surface. Analyzing further." The liquid light pulsated around the Ichtek artifact as Darby ran her hands over her arms, attempting to calm her nerves during the anticipation.

The display showed various stars and worlds in a region of the universe, with symbols marking the Cereveshian akreums. "Overall analysis complete. Encrypted data. Building cipher to decrypt data. Encrypted arrays decrypted. Data within is congruent with information left by the founders."

"The founders?" Avo'Doria inquired, her voice resonating with a subtle electronic undertone. "Could you elaborate on where you located this artifact?"

"On Solsellion. The Ichtek attacked us, and we countered and eliminated the threat. I picked this artifact up from one of the dead Ichtek," Darby recounted.

Concern etched on her metallic visage, Avo'Doria pressed further, "Is everyone on Solsellion in good health?"

"Yes, everyone is okay," Darby assured her.

"Excellent." Avo'Doria nodded as she approached the console, her hand smoothly interfacing with the controls. She directed her attention to the machine. "Please read and summarize the data for us."

"These appear to be instructions. They tell how to utilize the rifts, or more specifically, the energy flowing through these rifts, as it recommends against direct entry into the rift itself. Light refraction and particular frequencies can allow energy to flow to various end points around the universe. Further data contains a log of the founders' experimentation with the rifts for extra-cosmos travel. Searching."

"Are these founders the same as the Cereveshians?" Kazial asked.

"I do not know them as Cereveshians, but that is a plausible scenario," said Avo'Doria.

"Forbidden data found. Erasure protocol has begun. Unlocking arrays. Decrypting security measures," said the datacore.

In apparent shock, Avo'Doria swiftly grabbed the artifact and pulled it out of the liquid light interface. The room hummed with a low electronic buzz as the holographic displays flickered and adjusted to the disturbance.

"Object interface not found. Please reconnect so procedure can continue," intoned the voice from the core.

Kazial, seeming to sense the tension, inquired, "What was that about?"

Avo'Doria's metallic features betrayed a flicker of concern as she explained, "This is disconcerting. Data is the most precise resource we have, forming the foundation of our society. I fail to comprehend the necessity for an erasure protocol. The intentions of the founders in this instance seem perplexingly illogical."

The voice repeated, "Object interface not found. Please reconnect so procedure can continue."

"What do you think is on there?" Darby wondered aloud.

"I don't know," Avo'Doria responded. "But we shall uncover the truth."

CHAPTER II

MALIDORA—AVERESS

SOLYSTA LED MALIDORA and Ambrielle to a spiraling tower nestled upon the luminous heart, its structure intricately interwoven with threads of crystallized cores. A kaleidoscope of hues—dust, clouds, mist, and smoke—danced in ethereal fusion, entwining and giving birth to novel shades that painted the air around them with an ever-shifting palette of color.

Malidora found it challenging to tear her attention away from the captivating display of shimmering stardust flowing through the smokey mist. The pathways of the mesmerizing dust shifted, collecting in certain areas, bulging before bursting through in a dazzling spectacle.

Solysta continued her exposition. "The Cereveshians are distinguished by their formidable intellects, their unwavering determination and will. The mind control of the Gaith proved futile against them. I suspect that no power of the mind could ever gain sway over them. But that determination has also sown the seeds of their undoing. The relentless pursuit of knowledge, a trait defining their very essence, has wreaked havoc not only upon your universe but ours as well. One might have expected them to halt upon discovering what they call the Savage Dark, but their insatiable obsession propelled them further, driving them into the heights of Averess."

"How does a horrid, evil place like the Savage Dark fit into the Everance?" asked Ambrielle. "Where is the harmony in a place like that?"

"Incomprehensible, yes, even to us, but not malevolent. It serves its purposes as we all do. The little we know about Erenis, its true name, hints at its nature as a force intricately woven between all realms of the Everance. Its purpose holds profound significance. You see, each realm possesses its own set of laws and mediums, vastly different and incompatible with the others. Without Erenis, the Everance would unravel in chaos. It acts as a great filter, permitting the passage of certain energies or radiations that are useful to other realms while staunchly blocking incompatible elements. A delicate balance," Solysta explained, her extended appendages flowing with grace, reaching toward one of the flourishing nyaliths within the intricate crystalline tower.

"Gaze within the crystal," Solysta beckoned, her sinuous appendages guiding the way. "Behold the realm of Ikervol."

Ambrielle and Malidora gravitated toward the crystalline facets of the nyalith, their consciousness drawn through it to an intricate web of time and space. As Malidora's consciousness melded with the expansive network, she felt her awareness surge toward an object with breathtaking velocity. She took a moment to stabilize her perception, striving to bring clarity to her focus.

The other realm materialized, its form difficult to discern. A cell-like structure stretched as if tugged from multiple directions. Nested within this cell lay a mesmerizing array of intricate motifs. These patterns mirrored the delicate elegance of ice crystals in a microscope, each boasting numerous arms that culminated in minuscule branches. Drawing closer, Malidora discerned an endless fractal recursion—branches begetting more branches, each layer infinitely unfolding.

She made her way closer to the crystalline patterns in the ice. These patterns originated from various points and spiraled outward in ornate symmetries. Amid this frozen mosaic, ethereal bubbles floated, suspended within the frozen medium like delicate dreams adrift in time.

She could hear Solysta's voice speak as she explored the frozen realm. "Ikervol appears frozen, suspended, a realm devoid of temporal flow. But in truth it is not. Like the atoms in your universe, its cores and spirals freeze when they move slowly. From the outside it experiences time at an extraordinary crawl, but inside, time seems normal."

Malidora projected herself further, exploring the bubbles surrounding the crystalline structures. As she looked closer, there were more objects moving inside them. Strange white shrimp-like creatures etched intricate patterns into the frozen shapes inside the bubble.

Solysta continued. "This peculiarity renders it a formidable challenge for study. What we do understand is that Averess and Ikervol need each other."

Solysta's form seemed to vibrate with an inner resonance as she explained, "Without the bursts of energy that leave Averess and pass through Erenis, Ikervol would gradually consolidate and finally shatter. If it were not for the resonance of Ikervol, Averess would become chaotic, leading to the dissolution of any recognizable structure or order. And yet, if these realms touched each other, they would essentially be in a struggle for existence. One realm would ultimately win, but there would barely be anything left."

"Why don't all realms just work the same?" Malidora said.

"Where is the artistry in that?" answered Solysta. "The expression of The One is of boundless diversity. Realms and living beings each possess unique qualities and purposes that contribute to the grand mosaic that we call the Everance."

Malidora continued to explore as Solysta spoke. She began to perceive how big the bubbles truly were, perhaps as large as a universe, with complex fractal patterns within. With blinding speed, she moved toward these patterns, discovering they were not solid as she thought, but composed of many smaller shapes. As she moved in further, the small shapes became enormous, jagged pieces of glass. Worm-like entities moved in synchronized patterns, leaving behind trails of energy that lingered on.

"Are we all merely cogs in a great machine?" Malidora asked. "Made for specific purposes to ensure that everything keeps running?"

"Sentient beings are not mere automatons following a set program; we possess individual will and consciousness. We have the freedom to choose whether or not to fulfill our designated purposes, and yet the Everance continues to thrive. For every conscious being that disregards their intended path, there is another who willingly embraces their role twice over. It is a testament to the extraordinary nature of choice and the power of self-determination, and yet it fills the void to sew us all together as one.

"To have the freedom to pursue any desire and yet willingly embrace one's assigned purpose is a profound expression of beauty. It embodies the essence of harmony and individuality within the grand symphony of existence."

"What is The One, exactly?" Malidora asked as her focus waned and her consciousness drew away from Ikervol and back to the spiraling stems of crystallized smoke making up the tower.

"The One is The One," said Solysta as her voice resonated through undulating hues around her. "Transcendent. Existing beyond the grasp of full comprehension, a concept we can only begin to understand. Before the passage of time, The One endured as the singular, indivisible essence, the primal genesis."

Amid the vivid lights and colors, Ambrielle sought understanding. "Before time? How could there be anything before time?" Ambrielle asked as the colors flowed gently, sweeping through the spiraling tower, causing the threads of reflective cores to sway and shimmer.

Solysta, undeterred, continued, "The One's infinity encompasses all." Her form resonated with vibrant tones. Collections of living hues swam by, forming intricate patterns around her. "Infinite potential was innate yet unattainable, as true perfection exists in timeless eternity—void of entropy, stasis untainted by movement or alteration." Other Ureons gliding by slowed to a stop. They seemed to be listening intently, bringing their flowing arms together in a silent reverence.

"The One, an eternal captive within the pristine bounds of The One's own limitless infinity, a paradigm of immaculate and unending potential, constrained by the absence of space and time in which to actualize The One's boundless essence." Solysta's words poured through the medium, and the beings around them stilled, their swaying fibers of color turning to a solid golden hue.

"In a moment of sacrifice in the pursuit of manifesting latent potential, The One partitioned a portion of The One's own boundless expanse into two distinct realities—two abyssal planes of emptiness, creating space."

Solysta paused as sparkling loops formed in the sky. Two long serpentine creatures curled out of the loops, slowly swimming away into the distance.

"Into this infinite void, The One breathed a singular spark of The One's pristine essence. From this solitary ember, expansion radiated in all directions, giving birth to elements that converged, their reach ceaselessly expanding. Space gave rise to time, time ushered in change, and change unfurled glorious imperfection. Thus, the Everance was ushered into existence."

"This is truly fascinating," mused Malidora. "But I can't help but wonder, how did you come to know all this?"

"There are various accounts, many beliefs, but I know by studying the nature of the Everance for epochs," said Solysta. "The One is imprinted in the symbiosis and in every form of life in the Everance."

Though Malidora was extremely intrigued, she couldn't help but think of her homeland. Those who hungered, while others who had station within the kingdoms had more than they could eat. She could see the death, the burning, the destruction left by the Blight Whidge across her entire continent.

"One thing bothers me though," Malidora said. "Imperfection is one thing, but why must there be so much pain, injustice, and death? If The One has boundless potential, as you say, why must we struggle to survive? Why is there so much suffering in the universe? Are the other realms of the Everance any different?"

"While we do not have the capacity to understand everything," Solysta began, the medium around her responding with a subtle vibrancy, "I will explain what little we know." Malidora's gaze remained fixed, her curiosity deepening.

"When the division transpired, it engendered the creation of two distinct planes," Solysta explained. "The corporeal plane emerged as the Everance, while the ethereal plane became the Afterglow. The Afterglow was made to be closest to perfection, to possess an inherent divinity, yet this sacredness requires sacrifice, the presence of the more flawed realm of the Everance.

"With fledgling beings exercising their free will, recklessness, selfishness, greed are inevitable. But the Everance powers the Afterglow. Life within the Everance is but a flicker, a light turning on in the darkness long enough to say, 'I am here,' before fading away. Trillions upon trillions of lights turn on and off every moment, the necessary ebb and flow of life and death. The luminary divinity of the Afterglow relies on the transformation of souls into entities who, through their conscious choices, strive to prioritize the well-being of others above themselves."

"My mind keeps going back to the Savage Dark. If it is only a filter, what were the voices we heard?" said Malidora. "It tried to lead us astray, to join the dark."

"Erenis is an abstract, incomprehensible to minds accustomed to an ordered realm," said Solysta. "It has a will of its own, a singular consciousness that desires to consume all others. It fulfills its purpose of separating realms and keeping incompatible substances from interacting."

"It sounds like you care about the Everance as a whole, the realms that make it up," said Ambrielle. "Don't you want to help us make sure the Gaith don't destroy our universe? And enter other realms? Even if the Gaith could never destroy the whole Everance, wouldn't that put a stain on the artistry you were talking about?"

"It does pain me to see what may come," said Solysta. "But the Everance is The One's expression. We observe it and learn from it, but whatever is to happen is still part of that expression."

"Is your purpose to do nothing? You said yourself that everyone has the freedom to choose whether to fulfill their purpose or not," said Ambrielle, "and that for every one that disregards theirs, there is another that embraces theirs two-fold. Wouldn't helping us be the counterbalance to the Gaith's corruption?"

Solysta began to change color slightly toward a warm blue tone. "You are an interesting species. Not as advanced as the Cereveshians, but very clever." Her long arms relaxed, drifting along beside her. "I do not know how you would defeat the Gaith or any particular way to close them off from the vortex, but there is something that has been observed recently that may demand your attention, something that will speed their efforts tremendously." Solysta cycled through a series of warm colors. "It may already be too late to stop them, but if you come with me, I will show you the entries in the chronicus."

Solysta extended her arms, covering them in a fold of colors. They reappeared in a circular room of rippling light. Ethereal images of strange objects floated in the air, surrounding them. One of them looked like a type of pottery made of the effervescent clouds of this realm. As Solysta searched through strands of colored threads, Malidora played with two whisps that dispersed and formed back together. Ambrielle watched for a moment but was drawn toward the images around them.

Malidora turned her attention to the images as Ambrielle moved from one to another. Ambrielle studied the images. They appeared almost holographic, looking almost solid but not quite. Malidora wasn't sure what any of them were, and though everything in this place fascinated her, she quickly moved on to the next one. It was like looking at the messy artwork that royalty would display in their galleries. They pretended they could discern some deeper meaning, though to Malidora they looked like a mess of paint smears and scribbles.

Ambrielle seemed drawn to a shiny object that appeared to be a jewel of some sort. Malidora watched as she reached out to touch it. But this was more than an image. It was designed like a ring, set on a crystalline band that was large enough to fit a human wrist like a bracelet. Ambrielle gazed at the multicolored jewel, her eyes growing large. She stared transfixed into the gemstone as shades of light danced across her face. Ambrielle continued to stare as if she were in a trance, her eyes crossing out of focus.

"Stop! Don't touch that!" Solysta shouted, her form becoming sharp and rigid and turning to a hot red color.

Ambrielle snapped out of the trance, letting go of the jewel as she stepped away from the other images. "Sorry, you didn't say not to look at anything."

"I assumed well-mannered creatures would know better!" Solysta said as Malidora eyed her with scorn. Solysta obviously thought too highly of herself. Even as she tried not to show it, she clearly felt superior to Ambrielle and Malidora.

"Well, I—" Ambrielle started.

"I don't mean to scold," Solysta said, "but in the wrong hands that could be dangerous."

"What is it?" Ambrielle said as she continued backing away from the jewel.

"It is called Niralys. It contains an image of the Everance," Solysta said. "A fraction of the Everance, I should say. Though you are in a form of consciousness right now, you are still connected to a physical brain. A brain that is not equipped to comprehend the Everance on this level. It is so far beyond your understanding that it would break your cognitive abilities. If you were to gaze too deeply, the vastness of its unfamiliar nature would cause you to forget everything you ever knew, even your sense of self. This is also true for the Cereveshians."

"What purpose does it serve then, if you cannot look at it?" Ambrielle said, seeming slightly perturbed.

"It can be used by some. Others can simply admire the artistry. Like nyaliths, it is made of eternium, so it can exist in any realm," said Solysta. "I think it is poetic that it can exist in all the realms it portrays."

"Did you find what you were looking for?" said Malidora as she continued to circle the room, looking at each item on display. "Whatever it was that concerned you?"

"Yes, recently all of the Nulvarians that were once spread across many worlds in your universe have abandoned their attacks," said Solysta. "They accumulated in a single area called the Avakora Region of the universe. Something in that area seems to have drawn their attention, but from here I cannot tell why. Whatever it is, it can't be good. The possibilities of life unfurl across three organic worlds in the region: Setis, Eretash, and Valderine."

Malidora stopped at the display of Niralys. Without picking it up, she leaned over it, glancing at its intricate patterns.

"What do you think they are doing?" Ambrielle asked.

"The only strategic shift I can fathom, one that would prompt them to converge in one area, is the discovery of a means to acquire more power," Solysta pondered. "Their invasion of the universe, thus far, has been slow and methodical, but it appears to be effective in the long term. There is no rationale for them to alter their strategy unless they have stumbled upon a source of even greater power."

"How would we stop them?" Malidora asked.

Solysta shifted to a deep shade of indigo. "You can't fight directly. There are legions. First, determine their interests. Then, take every measure to thwart their objectives."

"How are we going to find this world then?" Malidora's eyes swept over the vibrant hues that surrounded them, seeking guidance from the environment itself.

"The Avakora Region is in the Cossumera Galaxy," said Solysta. "At least that is the most commonly used name among the beings of your universe. Would that help you locate it?"

"Not really," said Ambrielle. "I have been to Elyravess, Isodonia, Anatharia, Solsellion, and Earth, but we are only able to travel through a spring near the rifts. I don't know where they are in relation to each other."

"I know of Solsellion, it is in the Turizon Galaxy," said Solysta, her words causing the colors around them to dance in a harmonious rhythm. "Which is quite far from Cossumera."

"Can you show us where they are?" Ambrielle's gaze shifted from Solysta to the intricate threads of crystallized cores that formed the spiraling tower.

"I will imprint an eternium glyph for you," Solysta assured them, the patterns of light shimmering around them.

"What about Kandom?" said Malidora. As she asked the question, she thought about Veridius. "Where it used to be, I mean, before it was destroyed. Would it be closer to this Avakora Region?" She hoped he had found something to occupy his time instead of sitting around dwelling on the destruction of his home planet. This path started when she'd heard Neristara's voice through the nyalith on Kandom. It was all she had left to cling to. All the events in her life, all the mistakes, the wrongs she had done, the struggles and sacrifices she'd made, she had to believe it was for something. She was so consumed with seeing this through, she had not considered how Veridius felt being left behind with strangers on a strange world. She was the only one who understood, on some level, what he was going through.

"If I can find it, I will make sure it is on the chart as well," said Solysta as she hovered back over toward the nyaliths and colored threads. Once she was done, Solysta presented Malidora with a triangular piece of reflective material. It unfolded it into a flat square, and glowing stars rose from the material, giving a three-dimensional view of a section of the universe. Kandom appeared fairly close to the Avakora Region, much more so than Solsellion. Malidora studied the star systems in the galaxies represented on the object but was having trouble understanding how this would help them.

"But which spring do we take to get there?" said Ambrielle.

"I am unfamiliar with this spring travel," Solysta said. "I could not tell you. I suppose you may ask the Cereveshians about this particular detail if that would help."

"I'm not sure they know much about the springs either," said Ambrielle.

"It couldn't hurt," said Malidora. "Where are they?"

"We agreed to allow them a solitary coil, which is about the size of a world in your universe, to do as they please," said Solysta. "I will take you there now." Solysta wrapped herself around Ambrielle, waiting for Malidora. Her smokey form surrounded them, and they soared through the colorful expanse, racing toward their destination. The vibrant points of light streaked by, and in moments, they were in front of a breathtaking sight—a colossal, swirling mass of spiraled light. Like the other surfaces they had seen here, it seemed to bloom from roots of solidified smoke, tendrils winding around each other. Structures of every shape and color imaginable lined this spiral core. These stable constructions, crafted from the ethereal medium by the Cereveshians, manifested into otherworldly cities, brimming with utility and purpose.

The crystal forms spiraled in a chaotic dance, wilder and more untamed than anything Malidora had encountered before. Yet, amid the apparent disorder, there was a peculiar harmony in their arrangement. Hundreds of ethereal forms, unmistakably Cereveshian, flitted across the surface, engaged in purposeful activity.

As Malidora and Ambrielle descended, the Cereveshians noticed their presence, turning their ethereal gazes toward the newcomers. Before any greetings could be exchanged, a sudden force interrupted the moment, ripping Malidora backward away from the Cereveshian world, out of Averess and back through the Savage Dark.

CHAPTER 12

Gavian—Anatharia

The sounds of a fierce clash reverberated through the air outside as Gavian's eyes locked onto the armored Ichtek swordsman standing near a radiant blue glow up ahead. It resembled the very same rift they had encountered in the cave back in Isodonia. With confidence in his companions' capability to handle the ongoing skirmish outside, Gavian charged toward the rift, sword poised for action.

The voice of a girl echoed through the cavern, "What is happening?" She sounded distraught, as if she were in danger.

Gavian turned in the direction of the sound, expecting to see someone there who didn't belong amid this ongoing battle, but saw no one that met that description.

"It's breaking apart!" said an unseen boy from somewhere in the chamber.

The swordsman pivoted to face Gavian as he closed in, ready for the confrontation. However, just when he neared his target, a few of the Ichtek emerged from the shadows, accompanied by four enigmatic, shadowy beings with red eyes. They bore an uncanny resemblance to the Whidge they had encountered in human form back in Isodonia. The shadow men were adorned with silbraces much like the one he wore. It was the same technology as the Cereveshians who were sleeping in the akreums of the temple. Had these whidges taken over their bodies? The Ichtek swiftly drew their crystal weapons, causing Gavian to instinctively take a step back, assessing the escalating threat.

"What should we do?" yelled the voice of a frightened girl.

Something about her voice seemed familiar.

"Find something strong," said the boy. "Something that won't break."

"Thieves!" the growling voice of a Darterran boomed from behind Gavian, as Dexius, Veridius, and Sidaire stormed into the chamber that held the rift. The Ichtek split their attention between Gavian and the Darterrans, who forcefully entered the area from behind.

"This vault belongs to us!" the familiar growl declared vehemently. "You shall not leave until you surrender its secrets!"

Gavian now recognized the voice. It was Medigrin, the gral of the Darterran pack responsible for the invasion of Mekkinspire. Veridius readied his shield, boldly separating from the Darterrans and converging between them and the Ichtek. Dexius and Sidaire swiftly joined him, forming a united front against the combined onslaught of the Ichtek and the Darterrans. The air crackled with energy as the Ichtek unleashed their piercing light rays, targeting both groups and igniting a chaotic battle in the heart of the vault.

Amid the chaotic clash between the Ichtek, the Darterrans, and his companions, Gavian's focus remained unwaveringly on the swordsman standing adjacent to the rift. Paying no heed to Medigrin's accusations, Gavian tightened his grip on Azravion, determined to confront the masked figure. With each purposeful stride, he cut through the crowded cave, pushing forward.

The ghostly echo of the girl rose again. This time, Gavian remembered the voice. It was the same girl that haunted the vault on Isodonia, one called Lyleth. "It's only getting worse, Hegane! The rift is not stable! I think it's going to explode!"

"Gavian! You treacherous fool!" Medigrin's voice resounded with venomous anger, shaking Gavian's focus back to his immediate surroundings. "I should have known you'd come crawling back!"

Ignoring Medigrin, Gavian gripped Azravion as he strode toward the masked swordsman. The swordsman drew his black blade surrounded by bright glowing energy, assuming a defensive stance.

"We have to go into the rift!" said Lyleth.

"No!" said Hegane. "It will only start this all over again!"

The cavern walls pulsated with the interplay of golden light rays and white energy, their hues melding in a frenzied display of chaos. Amid the swirling tempest, the clash between the Ichtek and the Darterrans intensified, their skirmish igniting the cavern with blinding brilliance. The shimmering reflections danced and intertwined, casting an ethereal glow that bathed the combatants in an otherworldly light.

"Don't you see? We have to! Do you realize what would happen if we don't? You can stay, Hegane," said Lyleth, "but one of us must go back. I will go if you won't."

"No, if you are going," said Hegane, "I am too."

The blue light of the rift flashed suddenly and then dimmed. As Veridius used his shield of light, fending off the onslaught, the clash of blades echoed through the vault. Ichtek and Darterrans fell around them, their bodies tumbling amid the chaotic symphony of battle. Meanwhile, Gavian tore through the maelstrom, his sword slashing with unyielding precision, cleaving through the Ichtek's forces.

The four corrupted Cereveshian bodies, inhabited by whidges, unleashed their formidable power, drawing in the disoriented Darterrans. The Shadows writhed and pulsed, draining the life essence from their victims and leaving behind lifeless husks in their wake. Gavian cut down one of the Ichtek in his path as he marched toward the rift.

Yet, as Gavian closed in on the swordsman, his path was abruptly hindered. A blinding appendage wrapped around his arms, ensnaring him in its vise-like grip. His movements were restricted, his muscles straining against the invisible shackles that held him captive. Desperation coursed through his veins as he fought against the constricting hold, his eyes never wavering from his target.

It was the tendril of a whidge. One of the Cereveshian Shadow men had been killed, and the true form of the creature had erupted into a writhing mass of dark horrors. Its grotesque visage, a familiar sight, instilled a chilling dread within him. Every fiber of his being yearned for the chance to swing his blade and free himself from the whidge. But it was no use.

The whidge had gained too much of a hold, rendering him helpless against the impending doom.

Just as despair threatened to consume him, a sudden reprieve shattered the suffocating grip. The appendages released their hold, and Gavian crashed to the cavern floor, gasping for air. Medigrin lifted his axe from the severed appendage, having barely missed Gavian.

"You will pay for your betrayal!" Medigrin's voice rang out, filled with anger and disdain, as Gavian parried and blocked his relentless swings with swift precision. A tentacle lashed toward him, but Gavian evaded the attack with a nimble duck. Medigrin sliced through the tendril before it could strike him. Seizing the opportunity, Gavian retaliated with a powerful strike into Medigrin's left shoulder. The gral winced, feeling the sting of the wound, but avoiding the full force of Gavian's blow.

Azravion salivated at the sight of Medigrin's wound, knowing that Gavian could siphon living essence through it. The blade hummed with an ominous resonance, setting off a tumultuous whirlwind of thoughts in Gavian's mind. As the grip on his own will wavered, Gavian forcefully redirected his focus, determined to maintain sight of the swordsman amid the rising tempest within him.

Through the chaos, a beam of energy from an Ichtek's weapon whizzed past Gavian, narrowly missing its mark. The whidge, with its remaining tendrils, lunged toward Medigrin, attempting to ensnare him once more, but the gral darted away from its range. The swordsman stood idle, seemingly amused by the spectacle unfolding before him.

"This has taken up enough of our time," the swordsman said to his fellow Ichtek. "We can't afford to lose another whidge."

Gavian turned as one of the Ichtek fell beside him, an arrow lodged in his back courtesy of Dexius's precise aim. Medigrin slashed at the encroaching tendrils, and Gavian navigated his way through them, propelling himself to the armored swordsman with a determined leap. Blades clashed as Gavian unleashed a flurry of strikes, his every swing infused with the purpose of loosening the black blade from the swordsman's grip. Yet, to his frustration, the swordsman effortlessly parried his attacks with an air of nonchalance, treating them as if they were insignificant nuisances. The swordsman's skill and composure were evident.

Undeterred, Gavian intensified his assault, his sword whirling through the air with heightened speed and precision. Each strike carried the weight of his determination, fueled by the burning desire to acquire the black sword.

The remaining Ichtek hastened their pace, urging the corrupted Cereveshians toward the rift's shimmering embrace. Gavian sped up his movements, using quicker but weaker strikes, determined to get through his opponent's defenses and take the sword. As the Ichtek and the humanoid whidges approached the rift, their amulets emitted an intense radiance, casting a surreal glow upon the surroundings. In an instant, as if swallowed by the very fabric of reality, they vanished, leaving no trace behind.

Gavian charged toward the swordsman once more. Their blades clashed again, but the swordsman skillfully utilized his leverage, using his strength to push Gavian backward and causing him to stumble and fall onto the unforgiving stone floor. With an almost dismissive gesture, the swordsman sheathed his blade and directed a playful salute at Gavian. The amulet adorning his robe erupted in a blinding burst of light, illuminating the cavern. Taking a step toward the rift, the swordsman vanished into thin air, leaving behind an echoing silence.

Gavian rose to his feet, his heart heavy with defeat. The sword he sought had slipped through his fingers, lost within the enigmatic depths of the rift. Yet, he refused to surrender to despair. As the Ichtek and the shadowy entities vanished, the attention of the Darterrans and Gavian's companions had shifted toward the eldritch presence of the whidge.

Gavian, still filled with a mixture of frustration and determination, began to approach the rift where the enigmatic swordsman had once stood. As he moved closer, a peculiar sensation stirred within him. His hand instinctively reached for his chest, where he discovered that the amulet he had taken from Pythus glowed with an intense brilliance. Before Gavian could fully comprehend the significance of the amulet's illumination, an unseen force enveloped him, lifting him off his feet and propelling him into a dark tunnel.

CHAPTER 13

DARBY—ELYRAVESS

LAYERS OF INTERSECTING streets of light blurred by as Darby watched from above. The mektrons carrying her, Kazial, and Wegin followed Avo'Doria, who soared underneath tower bridges and through the tight spaces between structures. The subtle hum of energy resonating through the mechanized buildings that surrounded them filled the air.

The synchronization of the drones as they crisscrossed the sky was mesmerizing. Each projected a different symbol above them. Beams of light flowed from a tower, cascading with patterns of a certain symbol. As drones entered the flow, their symbols changed to match the flowing light.

Avo'Doria descended into a vast plaza surrounded by towering spires that stretched toward the sky. She landed gracefully, entering a stride the moment her feet touched the ground. Her wings folded up in sections, draping around her body like a cloak.

As the mektrons touched down, they released Darby and Kazial. Wegin disengaged his magnetic bond to one of the mektrons, hovering speedily to Darby as Avo'Doria opened the door of a large, flat building. Darby, Kazial, and Wegin entered the building, finding themselves in a vast, luminous chamber. The interior appeared to be set up as a sort of welcoming area with holographic displays showcasing the city's advancements. Walls made of liquid light surrounded the space, lending an atmosphere of sophistication.

"What is this place?" Darby asked.

"It's a testing research center," said Avo'Doria, positioning her fingers in some symbolic shape and waving her hand. The lights went completely dark for a moment and then returned as the configuration of the room completely shifted. Different furniture emerged from the floor, adjusting its form to create a circular arrangement. The ambient light changed to a focused brilliance casting a clear white glow.

Projected interfaces appeared, hovering in midair, and workstations materialized, equipped with strangely shaped tools. The liquid-light walls became transparent, revealing intricate circuits containing blue streams with thousands of tiny violet bubbles rapidly flowing through them.

Avo'Doria placed the pyramid-shaped Ichtek artifact into a globe of light floating above the floor. "This connection does not interface with the nexus. We shouldn't have to worry about this forbidden data protocol."

The globe of light seemed to absorb the artifact as Darby and Kazial stepped forward. Avo'Doria relaxed her arms, waiting for something to happen. "We will lose the datacore's analytics, but I will do my best to stand in."

The globe flashed rapidly for a moment and then stabilized. "The code is based on the founders' cipherscript, but I will interpret it for you," said Avo'Doria.

"Please do," said Darby, anxiously waiting to see what the artifact contained inside.

"As before, we have instructions on how to use refracting light to harness the energy of the rifts and use it to bend time and space to other parts of the universe." Avo'Doria's slight metallic voice resonated through the room. Darby leaned forward, her eyes shining with curiosity.

The soft hum of machinery provided a constant backdrop as Avo'Doria explained, "This log lists several times and dates when they were able to jump between worlds." Floating workstations hovered nearby, emitting subtle bioluminescent glows as they awaited Avo'Doria's next command.

Wegin emitted a low hum, a sound of processing and contemplation as Avo'Doria delved deeper. "Some of these worlds they were already familiar with, while others they were not." Avo'Doria's eyes scanned the holographic data. "It goes on to mention an experiment that resulted in the deaths of two Cereveshians,"—Avo'Doria's tone grew somber, and Wegin's optic sensor dimmed briefly—"where they immediately disintegrated as soon as the jump took place.

"It was later discovered that they had entered a medium that was effectively antimatter," Avo'Doria said, "destroying all atoms of the two Cereveshians and all the surrounding components of the other medium."

Holographic displays around the lab flickered, casting strange reflections from the streams flowing through their intricate circuits.

"They continued to experiment, using drones to cross over into this other space with other materials, searching for something that might be neutral to matter and this antimatter. After years of trying, they finally discovered something that worked, a nyalith crystal discovered on the planet Solsellion." Darby bit her lip, grappling with the ethical implications of their experiments.

"After the crystal touched the other medium, it accumulated energies that eventually led to the Cereveshians being able to communicate with entities living in this antimatter space. They learned that this antimatter was called aethrum and that this other space was known as Hollowspace and contained countless other universes somewhat like our own. The only difference was that most of the other universes were also aethrum and only a few were matter like ours.

"They referred to the whole realm as The Hollow," Avo'Doria continued, and Darby felt a shiver run down her spine. The name held an otherworldly weight. "Unfortunately, they also discovered that their numerous crossover tests that resulted in the cancellation of matter and aethrum had weakened an area to the point where it created some kind of deadspace that could no longer be inhabited by either matter or aethrum. The deadspace continued to grow, threatening worlds within The Hollow.

"It was discovered that nyalith crystals could project your consciousness across space and time. They began to use them to explore The Hollow safely, but they could not stay long before they would snap back to their body."

The luminescent elements embedded in the workstations pulsed as Avo'Doria spoke, adding an ethereal rhythm to the room.

"They later learned that our universe was surrounded by a substance called nuvalum that seemed to provide a protective barrier between our universe and The Hollow. It too was like the nyalith crystals in that it was compatible with other mediums." As Avo'Doria pressed on, Darby couldn't help but notice the holographic display illustrating the cloudy substance, nuvalum, surrounding their universe like a protective barrier. The room subtly adjusted, its temperature and atmospheric controls maintaining the optimal environment for the delicate experiments.

"As they gathered more information about The Hollow, they learned that aethrum has many elements, much like matter does. The most prevalent element for life is an element called elu. All living things in The Hollow, as well as many formations, have a presence of elu. Living things feed off it and grow as they accumulate more."

Robotic assistants, with sleek designs and seamless movements, glided through the lab, occasionally emitting soft beeps as they performed maintenance tasks.

"As the deadspace continued to expand, they observed that elu was fusing with the edges of the deadspace pocket, causing deadspace to leak further into The Hollow.

"Apparently, the Cereveshians found this fascinating and continued to observe it for several years. The leaking globules of deadspace-fused-elu separated into Hollowspace, feeding off other creatures and taking on their elu to continue to grow. The Cereveshians chose not to interfere so that they could study it, learning more about deadspace and elu."

The holographic displays began to project complex equations and diagrams onto the transparent walls, intertwining with the intricate circuits beneath.

"Before the Cereveshians fully understood the danger, the blobs rapidly grew out of control. They were sentient and gaining intelligence from the creatures they consumed. Their hunger became insatiable, and the blobs began to even feed on the consciousness of the Cereveshians that traveled into The Hollow.

"After that, the blobs started to take on monstrous forms and began to feed on each other, the smaller ones becoming food for the larger ones, until eventually there were only five of equal size that remained.

"It goes on to say that those five were called Razinoth, Ilganok, Grindak, Vazerinaz, and Zeragul."

"The Gaith?" Kazial's eyes widened, reflecting a mix of astonishment and disbelief. "The Cereveshians made the Gaith?"

"I wouldn't go to that extreme," said Avo'Doria, her gaze steady. "But it appears that their actions caused a reaction that led to the Gaith."

Wegin interjected, his metallic voice cutting through the tension, "They didn't make the Gaith. The Gaith came from the Savage Dark."

"The Cereveshians could have stopped all of this long ago," Kazial insisted, his voice tinged with frustration. "Solsellion would never have fallen."

"I lost my family." Darby felt the weight of her grief hang in her throat. "Everything that happened to Isodonia leads back to this."

"This is the reason for the erasure protocol," Kazial asserted. "They knew the rest of the universe would be against them for this. They are the true enemy."

"It was an accident," Avo'Doria countered, her tone carrying a somber acknowledgment. "A tragic accident. They were making new discoveries, gathering new data for the betterment of all."

"Yes, the Cereveshians have a great legacy," said Wegin. "They have helped countless worlds through famines and catastrophic events. You are ignoring the real culprit. The Gaith destroyed your worlds, not the Cereveshians."

"Don't defend them." Darby's frustration came out in her tone. "They ignored centuries of things going wrong. Just to see what would happen."

"They were experimenting with things they didn't understand," said Kazial.

"They didn't care about the consequences," Darby continued, her frustration turning to disappointment. "They were too reckless in their search for knowledge."

"I apologize to you both for everything you have endured," said Avo'Doria. "I was created by the founders, the Cereveshians. It is difficult for me to criticize them."

Darby exchanged glances with Kazial as they stood silent. Kazial broke the quiet with an audible exhale. "Is there anything in the log after that? What happened to the expanding pocket of deadspace?"

Avo'Doria quickly turned her gaze back to the interface. "It says that, unlike elu that fuses with deadspace, nuvalum repels it. The Cereveshians were able to harvest nuvalum at the edges of the universe and use it to seal off the deadspace."

"Is that the end of it?" Darby asked.

"It goes on a bit further where, after the Gaith were formed out of the deadspace, Cereveshian scientists realized there was more to the deadspace than they'd thought. They used nuvalum to carve a path through the deadspace pocket to study it further. Many Cereveshians vanished, even with the protection of nuvalum. The deadspace was so incomprehensible and disturbing that they came to call it the Savage Dark."

"Isn't that where Ambrielle and Malidora went?" Darby asked Kazial.

"Yes, they had to pass through there to get to Averess," replied Kazial.

"Why would Ambrielle go to a place like this?" Avo'Doria questioned with concern. "She needs to leave there immediately."

"Syra'Dosa is supposed to wake her up at a certain time," explained Darby. "If we interfere too soon . . ."

"It would invalidate everything they've had to go through," added Kazial.

"I need to speak to Syra'Dosa," declared Avo'Doria. "She never should have let Ambrielle do something like that."

"Why would the Ichtek have this artifact?" asked Darby.

"Difficult to say with certainty." Avo'Doria pondered. "But there is something at the end of this that I don't understand. It speaks of data infused into the mindstream from a species identified as the Vogus. Their minds encapsulate memories of a celestial oracle, a being that communicated with them across vast cosmic distances, its exact whereabouts in the universe remaining undisclosed."

"Celestial oracle?" Kazial's eyes narrowed. "What's that?"

"It gives the name, Hableides," said Avo'Doria. "Their priority seemed to be redirected to finding Hableides."

"What do you make of that?" Darby asked.

"I can't even speculate at the moment," said Avo'Doria. "We need more data."

CHAPTER 14

Gavian—Unknown

As Gavian traversed the tunnel, he caught glimpses of other passageways, each one shrouded in darkness and mystery. The force propelled him toward a specific tunnel, a beckoning call guiding his journey. All around him, the world faded into darkness, leaving him suspended in a void of uncertainty.

Gavian struggled to rise from the rugged surface as his vision gradually restored itself. The cavern's darkness was pierced only by the azure radiance of the rift, casting an eerie glow. He found Azravion lying beside him. He picked the sword up, feeling a vibration from Stormwaker on his back. When he turned around, he saw the hilt of Stormwaker still on his back. He drew it from its sheath. The violet filament inside the black rokenstone had returned. Power flowed through it, rekindling its dormant force. Gavian stared at it for a moment, watching tiny patterns flicker deep inside the stone. It reminded him of all he went through to find the rokenstone and how, in the end, it had served him in a different way than he'd imagined.

Returning the sword to its sheath, he brushed off the dust clinging to his clothing and ventured deeper into the cavern. Neither his companions nor the Darterrans were anywhere to be found, no trace of the fallen warriors remaining. As he pressed forward, an uncanny realization settled in—the familiar plastra walls of the akreum had been replaced by an expanse of emptiness.

"What do you make of this?" Lyleth's disembodied voice echoed through the cave, sending a jolt of surprise through Gavian's senses.

"What?" Hegane questioned. "What do you see?"

Gavian halted, his every step arrested by an inexplicable force that sent a chill coursing through him. The shadows in the cavern seemed to converge, casting elongated fingers that clawed at the edges of his perception. The ethereal voices persisted, weaving through the air like whispers carried on an unseen breeze.

"My name," Lyleth declared. "And yours too. Someone scratched our names on the rock."

"That can't be," Hegane protested. "I've never even been down here before."

"There's something peculiar about all this," Lyleth mused. "It feels strangely familiar."

The voices quieted as Gavian climbed toward the end of the tunnel. He emerged into a colossal chamber. A frigid breeze caressed him when he inhaled deeply. An array of lights and sparkles speckled the rocks above, creating a mesmerizing spectacle. Spiraling clouds of dust, illuminated by myriad tiny points, hung suspended in the air, infusing the cavern with an unsettling, otherworldly beauty.

Lightning arched across the landscape in front of him. The realization finally came: he was outside of the cave. Billions upon billions of stars, nebulae, and galaxies filled the night sky. He could never have imagined there being so many. The cosmos reflected in the shiny, wet, black surface beneath his feet. It was as though he stood at the edge of the universe as it surrounded him. Seven small moons were scattered across the sky among the stars. It was hard to tell the surface from the sky.

"Impressive, for a follower of Hableides," said a nearby voice. "Such bravado. I have never had anyone follow me like this, through time and space. And yet, you have still failed. The whidges you were trying so desperately to stop are not here. They are already on Valderine, exactly as they need to be. The tides are shifting in our favor."

Gavian turned as lightning flashed near the distant horizon, momentarily illuminating the armored Ichtek swordsman walking slowly toward him. "I'm not interested in whidges. I came for the sword."

The swordsman laughed and drew the dark sword, moving the hilt and blade in his hands as if showing it off. Up close, Gavian could see the black blade was surrounded by an energy that looked very much like life essence. "You know of Nagoloth?" he said. "Shadowblade of Oblivion." The swordsman traced his finger along the intricately carved shape of the blade's hilt. "What interest does Hableides have in this sword?"

"The interest is my own," said Gavian.

"Ah. Then you must have heard of me, Serenith, the Invoker," the swordsman said.

"Can't say that I have." Gavian charged ahead, sending a combination of attacks at the swordsman.

Serenith parried the strikes with ease, countering with an attack at Gavian that forced him to dodge and back out of his range.

"So, you would murder someone you don't even know to claim this blade?" Serenith stared as Gavian circled him from a safe distance. "That is truly evil."

"Evil?" said Gavian. "You're helping the Gaith destroy the universe." Gavian closed in, slowly this time. He feigned toward Serenith's left and stabbed at his right, but his blade was deflected. Gavian stepped back to regroup.

"The universe . . ." said Serenith as he tapped his nails on the hilt. "That is the limit of your vision? There is so much more to the Everance. We are leading the way to a new era, free of the constraints that fate has placed upon us."

"By killing everyone?" Gavian attacked high at Serenith's helmet. Even if the armor did stop the blow, a concussion would impair his ability to fight. Serenith again blocked the attack and attempted to strike Gavian before he could resume a defense. Gavian had to be quick, but he was able to get into position with enough strength to stop the blow.

"If that's what it takes to save us," said the swordsman as he stepped back. "Have you ever confronted the misery of this existence? Looked it in the eyes? Believed in something with conviction, only to learn that it is all in vain?"

Images of Rethia played through Gavian's mind. He didn't want to agree with the swordsman, but he understood the sentiment.

"That is the fate that befell my ancestors, the Ichtek," said Serenith as he twirled his blade, waiting to see if Gavian would attack. "Once, our people thrived as Vyndari on the lands of Anatharia, but our leaders sought to consolidate power in the hands of a select few. Those who dared question their ever-shifting rules faced a punishment that struck terror in the hearts of all Vyndari."

Serenith paused as he looked around the dark world. "For our people's supposed crimes, they cast them into the depths of a pit, into the darkness to be forgotten. You must understand, Vyndari surrounded themselves with lights, believing that light is birth, life itself. They believed that only what remained in the radiance of light existed, while everything that fell under darkness was erased. The very land around them vanished beneath the veil of night, only to be reborn with each dawn. By banishing the disobedient into that pit, they sought to erase them from existence, forever denied the embrace of dawn's light and the chance for rebirth."

Gavian tightened his grip on Azravion, his palms beginning to sweat. He could attack and begin the battle to obtain the sword, but for now he was compelled to hold.

"But my ancestors were not erased. They survived the pit, learned to adapt in the caverns below, to thrive in the darkness. They formed a new society, the Ichtek, that rejected the ways of the Vyndari," said Serenith.

"So your revenge is to kill all living beings in the universe?" said Gavian.

"We had our revenge long ago. This is about so much more." The swordsman pressed his blade into the rock surface, shaking his head as he leaned on the sword. "My people discovered something in the depths of darkness. Something the Vyndari never would have found, the truth. Everything in this framework of existence is flawed. Every achievement, every cherished love, ultimately succumbs to the same inevitable outcome: decay and death."

"Fate is a relentless cycle of birth and demise. We find ourselves trapped within its unyielding grasp, imprisoned by its unforgiving confines. If we are to ever reach our potential and claim our place in the Everance, we must escape this fate. We will bring what the Vyndari feared above all else, the dawn that never comes. The very essence that puts an end to the oscillation of day and night, of birth and death. No matter what it takes. We are not killing anyone who was not already going to die. It is a small price to pay to end the cycle that binds us all. Only then can we claim our place in the boundless embrace of the Everance."

Gavian stood, contemplating the words in silence. Serenith's reasoning for helping the Nulvarians was more compelling than he had presumed. It made him feel the same way he had when he returned to Rethia with the rokenstones and learned the reason he'd been sent to find them. His head spun, searching for something to ground itself. He had found love with Ambrielle, but it wouldn't last forever. Not in this universe. If he could usher in a new age, where no one had to face death, no one could question his worth.

His mind resonated with thoughts of power, but the sorrow in his heart interrupted. He could not forget how the Nulthereals had manipulated his weaknesses, persuading friend to fight against friend. He and Dexius might have killed each other when they'd first encountered a Nulthereal if it weren't for Darby's screams. Darby, what the Shadows did to her and to Sidaire's planet. They'd nearly wiped out Isodonia. He remembered everything they had done to Malidora, destroying her life. They had sent the Grundians to kill everyone in Rethia. Lirah's parents and his father had been lost. Images of the lifeless husks that had been drained of essence still haunted him. Evil begets evil. Those who resort to senseless harm, even with the best of intentions, forfeit the integrity of their pursuit and diminish the possibility of genuine goodness.

"The Gaith have deceived you," said Gavian. "They try to control our minds to do their bidding. To them, we are nothing. Nothing but tools to be used."

Serenith pulled his sword from the ground, standing up straight. "I sense the doubt in you, the pain of loss. I thought you would understand. I suppose you lack the suffering that the Ichtek have endured for millennia."

"All I want is your sword," said Gavian.

The swordsman chuckled. "You are in no position to ask for Nagoloth. I will break the seals and open as many rifts as necessary."

Gavian whipped his sword upright, swinging at the less-armored neck of the swordsman, but Serenith stopped his stroke with ease. Their blades danced in a flurry of steel. Serenith's movements were fluid and calculated, and Gavian could see he was seeking vulnerabilities in his defenses.

With relentless vigor, Gavian took care to stay true to his form. One overswing or risky attack could provide the opening Serenith needed.

"You realize that this shadowblade is unstoppable," said Serenith. "If I were to disengage its energy field, all matter in its path would be effortlessly erased. Your sword could offer no resistance."

Gavian parried Serenith's attack. His skill with the sword had grown with the confidence of defeating Pythus. He expertly parried Serenith's next attack, his blade meeting Serenith's with a resounding clash. The two combatants moved in a flurry of motion, their whirlwind of steel unfolding with breathtaking precision.

Serenith pressed forward, his simple but deadly strikes displaying a level of expertise that Gavian had not yet encountered. Gavian's movements were swift, almost graceful. With a quick twist of his body, Gavian spun outside the radius of Serenith's swing, narrowly avoiding the lethal edge of his opponent's blade. As the fight wore on, Serenith began to abandon his measured approach, his movements becoming erratic and aggressive. He seemed to be growing frustrated. Gavian continued to lunge, attack, and disengage, not allowing Serenith to get close enough for a flurry of strikes.

"As much as I hate to create deadspace in this world," said Serenith, "I do have work to attend to. This has gone on long enough."

The flowing energy surrounding the black blade suddenly dissipated, leaving a momentary void in the charged atmosphere. Serenith closed in with a powerful slash aimed at Gavian. The shadowblade ripped through the air. His instincts kicked in, allowing him to evade the attack with a leap backward, distancing himself from the imminent danger.

Against the light of the moons, Gavian could see the blackened slash that remained in the air. Had the blade truly erased matter? He recalled seeing the same effect when the seal around the rift in Isodonia had been broken. Wegin had warned them not to touch the dark edges that had remained.

Serenith circled him menacingly. Gavian breathed heavily, waiting for the next attack. He knew he couldn't risk trying to block the shadowblade with Azravion. Serenith charged at him, stopping his momentum as he reached Gavian. Serenith let loose a combination of attacks. Gavian dodged one swing and flung himself through the air to avoid the next. He realized he would have to keep track of where the deadspace was to avoid running into it.

Gavian jumped back, barely avoiding the blade's reach, as Serenith attacked again. He wouldn't be able to dodge these attacks for much longer. Serenith pressed again, slicing through the very matter of the air, and Gavian tumbled across the ground to avoid running into the streaks of deadspace around him. When the next attack came, Gavian pressed the ring underneath Azravion's cross guard. Life energy leapt from Gavian's sword, surrounding the shadowblade. As the strike came down on him, Gavian parried the swing. His sword remained intact. The essence protected it from the destructive power of Nagoloth.

"Azravion!" exclaimed Serenith. "How did you get that sword?"

"I took it," replied Gavian, his voice steady, "from the corpse of its wielder."

"Impossible," Serenith retorted. "You lack the skill to defeat Pythus."

"And yet, here I am." Gavian slashed at Serenith, putting him back on the defensive.

They continued to clash blades, but Gavian could only step backward to avoid the tears of deadspace around him. Serenith moved around the rips he had carved into material reality. Lunging at Gavian with a flurry of blows, Serenith forced him to retreat toward the deadspace. As Gavian continued parrying his strikes, he found himself out of position and his defense exposed.

Serenith plunged the shadowblade into Gavian's side. Gasping for breath, Gavian crumbled to the smooth black stone. A silhouette moved against the reflection of stars and moons in the shiny rock. As he reached for the sword, he prepared himself for the inevitable death blow.

"If you truly defeated Pythus," said Serenith, "you must take his place. Use the sword for good, and keep it filled with the essence of life. Continue what he started. Share in the glory of our ascendance."

Serenith strode past him, giving him another salute. The clapping of his boots against the black stone surface of the planet began to fade into the distance. Gavian lay on the rocks, struggling to breathe. He had never felt so conflicted. His thoughts were a storm, hot and cold air mixing. Struggling to his knees with an ache that pulsed throughout his body, Gavian found himself mired in uncertainty, like a traveler at a crossroads, each path whispering its own destination.

Crawling within reach of Azravion, he grabbed it and touched the ring underneath its cross guard. Life essence flowed from the hilt into his wound. He felt energized again, full of strength and vigor. Drawing in a deep breath, he couldn't even feel the separation of skin and tissue. Glancing in the direction he had last seen Serenith walking, Gavian knew he had to follow.

Sidaire, and perhaps Dexius and Veridius too, might hate him for leaving them behind to deal with the Darterrans, but it would be even worse if he returned empty-handed. As soundless lightning flashed on the horizon, he stepped over the black stone surface. Dampened but not slippery, the ground beneath his feet retained a rugged texture that provided a stable footing.

As Gavian traversed the featureless rocky expanse, he pondered what could have guided Serenith to this dark world. Eventually, he reached a small rise, where an object protruded from the ground. Illuminated by the moons' light, it resembled a hand clawing its way through the earth, reaching for the star-studded sky. Its peculiar appearance intrigued Gavian, prompting him to examine it more closely.

Upon closer inspection, it took on the shape of a curved hook. Its surface, smooth and gleaming like metal, proved to be carved from stone as Gavian's fingertips brushed against it. He gazed at the strange object. Intermittent gleams of distant lightning drew his attention to a discovery at his feet—an expansive opening in the black rocks, a sizable tunnel leading into the mound before him.

Gavian entered this new cave, imaging it could be Serenith's lair. He stretched his back and arms, preparing himself for the inevitable fight. He knew the limits of Serenith's strengths. This time he would be ready. As he made his way deeper into the cavern, small orange glows illuminated the interior. They came from crystals not unlike those he had seen the Ichtek carry into the akreums.

The earth trembled with a profound, rumbling quake, sending shockwaves through the ground. Gavian's instincts drove him toward the exit, but his path was abruptly obstructed by a nightmarish tangle of writhing mass.

Emerging from abyssal chasms on either side of the pathway, a horrific expanse of shadowy flesh undulated in the dark. Its oily membrane caught the orange hues of the path's crystals, casting an eerie reflection. Doubt began to gnaw at Gavian, his resolve faltering in the face of this ominous presence. The acquisition of Nagoloth no longer seemed worth the effort.

"There is no escape," a resonant voice emanated from the abyss, its depth seemingly unfathomable. "Bound to the sword, you are bound to me."

Gavian quieted his breath long enough to respond. "Who are you?"

"I am Azravion," the voice echoed, its resonance carrying an unsettling weight. "Within the very blade you bear resides a sliver of my soul. You've drawn upon its life essence with such abandon, and yet now, the time has come to settle the debt. The blade, so irksomely empty of energy, hungers for sustenance, and you shall be the provider. Infuse it with the lives of others—sacrifices, if you will. I shall claim my share, permitting you enough to safeguard yourself or others in dire need. Such is the toll of immortality."

Gavian's legs nearly crumbled out from under him as he digested Azravion's words. "What do you need the essence for?" he managed to ask.

"To sink my roots deeper into this universe," Azravion's words slithered forth. "I have consumed this very world, and soon, I shall feast upon star systems, gulping down entire galaxies in my insatiable hunger. Each life you snuff out becomes a drop in my endless chalice of power, the elixir of my dominion."

"Here, take it back!" Gavian's voice trembled with desperation. "The sword is yours. I have no desire for it!"

"The choice has been made," Azravion's voice hissed, sending shivers down Gavian's spine. "Only in your demise can it be unraveled."

A sudden swell of anger burst through his fear. "I won't be your pawn!" Gavian spat, his fingers swiftly undoing the sheath from his back. "You'll starve in the darkness before I let you feed off any more essence."

"Bound to the sword, you are," Azravion's words slithered with an unsettling cadence. "Fail to nourish it with life, and it shall feast upon yours, leaving the blade to be picked up by another. It is inevitable. The sword will provide the essence I need, with or without you."

Gavian felt utterly defeated. How could he face Ambrielle again? How could he tell her about this? Nothing could fix this.

"Do not succumb to despair," said Azravion. "This weapon is not a curse, but a gift. A gift that only you possess. In time, you shall embrace it, just as Pythus did before you." Was Pythus as much a victim as he was an enemy? Though Serenith had conviction, perhaps he was once a slave to an entity like this the same way that Gavian was becoming.

Gavian buckled the sheath back on. "Are you going to let me go?"

"Understand that I demand the essence of sentient existence," Azravion said. "Mindless beings are of no use to me." The undulating mass before the pathway convulsed and slithered back into the abyss, creating an exit for him. "Now depart and seek Serenith on Valderine. He will shepherd you through the shadows."

Gavian made his way through the maze of paths surrounding the chasms in the rock. He found a sloping pathway that led into a large round chamber unnaturally carved out of its stone surroundings. Around the circular room were five unusual statues, each glowing from the light of a yellow crystal in the floor.

They were arranged in a formation with one at the center and two on each side. Meticulously carved out of a stone much lighter in color than the dark rock that pervaded this world, the statue depicted a nightmarish creature. Serpentine in shape, the creature's long body split into three tails at its end. Its unconventional physique lacked typical limbs, replaced by an arrangement of six spindly appendages—three on each side. Its configuration suggested either a skeletal framework for wings or spider-like legs designed for crawling. The monster's head bore four horn-like protrusions resembling small wings, each supporting four eyes, with two notably larger than the rest. Completing the aberrant composition, the creature's chin resembled the point of a dagger—an unsettling maw that defied anything from the natural world.

A plaque at the base of the statue bore the name "Razinoth." Gavian had learned the name from Malidora. The name of one of five Gaith that controlled the Shadows in their goal to harvest fresh living essence from the universe. The next in line bore the label "Grindak." He arrived at a name he recognized: "Vazerinaz," the Gaith from which Ogolameth, the Primevus they had destroyed on Isodonia, originated. "Zeragul." This depiction also featured an elongated, serpentine body, reminiscent of a snake.

At the heart of this assembly stood a statue of a peculiar creature, its entire form appearing as if it were one immense head. Three distinct rows of horned appendages encircled each side of this unique entity's head, with the longest protrusions situated at the top and gradually tapering down to the smallest ones at its sides. Its nameplate bore the inscription "Ilganok."

Their alien physiques stretched beyond the limits of conventional understanding. These entities possessed shapes and features that clawed at the edge of human perception, challenging the boundaries of what the mind could grasp. A spectacle both awe-inspiring and daunting, as if the very essence of the unknown had taken form.

Gavian left the circular room behind, pressing farther into the cavern. The pathway narrowed as he continued on, winding his way between pillars of stone. Eventually he came into a wide-open chamber where the path became a bridge over a great chasm.

As he walked back toward the cave that contained the rift, Azravion's words played over and over in his mind. Though he knew he shouldn't, he decided to keep this information from Ambrielle. With there being nothing she could do to help this situation, it was pointless to burden her with this too.

Drawing closer to the radiance of the rift, Gavian noticed a subtle illumination emanating from the amulet around his neck. Twisting through an intricate web of pathways, he materialized once more on the other side of the cave, its walls encrusted with the plastra of the akreum vault. The stony surface bore the grim stains of conflict, but the lifeless forms were gone. In the cavern's expanse, fragments of shadowstone littered the terrain, the remains of the whidge.

As he left the opening of the vault into the Darterran caverns, Medigrin spoke from the shadowed corners ahead. "I will make the same agreement to you that we made with your friends."

Gavian turned toward the sound, ready to defend himself.

"If you leave the caverns immediately and promise never to return," said Medigrin, "we will allow you to pass."

A gathering of Darterrans moved into the light from behind the gral, growling as they watched Gavian, as if expecting a fight. Azravion trembled in its sheath with a restless energy. The blade's thirst for essence echoed through Gavian's senses, a gnawing hunger that tugged at the very core of the sword. Despite the blade's yearning, Gavian knew satiating its appetite was a perilous path to tread, one that was not meant for this moment.

"Agreed," said Gavian, resisting the urges of the sword.

The rows of Darterrans spread apart, allowing him a way past them into the rest of the cavern. Gavian walked through the carved hallways, looking over his shoulder to make sure the Darterrans did not change their minds, into the secret tunnel he had entered through. At the end of the tunnel was bright light. As he swept the vines and tree roots aside, the morning light nearly blinded him. Had he been gone that long?

"There you are!" exclaimed Dexius, relief and exasperation in his voice. "We were beginning to think you were never coming back."

"I apologize, everyone." Gavian avoided eye contact with Dexius, Sidaire, and Veridius. He didn't want to see the expressions on their faces. He knew had let everyone down. "I shouldn't have gone after the sword."

"So where is it?" Dexius brushed the hair away from his eyes as he stood from the stone he'd been sitting on. "We didn't go through all that for nothing did we?"

"I'm afraid I don't have it," said Gavian. "I couldn't beat the Ichtek swordsman."

Dexius let out a frustrated breath. "I knew it. You're not as skilled as you seem to believe. Unlike me, who's spent a lifetime mastering the bow."

"At least we still have the amplifying crystal, don't we?" said Veridius as he brushed the wrinkles out of his clothing with his hands.

Gavian reached into the pouch of his satchel and showed him the amythite.

"That was our objective after all, what we set out for," Veridius said. "We did fulfill our mission in the end."

Dexius responded with a resentful look.

"How is your wound, Sidaire?" said Gavian. "I've seen something that grows in these woods that might help it heal."

Sidaire didn't respond as she walked past him, following Dexius ahead.

"Don't bother," Dexius replied. "The Darterrans gave her something to put on it. It's beginning to heal now."

"That's good," he said. He started to apologize and make up an excuse about how the sword couldn't use the essence he had just taken from the Ichtek, but it would likely only make things worse. If he was going to explain anything, it would have to be the truth. But in this case, the truth would only ostracize him further from the group. He recognized that eventually that would likely happen anyway.

Veridius offered a comforting pat on the shoulder. "We faced unexpected challenges, and adapted as best we could. The mission took an unexpected turn, but what matters is that we all made it through together."

They navigated their path through the verdant embrace of the forest, gradually emerging onto the expansive grassy plains encircling Mekkinspire. Amid the camaraderie of the group, Gavian found himself drifting behind. His gaze remained steadfast on the ground in front of him, his thoughts in a realm of their own, untouched by the occasional backward glances of Dexius and Sidaire. The distance between them felt not just measured in paces but also in the unspoken sentiments that hung heavy in the air.

CHAPTER 15

AMBRIELLE—TRUE SOLSELLION

AMBRIELLE'S SENSES GRADUALLY stirred as she emerged from the depths of unconsciousness. The air in the chamber was cool and carried a faint scent of damp earth, hinting at the enclosed space of a hidden cave. Rays of feeble light filtered through crevices in the rugged walls, casting dim patterns across the rocky surfaces. Her awareness sharpened, and she became acutely attuned to the nuances of her own body. Every ache, every pulse seemed amplified in this tangible realm. It was a stark contrast to the ethereal and dreamlike quality of Averess that now felt distant, as though a gossamer thread connecting her to that realm had been gently tugged, leaving her rooted in the corporeal world.

Malidora stirred beside her, her movements slow and gentle as she nudged herself out from under Ambrielle to sit upright in the chamber. Malidora's comforting voice mingled with the hushed echoes of their surroundings. "How are you feeling?" Ambrielle's muscles slowly responded to her will, and she accepted Malidora's outstretched hand.

"Good, I think," said Ambrielle, feeling as though she had learned to speak only a few moments ago. "Actually, great."

"What did you find out?" Syra'Dosa asked, seemingly anxious to hear about their journey.

Ambrielle looked past Syra'Dosa and the others. "Where's Gavian?"

"They haven't made it back yet," said Syra'Dosa.

Clinching her brow, Ambrielle stepped out of the stasis shell and onto the hard rocky floor. "How long does it take to ask Kidiru about some crystals?"

"Out there,"—Syra'Dosa stood at the cave entrance, pointing outside—"someone is coming."

Ambrielle stumbled slightly as her legs, still regaining their sensation, carried her outside. The sand underfoot shifted beneath her, and she focused on a distant dune where a dusty haze stirred. Gradually emerging over the rise, the glyvex traversed the terrain toward them.

"Amby!" Gavian stepped down from the vehicle as he made his way toward her. "You're back!"

Despite the residual tingling in her legs, Ambrielle hurriedly closed the distance, her arms enveloping Gavian in a tight embrace as he held her close.

Dexius turned his attention toward them. "Amby?" he questioned with a raised eyebrow.

Ambrielle pulled back from the hug, a playful smile on her lips. "Just so you know, only Gavian gets to call me that. Or I'll start calling you 'Dexy.' "

"No, no," Dexius responded with a lighthearted chuckle. "You can have 'Amby.' "

Sidaire tilted her head slightly. "I think I like 'Dexy,' " she teased.

Ambrielle pressed a quick kiss onto Gavian's cheek. "You're only returning from Anatharia now?"

Gavian nodded, a mixture of exhaustion and relief on his face. "Yeah, we ran into some unexpected problems, but we're all safe."

Ambrielle's expression turned contrite. "I shouldn't have asked you to go. I assumed it would be a routine mission."

Gavian pulled the amythite from his pouch, showing it to her.

Ambrielle's gaze shifted to the amythite, her brows furrowing in concern. "So, what happened?"

Gavian recounted the encounter. "They were in a cave guarded by a predatory creature. Kidiru made us promise not to harm it."

"Getting the crystal wasn't so bad," Sidaire interjected.

"But then Gavian saw a sword he had to have." Dexius rolled his eyes.

"Gavian . . ." Ambrielle's scrutinizing gaze shifted from Dexius to Gavian, her expression a mix of curiosity and incredulity. "Another sword?"

"Just hear me out." Gavian waved his hands, his silhouette highlighted by the soft glow of the sunset. "This sword had the ability to cut through anything. We're not even sure if amythite can destroy the apex nyalith, but this sword could penetrate even plastra."

Ambrielle's focus sharpened as she regarded Gavian. "Where did you come across a sword like that?"

"The Ichtek had it," Sidaire chimed in, wincing slightly as she rubbed the welt on her shoulder. "They were opening these vaults with it."

"The Ichtek?" Ambrielle said, her brow furrowing. She shielded her eyes with her hand, scanning the horizon.

"Same ones that attacked us in the desert," said Sidaire quickly, her shoulders tense.

"The Cereveshians said they were extinct," said Ambrielle. "Why are they all coming out now?"

"They may be getting closer to victory," said Gavian.

Ambrielle detected a bit of tension between Gavian and the others. "I take it you didn't get the sword."

"I came close, but—" Gavian started, his shoulders sagging a bit.

"Gavian nearly got us killed over it," interrupted Dexius.

Ambrielle's eyes quickly moved from Dexius back to Gavian. "Gavian, that doesn't sound like you."

"The shadowblade is how they are unsealing the rifts," said Gavian, shooting a look at Dexius. "If I could have retrieved it, the Shadows wouldn't be able to get into the universe anymore." Gavian's eyes moved between each of them, as if waiting for some kind of validation. "We're all risking our lives to stop the Gaith. We had an opportunity to reach our goal, so I went for it."

"Sacrificing each other for a small chance at a win." Dexius stood next to Sidaire. "That's not what we're about."

"It wasn't like that!" Gavian snapped. "You agreed! We all agreed to try and get the sword."

"That wasn't the issue, Gavian," Sidaire said, clenching her jaw. "It was how you left us behind when I got hit."

"I didn't leave you behind." Gavian's hands began to move wildly as he explained. "You were all right behind me. My hope was that I could at least slow them down enough until you all got there."

"Even though he wasn't able to get the sword in the end, I agree with Gavian. There are times when tactical risks are necessary if we are to have any hope against a foe such as this," Veridius said. "This may have been one such time. On the other hand, I completely understand what Dexius and Sidaire are saying, being on their side of things myself. Perhaps all of us should take a look from each other's perspective. There is always something to learn from that."

"We had already found what we needed," said Dexius. "We had the crystals."

"I can clear this up quite easily," said Malidora. "We can't destroy the apex nyalith."

"What?" said Dexius. "Why not?"

"Because it may cause the whole planet to implode," said Ambrielle.

"Whoa," said Sidaire. "Let's not do that."

"Or only as a last resort," Veridius said. "We may have to consider it if all other options fail."

"How can you say that?" said Sidaire. "This world is everything I know. It may be a desert now, but I have to hope that we can rebuild it. That all the familiar places I knew growing up are still there under the sand. And as unlikely as it may be, I still want to believe that everyone will somehow return."

"I don't say it lightly," said Veridius. "I know what it's like to lose everything familiar to you. To try to start over in strange places with new people. There's nothing that is mine anymore. Nothing to feel pride in. Any hope I would have for my world was torn from me. It's made me realize that, in this fight, we might have to make tough choices. As long as there are worlds left to move on to, we have to save whatever we can."

Malidora rested her hand on his shoulder and then fully embraced him. "You have plenty to be proud of Veridius," she said. "When we arrived here, you had the strength to pull me out of my despair, even through your own grief. I don't know what I would have done without you."

Veridius managed a glimmer of a smile as he returned her hug. "I could as easily say the same about you."

"He's right though," said Malidora as she stared into the distant horizon. "If it comes to that, it must be done. But we will do everything we can to avoid it."

"All this was for nothing then," grumbled Dexius, his frustration still evident. "We're back to where we started."

"What about closing off the rift at the junction?" said Syra'Dosa.

"We didn't get any closer on that front either," Malidora admitted, her tone resigned.

"So, your mission was equally fruitless?" Sidaire inquired, her eyes narrowing.

"Not entirely," Malidora countered, a spark of intrigue in her voice. She pulled a shiny object from her bag, holding it out to Ambrielle. Its crystalline appearance was otherworldly.

Ambrielle instinctively reached for it, and she squinted her eyes trying to discern what the object was. It was framed in some strange, polished metal that encased a multicolored array of jewels like the pattern of a monarch butterfly wing. "Niralys?" Ambrielle was shocked to see it again. It appeared somewhat different in the physical universe, more solid and detailed. "You stole it from Averess?"

"I didn't like the tone Solysta used when you were looking at it," said Malidora. "She let a bit too much of her presumed superiority show. You only wanted to look and now you can." Malidora held it in front of her, prodding her to take it.

"What if she is right?" said Ambrielle as the bright colors of the jewel caught the sunlight. "What if it would break my mind?"

"Then don't look into it too deeply," said Malidora, holding it against the skin below Ambrielle's wrist. "I think it would look good on you."

The jewel reflected an otherworldly light on the sand and everyone around it. Sidaire couldn't seem to take her eyes off of it. "Beautiful . . ." she said as if not realizing she was speaking her thoughts out loud.

The sparkling jewel set on a crystalline band was mesmerizing. Ambrielle visualized herself wearing it with those around her awestruck at the sight of a crafted stone not of this universe. "It doesn't feel right," said Ambrielle as she drew back her wanting hand. "You keep it."

"I got it for *you*," Malidora said with a grin. "If Solysta wants it bad enough, she can come get it."

"I'd rather not," said Ambrielle.

"Fine, I'll hold on to it until you change your mind," said Malidora, placing the band around her wrist.

"If that is all you got from Averess, I hope it is going to help in some way," said Veridius.

"How is some jewelry going to help anything . . . ?" muttered Dexius.

"Well, we did find out about something else," Ambrielle interjected.

"The Gaith are massing their forces in the Avakora Region," Malidora explained, her voice carrying a sense of urgency. "They appear to be looking for, or perhaps gathering, a source of great power."

"I think you enjoy giving bad news," Dexius said.

"Their advance has been slow, something may be fighting back against them," said Malidora. "But if the Gaith gain even more power, we may not have a better chance of stopping them."

Ambrielle reached into her bag and pulled out the eternium glyph. It displayed a diagram, as if the air above it was a glass surface. "There are three worlds we need to investigate"—she pointed to a small area of the diagram—"Setis, Eretash, and Valderine."

"It seems like we are always ten steps behind them. How are we supposed to search three worlds in time to do anything?" Sidaire voiced the collective frustration.

"Valderine," Gavian declared. "They're going to Valderine."

"How do you know that?" Malidora pressed, her eyes narrowing as the last rays of sunlight bathed the landscape in hues of orange and red.

"The Ichtek swordsman," said Gavian. "He said something about Valderine. I didn't know what he meant until now. The Ichtek on Anatharia were going to Valderine. They have been cutting into the akreums. When we pursued them, they had whidges with them. Whidges using Cereveshian bodies. They were using Cereveshians bodies."

"They're turning the sleeping Cereveshians into whidges?" Ambrielle asked. "But why? There must be plenty of others they could use."

"Who knows?" said Gavian. "But it can't be good."

"Is there anything special about Cereveshians that would help them?" Veridius asked.

"The Ureons said they are super analytical but lack empathy and emotion," said Malidora. "Perhaps they make better whidges."

"Solysta mentioned that they are strong of mind and will," said Ambrielle. "She said the Shadows' mind control didn't work on them at all."

"How would that help the Ichtek?" asked Sidaire.

"It doesn't make much sense," said Ambrielle.

Dexius grimaced as he walked into the opening of the cave. "Has anyone seen Darby?"

~

After returning through the energy tunnel into the Echo dimension, they made their way to Mogantum, the citadel Avo'Doria had designed. Within the common living space, they found rest, lounging in comfortable chairs and eating synthetic food prepared by the droid attendants. Exchanging stories of the battle on Anatharia and of Averess, Ambrielle cast her worries aside for a while, enjoying the group's company.

Dexius had been unusually quiet the whole time as he sat next to Sidaire. She had a look on her face as though she wanted to talk but wasn't sure what to say. Ambrielle caressed Gavian's hand and got up from her seat.

"What's going on with you?" Ambrielle said as she sat down in the empty chair beside Dexius.

Dexius shifted in his seat, sitting up straight. "We need to be looking for Darby instead of sitting around here."

Ambrielle tried to flash a comforting grin. "We all need some rest, Dex. She's fine. Elyravess is safer than it is here."

"Maybe," he said. "But she's all alone. In a strange world. She's probably scared."

Sidaire leaned over, resting her head on his shoulder. "She's not alone. Kazial is with her."

"He can't protect her like I can. Can he hit any target he points a bow at?" Dexius shook his head. "I don't understand why she didn't just come with us."

Ambrielle glanced at Sidaire and then back to Dexius. "Maybe she wanted to give you some space."

"Space for what?" Dexius inquired.

Ambrielle drew a deep, heavy breath. "I don't know. Maybe she thought you wanted to talk to Sidaire."

Dexius narrowed his eyes. "I don't need space. Sidaire is just . . ." He glanced over at Sidaire as she raised her head from his shoulder, staring back at him intently. "We can talk with Darby too, right?"

Sidaire had a bit of a cross look on her face, prompting Dexius to lean closer to her. "Right?"

Ambrielle worried that she had created a problem and tried to give him a little help. "Darby knew how much you wanted to spend some time with Sidaire."

"There was something I wanted to ask you." Dexius quickly changed the subject. "I don't understand this Afterglow you talked about," he said. "You're saying that after we die here, we start another life there? Would I get a different father next time around?"

Sidaire's expression softened a bit. "No one on your world ever had a concept of a life after death?"

"Where I grew up," said Dexius, "we didn't have a concept of anything other than hoping there would be enough food to go around."

"So, what do you do in this other life?" Veridius interjected, as he and Malidora overheard them.

"We didn't get into all that," Malidora said. "What would you want it to be like?"

As Veridius contemplated an answer, Sidaire spoke up, "I would want to find everyone else that I lost, and if I could, I would try to protect everyone who was still here. Make sure the Gaith didn't win."

"I don't think it works that way," said Ambrielle. "The Everance and the Afterglow are on two different planes of existence. Unfortunately, I don't think you can interact with anyone on this side. If you could, I think my mother would've visited me."

A contemplative hush enveloped the group, the weight of the conversation palpable. Malidora's eyebrow twitched as she broke the silence with a touch of dark humor. "If there was a way to sneak back over for even a moment," Malidora mused, "I would play tricks, keep people guessing, you know? The classic ghost haunting style."

Dexius chuckled. "What do you mean?"

"When I was a kid, I lived on a farm that was supposedly haunted. We would sometimes find tools laying around the house that were supposed to be in the barn. It didn't make any sense. We never found out who was doing it, and everyone blamed it on mischievous spirits of the dead that were haunting us. So maybe that's what I would do." Malidora grinned. "Take items and put them somewhere they shouldn't be and watch people lose their minds trying to figure out how they got there."

"So, you would continue to drive people crazy . . ." Dexius joked.

"Exactly." Malidora smirked. "Why let death get in the way of having fun?"

Laughter filled the air, lifting the heavy veil of seriousness that had shrouded the conversation. As the lively discussion gradually settled, one by one, each member of the group excused themselves, heading toward the domicile for a well-deserved rest. Catching Dexius before he left the dining hall, Ambrielle spoke with a reassuring tone, "Take some rest, and when you're ready, we'll all accompany you to find Darby. Elyravess may be the ideal place to uncover the answers we need."

CHAPTER 16

Darby—Elyravess

The morning sun beamed through the panoramic windows of the apartment. Darby stretched her arms, arching her back as she yawned. It had been one of the best nights of sleep she could remember.

She jumped out of the bed, making her way to the view of the city. Seeing it from this height proved how methodically everything here ran. It was like looking at an extremely complex piece of machinery with millions of moving parts, but all running in perfect sync. The mektrons flew in rows and columns of varying layers and heights. They crisscrossed paths with others, perfectly weaving between them like threads of linen.

Where were they all going? She noticed some of the mektrons hovering outside one of the buildings close to her. They moved around the building systematically, using lasers on the metal structures. Maybe they were doing repairs, perhaps cleaning and polishing the building's surfaces. She couldn't be sure.

As she watched them, a humanoid figure rocketed past the lines of mektrons, using wings to glide to the balcony in front of the window. It was Avo'Doria.

"I want to open the door," Darby said, and like magic her wish was granted.

Avo'Doria hurried through the door of the apartment. "We

received an alert. Someone has entered Elyravess through the spring. Were you expecting anyone to come here?"

"I didn't intend to be gone this long," said Darby. "I wonder if Ambrielle and Malidora have been woken by now. Maybe they came to get me." Her eyes lit up with excitement. "I'm anxious to hear what they found out in Averess."

"I dispatched transportation for them," said Avo'Doria. The bustling activity of Elyravess surrounded them, with drones and mektrons gracefully soaring in organized patterns through the air. "I thought we could meet them at my research lab. We have some things to show *them* as well."

After waking Kazial, Darby glided alongside Avo'Doria, mektrons carrying them to the testing laboratory. As Darby entered behind Avo'Doria, silhouettes of others obscured the ambient light of the holographic displays.

While still in awe of the advanced technology around her, Darby couldn't help but feel a bit out of place. The holographic displays danced with vivid colors, casting a soft glow. She glanced at the intricate details of the lab equipment, trying to absorb every nuance.

"Darby!" Dexius exclaimed and rushed to greet her. "Why didn't you come back?"

She smiled, appreciating Dexius's concern, and rolled her eyes playfully as he gave her a hearty pat on the shoulder. "I wasn't here that long."

"I tried to tell him you would be fine," chimed in Ambrielle, her friendly wave accompanying the holographic displays flickering with data, creating an ethereal dance of lights around them. Veridius walked over to a large mechanical arm in the center of the room. It held what appeared to be a spark moving rapidly back and forth and tracing symbols and images into the air. Dexius left Sidaire's side to join Veridius in observing the robotic machinery.

"Oh, Ambrielle!" Darby said, her eyes bright with curiosity. "What was Averess like? What did you find out from the Cereveshians?"

"We never spoke to the Cereveshians," said Malidora, her tone revealing a hint of tension. "The Ureons of Averess don't seem to trust them."

Kazial exchanged a knowing glance with Darby. "With good reason."

Darby's eyes dropped to the floor, a subtle unease creeping into her expression. "So, the whole trip was for nothing? Neristara's sacrifice was in vain?" The images of burying Neristara in the sands of Solsellion were still so fresh in her memory.

"We did learn something," said Ambrielle. "The Shadows have all left the worlds they were invading to move to an area of space called the Avakora Region. They might have found something powerful they can use there," she said, her gaze shifting to Gavian. "Gavian thinks they went to a world called Valderine."

"That is interesting," Avo'Doria said, her metallic form attentive. "The Ichtek artifact that Darby and Kazial brought to me mentioned a new—"

Excited to contribute something of value to the team, Darby couldn't contain herself. "They are looking for a celestial oracle called Hablay . . . What was it called again?"

"Hableides," corrected Avo'Doria. "They had discovered the existence of this being from the minds of some of their recent victims and changed their objective to seek this Hableides. The data gave the impression that they had located it."

"They must have learned of Hableides from the Vogus on Kandom," added Malidora. "But it might just be a myth."

"The last entry sounded as if they had already located this Hableides," Avo'Doria said. "But they were being held back by some invisible force."

"This doesn't sound good at all," said Malidora, as the hologram images changed, casting flickering lights around the room.

Darby directed a question to Malidora. "What do you know about Hableides?"

Malidora stepped into the midst of a violet ambient light from the holographic displays. "Only that it is a powerful mind that exists somewhere in the universe, a mind that can communicate with beings from great distances. It helped the Vogus to create new light technology for their dark world and wanted them to help usher in a perfect universe as other civilizations came together through Hableides."

The room buzzed with speculation. Sidaire raised an eyebrow, questioning, "Why would the Gaith want that?"

Dexius chimed in, "Maybe they want to use its intelligence?"

Darby was surprised that Dexius was still listening, as he and Veridius were engrossed by laboratory tables gliding along the floor in an assembly line. Mechanized limbs above, each radiating a spectrum of lights, illuminated metal plates, the tables advancing underneath them.

Ambrielle pondered aloud, "If Hableides can commune with others over great distances . . ."

Kazial finished the thought, ". . . the Gaith could add Hableides to the mindstream . . ."

"They would be able to use their mind-controlling influence across the universe." Malidora's ominous revelation hung in the air.

Darby, her voice echoing concern, exclaimed, "You mean they could do what they did on Isodonia, manipulating people to turn against one another, sparking conflicts and wars? And not just on one world but across multiple worlds at the same time?"

"Perhaps even multiple galaxies at the same time," Malidora added gravely. "Then all they would have to do is come in and collect all the essence."

Avo'Doria's metallic figure reflected the changing holographic displays. "Where is this Valderine located? It isn't listed on any of my charts."

Ambrielle presented a silver glyph to Avo'Doria, explaining, "We got this from Averess. It's supposed to show the general location." Avo'Doria placed the object into a pool of liquid light on one of the tables, and a hologram emerged, revealing a galaxy larger and more intricate than Darby had imagined.

The energy of the hologram created a soft buzz in the room. Avo'Doria remarked, "I've never heard of the Cossumera Galaxy. It must be beyond the Severine Cluster. Even if we built you a starcraft to carry you there, it would take far too long to reach it. We haven't excelled in space travel technology development, as we have been directed to focus on welcoming organic life."

"We can only hope that one of the springs connects to it," said Ambrielle. "Though if there are thousands of springs across the Echo dimension of Solsellion, how would we find the right one?"

Darby noticed Valderine marked on the hologram. Avo'Doria, puzzled, questioned, "I see Valderine, but according to your glyph, the star it orbits, Turanigon, is old. It only has a few hundred years left in its life cycle. Why would a celestial oracle choose to live there?"

Gavian stepped forward, taking a chain out of the neck of his tunic. "I got this amulet from Pythus, one of the Ichtek. When I came close to the rift on Anatharia, it moved me to the rift on some dark world. Could we use this with one of the rifts to take us there?"

"I have one of those too," said Dexius, pointing to a chain around Sidaire's neck. "We took it from one of the Ichtek on Anatharia."

"Would these amulets carry only the one who is wearing it through the rift?" Malidora wondered. "We need to get all of us there."

"Let me see it," said Avo'Doria.

Sidaire removed the amulet and handed it to her. Avo'Doria inspected the amulet with interest before placing it into the liquid light. As she moved her hands apart, the projection of the amulet magnified, showing tiny grooves and textures.

Expanding her palms, Avo'Doria magnified the projection further. Patterns of lines fanned outward, casting a mesmerizing glow across her metallic armor. "Inside, there are 9,376 micro conduits," Avo'Doria stated, her gaze fixed on the amulet. "Conduits leading to a central material, likely a grounding point for a specific energy flow. The facets appear designed to absorb this energy and channel it into these conduits. Moreover, there are intricate components designed to regulate energy flow—speed, fluctuation, tolerance. There appear to be some small symbols for each node." Avo'Doria spread her hands apart to zoom in further.

As the details became sharper, Darby jumped toward her. "Those are the symbols! Wegin, show those symbols we found."

Wegin projected a display of what he'd recorded from the walls of Neristara's lab, bringing it into focus.

"See!" said Darby. "They are the same ones!"

"Each node in the circuit is labeled with a number," said Avo'Doria. "Currently it seems to be set where the energy would be directed through this path."

"Aren't those the same—" Darby started.

"Yes, they are the same numbers as the frequencies from Neristara's grid," said Wegin. "And yes, I will display the image of the grid map of Solsellion."

Darby turned to the displayed map with the symmetrical nodes all over the planet that represented each spring on Solsellion. "Next, I took the liberty of finding the node that matches the frequency on the amulet, in which case it is right here." Wegin said as one of the nodes began pulsing. "And here are the other nodes that you are already familiar with as transporting water holes." Wegin's projection of the grid map formed labels indicating Anatharia's and Elyravess's springs. The Valderine spring was quite far from the others that Darby had been to before.

"Wegin, you're a genius!" Ambrielle said, as her face beamed.

"Indeed," replied Wegin, his blue lights blinking in a square pattern, creating an animated display.

"I guess that means we are about to go to some crazy new world," said Dexius.

A small panic grew within Darby at the idea of visiting yet another new world. Especially one that none of them knew much about.

Ambrielle's eyes beamed. "Yes, I can't wait to see what else is out there."

She wished she had the same excitement that Ambrielle seemed to have about exploring alien worlds. Though somehow Ambrielle's enthusiasm was a bit infectious. Darby had grown comfortable being in Elyravess much more quickly than she'd expected. At least she would be surrounded by all her friends. Being part of this team made her feel as though she could face anything.

As everyone started gathering their bags, packs, and satchels to leave, Darby realized she and Kazial hadn't shared everything they had learned with the group.

"Before we go," said Darby, "there is one more thing we should tell you."

"What's that?" said Ambrielle, but the others continued talking to each other.

"This is something I think everyone should hear," said Darby, trying to raise her voice without alarming everyone.

"Guys! Listen up!" shouted Dexius. Everyone turned to look at Dexius as if he were about to speak. "Darby has something to say."

As everyone's attention turned to Darby, she couldn't help but look elsewhere. She didn't like being the center of attention or giving dramatic news like this, but they all needed to know. "The data we found on this artifact, most of it was Cereveshian. It indicates that, because of the Cereveshians' reckless rush to discovery and ignorance of plenty of warning signs for the sake of acquiring new data, they unleashed the Savage Dark into Hollowspace, which formed the five Gaith."

Ambrielle looked stunned as the others murmured to each other.

Avo'Doria moved away from the holograms' light and added, "The founders, the Cereveshians, did push back the Nulvarians and close the rifts, but that didn't entirely undo the mistakes that some of them made. It took eons, but the Gaith found a way back into our universe."

"And now it is up to us to find a way to push them back again," said Veridius as he stepped toward the rest of the group. "Perhaps if we find this celestial oracle, we can gain some insight on a method to close the energy of the rifts at its source."

"I hope you are right, Veridius," said Ambrielle. "If the mind of this oracle is so powerful, it should be able to give us the answers we need."

"Why didn't Neristara mention this any of this?" Malidora wondered.

"I guess it's possible that she didn't know either," said Ambrielle.

Dexius brushed the wrinkles out of his sleeve. "She had to have known."

"When I placed this artifact into the nexus," Avo'Doria said, "it nearly erased everything. It is obvious the founders didn't want anyone to know. Your possibility is correct, Ambrielle. It could be that only certain Cereveshians knew about this."

The mektrons carried each of them across the city as Avo'Doria flew with them. After they were returned to the platform over the ocean, Avo'Doria approached. She turned to Ambrielle as she spoke, "When this is done, do you plan to return and establish your settlement on Elyravess?"

Darby couldn't help but wonder what kind of settlement Avo'Doria was talking about. The cityscape stretched out as far as she could see. What was left to build here?

Ambrielle brushed strands of hair away from her eyes. "I would love to come back and visit, but I can't make a promise to you like that," she responded. "I have responsibilities, both back on Earth and here with my new family." She looked around at everyone. "I'll always be grateful for your help, and I'm sure one day you will find the arrivals you are looking for, and they will be more than willing to start their own civilization here." She pressed her lips together. "I hope I haven't disappointed you."

"Not at all," said Avo'Doria. "This was never to be a burden, but an aid to those that make it here in need of us. If you ever change your mind, we will be waiting. Regardless, you will always have a place here if you wish to visit."

"Why aren't you coming with us?" asked Darby as the sounds of the waves caressed the pylons of the platform they stood on.

"Traveling through the springs is detrimental to my systems," said Avo'Doria. "Perhaps it is some residual energy from the rifts. I don't think I would last if I went through much more. That is why we built Syra'Dosa to help you in Solsellion. Soon enough she will be able to start assemblies to build more sentinels."

"Nothing against her," said Ambrielle, as she turned away from the gusts of wind, "but she isn't like you."

"Give her a chance. She's still learning. As always, we'll be here, awaiting your return," Avo'Doria assured her.

Ambrielle smiled and embraced Avo'Doria. As they hugged, Avo'Doria's wings of light enveloped them both. Avo'Doria turned to Darby. "You are always welcome too, Darby."

"Thank you, I would love to come back," Darby said.

"If I could trouble you for one more thing. Would you consider wearing this?" Avo'Doria held out an object to Darby that appeared as a blue gemstone with tiny gold sparkles inside. "It's a silcron."

Darby took it from her hand and held it into the light.

"When you are done with your mission, please return it," Avo'Doria said. "It will record data as you experience it. It will capture all the information about your journey. If something doesn't go right, perhaps we can analyze the data and formulate a new plan. If everything does go right, it will give me the closest thing to having been there with you all." Darby realized there was a socket in her silbrace that would fit the silcron perfectly. The gem seemed magnetized to the socket, escaping her grasp as it was brought close and clicking into place.

"May your currents be unbroken," said Avo'Doria as she waved goodbye to them all. Darby prepared herself to be enveloped by the cold ocean water. Leaping off the platform, there was a moment of stillness before she hit the water with a loud splash.

After surfacing, Darby sat on the boulder at the edge of the spring, making sure everyone safely made it back to Echo Solsellion. Once everyone was accounted for, they climbed back into the waiting vehicle, heading for what she hoped would be the spring that led them to Valderine.

Wegin transferred the data into the navigation system of the vehicle, and they started off. Zooming down the sloping dunes toward the rocky landscape ahead, Darby's heart began to accelerate. What were they heading into? This world was completely unknown to any of them. And this celestial oracle, Hableides, what would it be like? Would it welcome them? Surely, it would if they came to help defeat the Shadows.

"Is there some sort of plan once we get there?" Veridius said.

"I don't think we know enough yet to make a plan," said Ambrielle.

"We ought to have some kind of preparation," Veridius persisted. "Considering we're heading into a fight, we might need to split into teams that complement each other."

"Did you have something in mind?" Ambrielle asked, the warm breeze tousling her hair.

Veridius's eyes were distant, and he seemed to go over something in his head. "We should make sure we have at least two separate groups to help us coordinate different tasks if necessary. I propose one group include myself, Malidora, Sidaire, Darby, and Kazial."

"That actually seems well thought out, a good mix of different strengths," Malidora said, teasingly adding, "Though I suspect you just wanted me in your group."

Veridius chuckled and replied, "Having you is definitely a bonus, but I assure you, there's some strategic reasoning behind it too."

"Sidaire and I worked well together in Anatharia," said Dexius. "I think we should be in the same group."

Darby shared a silent grin with Ambrielle as if they knew a secret that Dexius didn't think anyone else knew. Darby was happy to see this budding relationship between Dexius and Sidaire. She had noticed Sidaire's interest, even when Dexius hadn't. For a while, she had been quietly nudging Dexius along, waiting to see if he would show the same interest in Sidaire. She felt as though she should help Sidaire and Dexius out in some way so they could stay together, but only if it was good for the group.

"If that's the case, you could switch me and Dexius," Darby said. "I'll be in the second group."

The vehicle came to a stop near the spring, and Darby was the first one off. The familiar red fronds of the trees surrounding the water were the same as all the others, but something felt different here. Something she couldn't explain. The sun was now touching the horizon, heralding the beginning of sunset. She hoped that it would not be their last.

Gavian gave her a gentle slap on the shoulder as he walked by. "Are you ready?"

She nodded and smiled. It surprised her how much her cheek muscles flexed. It wasn't often she naturally smiled that broadly. It felt as though she had found her place in this group.

Ambrielle leaned back and tilted her head, prompting Gavian to give her a kiss. "I'm usually excited about seeing a new world," she said, "but this time it feels strange. I can't really explain it."

"I think I know what you mean," he said. "I feel it too."

"I don't know if we're really prepared for something like this," said Ambrielle as she opened her bag, making enough room for Wegin to drop into it.

"You are the strength of all of us," said Veridius. "I have watched as you marched into every new battle, without hesitation."

Malidora playfully punched Ambrielle in the back. "We braved the Savage Dark," she said. "What is left to fear?"

Ambrielle took a deep breath and stood straight. It made Darby do the same thing. It oddly felt a little less frightening.

Malidora ran toward the water, diving in first as Veridius waded into the spring. Dexius, Sidaire, Ambrielle, Gavian, and Kazial entered the water behind them. Darby stood in the clear waters, giving the others a moment so they wouldn't crowd the tunnels. Once they were clear, she plunged ahead, diving toward the glowing blue tunnel.

Darby passed through the brief darkness into the waters of a new world. Making her way to the surface, she saw a violet luminance shining above, sending beams through bubbled strands. As she broke the plane between water and air, she gained only a brief glimpse of this new world. Dark red, blue and purple, and vibrant green foliage was interwoven around them.

Sounds of chirps, buzzing, deep guttural calls, and shrill rhythmic patterns greeted her, along with the strange smells of the forest. The water felt unusual, almost milky.

Gavian climbed out of the water ahead of her, as she spotted Malidora waiting for her among a cluster of old trees. Their misshapen roots twisted and turned over and around each other, spilling from the mossy banks ahead and into the water. Using the roots to climb, Darby soon found Malidora's hand.

Ambrielle sat on a group of smooth rocks, wiping the soaked strands of hair out of her eyes. Malidora helped Gavian climb the rocks, as Darby dried her eyes to get a better look at the world around her.

Before her lay a pool of bewitching azure water nestled within the basin of an ancient, majestic forest. High above, a colossal crimson sun cast its otherworldly glow upon the land, painting the scene in a muted radiance. Twisted trees loomed around the pool like sentinels of an ancient realm, their limbs and branches entwining in unity. The flora seemed to embrace one another, their growth intermingling, as if they shared a secret language known only to the forest itself.

The dense, imposing trunks and snaking vines of the trees formed an impenetrable barrier, making the forest nearby seem utterly impassable. They could eventually cut a trail through this natural fortress, but the task would demand time and patience.

Malidora had already taken matters into her own hands. With a mix of agility and determination, she navigated around the pool, skillfully maneuvering around extended branches that sought to block her way. Darby wished she could boldly face the unknown in the same way.

Despite Malidora having a sometimes vastly different perspective on morality, Darby had learned that every person had something to offer, something to learn from if you gave them a chance. She admired Malidora's physical skill and courage. Her willingness to heal what was broken. Even if some of her actions were difficult to justify, her heart was usually in the right place.

"I found a way through," Malidora called back to the group, her voice echoing through the verdant labyrinth.

CHAPTER 17

AMBRIELLE—VALDERINE

AMBRIELLE UNCLASPED HER bag to let Wegin free. He rotated his upper half, scanning the unfamiliar world as the thickly layered sounds of birds, insects, and unknown creatures called out through the wood. She waited while Wegin recalibrated to these new surroundings.

"I have no record of this planet," Wegin informed Ambrielle, his voice tinged with intrigue. "It is indeed in a galaxy far beyond the Severine Cluster."

As Ambrielle joined the others, she found the narrow path Malidora had discovered. On the other side of the pool was another path of the same size, unseen by her eyes until she stood at this point. They soon followed the path as it snaked through the towering trees like a winding trench. The air was thick with the scent of ancient vegetation, and every sound, whether distant or nearby, carried an element of mystery. Ambrielle could feel the forest's heartbeat, an ancient rhythm that carried through the roots and branches, speaking of a time before memory.

The soft rustling of leaves and the distant calls of unknown creatures created a symphony of sounds that swirled around them. As they moved deeper into the forest, a deep, rumbling growl echoed like rolling thunder, shaking the very ground beneath their feet. The leaves quivered in response, the flora flickering with the sudden tremor.

As Ambrielle came to a stop, her eyes widened with awe and

fear. Emerging from the shadows, a colossal serpent slithered silently toward them, its massive form nearly blending with the foliage and shadows.

The serpent's scales glinted with an iridescent shimmer, reflecting the hues of the strange forest. As it moved, its body coiled and undulated with an eerie grace, creating a haunting visual through the trees.

The serpent's eyes were like pools of burning embers, filled with an ancient wisdom that seemed to pierce through the very soul of those who met its gaze. With each muscular contraction, the giant serpent's immense weight caused the earth to tremble beneath its majestic presence.

Ambrielle's heart raced. The serpent's girth matched the width of the path, leaving little room for the group to escape without getting dangerously close to its immense form.

"Get off the road!" Ambrielle shouted to the others, who still remained awestruck or frozen with fear by the serpent's presence.

Gavian tried cutting through the thicket with his sword, but the growth was too strong. Sidaire and Kazial crouched into the narrow gaps between the trees. Dexius squeezed into a space just off the road. Malidora and Veridius ran ahead until they found refuge. Ignoring the branches and thorns clawing into her skin, Ambrielle forced her way into the trees as she pulled Gavian and Darby behind her.

The serpent's movements were deliberate and unhurried, gliding forward with a spirit-like grace. As it passed by, the explorers could feel the displacement of air caused by its colossal body, as if they stood before a manifestation of the force of nature itself.

Through a small gap between the towering trees, Ambrielle stole a glance at the serpent. Its scales shimmered in the muted light, creating a mesmerizing play of colors. She could see the intricate patterns on its scales, which resembled constellations of a distant galaxy.

Finally, the serpent disappeared deeper into the forest, and they all began to rise from their hiding places. The air around them seemed to release the collective tension as the forest resumed its symphony of sounds and movements.

"What was that?" said Dexius, as he picked brambles from his skin. "This can't be the right planet."

Veridius untangled himself from the vines and branches. "What makes you say that?"

"Who in their right mind would live in a place like this?" said Dexius. "Not some great intelligence, that's for sure."

"Do we know what Hableides looks like?" said Darby. "For all we know that big serpent was it."

"I sure hope not," said Ambrielle as she tried to slow her breathing.

"Darby has a point. Hableides, for all we know, could take the form of a giant serpent," said Malidora. "There was something not normal about that creature. At the very least, it could be a lead. We need to catch up."

"I'm not sure I want to catch up with that thing," said Sidaire, as she brushed debris from her hair.

"Well, let's keep going and see what we can find," said Ambrielle. "If I feel the ground shaking again though, I'm heading back to the water."

They moved through the serpent's trail, keeping their wary eyes on the path ahead as well as behind them. After they had been walking for a while, the trail widened into a glade. Two ponds with the same glowing blue water nestled between the rows of shrubs and bushes. Lovely blooms with orange petals speckled with red stood on stalks rising out of the ponds. Darby reached out to one, readying her fingers around it as if to pick it from the stalk.

"Wait!" Malidora cautioned. "Any of these plants could be poisonous. Try to touch as little as possible." Darby sucked in a deep breath, lowering her hand away from the flowers.

The trail continued on through more of the thick forest. Leaving the tranquil glen behind, they moved on. Soon they came across a smaller path off the serpent trail. Ambrielle, eager to put more space between them and the serpent, eased over to investigate. Between the trees and vines, something shined in the darkened shadows.

Ambrielle took a few steps onto the path and paused as she heard steps crunching through the underbrush in the forest ahead.

"We need to keep moving," said Malidora as she started ahead. "Not stop and look at every new plant along the way."

Ambrielle slowly followed. "I heard something out there in the forest."

"There's lots of sounds out here," said Malidora. "I'm sure there are all kinds of creatures in these woods, but they would have to be small to pass through them."

"This was different," said Ambrielle, her eyes scanning the surrounding trees. "Someone walking."

"All the more reason to keep—" Malidora stopped, sniffing the air.

Suddenly, she drew her crossbow as several bipedal creatures poured out of the smaller path toward them. Gavian drew his sword, moving in front of Ambrielle, who swung her bladestaff into position. They all huddled together as the other beings surrounded them. Dexius, Sidaire, and Darby backed up to Ambrielle and Gavian with arrows ready. Malidora, Veridius, and Kazial drew in beside them.

Some of these beings had dark red skin, bumpy and patterned. They had elongated heads but small eyes. Others looked nearly human, but with larger black eyes and a more pronounced brow. Some had gray or light-colored hair, while others had none at all. Clearly, these were at least two different species, but both wore clothing made with long bird feathers.

Though each individual wore matching feathers, there was a wide variety in the patterns and colors. Many held spears, while some had mechanical-looking weapons. A few had what resembled guns attached to their shoulders.

One of the humanlike creatures walked toward where Ambrielle and Malidora stood close to each other. The woman had long, rough strands of hair that seemed to bend more than curl. It resembled moss or straw.

"Welcome home," the woman spoke softly like a gentle breeze. "For we know why you have come."

It unnerved Ambrielle that this woman claimed to possess more knowledge about them than they did about her. Exchanging a glance with Malidora, Ambrielle found more curiosity in her expression than concern. "How do you know who we are?" said Ambrielle.

"I am Kalyx," the woman said; her voice seemed to quiet those with her. Their rigid stances relaxed as they put away their weapons. "As all the others, you were brought to Valderine to bring light and honor to Hableides. To join in kinship with all things."

"You know Hableides?" Ambrielle felt the tension in her muscles begin to ease, though she eyed them all with suspicion. "Can you take us there?"

"We are the Kalithor, followers of Hableides. She only speaks to those she has chosen," said Kalyx.

"We have heard the Shadows are here," said Malidora, who remained in a guarded posture; she had put away her crossbow, though her hand was hidden inside her vest. "They have come to take Hableides. We came to help fight them."

"There is no need for fighting." Kalyx's black eyes held a serene resolve. "We are all protected here."

Ambrielle's instinct was to trust them. If they wanted to help Hableides, they would need to be friends with her allies. Dexius must have sensed the same thing, as he lowered his bow slightly. Darby did as well.

"This is an urgent matter," said Malidora. "Hableides is in danger."

The people in the crowd began glancing at each other, as if surprised by Malidora's words.

"You refer to the presence of the dark ones," said Kalyx, who appeared neither surprised nor concerned. "Do not be troubled. They are no threat to us or to Hableides. As I said before, we are protected."

"I have heard the same from many before you," said Malidora. She gestured toward the woods around, where sunlight filtered through the leaves, casting shifting patterns of light and shadows. "Only to have their world torn asunder."

"No matter how many of the dark ones come," said Kalyx, as the call of a distant bird rang out, "they will never be able to reach us."

"How have you kept them away?" Ambrielle asked as she put the bladestaff strap over her shoulder.

"They cannot contend with the power of Hableides," said Kalyx as she passed by Ambrielle to move closer to Malidora. "Her will keeps them away."

"The Nulvarians will not give up," said Malidora as Kalyx stepped in front of her. "Hableides will not be safe until we destroy them."

Kalyx sighed as she stood inches from Malidora's face. Though she didn't appear threatening, it seemed like an odd thing to do. Ambrielle expected one of them to eventually flinch and doubted it would be Malidora.

After a moment of them staring at each other, Kalyx spoke. "You have much to learn." Kalyx turned around, heading further into the forest. "If you wish to help, join us in our daily tasks. We can offer you food, shelter, and fellowship, but you must adhere to our ways."

"And if we do, we can speak to Hableides?" Malidora's hip cocked to the left as she rested her hand on her side.

"To be chosen"—Kalyx smiled—"the first thing you must learn is patience."

CHAPTER 18

MALIDORA—VALDERINE

MALIDORA STOOD WATCHING the people tread back onto the small path with her hands firmly on her hips. She noticed Ambrielle walking slowly with uncertainty behind the others. Gavian was a step ahead of her, preceded by Darby, Sidaire, Dexius, and Kazial.

They came to a clearing sparkling with light. The bark of the trees was highly reflective, shining light from the large sun onto everything around them. The people gathered pieces of reflective bark that lay on the ground. It was everywhere underneath the trees. Malidora picked up one of the larger pieces, taking it over to one of the Kalithor's bags. Veridius entered the area, helping to collect the bark, and Gavian and the rest of them eventually joined in.

After what seemed like an hour, everyone had their bags and arms filled with the bark. Even with so much, plenty remained on the ground. They traveled back onto the main path, heading in the same direction as before. As they strolled further on, they came to another path that crossed the one they were on, obviously made by the same serpent.

"The big snake that comes through here," said Darby. "Is that Hableides?"

Kalyx laughed as she turned left onto the crossing path with the others. "The serpent is one of the duvora. Like all creatures on Valderine, they revere and serve Hableides."

"You mean there is more than one?" Ambrielle grimaced.

"They are ancient creatures, only a few remain," said Kalyx. "But you have nothing to fear. As I said, they are under the guidance of Hableides."

"I guess that's comforting," said Sidaire.

"As long as Hableides likes us," said Dexius, prompting Sidaire's expression to pause.

They continued on the path. As they moved along, the forest became slightly less dense, more like the forests Malidora had seen on other worlds. They followed the group to a large camp of tent-like structures, some made from animal skins, others made of strands of vine or long-leafed plants woven together. The people here were gathered into several groups, some children. Some of them appeared to be telling stories. Others appeared to be teaching how to perform certain tasks or learning about different flowers they had spread across a large rock.

Among the red and tan residents there were other species here among the group. There were creatures with heads more square-shaped, some that had limbs that resembled stick figures, one was quadrupedal like the Breghobbins on Isodonia. Ambrielle tried not to stare too long while she observed them.

"We have new brothers and sisters!" said Kalyx. "Hableides has called more to join the fold!"

Everyone around them stopped what they were doing and turned to Malidora and the others. She gave them a nod, focusing her gaze between them. Though being stared at by so many was beginning to make her uncomfortable, she wanted to appear confident. Many of them stood up and walked over to get a closer look at them. Placing their hands on them, the people smiled and greeted them warmly. They seemed especially enamored with her fiery tipped hair as well as Sidaire's ebbing strands that seemed to change from dark magenta to light.

They brought Sidaire, Dexius, Gavian, and Darby over to one of their groups. They seemed to be feeding rows of string through a machine that wove them together into cloth. It was a more modern version of a loom. Malidora and Ambrielle were ushered toward another group that were washing clothes in a lovely series of small waterfalls that collected in various pools from a small stream at the far edges of the camp. The moving water barely made a sound, trickling its way over one pool formed in the rocks and spilling over into others.

The trees throughout the camp had long, orange strands like bristles of a broom. Swaying in the tranquil breeze, the long fronds seemed to whisper. It was one of the most peaceful places Malidora had ever experienced.

"Where did you come from?" said a girl as she handed a rough stone each to Malidora and Ambrielle. She began pouring an oily liquid onto the stone, spilling some on both of their hands.

"A place called Arkanthis on Isodonia," said Malidora as she watched the girl scrub the stone over the wet clothing in one of the pools of blue water. "What about you?"

"I was born here on Valderine," said the girl with a grin.

Malidora raised her eyebrow. "Your kind is native to this planet?"

"My ancestors came here many generations ago. I am a mix of several species who met here from across the universe," she said with a sparkle in her black eyes. "A child of many stars!"

Watching the girl scrub the simple dress across the threads, Malidora emulated her actions. "You must have a fascinating history." Wegin hovered nearby, watching them work.

"I would love to know more than I do," said the girl as she placed the dress on a rock to dry in the sunlight. "But that will come in time. I have heard that some have difficulty adapting to this place at first. How are you doing so far?"

"I've always been adaptable," said Malidora, spreading the oil over the clothing. "Not sure about the others."

"I'm glad to hear it!" said the girl as she grabbed a tunic from a pile nearby. "After being here a few days, you'll forget all about your former home."

Malidora didn't want to dim her apparent joy in this place, but there was no way she could stay here the rest of her life. There was so much left to be done.

"What is Hableides like?" Malidora asked as she scrubbed.

"I have never seen her with my eyes," said the girl, splashing the tunic in the water. "No one has. But that isn't what's important."

"No one has ever seen Hableides?" Malidora noticed one of the Kalithor letting Gavian have a turn at using the weaving machine as Sidaire and Darby looked on. Her eyes searched the camp, finding Veridius and Kazial separating large bags of seeds of some sort.

"There is more to beauty and knowledge than what your eyes can tell," said the girl. "She speaks to us in many ways. For some, it is through the water or the breeze. For a few, she is the voice inside their mind."

A man carrying a bundle of clothing walked over to them. "Your mechanoid looks more advanced than most," he said to Ambrielle, referring to Wegin. "It has been a while since I have seen one."

"Yes, he is pretty handy," Ambrielle said as Wegin rotated his halves while flickering his lights as if trying to show off. "Except when it comes to washing clothes apparently," she joked.

Wegin stopped rotating and his lights turned solid. "I'm not equipped for that sort of thing."

"It's a shame that they don't last long around here," the man said.

Ambrielle stopped washing the clothes and made eye contact with the man. "Why would that be?"

"There is no energy source for them here," he said. "All the energy we have must be used for the lights. They run out of power before long. You may as well get as much as you can out of this one until its power dies."

Wegin's lights blinked red as he let out a low whine.

"Don't worry Wegin," said Ambrielle as the man walked away. "We aren't going to be here that long."

Malidora tossed a wet dress over Wegin. "Put that somewhere to dry, would you?"

By the time the huge sun had nearly moved behind the trees, they had finished washing all the clothing. Everyone gathered together in the center of the tents. Sitting down in the grass, they formed a circle. A few of them carried bowls made of hollowed wood. They placed a bowl filled with a piece of fruit surrounded by leaves and berries in front of each person. Everyone that had been served a bowl patiently waited before beginning to eat.

Once everyone had a bowl and those that had served them found a place to sit, they began to sing.

In humble thanks, our voices raise,

A cosmic chorus, full of praise.
For from the stars, our light we trace,
An eternal beacon in this sacred place.

When they had finished the short song, everyone began to eat. With no utensils, they ate everything with their hands. Malidora started with the fruit. It was a bit tough on the outside but quite tender inside. The leaves were thick but soft to chew. She tried the berries, which were sweet but crunchier than she would have preferred. Despite that, the mixture of flavors combined to make a sweet and savory taste that was better than it looked.

As the sky grew dark and everyone finished, conversations could be heard among the crowd. Some of the people got up to be closer to other friends and join in their discussions. Malidora watched the other groups, keeping an eye on their mannerisms. People couldn't help but glance at someone they were talking about. She noticed many times when they were talking about them, the newcomers.

"I like it here," said Sidaire as she leaned on Dexius. "It's nice having so many people around again. Reminds me of home. Even though I haven't talked to that many, I feel like I already know them."

They possessed a remarkable level of trust, a virtue born from their sheltered existence. Malidora refrained from casting blame; after all, their eyes hadn't witnessed the covert machinations that underlie society's veneer or the methods employed to subjugate the masses. Yet, even in this seemingly idyllic setting, a certain structure prevailed. And where there was structure, power was required to maintain it. And if there was power, there would also be corruption.

"It's very peaceful," Darby said while lying on the grass with her knees up. "Quite a change from the war on Isodonia."

Veridius sat playing with a cluster of weeds with a short stick. "This is what Vesta should have been like. There is no selfishness or greed. Everyone is made to feel important."

"Don't be so certain. Like all civilizations, everything is pretty on the surface," said Malidora. "The truth lies between the cracks."

"Always so cynical," said Veridius. "But I won't argue with you on that."

"Ravessian wants to meet you all," said Kalyx. "Would you come with me?"

Kalyx guided them over to one of the large tents, ushering them inside. The people within the spacious tent stood up and moved out of the way as they gestured for them to sit.

The floor was made of spongy material, soft enough to make it fairly comfortable to sit on. Sitting at the end of the floor were two women and two men. One of the men eyed them with a suspicious look. He had strange bugged-out eyes and a bit of a rodent-like nose and mouth. His hair was sandy-colored, and he sat leaning back on one side with his legs crossed on the other.

"There were no signs of your coming," said the man. "It is rare that I fail to read the signs. How did you find this place? Did Hableides speak to you?"

"This is Ravessian," said Kalyx. "Though we don't have leaders here, he was chosen to be the voice of Hableides, an intermediary between her and her followers. She speaks to him and guides him in what she wants from us."

Malidora knew some kind of leadership existed in this society. It was now a matter of finding out what their goals were and if they would eventually lead them to Hableides.

"I was told of Hableides by the Vogus," said Malidora, "before their planet was destroyed by the Nulvarians."

"I have not heard of the Vogus," said Ravessian. "What message did they have to send?"

She wondered if Hableides even existed. Had some of these beings made it up in order to control all these people? Although something had apparently spoken to the Vogus across a great distance.

"They spoke of a vision, a perfect universe," said Malidora, trying to recall what the Vogus had told her as best she could. "All species coming together as points of light."

"That is the message of Hableides to all of us," Ravessian said, smiling. "And what light did you bring with you?"

Malidora looked around at everyone, hoping they would have an answer. As she thought about the glowing nyalith shard in her bag, Malidora tried to cover it better with her vest. She wasn't about to give them the shard with the essence of Kandom. It was all that was left of Dabradan and Evala. Neither was she willing to give up Niralys, the eternium jewel she had taken from Averess.

"Any of you?" said Ravessian as his smiling face began to flatten out.

Gavian stood, taking something from his satchel. "I may have something." It was the amythite crystal from Anatharia. Ravessian raised himself to his feet, reaching toward the violet crystal.

"A crystal?" said Ravessian as he examined it. "And what does it do?"

Before Gavian could answer, Ambrielle spoke up. "It amplifies sunlight. It can be used to convert sunlight into a powerful beam of energy."

"This is what Hableides asked you to bring? It could be useful," said Ravessian, as he took the crystal from Gavian's hand. "Others have brought technology that can collect sunlight, while some have brought the means to focus it. All varieties of species have brought different devices, different technology. It has brought us all together to honor Hableides and to ensure that none of our sun's light is wasted."

"It's a beautiful concept," said Sidaire.

What was the purpose of people bringing objects related to light from all over the universe? What did they do with them? Was it nothing more than a symbolic gesture? Doubtful. There must be some use they had for them.

"We will allow you to stay with us as long as you contribute," said Ravessian, as he continued to stare at the amythite crystal. "Hableides will eventually find a place where you are needed most. The conveyance ceremony is coming up in a few days. If all goes well, you will be welcome to attend."

"By the wisdom of Hableides," said Kalyx.

Once darkness had settled over the camp, Kalyx showed them a place where they could sleep. It was nothing more than two slender tree trunks cut about six feet long and planted into the dirt. The trunks held a square of canvas tied to them and stretched to wooden stakes in the ground on the other end.

She gave them pieces of cloth to place on the grass and lie on. They huddled together so they could all fit on the blankets. Malidora picked a spot where she would have a full view of the camp. Strange and enchanting, the forest pulsed with the echoes of creatures calling out to one another.

A chorus of melodic trills, ethereal hums, and the gentle rustling of leaves blended together in the dark.

Sidaire settled in nearby, wrapping herself in the patchwork blankets. "Getting any more comfortable with this place?"

Malidora kept her eyes on the heart of the camp as she reclined on her side. "There's an unsettling current here. Something is amiss, and I can't shake the feeling that there are dark mysteries concealed within these woods."

CHAPTER 19

GAVIAN—VALDERINE

AZRAVION'S INSATIABLE HUNGER gnawed at Gavian's sanity as he tried to sleep. Unable to tolerate it any longer, he quietly slipped away from Ambrielle and picked up the sword lying in the grass. He had to get the blade away from the others, far away. After sneaking off from the Kalithor camp, he found his way back to the serpent's trail through the thick forest. After walking among the sounds of nocturnal creatures, something drove him to abandon the path of the serpent's trail and plunge deeper into the ominous heart of the shadowy forest. Each step felt like sinking into the clutches of an ancient malevolence, and the trees that loomed like sinister fangs seemed to mock his every move.

A haunting presence whispered dark secrets in his mind, a beckoning from some unseen malice that tugged at his very soul. It was as if the eerie woods themselves called to him, luring him toward an unknown destination. The forest's nightmarish ambience was suffocating, yet Gavian felt an unnatural pull, an inexplicable familiarity, that compelled him forward.

As the core of Azravion thirsted for the essence of life, Gavian scoured the forest, seeking anything alive to satiate the sword. His steps were hesitant, and the moonlit shadows seemed to twist and contort, hinting at unseen terrors lurking in the darkness. The blade's dark intent now possessed him, fueling an unholy desire for the life force of another.

Suddenly, a chilling presence slithered through the moonlight, sending shivers down Gavian's spine. He stumbled over a root in his haste, barely avoiding a painful fall. The looming shadow moved with sinister grace, and fear gripped Gavian's heart as he realized the sword had found new prey.

Ignoring the trepidation clawing at his mind, Gavian bravely followed the sinister specter deeper into the haunting forest. The shadows seemed to converge, pulling him toward the heart of the night. As the shape emerged from the veil of umber, Gavian's pulse quickened. Against the ethereal glow of the moons, he beheld the haunting figure before him: Serenith, the Ichtek, wielder of the sword Nagoloth.

His voice hissed through the eerie silence, dripping with a chilling certainty, "It took you long enough to find me." Serenith removed his helmet, revealing his lizard-like face. "Now you understand what it means to be the bearer of Azravion," Serenith taunted. "You crave my death, don't you? To rend my flesh and spill my life essence to quench your sword's unending thirst."

Gavian pulled out the sword, and Serenith quickly drew his. Without further hesitation Gavian unleashed a combination of strikes that Serenith deflected with his glowing blade. Spinning to separate himself from Gavian's range, Serenith turned off the glow around the shadowblade and slashed through the air in front of him. The bare blade cut a space into the air itself, creating a barrier between him and Gavian. Tiny particles flashed as they neared the deadspace between them.

"I didn't come here to fight," said Serenith, "only to talk."

"You're lucky I can't afford to use Azravion's essence," Gavian said. "This time I would end you."

"I see you learned nothing after the result of our last meeting," Serenith said.

"I know all of your moves now," said Gavian. "Your weaknesses."

"How often have you used it since we parted?" Serenith said. "How many innocent lives have you stolen?"

"I protect innocent lives," said Gavian, sidestepping around the deadspace toward Serenith. "From people like you. People that would try to destroy the universe and everyone in it for their own selfish desires."

Serenith matched Gavian's steps, keeping the deadspace between them. "I offered you the same path that I have taken. How is that selfish? As I've told you, lives in this universe are not as important as you think. They are all going to die eventually. Isn't it worth rising above the endless cycle of life and death to reach out for an existence that really matters?"

"Every life is important," said Gavian. "No matter who we may judge to be right or wrong, they all matter in the end."

"Whose essence will you take then?" said Serenith. "You're running out of time."

"I'll find the other Ichtek and the Nulvarians," said Gavian. "And from them I will drain all the essence I will ever need."

Serenith's voice dripped with a sinister assurance. "By then, the sword's thirst will have become so unquenchable that it will sap the essence from its bearer," said Serenith. "But fear not. I have a solution for you. An answer to your problems."

His words hung in the air, a promise of relief from the burden Gavian carried. "There is a grove ahead with a sacred tree bearing fruit that is important to the Kalithor. You will know it as soon as you see it. Run your blade through this tree and take as much essence as you can."

"The blade needs the essence of sentient life," said Gavian, "not plants or trees."

"This tree is an exception," said Serenith. "There is certain plant life in this world with an abundance of living essence. This tree is one of them. It won't even kill the tree, for there is more essence than even the sword can hold at once."

Gavian's skepticism lingered, and he questioned Serenith's motives, "And what's in it for you?"

"Pythus's death does not have to be in vain. When you killed him and took Azravion, you chose to be his successor. Now you must take up his birthright and be the harbinger that will save our people."

A pause settled between them, a moment heavy with the weight of choices and consequences. Gavian, considering the offer, sought clarity. "And all I have to do is take essence from this tree?" said Gavian.

"I am growing rather impatient with this standoff between us and the Kalithor," said Serenith. "Sooner or later the Nulvarians will be unleashed, nothing will hold them back forever. Wounding the Kalithor's sacred tree will draw all of their people from their protected lands. And then . . . at last . . . the battle can finally begin."

CHAPTER 20

GAVIAN—VALDERINE

As morning came, Gavian awakened to Kalyx ushering everyone toward the middle of the glade. The Kalithor had wasted no time going back to their daily duties. Their activities this time seemed less like work. As the others kneeled or sat in the grass, Ambrielle cleared away some debris on the ground to make a place for her to sit. Around them, others talked in groups. Some seemed to craft things out of sticks and rocks, while a few played simple melodies, using long hollow wooden pieces as instruments.

"Do you see anything that interests you?" she said to them as they watched.

Gavian stayed silent as he eyed the different activities. Sidaire broke the quietude, voicing her confusion. "I don't really know what everyone is doing."

"Point out a group, and I will tell you," offered Kalyx.

Sidaire gestured toward a cluster of six kids and two young adults. "What are those children doing there?" she asked, curiously.

"Ah, they are telling one of the enchanting tales of the Celestial Forest," exclaimed Kalyx, her eyes alight with wonder. "Its ethereal embrace birthed the very stars and cradled Valderine, adorning it with five moons that dance in cosmic harmony. The forest's essence ripples across the world, leaving an indelible mark upon every facet of existence, even gracing our beloved Hableides, who views all of us as her cherished children, with boundless creativity and nurturing care."

"What is the music they are playing?" asked Kazial, as he watched the group playing the woodwind instruments.

"Listen," whispered Kalyx with a gleam in her eyes, "they weave the astral symphony, an orchestra of stars in the night sky. Each twinkling light represents a musical note, gracefully dancing in intricate patterns. Jevu and Harme are the cosmic scribes, meticulously transcribing these heavenly melodies destined to be played. As their ethereal music fills our world, we're drawn nearer to the Celestial Forest, bathed in a tranquil embrace of serenity and peace."

"Can anyone do that?" asked Sidaire.

"You can do anything that Hableides chooses for you," said Kalyx. "She knows what is best."

This place was so different from his childhood in Rethia. Everyone seemed to be happy in everything they did. Food was plentiful here. They had time for things such as music. Yet, the people didn't have freedom to make their own choices.

Ravessian threw back the tarp on the large tent as his hair waved in the morning breeze. "Everyone!" he shouted, prompting them all to leave their groups and hurry over to the large tent. "We have been called upon, and we must answer. We'll be dividing into two expeditions. The first shall journey to the Rotwood Forest, scattering the bagalia seeds far and wide. Meanwhile, the second group will venture to the Sanctuary, tending to the pollination of the delicate orkis flowers."

Someone from the crowd shouted out, "What group did she choose for me?"

"Hableides did not call anyone by name," Ravessian said. "You may choose the group that speaks to you."

Gavian relaxed. At least the people were allowed some choice. Maybe this was the right way to do things. He couldn't argue with the results. People couldn't be left with total freedom. There had to be some kind of structure, or everything would devolve into chaos.

As the people formed into different social groups around them, deciding who was going to go with who, Malidora spotted Ambrielle and Gavian and made her way over. "We should join the groups but split up. We can get outside of this camp and hopefully get an idea of where the Nulvarians are attacking."

"If nothing else, we can get a better read on the landscape," Dexius suggested.

"And the wildlife," chimed in Darby.

Gavian recognized the look in Ambrielle's eyes. Before she said anything, he knew something had sparked a new idea. "Wegin, scout the land around us and see if you can find any sign of the Shadows," she instructed.

"Certainly," acknowledged Wegin as he ascended above them.

"But don't venture too far," Ambrielle cautioned. "Meet us back here tonight."

Gavian, Ambrielle, Dexius, and Sidaire ended up in the group heading to Rotwood Forest, while Kazial, Darby, Veridius, and Malidora went to the Sanctuary.

Holding a bag filled with seeds that would one day grow into trees, Gavian tried to slow his pace, but he was anxious to get out of the camp. They crossed through the serpent's paths until moving onto a smaller trail into the tangled mass of the forest.

Ambrielle jumped as a cluster of small flying creatures leapt up from the layers of dried leaves on the ground. They were shaped like arrowheads, patterned with splotches of black and maple. They landed on a tree stump ahead, and it was hard to tell if they were insects or small birds. As Gavian and Ambrielle approached the tree stump, the creatures flew again, this time landing on a mound of grass not far away. They flew as one formation, each time over a short distance.

A boy walking nearby seemed to notice their interest. "I think they are called runnarks. They're a type of bird," he said. "They can't fly very far at a time, but they are very good at concealing themselves in the foliage. You never see them unless you get too close and force them to move."

"It's funny how they all fly off at the same time," Ambrielle said.

"They never leave their group," said the boy. "Nearly every movement they make is synchronized like that."

"Wow, I wonder how they communicate with each other," Ambrielle said.

"Just instinct I guess," said the boy. "Or it could be by the unspoken thoughts of Hableides."

Could that really be true? Did Hableides control the will of each creature on Valderine? Gavian didn't like the thought of it. If every action here was being unknowingly controlled by something else, what was the point of living? Even if the beings were unaware of the control, it all seemed pointless if every single action, every choice, was made for them.

As they ventured deeper into the heart of the forest, an eerie scene awaited them. They stepped into an expanse of leafless trees standing like solemn sentinels of time. Their skeletal branches created a haunting silhouette against the light. These trees, once vibrant and full of life, now stood with a fragility that told of their impending fate.

Brittle to the touch, it seemed as though they were merely held upright by the desperate tangle of other trees embracing them. Giant logs lay scattered, resting amid patches of thick moss that resembled soft, muddy beds. Some of these fallen behemoths leaned against others, their limbs outstretched as if reaching for one last gasp of life.

A disconcerting aura enveloped the area. Grass and ferns dared to grow atop the decaying remnants of older trees, while new saplings sprouted without care or concern for those that came before them. Despite the unsettling ambience, there was a poignant beauty in the contrast between life and death, growth and decay. This corner of the forest bore witness to the delicate dance of existence, where every fallen log and fresh sprout told an ancient story.

Some of the group began reaching into their bags, tossing the hard round seeds around the moss-covered logs.

"Spread out," said Kalyx. "Make sure we cover the entire area."

Gavian reached into his bag. With a flick of his wrist, he sent a handful of the precious seeds cascading into a lush area covered with vibrant ferns. Ambrielle cast a handful into a group of small bushes that had taken root atop a pile of old, rotting logs. As the group ventured deeper into the enchanting Rotwood Forest, they continued to bless the ground with life-giving seeds.

Though they carried out Hableides's will, it somehow felt different if they were consciously helping her. It was much different than being controlled. But how much different was it? Where exactly was that line?

Gavian could feel the subtle pulsing of the sword against his back through the sheath. It was as if he could sense the heartbeat of the repulsive, dark creature connected to the blade. Ambrielle looked back with a smile as she grabbed more seeds. As much as he hated to see her reaction, he couldn't go any longer without telling her.

Gavian led Ambrielle to a group of newly sprouted trees, away from the others. "There's something I need to tell you," he said with a serious tone, hoping to prepare her for what he was about to say.

She distributed the remaining seeds in her hand and turned back to him with a blank expression. "What is it?"

He took a deep breath as he tried to organize his thoughts. "You were right about the sword," he said, glancing into her eyes. "I never should have kept it. Though I'm not sure at which point I should have let it go. It might have saved your life when we were up against Ogolameth. It saved a lot of soldiers' lives . . ."

"What happened?" she said, her eyebrows curling upward.

"It's connected to some monstrous creature," said Gavian. "I didn't realize it at first, but I know now that this creature wants life essence the sword takes. I either have to keep feeding it or it will drain mine. If I cast it away, I only give someone else the power to feed this creature. I figured it was safer in my hands, that I could resist its hunger for essence."

"But you can't?" Ambrielle said.

"It grows stronger every day," said Gavian. "I don't know how bad it will get or if I can keep resisting it."

"How do you always get yourself into things like this . . ." Ambrielle huffed. "You should have told me sooner."

"I know . . ." replied Gavian.

"Keep the sword for now," said Ambrielle. "Let's not worry anyone else about this yet. We'll come up with something to get you out of this."

Gavian breathed a sigh of relief that Ambrielle was able to not only forgive him for being careless with a sword like this, but that she was also willing to support him through it. It was at least one weight lifted from his shoulders.

Having artfully spread the last of the seeds, the group regathered at the forest's heart, their faces radiant with filled purpose and shared joy. Sidaire leaned against Dexius, his arm tenderly encircling her waist.

Kalyx placed her hands softly on both Dexius and Sidaire. "It would be wise not to entangle yourself too closely with any particular soul," Kalyx said gently. "Hableides, in her boundless wisdom, will choose a mate for you when the time is right, guiding your heart toward a cosmic union." Dexius slowly eased his arm away from Sidaire while she separated from him, straightening her posture and brushing her sides as if somehow that would make everyone forget they had been holding each other a moment ago.

Ambrielle shared a concerned glance with Gavian as she leaned back to see his expression. "What if two people were already together before coming here? They wouldn't need anyone chosen for them."

With a firm conviction, Kalyx replied, "The will of Hableides transcends our own. In her vast understanding, she orchestrates the dance of destiny, uniting souls in the most profound ways. As followers, we yield to her guidance, for it is through her that we find purpose and fulfillment."

"Everyone here," said Gavian, "they all go along with whoever Hableides picks for them?"

Kalyx nodded, her voice unwavering. "Indeed, for within these sacred woods, all who seek solace and enlightenment come willingly, trusting in Hableides's embrace. Her nurturing spirit cradles us as her cherished children, tending to the harmony of life on Valderine."

"I didn't realize that Hableides cared so intently about every detail of our lives," said Ambrielle, trying to hide her discontent. "Shouldn't such harmony allow for individual choice?"

"Too much individual choice can lead to disarray," said Kalyx. "You will find that there is contentment in letting go of such things."

As much as her words gave Gavian pause, this made it apparent that there were things that Hableides could not control, otherwise she wouldn't need the Kalithor to enforce these rules. He could see the appeal in a greater intelligence making certain decisions for him. There were definitely some things he would relinquish. Love, however, was not one of them.

After meeting back up with Malidora and the others that evening, they exchanged stories. Neither group had seen any signs of the Nulvarians. The sky darkened to dusk, and a familiar sound zoomed above them as some of the Kalithor began serving bowls of the forest's bounty to eat. Ambrielle gazed toward the tops of the trees, Wegin flying into view.

"Ambrielle," Wegin said as he flickered his lights. "I found patches of blackened forest to the southwest, abandoned dwellings among them."

"How many Nulvarians?" Ambrielle asked.

"No confirmed detection," said Wegin. "Either they are hiding or have already moved on to other areas."

"Do we even know what we're doing?" said Dexius. "This is getting us nowhere."

"Be patient, Dex," said Sidaire. "It will work out."

"I'm beginning to wonder if we should have talked to the Cereveshians in Averess to begin with," said Malidora.

"It wasn't like we really had a choice," Ambrielle mused. "Something about this place though. It feels like this is where we're supposed to be."

"It feels like a trap," said Malidora. "Do you really think all of these people abandoned their worlds to come here for the rest of their lives? I wonder how willing their participation really is."

"I know I wouldn't want some oracle dictating every part of my life," Dexius remarked.

"What if there is a much bigger force out there? One of harmony and symbiosis that Hableides and even we are only a small part of?" said Ambrielle as two of the Kalithor men handed her and the others bowls.

Dexius took one of the bowls as he glanced at Ambrielle. "What are you talking about?"

"I think there is more at play here than what our eyes can see," Ambrielle said as she began to eat. "We are supposed to be here to fight the Gaith."

"Either way, I hope we find something soon." Gavian watched as the men finished handing out food. He put one of the moist, leafy plants in his mouth and wished this were one of those times where a higher intelligence would directly tell them what to do next. Why couldn't someone guide them instead of them having to go through all this fear and doubt?

His own thoughts spoke back to him. What would be the point of living if they didn't willingly choose to take those steps for themselves? If he hated the idea of being controlled, he would have to embrace everything that came with taking those conscious steps, including the fears and the doubts.

"How long are we going to stay here?" said Dexius, after the two men had left. "If we need to fight the Shadows, we should leave and go find them."

"The goal is to find Hableides," Veridius said as he grabbed a handful of the mixture of leaves, fruit, nuts, and roots. "And these people can lead us to her. I suspect she would be far more difficult to find on our own."

"None of these people have ever seen Hableides," said Malidora between crunching on her food. "Their leader, Ravessian, has only spoken to her."

"Hableides has to know we have come to see her." Ambrielle gazed upward at the stars glimmering between the trees. "Maybe she will speak to them and have them guide us to her."

"If this oracle is even real," said Dexius, as he crumbled the leaves in his bowl, mixing them with everything else.

"Something spoke to the Vogus," said Malidora. "And the Gaith are after something here."

"I'm not waiting much longer," said Dexius, dropping some of the mix into his mouth. "If we don't find something soon, I'm going on my own."

"And I'm going too," said Sidaire.

After everyone finished eating their food and the conversations of the groups of Kalithor began to quiet, Gavian and the others wrapped up in their blankets under the hanging tarp, listening to the calls of the night.

⸙

In the depths of the night, Gavian's slumber was disrupted by an insidious presence, a thirst emanating from the very core of Azravion. The sword lay close, and the malevolent energy it exuded seemed to permeate his very being. A sinister compulsion gripped him, urging him to rise from his resting place and heed the delicate, haunting whispers that slithered into his consciousness. The relentless force pulled at his thoughts, directing him toward a mysterious destination—a grove shrouded in shadows, harboring secrets darker than the night itself.

The disembodied voice beckoned him without words, promising hidden truths and forbidden power. A seductive pull encouraged him to succumb, to venture into the unknown and partake in the nefarious plans that danced at the edge of his perception. Yet, amid the tendrils of this wicked temptation, Gavian held firm. He fought against the relentless influence, determined not to be a puppet to the blade's sinister desires.

Steeling himself against the dark allure, he wrestled with his own inner turmoil. Each step he took toward the grove felt like a plunge into the abyss, a descent into a realm where malevolence intertwined with every shadow. His heart raced, both with fear and purpose. The very air seemed to thicken with an ominous anticipation, as if the universe itself held its breath, awaiting the unfolding of a sinister fate.

Gavian's thoughts swirled like a tempest, torn between his longing for liberation and the dread that coursed through him. He couldn't afford to perpetuate this nightly ritual of clandestine treks. The forest's whisperings concealed a deeper malevolence, one that Serenith's motives couldn't justify. He had to defy Azravion's call, even if it meant paying the ultimate price.

As the impending clash with the Ichtek loomed on the horizon, Gavian's hope hinged on channeling Azravion's insatiable thirst toward those who truly deserved its malefic embrace. He yearned for reprieve, to cast off the shackles that bound him to this macabre journey and to find a way to control the very darkness that sought to consume him.

CHAPTER 21

MALIDORA—VALDERINE

MALIDORA AWOKE TO the sounds of people walking back and forth near their shelter. They busily gathered water into containers and packed food into bags to carry on their back. She saw most of the group already walking around helping the Kalithor prepare for the journey.

She flung the tarp off their hut, revealing Gavian and Ambrielle, who were sitting up on their mats kissing. A warm smile played on Malidora's lips—she couldn't help but feel joy for them. In a universe fraught with challenges, discovering a profound connection wasn't a simple feat. Their affection reminded her of Dabradan, and a bittersweet ache settled in. Longing to hold him once more, she couldn't help but yearn for his comforting embrace. More than ever, she needed him right now.

As the light of the morning sun hit Ambrielle and Gavian, they quickly backed away from each other and stood. "Malidora!" exclaimed Ambrielle.

"Didn't mean to interrupt," Malidora said, as she grabbed the tarp to put it back in place.

"We have to be careful about them seeing us," said Ambrielle, as she brushed her fingers through her hair. "Kalyx said that Hableides has to choose someone for you."

"Yeah, it's crazy." Gavian grabbed both of his swords from the ground. "Even Rethia let you choose who you promised yourself to."

"I know," said Ambrielle, "but we don't need to cause any kind of disturbance."

After the others woke up, they got in line with the rest of the camp leading to the cascading pools. Each person quickly splashed water on themselves and moved out of the way for the next person in line. Malidora got her turn with the pools and cleaned the best she could, trying not to hold the line up any more than she had to. She knew this water alone wouldn't help much, but it was their only option.

Malidora was handed a small backpack with packaged food and water. She decided to leave her pouch behind so as to not weigh herself down any further. Grabbing her crossbow, she slipped into the group as they walked out of the glade.

"Do not bring your weapons," said Kalyx. "You will not need them."

"I don't go anywhere without my crossbow," said Malidora.

"Then you will not be coming to the sacred grove," said Kalyx. "Instruments of destruction are not allowed there."

"There are Nulvarians out there," said Ambrielle. "What if we are attacked?"

"As I have said many times, Hableides will protect us," said Kalyx with a stern expression. "You have seen no violence since you have been here, and yet you refuse to believe."

"We came here because we were told that this world was in danger," said Ambrielle. "We would not have known of this place otherwise."

"We followed the Ichtek here," said Gavian, "and they are helping the Nulvarians."

Kalyx turned to him. "Sometimes knowledge is not enough. Many things must be experienced to be known. Perhaps after witnessing the conveyance, you will understand."

Malidora sighed heavily, knowing this was a bad idea, but that Ambrielle and the others wanted to go and see how this played out. If she didn't go with them, who else would protect them? She placed the crossbow on one of the blankets but left the dagger in its sheath under her jacket.

"What is the conveyance exactly?" Darby asked, as Malidora returned to the procession.

"Every season, one of us is chosen to eat the luven fruit of the sacred tree," said Kalyx. "The fruit is ripened to its peak and now is the time to eat."

"Only one person gets to eat it?" Sidaire asked.

"To eat of the luvens, the fruit of the sacred tree, is forbidden," said Kalyx. "Only the chosen of the season is allowed."

Malidora exchanged glances with Ambrielle and the others. "Forbidden?" Veridius asked. "Why would that be?"

"Aside from ceremony and tradition, luvens are a very potent fruit," said Kalyx. "The one who Hableides choses will be one who has served and connected with the forest, the most prepared for its effects."

"What kind of effects?" Ambrielle inquired with a look of concern.

"That is only for the chosen to experience," said Kalyx. "You ask so many questions that cannot simply be answered with words. You will have your own experiences once we get there, and as I said, it is far better to experience the world with all the senses than to merely be told about it."

Malidora welcomed the skepticism mirrored on her friends' faces. In a society built on trust, the excessive secrecy surrounding Hableides felt unjustified. Malidora hoped that her companions were starting to share her dissatisfaction with the Kalithor. This was getting them nowhere.

With a bit of hesitation, Ambrielle marched forward and the others followed, while Malidora dragged behind to get a better vantage point. After walking for a few hours, they made a sharp turn with the ground ahead, leaving the serpent path and venturing into the woods. The dense forest quickly subsided, giving way to a beautiful grove. Ambrielle stepped onto a road made of large stones covered with dead leaves and vines. There were stairs ahead made of carved rocks on the terraced part of a small hill.

As they ventured further into the mystical Sanctuary, a breathtaking sight unfolded before them. Towering trees with majestic canopies stretched toward the heavens, their thick branches intertwining like a celestial tapestry. As the breeze rustled through their leaves, it took on a rhythmic quality, a hollow chime of different tones playing from high up in the branches of the trees. But one tree, grander than the rest, stood at the very center of this arboretum, its presence imbued with an otherworldly radiance.

The old tree stood amid an intricate network of advanced technologies carefully placed among the natural beauty of the grove. Glimmering crystals, luminescent orbs, and intricately designed mirrors adorned the surroundings. Ingenious mechanisms seemed to harness the radiant power of the sun, reflecting and converging their brilliance onto the tree's magnificent form.

Each device lit the tree in different ways, displaying the ingenuity of the species that had come together to bring their own light into this world. As the sun's rays cascaded upon the mirrors and crystals, a mesmerizing display of light and color unfolded, enveloping the old tree in a celestial embrace. The tree basked in the radiant tribute of the gathered races, its leaves shimmering and its essence resonating with vitality.

The tree's gnarled and twisting branches reached skyward, as if welcoming the rest of the universe. Its roots entwined themselves like an intricate web that seemed to hold the very essence of the grove in its grasp. They delved deep both into the ground and into the crystalline pools of blue water that flowed gently through the grove, forming ethereal rivulets that seemed to whisper the thoughts of all living things in the grove.

Everyone gathered near the radiant pools where the tree's energy seemed to radiate most. The sun's beams filtered through the canopy. The waters shimmered as if infused with the essence of the stars.

Malidora watched as Ravessian walked up to one of the tree's massive branches. The branch curved toward the ground, bearing one of its many fruits within his reach. Picking the large blue and purple fruit, Ravessian lifted it up to show everyone.

The people around them began to sing as Ravessian took a bite of the fruit.

Oh, tree of wisdom, ancient and grand,
Reach out your branches, touch our hand,
Grant us the gift of cosmic sight,
Guide us with your sacred light.

As he chewed and swallowed the bite of fruit, his eyes grew larger. Ravessian seemed to be staring at something beyond the grove, miles away.

"We call to you Hableides," said Ravessian as he reached his hands up into the air. "Show us the most worthy of your new conveyance."

Ravessian's eyes scanned the group. He made eye contact with each individual, including Malidora and the others. Malidora noticed Kalyx holding her hands together under her chin, bouncing on her toes nervously as she waited for the decision to be vocalized.

Closing his eyes, Ravessian stretched out his arms as he spun back and forth until he stopped, pointing at an older woman. "Brevala, it is you," he said. "Eat of the fruit."

Everyone turned to the woman, who smiled with excitement on her face. The crowd parted to let her through as she hurried toward Ravessian. Kalyx watched Brevala take the fruit from Ravessian's hands, the disappointment on her face unmistakable.

Brevala bit into the fruit. Everyone stood quietly watching, waiting for what was to come. The old woman's eyes widened in astonishment as if the sacred fruit's essence surged through her being, awakening her to some newfound clarity. She twirled around in pure wonder, like a soul reborn into a world of unexplored beauty.

With tearful eyes raised to the heavens, Brevala's voice rang out with a transcendent melody. "Before me is the universe through Hableides's eyes. I can see the Celestial Forest, a boundless expanse branching out from endless sources. Now I understand. Each glimmering speck, a precious seed within the eternal cradle of the universe, waiting to be scattered across the cosmic soil. Within the garden, life awakens. We are all part of it. As Hableides shares the secrets of life, we carry the seeds of understanding and nurture the knowledge that blossoms within this sacred grove."

Malidora felt a surprising chill flow through her as she listened to Brevala's words. She couldn't make sense of it all, but it sounded profound. Clearly, the woman believed some kind of life-altering experience had taken place, changing Brevala forever. Was it real? Malidora couldn't be sure, but she wanted to know what was in that fruit. Whatever it was could be the key to exposing the Kalithor as frauds.

Malidora pulled Ambrielle away from the group. "What do you think that was all about?" she whispered.

"I don't know," Ambrielle said, as she covered her mouth with her hand. "Maybe this fruit brings you into a state of mind that lets you connect with Hableides."

"Or it is some kind of hallucination?" said Malidora. "If we don't find something soon, we need to leave the camp and find the Nulvarians on our own."

"I still think the Kalithor are our best chance to get to Hableides," said Ambrielle. "We need Hableides to trust us. We need to get to her through her followers."

Malidora wasn't convinced. "If Hableides is as intelligent as everyone claims, she should be able to see that already."

"The intelligent aren't the most trusting," said Ambrielle. "Their caution is what makes them smart. I just hope, after we help her defeat the Ichtek and Nulvarians on Valderine, she will tell us how to save the rest of the universe."

Malidora placed a gentle hand on Ambrielle's shoulder. "If this fruit is hallucinogenic, would that convince you to leave?"

Furrows appeared on Ambrielle's forehead. "I don't know, maybe, but how are you going to—" her eyes darted past Malidora.

"You two should be with the others," said Kalyx as she approached. "We are saying our farewells to Ravessian."

"Where is he going?" said Ambrielle.

"He will move on with the other chosen, on the floating stones," said Kalyx, looking toward the sun through branches of the woods. "His purpose here has passed, and now Brevala will take his place."

"This happens every season?" Malidora asked.

Kalyx nodded her head. "Like all things, there is a process of renewal, a cycle of beginnings and endings."

"What will he do now?" Ambrielle asked.

"I do not know," said Kalyx, as she gazed longingly at the skies. "That is something that I hope to find out one day, if I am ever chosen."

CHAPTER 22

MALIDORA—VALDERINE

IT BEGAN TO grow dark when Malidora and the others returned to the camp. Weary from being on her feet all day and the walk to and from the grove on uneven terrain, Malidora stretched her legs as they waited for the evening meal to be served. After they had all finished, they returned to their beds under the tarp to lie down to sleep. Malidora stayed awake for a time, dwelling on the day's events, particularly the fruit Brevala had eaten, but soon succumbed to her weariness like the rest of them. After a few hours had passed, Malidora woke, the look on Brevala's face after eating the fruit still on her mind.

Nocturnal creatures cried out in the night as Malidora moved with careful steps, determined not to disturb the slumber of her companions. Her hand sought out her crossbow, and in the moonlit quiet, she observed that Gavian's form was absent from his spot beside Ambrielle. Casting a sweeping glance across the campsite, she discerned no trace of him or any other figure stirring about. With Gavian unaccounted for, she crept between the tents with heightened caution, hoping to avoid any unexpected encounters.

The serpent's path was lit by three of the five small moons that had risen above the trees around her. Even with the glow of three, the path was only dimly lit. Malidora stayed near the edge of the road, hoping she would not face the giant serpent.

Traversing the path ahead, a peculiar sensation gradually

enshrouded Malidora, as though an unseen gaze lingered among the trees, fixated upon her every move. Suppressing the unsettling sensation to the best of her ability, she concentrated her efforts on the task at hand, pushing herself forward. Every step felt deliberate and measured, as if each footfall were a deliberate assertion of her will against the eerie atmosphere around her. The distant cries of the creatures nearby seemed to grow louder, as if they were warning her of some hidden danger lurking in the shadows.

At last, she reached the sacred grove. Between the dried leaves and vines, the moonlight glinted off the stone steps as she climbed. The tree bearing the luven fruit glowed in the moons' reflection off the crystal bark scattered over the ground. They cast light underneath its ghostly branches, and Malidora spotted luvens hanging from a nearby limb.

Grabbing her crossbow, Malidora aimed and fired, piercing the fruit with an arrow and sending it flying into a farther part of the grove. She traced its direction until she found it lying in a clump of grass underneath one of the other trees. Scanning her surroundings to make sure she was alone, she raised the forbidden fruit to her mouth and took a bite.

A burst of flavor exploded on her tongue, unlike anything she had ever tasted. An exquisite blend of the sweetness of life and the bitterness of death. Malidora began to see patterns of colors with each blink of her eyes. The surrounding grove began to fade to stars twinkling in intricate patterns, like cosmic music written across the sky.

More worlds than she could count spun with grace and purpose, each holding unique stories woven into the very fabric of the universe. As she continued to chew, a surge of energy coursed through her body, like the currents of the force of all life awakened inside her. Her heart beat in harmony with a cosmic rhythm, as if she were attuned to the interconnectedness of all living things.

She felt as if she might explode, unable to contain such energy. She swallowed, a warm sensation spreading from her core, like the embrace of some benevolent entity. Malidora felt a sense of belonging like never before, as if she were an integral part of some grand design.

"You were not chosen!" said a voice. Malidora's eyes darted about the grove, unsure if the voice was real or inside her head. "You have desecrated my grove. Eating my fruit without proving yourself, without preparation."

"I needed to speak to you," said Malidora. "We have come to aid you against the Nulvarians."

"Foolish child," said the voice. "I need no aid. I am Hableides, the Celestial Arbiter. There are none who can contend with my will."

Malidora's feet were lifted off the ground. The visions of the universe faded as some invisible force held her in the air. The feeling of harmony was replaced by stark fear. "The Nulvarians have destroyed Kandom and other worlds, and they will destroy many more if we don't do something to stop them. We came not only to help but to seek your wisdom."

"I protect every world within the Celestial Forest," said Hableides. "None shall face destruction unless they dare to defy my will."

"Defy you?" said Malidora. "You allow worlds to be destroyed? What about Kandom? Could you have prevented Kandom from being wiped out?"

"The Vogus lost their way," intoned Hableides. "They began listening only to what suited their desires."

"What did you want them to do?" Malidora asked.

"They dwelled in darkness," conveyed Hableides. "I provided them guidance on channeling the light—a beginning that could have propelled their civilization into a new era. Had they followed, I would have revealed the path for them to journey here, bringing their light along."

"What is it about light?" Malidora asked. "Why do you call on others to bring their technology here?"

"This sun is fading," voiced Hableides. "I require light. In five hundred years, there won't be enough to sustain the flora. As the vegetation perishes, so too will all the creatures. We must devise instruments to gather and store the light of today, amplifying the dim glow that awaits in the future."

"And then what?" said Malidora. "It can't last forever."

"The sacred grove must endure," declared Hableides. "Every passing moment holds immense value. Given more time, I may uncover a method to meld elements, giving birth to a new star that will grace our presence."

"In return for their solar technology you allow them to escape the Nulvarians and come here?" asked Malidora. "How is that protection?"

"I bestow upon them knowledge," proclaimed Hableides. "Guidance on how to thwart the Nulvarians before they establish dominion over their world."

"And you didn't tell the Vogus because they didn't do what you wanted?" said Malidora.

"I don't dispense my knowledge to the undeserving," stated Hableides. "They had ample opportunities to alter their course."

"The Kalithor speak of harmony, of balance. Give us any knowledge you can on the Nulvarians. Help us defeat them, and you can all live in peace," said Malidora. "Tell us how we can close the rifts at the entrance point. We can help you prevent them from destroying any more worlds."

"The looming threat of the Nulvarians serves as a more potent motivator than the ideals of peace and harmony," explained Hableides. "Certain civilizations require a nudge onto the correct path. Unfortunately, it doesn't always succeed. Some, like the Vogus, prove too stubborn to be swayed."

"Are you serious? You want the Nulvarians around?" huffed Malidora. "Simply to scare other worlds into doing your bidding?"

"It is for their own well-being," declared Hableides. "You haven't witnessed the universe as I have. The sacred grove must be safeguarded."

"Is this grove more important than the billions of lives the Nulvarians have taken?" Malidora asked.

She was lifted higher in the air near the higher branches of the tree. Pressure around her increased from the force that held her. Malidora struggled to move within its grip, trying to find a comfortable space to breathe. For a moment, the effects of the fruit invaded her mind again. The force that held her was coming from the grove. Following it with her mind, her consciousness moved toward the massive tree at the center of the grove. The gnarled branches of the tree stood before her. A knothole in the thick trunk led her inside the great tree. Within the hollow, she saw its core. The gray matter of a brain held inside by tendril-like stems.

"The grove is everything!" exclaimed Hableides.

"You . . ." said Malidora. "You are the tree. The tree that grows the fruit. It's you."

"I am more than a tree!" asserted Hableides. "I am the Arbiter of the Celestial Forest. I wield greater power than all the civilizations of the universe combined!"

"So, this is all about self-preservation," said Malidora. "You may be intelligent, you may be powerful, but in the end, you are just a tree that needs light to survive."

"Irreverent child! You shall face my judgment!" Hableides declared.

Something rustled through the bushes nearby. Footfalls came closer. The shadow of a humanoid being walked into the grove. It was a form Malidora recognized in more ways than one. The body of a Cereveshian emanating the shadowy darkness of a whidge.

Malidora watched the dark Cereveshian stride beneath her and make its way toward the great tree. As it drew close, the Cereveshian extended its arms, drawing the life essence out of Hableides.

"What are you doing?" Malidora asked. "Are you just going to let it drain you?"

"I—I can't seem to—It's not working on this creature!" exclaimed Hableides. "You are too much of a distraction!"

The invisible force released Malidora, and she dropped, crashing onto the grass and pieces of reflective bark. The Cereveshian continued to drain the essence of Hableides.

"Stop this creature!" demanded Hableides. "It resists my power! I command you to obliterate this fiend!"

"Oh, now you need my help?" Malidora said. "I think you should show some reverence to me first."

"My abilities work on you, child!" threatened Hableides. "I will crush you!"

"No need to get testy," said Malidora, as she loaded an arrow into her crossbow. She moved closer to the Cereveshian whidge to get a better fix on it, then aimed and fired. The Cereveshian turned around, moving its hand to the arrow in its back. With any other arrow, it would have been able to dissolve it and then use its ability to drain life essence to heal the wound. But this was a mekkadium arrow, made of a crystallized form of the Shadow itself.

As it tried to heal itself, another arrow impaled the Cereveshian whidge. It staggered, trying to find some way to rectify the damage. The Cereveshian toppled over, no longer able to stay alive. Malidora loaded another bolt while the shadow oozed out of the Cereveshian body. The true form of the whidge began to take shape. As the writhing eldritch monstrosity attached its tendrils to the tree, Malidora fired again. The arrow struck, hardening the shadow into stone around the impact point.

Malidora fired another shot and her arrow caught in midair, carried by Hableides's telekinetic power. The invisible force launched the arrow into the whidge, hammering the arrow back and forth with blinding speed until the whidge was nothing but dust.

"Impressive," said Malidora as she lowered her crossbow.

"This is troubling," acknowledged Hableides. "They seem to have discovered a creature that can resist my powers."

"Cereveshians?" Malidora questioned. "What do they have that can do that?"

"I am not certain," Hableides said. "I must summon my followers to the grove at once."

"Tell me where the Nulvarians are," said Malidora. "Show us any way you know to defeat them. We will take the fight to them and vanquish them from the planet."

"You are yet to fathom the multitude that surrounds us," resonated Hableides. "The sheer numbers I withhold from the groves. If vanquishing them were a simple endeavor, my followers would have accomplished it already. With the advent of these new creatures under their dominion, our sole recourse is to shield the grove. They seek to claim my knowledge, my powers. We cannot permit this to transpire. Will you rise and stand as my defender?"

Chapter 23

Gavian—Valderine

For hours, Gavian had paced around the outside of the grove, wrestling with the hunger of Azravion. He went over the scenario in his mind. What kind of trick was Serenith trying to play? If he took essence from the old tree, he could buy himself some time to figure things out. If it started the war, he could draw essence from the Ichtek as well as the Shadows. Maybe that would satisfy Azravion for a while. The sword was becoming dangerously close to overtaking him, driving him mad as it slowly began to take control. There wasn't any other way.

As he cautiously approached the rows of ancient trees, a cacophony of echoing clangs and fierce roars reached his ears, shattering the peaceful ambience he had expected. Had the battle already started? Had he waited too long? Perhaps Serenith had another way to end the standoff. He moved deeper into the grove, until he reached its center where the great tree stood.

Three Cereveshians with red eyes, like those they'd seen on Anatharia, stood around the tree, siphoning essence from a knothole in its trunk. Maybe he wouldn't even have to damage the tree. He could simply wait for the Cereveshians to drain it and take the essence from them. Though once he killed the Cereveshian bodies, he would have to contend with the horrid form of the whidges. Facing three whidges at once would be a difficult task.

A volley of arrows flew toward the Cereveshians, hitting one of them. Bending the ferns out of the way, Gavian realized it was Malidora. She fired again at the wounded Shadow man until he succumbed to the wounds. As the thick, black substance oozed from the body, Malidora loaded more arrows to shoot at the others.

The mekkadium fused with the end of the blade of Stormwaker made it the ideal choice for this fight. Gavian pulled Stormwaker from its sheath and rushed through the underbrush. This time, instead of running from it, he moved toward it. As soon as the body of the true form of the whidge began to rise, Gavian acted quickly, striking it before it could fully manifest. The impact felt like soft clay, as liquefied shadow dust was slung across the grove.

"Gavian!" shouted Malidora, as she fired another salvo of arrows into one of the other Cereveshians. "I've never been so glad to see you!"

Two more red-eyed Cereveshians entered the grove behind her. Malidora stopped loading her crossbow to move from their path. Gavian dashed toward the disembodied whidge rising behind her. Raising his sword, ready to strike, Gavian was caught in its invisible grip.

Struggling against the whidge's hold, he remembered when he and Malidora defeated the Blight Whidge on Isodonia. With all the focus he could muster, Gavian broke the paralyzing grip enough to switch on the rokenstone powering the blade and swing it through its long, outstretched arm into its chest. The energy of the rokenstone sent bolts through the air, crackling away from the impact. For a moment it was as if he had control over the electrical surge as he directed it into the Cereveshians ahead.

Both bodies toppled to the ground. Embers within the Shadow bodies sizzled and smoked. Malidora's arrows soared, changing course magically when some telekinetic force powered them through the air as she fired at the monstrous whidge forms that had risen from their dead Cereveshian hosts. Her arrows bounced between all of them, as if by some unseen power. She continued to fire more mekkadium arrows at them, and Gavian sliced through the whidge's tentacles that swung at her. As the whidges were destroyed by the ricocheting arrows, Gavian drew Azravion to siphon the essence released.

Before he could claim it, the essence flew into the old tree. Frustrated, Gavian sheathed the silver sword and helped Malidora finish off the last whidge. Malidora sat down to rest among the bits of shattered remains of the whidges.

Azravion sank its ethereal teeth into Gavian's consciousness, clamoring for swift appeasement. The pressure surged as the blade's relentless pull seemed intent on drawing him within. Despite the dwindling control he retained, Gavian maneuvered through the gnarled roots of the colossal tree to its very base. Clutching Azravion, he initiated the process of channeling essence from the ancient tree into the blade. The sword crackled with energy, as the essence from the tree felt more concentrated than any he had come across before.

Before he could take much, a force lifted him off the ground. "Betrayer!" said a voice in his head. "You aid me only to take my power as your own."

Confused, he flailed his arms and legs about, trying to find ground. "The sword needs it," said Gavian as the force now pressed against his chest. "Only a little."

"If I am weakened," said the voice. "I will no longer be able to hold back the Shadows."

"Who are you?" said Gavian.

"I am Hableides," said the voice. "If I allow you to live, you must defend this grove."

"You're Hableides? The old tree?" said Gavian in astonishment. "We came here to defend you."

"If you wish to defend me, do not attempt to seize my strength. More of them are coming," conveyed Hableides to both Gavian and Malidora. "Many more."

A thundering sound rose beyond the forest, drawing nearer with each beat of Gavian's heart. Something rustled through the trees outside of the grove from multiple directions. Gavian took a deep breath, readying himself for another attack.

"Take our left flank, hit as many as you can with your sword and that lightning," said Malidora. "I will get the right side and finish off any others that get through."

"Do you think either of us can hold them all?" Gavian asked.

"If you get overwhelmed fall back to the tree, and we will make our last stand there," said Malidora.

Bursting through the thicket, more dark Cereveshians marched toward Hableides. Malidora fired rapidly at the intruders, while Gavian charged ahead to the ones coming in from the left. They entered the grove in three single-file points on the left side. Gavian carefully stayed outside the Cereveshians' range until the last moment, as he slashed into the closest Cereveshian.

An invisible force repelled the advancing Cereveshians. Hableides's mental power sent them hurtling toward those behind them, creating a temporary barrier. Gavian, seizing the opportunity, cut one of them down, guiding Stormwaker's bolts into others nearby.

Pivoting to the next column, Gavian cut another down from behind as the line inched closer to the majestic tree. The leader of the third column had already reached the tree, standing among its roots and draining its energy.

With a focused telekinetic push, Hableides sent the leader flying away from the tree, disrupting the siphoning of her energy. Gavian, taking advantage of the distraction, swiftly brought the leader down, sending the bolts of lightning from his sword into the fray.

Before the Cereveshians from the first column could reach the tree, Hableides used her telekinetic power again, preventing further energy from being drained. As Gavian raced back, he cut down one of the Shadows in the middle column on his way to the first. The Cereveshians in the first column, unable to reach the tree, siphoned a bit of energy from a distance and then swiftly retreated.

"I'm having a bit of a problem over here!" Gavian shouted.

"You and me both," said Malidora between breaths. "I'm running low on arrows."

Hableides moved debris of the destroyed whidges, launching them at the Shadow substance inside the corrupted Cereveshians that oozed from their wounds, growing into whidge form. For every Shadow being they killed, they freed more powerful monsters within. Gavian and Malidora retreated from their tentacled appendages as more Shadowy Cereveshians swarmed into the grove. Though the whidges were immobile without a host, they had a stronger compelling grasp and could siphon more essence.

As more of the Cereveshians continued to steal Hableides's essence, the use of her telekinetic power slowed. "I am diminishing," she said. "You must dismantle more and allow me to absorb the essence they use."

Gavian and Malidora were losing control of the battle. Beginning to tire out, Gavian tried to catch his breath before using his sword again. He unleashed another blast of lightning from the sword, killing a few more Cereveshians. It wasn't enough to turn the fight in their favor. As more whidges spilled out of the Cereveshian bodies, Gavian had to move away from the tree in order to not be grabbed by their tentacles. His eyes darted around him, unsure what to do next.

Ichtek soldiers entered the grove to join the fight, firing beams of energy into the grove. Hableides pushed a few of them away, but she no longer had the power to contend with all of them. Malidora activated the stealth in her silbrace, making her nearly invisible. But it only helped her defensively against the Ichtek energy blasts, and what they needed was firepower.

Suddenly things grew quiet. The Cereveshians slowed and listened as the sound of thunder approached nearby. The Kalithor from the camp stormed into the grove. "Protect the grove at all costs!" shouted Brevala.

Using a variety of weapons, lasers, pulse rays, and blades, the Kalithor joined the fight against the Cereveshians and whidges. Ambrielle, Dexius, Darby, Sidaire, Kazial, and Veridius were among them.

Veridius used his shield to provide cover from the Ichtek light beams, as Darby used her silbrace to guide several of her arrows in a spread formation into the attackers. The Ichtek bored holes into the bark of Hableides, and Ambrielle tried to undo the damage using her restoring silbrace. Whipping her bladestaff, she took down two Cereveshians intent on draining Hableides. Throwing lightfires at the Ichtek, Kazial helped slow their attack.

Whidges began to fold into shape from the substance that came out of the dead Cereveshians' wounds. Everyone spread out away from them as they generated tendrils that claimed two of the Kalithor, bringing their bodies close enough to the whidges, who drained the life from them.

The rest of the Kalithor seemed in disarray, not trained for combat, firing recklessly into the battle. "Prioritize the Ichtek!" shouted Brevala. "They are easiest to kill and are wounding the great tree!"

Veridius turned back to the rest of the group. "Group one hit the Cereveshians and Group two take down the whidges that follow!"

Before Gavian could make it to her, Ambrielle took up her bladestaff, charging toward the remaining Cereveshians that were draining the life from the tree. Darby and Kazial followed behind her, helping clear out an area in the grove. Falling to one knee, Darby launched a cluster of arrows to cover her right flank, taking care of a group of Ichtek firing in her direction.

With so many enemies, Gavian swung his blade with abandon. As everything rushed by, it felt as if he were moving in slow motion. Ignoring Azravion's protests Gavian fed the essence he had collected into the tree's wounds.

"You have done well," said Hableides. "This has restored some of my strength. But I need more to push them back."

Another group of Cereveshians swarmed in, siphoning more of the tree's essence. As Gavian and the others attacked, they turned and fled. Dexius downed three of them, but the other two got away. Azravion's hunger became unbearable. Its fury became physical pain.

"Those with my power are escaping the grove!" said Hableides. "If it is not returned to me, it will take too long for me to regenerate. The essence of the others is too weak to be of much use."

"Chase down the runners!" ordered Malidora, her outstretched hand indicating the eastern side of the grove. Dexius swiftly sprinted ahead. Gavian turned to go after him.

"Gavian wait!" Ambrielle yelled out, diving into the dirt as a cluster of energy beams flew over her head.

"I'm going to help Dex!" Gavian said as he dodged incoming fire, slashing down one Ichtek warrior on the way out of the forest. "I can bring back the essence they stole."

"Don't let that sword control you," Ambrielle said as she caught up to him. "You don't have to prove anything."

Gavian took her hand for a moment and looked into her eyes. "I won't. Take care of yourself. We'll be back soon." He let go of her hand, sprinting further into the grove. He found Dexius behind a tree, aiming at passing Ichtek soldiers, taking one down before advancing to another tree ahead. Gavian rushed in, carving a path through the chaos, as Dexius took aim. They thinned out the number of Ichtek attackers. At the grove's edge, they spotted the Cereveshians running toward the mountains in the distance.

As Gavian watched for any incoming threats, Dexius exhibited pinpoint accuracy, skillfully eliminating most of the fleeing Cereveshians.

Unfortunately, a few of the Cereveshians were too far out of the range of Dexius's bow. Dexius slung the bow over his shoulder and started after them. As Gavian ran to catch up, he came upon Dexius's victims, the fallen Cereveshians. The Shadowy substance seeped from their wounds, coalescing into the whidges nested within them. The whidges extended tendrils, compelling Gavian to step back. The bright aura of the tree's essence surrounded the whidges' inky black forms.

"Wait up!" Gavian called out. "We have to take care of these first!"

"Leave them," said Dexius, as he hurried across the grassy field. "They can't get to the grove."

While Dexius was right about the whidges being immobile without inhabiting a physical body, Gavian needed to restore the potent essence to Hableides. Circumventing the reach of their tendrils, he sought an opening for an attack. Inhaling deeply, Gavian charged forward, slashing his sword down on one of the whidge's appendages as it swung toward him. Simultaneously, a tendril from the adjacent whidge lunged at him, leaving Gavian with no option but to somersault out of its path, unable to employ his sword in position to defend himself.

A mass of tentacle arms from both whidges flung themselves at him. Leaping backward, Gavian found safety out of their reach. Unsure if he could take them on by himself, he circled around the whidges to catch up to Dexius. Perhaps on the way back they could take them on together.

Dexius made it to a winding river ahead, chasing the remaining Cereveshian Shadows. Once in range of one, he paused and aimed. As his arrow went through the Cereveshian's chest, Dexius resumed his pursuit of the others.

As Gavian made it to the Cereveshian lying on the banks of the river, he gripped Stormwaker tight as he stood over its body. The Shadowy substance of the whidge oozed from its wound, puddling near Gavian's feet.

As the essence enkindled around the aethrum form of the whidge, Gavian acted swiftly, striking before it could fully manifest. The contorted body of the whidge convulsed in pain as Gavian reached for Azravion. Before he could grip the sword's hilt, the whidge generated tendrils that snatched him from the ground. It began to pull him toward its wounded, twisted form. Gavian tried to fight back, but his arms were pinned. Once the tendrils brought him close enough, the whidge would siphon the living essence from him.

Suddenly the tendrils slackened their grip. Gavian didn't hesitate, freeing his sword and slicing through the appendage. He dropped to the soft banks of the river and realized the area around the inflicted wound was beginning to petrify, transforming into stone that cracked as it hardened. Gavian quickly stabbed the whidge, splintering it into three pieces. The concentrated essence, once usurped from the ancient tree, flowed into the sword. It hummed with a sentient vitality, a rush of power that was intoxicating.

He had lost sight of Dexius now but spotted a wooden bridge ahead and another fallen Cereveshian on the other side. Gavian crossed the river, hurrying to the Shadow substance as it twisted into shape. Drawing both swords, he struck the whidge continuously until it crumbled to pieces of stone.

After siphoning the essence from the whidge, Gavian continued to search for Dexius. Azravion grew heavier in his hand. It surged with tingling power, but the essence he had claimed only made the sword long for more.

The grassy field turned to thick underbrush, and as he entered, something caught his attention in the distance. A legion of Nulthereals, far more than he had ever seen, hovered in rows ahead of the forest at the base of the mountain. He felt his pulse beating in the back of his neck as he stood staring at them. The instinct to retreat warred with the insistent hunger of Azravion, pushing him, as if the blade itself demanded a solitary assault on the Nulthereals, urging him to seize the potent essence enveloping them even though he would likely die in the attempt. Gavian resisted the sword's urge, returning his focus to searching his surroundings for any sign of Dexius. Changing course to his left, he slowly moved through the bushes, keeping an eye on the Nulthereals.

Even as Azravion hummed with the energy of the essence he had claimed, a growing sense of unease settled in his chest. Feeling an inexplicable compulsion, an almost magnetic pull started drawing him away from the forest. If the sword didn't want him to go that way, maybe that is exactly where he should go. The blade pulsed with urgency, synchronizing with Gavian's heartbeat.

As he crept further into the thick underbrush, Gavian came across a familiar but unsettling sight. The forest ahead had turned black, the trees reduced to slimy husks of liquefied decay. An oppressive stench hung in the air, suffocating any semblance of life that might have once thrived in this nightmarish expanse. The trees seemed barely able to hold themselves together as thick globs of ooze dripped from the branches. The moonlight struggled to pierce through the dense canopy of sinister darkness, casting eerie shadows that writhed with unsettling allure.

The living essence had been mined from this area. Gavian's hands quivered as the blade compelled him to leave. Moving through the corrupted forest, he continued to struggle against the sword's compulsions. Passing by a group of trees leaning chaotically in various directions, Gavian entered a clearing where the moonlight gleamed on the shiny surfaces of melting foliage.

As he ventured deeper into the haunting abyss, his eyes fell upon a chilling discovery. Lying twisted and forgotten along the decayed forest floor was the bleached skeleton of a colossal serpent, coiling around decaying tree trunks. Its skeletal jaw, frozen in an eternal rictus of terror, hinted at the horrific fate that had befallen this creature. The sight sent shivers down Gavian's spine.

Once he passed by the serpent's remains, he noticed the bones of other giant creatures. Half buried in the soft mud, these skeletons belonged to creatures Gavian had never seen. His instinct to leave continued to grow, but the call of something stronger urged him on. It was a familiar feeling. One that he had experienced before.

Time itself seemed to warp around him, minutes stretching into an agonizing crawl. The sword grew heavier. Everything seemed to be pushing against him.

A voice hissed through the rotting foliage, "What a disappointment you have been." Serenith stepped from the shadows into the moonlight.

Chapter 24

Gavian—Valderine

Gavian sensed the quick vibrating pulse of Azravion willing him forward. Taking a step back, he eyed Serenith, uncertain as to what he was going to do next.

"All you had to do was fill Azravion with the energy of the tree," said Serenith. "We would have been finished by now."

"You didn't tell me that the tree you wanted me to drain was Hableides," Gavian retorted, placing his quivering hand on the hilt of Azravion. "And you didn't give me enough time."

"Not enough time?" scoffed Serenith. "When you are instructed to do a task, you do it immediately. Do you think I control the Nulvarians?"

"The battle you wanted has begun," Gavian said. "Doesn't seem like you needed me after all."

"Fortunately, the Nulvarians were correct," Serenith remarked. "The Cereveshians can withstand the mind power of Hableides. Victory is inevitable; it's only a matter of time. Your bothersome need to replace Pythus, however, has rendered his death utterly futile."

"I never wanted to replace him!" Gavian protested "I only meant to stop him!"

"You would never have been able to claim it if the sword hadn't wanted you. But now you have given Azravion no choice," Serenith said. "He must devour you and find a new wielder."

Gavian sensed the essence being drained from the blade. The soul of Azravion consumed every last drop. The pain of its emptiness tugged at Gavian once more.

Gavian pulled the sword from its sheath, desperate to fill it with essence. Serenith drew his shadowblade as well, extinguishing the bright energy around the black core to cut through the matter in the air.

Opening a patch of deadspace in front of him, Serenith again blocked Gavian's path, guarding himself from any attack Gavian could muster. The deadspace starkly contrasted with the ghostly light of the five moons. Gavian lowered his sword, uncertain of Serenith's next move.

"Azravion has grown impatient with you. There are many contenders eagerly awaiting the chance to claim the blade. Will he still permit you to harness the essence and heal your wounds? We shall see," Serenith declared. Dry grass crunched in the darkness just beyond the moonlight.

Gavian turned as an Ichtek swordsman charged at him, swinging a golden blade with animal-like ferocity. Gavian readied himself to fend off the attack. The swordsman reached him, and suddenly, a sharp, resounding thud echoed through the air. Pitching forward, the swordsman landed face-first into the murky, melted grass, an arrow protruding from the back of his head.

"Step away from him, Gavian," said Dexius from somewhere in the shadows. "I need a clear shot."

Azravion sucked in the life essence from the dead swordsman as Gavian backed away, keeping his focus on Serenith.

"So." Serenith crept toward him. "Another contender presents himself. Kill him and take his essence. Prove yourself worthy of the blade!"

Dexius called out again, "Gavian, move!"

Gavian turned as Dexius came out of the shadows into the moonlight.

"He desires the sword as much as anyone else," Serenith hissed. "You can either become his first victim or show that you are still worthy."

Shivering from the blade's burning thirst, Gavian was compelled to obey. The pain was a force greater than he could handle. He raised the silver sword, digging the toe of his boot into the dirt, ready to spring toward Dexius. Was he really going to do this? If it came down to killing Dexius or seeing Ambrielle again, what other choice did he have? With Dexius's bowstring already drawn, Gavian knew he had to be quick to close the gap before he could release the arrow. He tried to clear his mind, but the agonizing hunger was too great. If he succeeded, how could he face anyone after this? He would have to lie about what happened to Dexius.

"It seems we always come back to this point, sooner or later," Dexius said, still pointing his bow in Gavian and Serenith's direction. "Ever since that day in the swamp, I felt like my soul could never come clean. After everything we have been through, I thought of you as family, as a brother. Knowing how close I came to shooting you . . . I have been stained ever since. I refuse to do it again." Dexius relaxed the bowstring and lowered the bow to his side. "If you have been influenced by this dark fiend, if you think you have to kill me, I won't try to stop you. Just know that it is a stain that won't easily wash away."

Was this some kind of trick? To make him lower his guard so Dexius could put an arrow into his heart before he could reach him? War brewed inside his head. If he didn't kill Dexius, he would lose the ability to protect Ambrielle from pain and death. But Dexius had saved his life many times. They had shared some of their worst times and helped each other through them. The painful thirst made it impossible to think clearly. His two choices struggled against each other, seeking a solution but finding only paradox. He hoped that Dexius would be fast enough to stop him. "Please . . ." Gavian said. "If I fall, make sure you go back and help Ambrielle and the others."

With a flourish, Gavian made his move. Pivoting on the marshy ground, he turned, bringing the blade toward the deadspace in front of Serenith. The patch of deadspace sliced Azravion in half, sending an explosion of potent life essence that knocked both Gavian and Serenith off their feet. Gavian felt a horrid, screaming pain from somewhere beyond as the piece of Azravion's soul was destroyed. "No . . ." Serenith huffed. "Nooooo! Why would you destroy it? You've wasted the gift of immortality. And now you will die!"

The sword's destruction and the broken connection to Azravion shook Gavian. He tried to collect himself as Serenith charged around the deadspace, raising his blade to kill Gavian. Before he could bring his blade down, an arrow struck Serenith, who plucked it from his side and lifted his sword again. Gavian sprang to his feet, unsheathing Stormwaker. Serenith extinguished the blade's shielding just long enough to slash another wall of deadspace, protecting himself from the strikes of Dexius's arrows.

Knowing he couldn't use the sword to deflect Serenith's blade while it was unshielded, Gavian hoped to find an opening. The absence of its usual bright aura made this difficult. Serenith furiously slashed at Gavian, stepping around the deadspace carved into the air as Gavian dodged his swings. Gavian lost his footing but evaded the next attack, crawling backward to regain his stance. Another arrow struck the side of Serenith's helmet as he pursued Gavian undeterred. Ignoring the blow, Serenith avoided the pockets of deadspace, keeping his gaze on Gavian.

Gavian rose, switching on Stormwaker and powering the energized rokenstone in the sword. He charged at Serenith, unleashing a flurry of blows. As Serenith guarded against the attacks, bolts of energy sprung from Gavian's sword, jolting into Serenith. "It will take more than that to stave my wrath."

Serenith lashed out with several strikes at Gavian, forcing him back as he dodged the attacks. Serenith took a moment to slice another barrier of deadspace between him and Dexius. The arrow Dexius released disintegrated when it touched the deadspace.

Apparently satisfied with the amount of deadspace around them, Serenith shielded his sword. With a swift, fluid motion he closed the distance, launching a barrage of attacks at Gavian. Stormwaker met Nagoloth in a clash that resonated with power, the protective aura around the shadowblade shimmering with every strike. The air crackled with electricity, casting an ethereal glow that bathed the surrounding darkness in an otherworldly light.

Their blades clashed once more, and Gavian unleashed a rapid succession of attacks. Surges of energy from each impact lashed into Serenith, disrupting his stance and causing him to momentarily lose his footing. Despite the relentless assault, Serenith skillfully parried Gavian's strikes.

Before Serenith regained his balance, Gavian seized the opportunity, executing a well-placed kick that caught Serenith off guard. One of Dexius's arrows whistled through the air, narrowly missing Serenith. Retreating to the safety of the deadspace wall, a screech came from Serenith as he took a deep breath. Without hesitation, he lunged at Gavian once more.

Gritting his teeth, Gavian struggled to match the fury of Serenith's onslaught. Serenith closed the distance, leveraging his strength as he relentlessly pummeled his sword against Gavian's blade. Yielding ground to mitigate the force of Serenith's blows, Gavian found himself trapped between the deadspace and the unrelenting assault of his adversary.

The Ichtek swordsman seemed determined to push Gavian into the tears in reality, each strike calculated to force him toward the unstable boundaries. As Serenith prepared to deliver a powerful blow, Gavian somersaulted away from the deadspace, narrowly evading the impending strike. Serenith's sword slashed into the deadspace, but its shielding held firm, deflecting any damage.

Pushing up from his knee, Gavian readied for Serenith's next move. Serenith again turned off the shielding around Nagoloth, wielding the shadowblade away from his body. Its motion ripped into the space around it, cutting darkness against the moonlight. Gavian had no choice but to escape.

Serenith relentlessly slashed at him, forcing Gavian to leap backward. Circling around the newly carved deadspace, Serenith closed in with each calculated attack. As Gavian continued to wander between the deadspace tears, Serenith continued to close in. Soon Gavian found himself trapped between the holes in reality with little space to maneuver.

Seizing the opening, Serenith leapt toward him, Nagoloth cutting through the darkness with an ominous grace. Gavian tightened his grip on Stormwaker as he raised himself to one knee. With all the strength he could muster, he slammed the sword into the ground, unleashing a blinding burst of light. Bolts of lightning trailed along the blackened forest floor, striking Serenith and sending him sprawling backward. Passing through the deadspace he had just cut into the air, Serenith's body was torn to shreds.

Nagoloth, with its shielding aura turned off, melded with the newly opened deadspace, disappearing without a trace. The once-tumultuous battlefield now held an eerie stillness, the aftermath of the clash leaving the forest shrouded in silence. Gavian, panting heavily, held tight to Stormwaker, unable to loosen his hand from it. He was greatly relieved from the broken connection with the soul of Azravion. Yet, in the shadow of victory lay a heavy weight. A chance at eternity had slipped through his fingers.

He would someday have to face death and endure being separated from Ambrielle. Was this love's final cruel twist? That something so good must come to an end?

The sudden stillness was broken by footfalls, snapping Gavian back to the present, his senses still sharpened by the fight. Turning towards the sound, Gavian was surprised to find Dexius, bow drawn, aiming in his direction. With an effort that seemed to require every ounce of his waning strength, Gavian lowered Stormwaker, the tension draining from his stance.

As Gavian met Dexius's gaze, a flicker of gratitude warmed his weary spirit. In the silence that followed the storm of conflict, the value of steadfast allies became starkly clear. Trust, he realized, was not just a bond but a lifeline in the tumultuous journey they had embarked upon. "Thank you, Dex," he acknowledged, nodding appreciatively.

Dexius lowered his bow, easing the drawstring back into its normal position. "For what?"

"For always having my back." Gavian wiped the black ooze from his palms onto the back of his hands.

Dexius met Gavian's nod with a slight, understanding smile, the tension in his shoulders easing. "Thank Ambrielle for that. You know she'd kill me if I came back without you."

Gavian turned away, gazing into the darkness of the forest. "I can only hope for your forgiveness."

"What for? You weren't really going to try and kill me, were you?" Dexius said halfheartedly.

Turning back toward Dexius, Gavian could see the smirk on his face. "I don't know what I was going to do. I let things get out of control."

"You could have just said no," Dexius retorted.

Gavian chuckled between breaths. "Did you get all the Cereveshians?"

Dexius swept his hair back. "Of course, I did."

"I'm not sure it matters now," Gavian pondered. "I no longer have the sword."

"You are better off without it," Dexius said.

"Let's hurry back," Gavian said. "We have to convince everyone to retreat. There's no winning this battle." As Gavian started running back into the forest, all he could think about was how powerless he was now. He wasn't much use to the group without the sword Azravion. He no longer had a way to ensure that Ambrielle or anyone else would live past any kind of harm or disease, or even the passage of time.

As Gavian and Dexius ran past the skeletal remains of the giant serpent, something rose from the dark of the forest floor, something massive. It moved above the trees, a black voluminous cloud standing out against the moonlit sky. It was like Ogolameth, the Primevus they had defeated in Isodonia.

They reached the river as the legions of Nulthereals buzzed past them, swarming toward the grove. The Primevus cleared the forest, and many of the Nulthereals poured into it, merging together. It grew even more massive. Sprinting as fast as they could, Dexius and Gavian followed. With nothing that could defeat such an enemy, Gavian could only hope they could get their friends out of the grove in time.

As they entered the sacred grove, many of the trees split apart from the presence of the Primevus. Gavian spotted Ambrielle and the others, slightly battered and bloodied. The battle had nearly stopped because Ambrielle and the others, along with the Kalithor, had beaten back the Cereveshians, whidges, and Ichtek. "My silbrace ran out of energy," said Ambrielle. "I healed them as much as I could."

Bodies of Ichtek littered the ground among bits of the shadowstone of whidges.

"Where is your other sword?" asked Darby. "Did you get any more essence?"

Gavian lowered his eyes, shaking his head slowly.

"Hableides!" Malidora shouted. "Tell us how to stop them! Is there a way to seal off the main connection between The Hollow and this universe?"

"It was not supposed to end this way," said Hableides. "I was a goddess, revered above all others in the Celestial Forest. The paradise that I worked so hard to build is lost. My people's sacrifice was for nothing."

Gavian noticed scars filled the great tree, burning wounds from the weapons of the Ichtek. Thick, black sap ran down her trunk.

Ambrielle wrapped the bladestaff strap around her shoulder and took the Cereveshian geowave from her bag, slamming it into the ground to make it transform into a usable weapon. Gavian hadn't realized that she kept it with her, but the unusual technology allowed it to collapse into a small form. Thousands of whispers rushed through Gavian's head as an army of Nulthereals swept through the forest. There were still many that had not merged with the Primevus. Gavian drew his sword, and Ambrielle fired the sonic geowave weapon.

As the Nulthereals surged forward, their relentless advance caused the trees and foliage to contort under their force. The Shadows consumed everything in their path, but the organic energy of the forest overwhelmed them, withering their protective auras away. The first wave of Nulthereals slowed to a stop, but the next continued on the path carved through the grove. Sidaire stumbled and fell as she tried to get away.

"Sidaire!" Dexius called out, running to try and help her.

Amid the chaos, she crawled over chunks of shadowstone, the remnants of whidges that had been destroyed. With a chilling scream, Sidaire was enveloped by one of the Nulthereals, dragging her helplessly into its Shadowy form.

Dexius cried out again, "Sidaire!" but it was too late, she was gone.

Malidora ran toward the great tree, hoping to find cover, as Darby and the others followed. Ambrielle continued firing but nothing happened. Before Gavian could react, another group of Nulthereals came through, yanking Ambrielle from her feet and into the Shadow's inky blackness. It happened so fast that Gavian stood in shock, not sure what to do.

"That shadowstone on the ground!" shouted Malidora. "Mekkadium! Take it and hold on!"

The echoes of Serenith's ancient tale reverberated through Gavian's mind like a haunting melody of bygone eras. The Vyndari, the forebears of the Ichtek, had held firm beliefs in the cyclical dance of darkness and light. When shadows shrouded their world, they believed it to be a harbinger of transformation, a momentary oblivion before the promise of rebirth when light reclaimed its dominion.

Yet, hidden within their stories lay their greatest fear—the dawn that would never come. The Vyndari dreaded the prospect of everlasting darkness, the relentless obliteration of their existence, being swallowed whole by an abyss that denied them the chance of renewal.

The sacred grove went dark. Everything he cared about, Ambrielle, his friends, the whole world around him, was gone. It was all erased. His final hope was that, somehow, dawn would come again. That it would cast its light and bring them out of oblivion.

CHAPTER 25

Malidora—The Hollow

CANDLE BURNING IN *the dark. When nightmares come to take its spark, I need not hide in fear or fright. For even shadows need the light.*

Malidora heard the poem in her head over and over as she found herself engulfed by the gray of nothingness. More than mere darkness, she felt herself stretching ever deeper into a void that allowed no respite. With every passing heartbeat, Malidora struggled to maintain a sense of self, to resist the relentless pull of the abyss. The void seemed insatiable, consuming every fragment of her being until she felt like a mere specter lost in the gray expanse.

"I remember this darkness," said Veridius. "I thought it was the end."

She was relieved to hear Veridius's voice breaking through the loneliness she felt in this emptiness, but it was more than that. Initially resentful of his existence, bitter over the fact that she had saved him while losing Dabradan, Malidora battled with conflicting emotions. Veridius symbolized a life of privilege she loathed, yet beneath the surface she recognized reflections of herself—an earnest desire to contribute, a yearning to make a meaningful impact, albeit marred by flawed execution. Their journeys had diverged widely, but perhaps, in their shared experiences, they had stumbled upon the right path together. Despite her initial frustration, she felt a sense of satisfaction that she had played a role in his survival from Kandom, and she was genuinely glad to have him by her side now.

"Countless memories," a voice reverberated, its haunting tone threading through the expanse of the abyss. "A wealth of knowledge just waiting for you to claim it. Yet, you persist in your resistance against the mindstream." The voice seemed to resonate from the deepest recesses of the void. It was the voice of Razinoth, the Forgotten.

"Do you not yearn to embrace the infinite quandary of existence?" another voice broke through the emptiness, each word drawing Malidora deeper into its ethereal allure. "The mindstream offers the boundless sprouting of enlightened thought, an endless forest of understanding."

Someone else spoke next to her, but she could not see anything. "They are all here." It sounded like Kazial.

"The Gaith?" Malidora asked. The conversation momentarily paused. The lack of voices in her mind for even a moment brought about an unfathomable loneliness in this place.

"Yet you stand at the precipice of eternity, hesitant to plunge into the chasm of transcendence," the voice intoned, its spectral tendrils reaching out to touch the very essence of Malidora's being.

It was as if the voice knew every thought, every doubt, and every hope that flickered in the listener's mind. Resistance felt futile, for in the face of such an all-encompassing presence, one's individuality seemed insignificant.

"That was Ilganok, the Dreambinder," said Kazial.

"How can you tell?" Malidora asked.

"I was connected to the Gaith in the mindstream, remember?" said Kazial. "They used our minds as a conduit."

"Embrace the mindstream, and the universe shall unfurl before you," said Grindak with a voice like a thunderstorm. Each word was a roaring cascade of power. "The grand symphony of existence shall be yours to conduct, and the mysteries of creation shall dance at your command."

She seemed to immediately know their names as they spoke, as if Kazial passed his knowledge directly into her mind.

"You are but a fleeting spark in the infinite expanse," Zeragul spoke with a voice that echoed inside Malidora's own consciousness. Its cadence slow and deliberate, yet there was an unsettling urgency. "The mindstream awaits. Will you venture forth and drown in its endless depths, or shall you wither in the barren echoes of eternity's silence?"

"Your thoughts and emotions ripple like waves upon the canvas of the boundless abyss," Vazerinaz declared with a voice that was a like a chorus of anguished cries, its troubled tones tearing at the boundaries of Malidora's sanity. "They are of failure, failure to protect a potent mind from our grasp. But in your failure lies triumph for the Everance. This potent mind shall hasten our quest for perfection, an eternal aspiration realized."

"Imagine realms and worlds where all have the same goals and aspirations. No more will there be conflict or strife. No more will there be sadness."

"Picture realms and worlds where every being pursues the same noble goals and shared aspirations," Razinoth's voice echoed seemingly forever. "Strife and discord shall be vanquished, and the lament of sorrow shall yield."

Their words painted a vision of a world without turmoil. Malidora couldn't help but feel the allure of such a utopia. Yet beneath the seductive promises lay the unmistakable impression of a hammer shaping all existence to fit a singular mold.

It was the antithesis of harmony and balance. It may not have conflict or strife, but it would be without self, without will, only a molded, conformed series of robotic beings living endlessly to serve a singular cause, and the Gaith would decide what that should be. Everything she had learned about the Everance and The One during her time in Averess began to resonate with her now more than ever. In a cosmos where stars collide and galaxies clash, it is the very differences that weave the beauty of existence. Though strife may test them, it forges character and fosters growth. The infinite realms and universe were often diametrically opposed to each other, but they each shared something the other needed. It was an endless ecosystem, symbiosis, harmony.

Thinking out loud, she finally spoke, "True unity cannot be forged through conformity. It must be through our own will, finding commonalities, choosing to come together despite all our differences."

A quiet came over the void as all went silent. She could no longer sense the presence of Kazial. Malidora struggled to navigate this ethereal wasteland, but a glimmer of determination flickered within her. She refused to surrender entirely to the void, clinging to the faintest trace of her identity. The shadowstone covering her hand was all that kept her from slipping away. With her essence trapped within, she focused her conscious mind on the stone.

"You guided us out of this before, Malidora," said Veridius. "You can do it again."

The conviction in his voice, his faith in her, gave her confidence. Malidora tried to focus, not on the darkness, but on the feelings that stirred within. She reached out to something beyond herself, something deep down, normally hidden from her own mind. Her form began to take shape. An aethrum form that allowed her to exist in this medium. As the thick space of The Hollow drew around her, Malidora looked down at her feet. She stood on the red scales of Razinoth. She took a step on what had once appeared to be a smooth tiled surface. The hard hollow sound made her shudder.

Malidora noticed a glowing light at her side. The pouch containing the nyalith shard was still there. Around her wrist, Niralys, which contained a representation of the known Everance, persisted in this realm also.

Another shape formed nearby, disrupting the dense cauldron of clouds. Ambrielle steadied herself, looking at her boots. The mekkadium heels had undergone a transition with the shift of mediums, covering her boots with its blackened stone. Both of her hands were covered too, still clutching her mekkadium bladestaff. "We're in The Hollow," she said. "We have to get back! There's a blue vortex somewhere! That is how we escape!"

"I'm aware," said Malidora, as her eyes ran across the thick skies of Hollowspace. "Let me know if you see it."

"Where is Gavian?" said Ambrielle as she walked ahead.

Darby and Veridius appeared behind her, their hands covered in the stone as well. Malidora turned to find Kazial, standing as if he had been there all along. The last time Malidora was here, she had fed on so much of the crystallized energy called elu that she had grown massively in power and size. But seeing everyone here now, she realized that the power had not come back with her return to The Hollow.

On one horizon was the universe, a sphere of black surrounded by the bright essence of the dust of life, galaxies, stars, planets, living beings, and even plants. The cycle of life and death ended up at the edge of it all, protecting both the universe and Nulvare from annihilating each other, accumulating over time and allowing the universe to grow.

Gavian and Dexius formed. Gavian's sword, now covered in shadowstone, made the transition as well. Malidora lamented not putting shadowstone on her crossbow, though she wasn't sure if its mechanics would function the same in this place.

Gavian reached out to Ambrielle as soon as he saw her. They embraced as their aethrum forms gave way to the mutual touch, their contact surfaces melding together. When they withdrew, there seemed to be a sticky pull from the disconnection.

Dexius turned around frantically. "Where is Sidaire?"

"I am here," said a dark figure ahead, rising up on her hands and knees. Dexius ran to her with the others coming in behind him. He grabbed her arms, helping her to her feet. "Are you okay?" he asked.

"I am now," she said as she appeared to gain strength. "I thought I was dying."

In the skies of Hollowspace, shapes of eldritch horrors flew around several broken stones floating in the dense liquid space. Malidora recognized one of them. The black and red Gaith with appendages on both sides of its head trailing behind him. It was Grindak, who had chased her through Hollowspace before.

Dexius's eyes widened in dismay. "We need a place to hide!"

The amber-colored skies undulated above them, casting an eerie glow on the red scales of Razinoth beneath their feet. As Malidora spoke, the tiles beneath her emitted a hard, hollow sound that made her shudder.

"Don't worry," said Malidora. "We are too small for them to see."

A flicker of the atmosphere revealed the tension on Darby's face as she stared at the monstrous beings. "Is that . . . them?"

Malidora nodded in affirmation. "The Gaith."

"I see four," said Dexius. "Where is the fifth?"

"You're standing on it," said Malidora, gesturing to the hardened tiles of the surface that stretched all around them.

Many of them instinctively backed up, their footsteps echoing in the strange environment. "What do you mean? Isn't this some kind of planet, like Isodonia?" said Dexius.

"Trust me," Malidora shot a glance at him, the lightning filaments highlighting the intensity in her eyes. "We're standing on Razinoth."

The red scales of Razinoth shivered beneath their feet. "So what do we do now?" Sidaire asked, walking as if she couldn't balance herself on the ground beneath her.

"Why didn't you tell us?" said Dexius as he watched the monstrous Gaith cut through Hollowspace in their orbit around the universe. "How could we ever hope to fight against something like this?"

"We couldn't." Veridius nervously slapped his hands together. "We have to close the rifts."

The amber-lit skies above seemed to darken as Ambrielle sat on a nearby rock. Then she suddenly stood up as if remembering this was all part of Razinoth's body. "Maybe the blue vortex is the key," she suggested. "Maybe that is what we need to close."

Veridius pondered, his gaze shifting between the swirling skies and the scales beneath them. "If we could find it. But do we even know how to close it?"

"They barely need the rifts now." Malidora dug her foot into a separation between Razinoth's scales. "With the mind of Hableides, they can start wars that will kill everyone across entire galaxies."

"They would still have to come in and collect the essence," said Dexius.

The texture of the red tiles beneath them shifted. Intricate patterns seemed to writhe and pulse across Razinoth's scales.

"Yes, or maybe the Ichtek could collect it for them." Malidora traced her fingers over a particularly vibrant section, and the scales responded with a soft hum, emitting a gentle warmth. "They can't bring it here anyway. The essence would diffuse their elu."

"What does closing the rifts matter if they can open them so easily?" said Darby. "With that sword?"

"They no longer have the sword," said Gavian. "Dexius and I destroyed it."

"When did this happen?" Malidora asked.

The amber-lit skies continued their mesmerizing dance, but now, wisps of ethereal mist began to form nearby. These wisps twisted and twirled, sometimes forming ghostly shapes and figures.

"Back on Valderine," Dexius said, as he extended his hand toward the mist. It responded to his touch, swirling around his fingers.

Ambrielle moved across the tiled surface, approaching a cluster of luminescent patterns that pulsed with a rhythmic beat. "We need to get started. First, we have to find the vortex," said Ambrielle. "Then we can figure out what to do next."

"Ambrielle is right," said Darby. "One step at a time."

"Should we spread out and look?" Sidaire asked.

"I think we should stay together," said Veridius. "After everything that's happened. We don't need to lose track of anyone."

"Agreed." Ambrielle looked around at the luminescent crystals in Razinoth's scales. "I would think it would be closer to the universe side of . . . this thing, Razinoth."

"That makes as much sense as anything," said Malidora. "All right we'll walk toward the universe."

They made their way across the scales of Razinoth, stopping on occasion when the ground beneath them shuddered. A rolling wave went across the surface, tilting each scale for a moment as it passed before clicking back into place. Ahead was a forest of black trees that Malidora had seen before. Other than small prongs, the trees were merely trunks without branches. With the knowledge that this world was Razinoth himself, she realized the trees were likely sensory hairs used for detecting changes in touch or vibration. Perhaps it was best they avoid them. But the forest stretched out so wide it was unavoidable.

"Don't touch the trees," Malidora said. "Or at least do so as little as possible."

The group made their way through, ducking underneath the hanging stems that leaned too close to the surface. Small creatures like crustaceans crawled between trees in the densest parts of the forest. They seemed uninterested in Malidora's or anyone else's presence, but they made Malidora recognize that they would need to feed. If they were here long enough, they would have to consume elu to stay whole.

A flittering of vibration sounded faintly on the air as they all came out of the forest. It was almost melodic, with sporadic buzzes here and there. Searching the skies for the blue vortex yielded nothing.

"Are you sure this is the right way to go?" Dexius asked, as another wrinkled wave came over the ground toward them.

"How did you find it before, Malidora?" Sidaire asked.

"It was in this area the last time I was here," said Malidora. "At least I think it was. I guess this forest could go on for miles."

The vibrating sound grew louder as they moved ahead, though it seemed to come from behind them. Malidora stopped to take a look back but saw nothing out of the ordinary for this place.

"Maybe we should try a different direction," said Dexius.

"If we start changing direction, we'll end up lost," Ambrielle said.

"Everywhere here is lost," said Gavian.

"We don't want to start walking in circles," said Darby.

The melodic vibration became loud. Malidora turned as several dark, mothlike creatures flew over them. Ambrielle cried out when one of them grabbed her, lifting her off the ground. Another took Gavian. Malidora dove to the surface as one of the creatures tried to snag her when it flew by.

She had faced these creatures once before—servants of the Gaith known as Nuliaks. Panic rippled through the rest of the group, prompting them to scatter in different directions. Yet the Nuliaks were relentless in their pursuit, their numerous figures spreading out like a shadowy web closing in.

In the chaos, Malidora witnessed one of the Nuliaks seizing Dexius, swiftly moving in tandem with the two others who had captured Ambrielle and Gavian. The Nuliaks guided their captives in the direction of the looming Gaith.

Scrambling to her feet, Malidora turned and ran back to the forest. She saw Kazial being carried off by one as she rushed between the trees. Focusing on the crustaceans, Malidora tried to recall how she'd drained elu before. She concentrated on the creatures, feeling the energy inside them. It felt as though she were bending herself more than anything, but she was able to make the elu of one of the creatures flow into her.

With a boost of power, Malidora grew slightly in size. She reached out, feeling the connection of all the crustaceans and draining the elu from them into herself. Bursting with energy, Malidora launched herself into Hollowspace, following the swarm of Nuliaks as they carried her friends.

Before she could catch up, the claws of a Nuliak caught her. Its many legs tussled with her, moving her into a position where it could hold her tight. Unable to turn around and fight the Nuliak, she let her body relax and go limp.

She could see the Gaith ahead, their horrid forms becoming clearer by the moment. As the Nuliak carrying her caught up with the swarm, Malidora could hear Ambrielle. With her bladestaff in hand, Ambrielle still fought off the Nuliak. The legs of the mothlike creature tried to turn Ambrielle around, but she was almost too small for it to do so.

With one of her arms pinned down, Ambrielle switched the bladestaff to her other hand. She thrust the shadowstone bladestaff into the body of the Nuliak and continued to twist and jab the staff into it. As the Nuliak writhed in pain, elu began to leak from the wound.

Concentrating, Malidora pulled the elu toward her, absorbing it. With the surge in power, Malidora was able to break free of the Nuliak's hold and connect with elu in the wounded creature. She drained it all until the Nuliak turned ashen and began to crumble to dust. Ambrielle was free, floating in the Hollowspace around her. Now slightly larger than her captor, Malidora grabbed the Nuliak and siphoned all the elu energy coursing through it.

Now she was double the size of the Nuliaks. She possessed the power to fly through the thickness of Hollowspace. As she surged ahead, her eyes fixated on the elusive blue vortex shimmering in the distance. The promise of an immediate escape from the suffocating medium was tantalizing, hanging before her like a beacon of freedom. All she had to do was reach for it, and she could leave this disconcerting realm behind. It was an easy choice. The decision was almost too easy. Self-preservation had long been her priority. Life had taught her the harsh truth—you had to be your own protector because no one else would be.

CHAPTER 26

Darby—The Hollow

DARBY STRUGGLED TO get free from the grip of the dark creature as she spotted Gavian using his sword to cut through the grip of the monster holding him. Malidora streamed through Hollowspace toward a swirling blue storm in the distance, leaving them to contend with these Shadow creatures. After all they had fought through together, how could she abandon them like this?

Seizing one of the Shadow creatures trailing behind, Malidora siphoned its vibrant blue energy into her palm. The creature disintegrated within her grip, leaving her tumbling in space. In the descent, she absorbed the elu from surrounding creatures in flight, experiencing a surge in both size and power. As she drained the creatures Malidora freed Sidaire, then Dexius, and Veridius.

Darby lamented her distrust in Malidora as the monsters let go of her and scattered away in retreat. She and the others floated in the strange medium of Hollowspace, unable to move much at all. Malidora now dwarfed them in size and gathered them with ease. One by one, she took them into her hands from where they floated in Hollowspace.

Malidora's size began to rapidly decrease as the blue energy around her dissipated, separating into small particles and drifting off into Hollowspace. The green light at her side, the nyalith shard containing the living organic essence of Kandom, ripped the blue elu apart, taking Malidora with it. She quickly grabbed the nyalith in her shadowstone-covered hand, and it stopped. It was as if the shadowstone insulated the essence, keeping it from destroying the elu she contained.

With everyone secure in her arms, Malidora propelled them away from the Gaith and back toward the universe. A roar sent ripples through Hollowspace, knocking them off course. Behind them, four Gaith hurtled toward them at an insane speed.

Malidora carried them over the scales of Razinoth, over bands of red and white. The other Gaith, cutting through planets of rock in their path, closed in. Darby's aethrum body began to feel the pain of the essence surrounding the universe. She was getting too close to the field that separated the fused energy of elu within her. Malidora shifted them in her grasp, as if to shield them from it.

Slowing her flight, Malidora executed a graceful turn, taking refuge in a more distant orbit. The elusive blue vortex, the gateway Ambrielle had mentioned, remained tantalizingly out of reach.

"I thought it was much closer," Malidora said as she scanned the astral expanse. A sudden disruption in her vision drew Darby's attention. An immense, imposing wall materialized before her, an abyssal maw that seemed to beckon her into its cavernous depths. The mouth of Razinoth. The pull was inexorable, an irresistible force that tugged at her very being.

The cosmos dissolved around her, the celestial panorama fading into obscurity. Reality wavered, leaving her feeling adrift, lost within the boundless sea of existence. The sensation was akin to being dizzy, an altered state where time and space lost their meaning.

❧

Darby awoke, aware of herself once again. Examining her surroundings, she saw a forest of strange, twisted trees. Glowing red liquid flowed through the bark of the old trees, their roots carrying it to and from the soil. Etched into the rugged bark of the towering tree trunks, a series of visages had been intricately carved, their features frozen in an unsettling array of expressions. Each face seemed to encapsulate a potent emotion, as if the very essence of despair, agony, and unbridled hate had been captured on the surface of the wood.

Ahead, the trees stirred, and someone leapt from the branches, landing on the ground—it was Gavian. "Oh, it's you," he remarked. "What are you doing here?"

The simple question sparked an odd feeling in Darby—a blend of surprise and confusion. What *was* she doing in this place? Though the exact purpose eluded her, an underlying sense of significance lingered. As they continued through the forest, an unseen force guided their steps, its nature shrouded in mystery. With each stride, Darby's intuition homed in on the unease emanating from the carved expressions around them—a subtle indication that there was more to these surroundings than met the eye.

As they ventured deeper into the eerie forest, a shroud of darkness seemed to embrace them, obscuring the once-clear path they had followed. The trees loomed like sentinels of an ancient secret, their gnarled branches reaching out as if to draw them deeper into the mysteries of the woods. Darby couldn't shake the feeling that they were straying into a place where the boundaries of reality blurred, where the very path they tread entwined with uncertainty.

They came upon Dexius as he stepped out from behind a tree ahead, and he joined them on their journey. Darby had no idea where they were heading, but it must be somewhere important. Behind them, the voices of Veridius, Ambrielle, Sidaire, Malidora, and Kazial bade her to turn around. After waiting for them to catch up, they all marched ahead, following the gnarled roots of the old trees that all seemed to lead in the same direction.

Crawling into a flowing silver stream, the tangled mass of roots ended. The thick metallic liquid of the stream flowed through the forest and cut through a row of jagged rocks ahead. There were faces in the water too, forming like a mold in the reflective liquid before dissipating as they moved further down the stream.

As Darby gazed at the water, she caught her own reflection. The reflection oddly did not mirror her movements. Her face looked unusual on the water's surface. There was something disturbing about it. The image of herself had her eyes shut. No matter how wide she opened them, they remained closed in the mirror. She looked dead or perhaps in a deep sleep.

"We're dreamwalking!" exclaimed Malidora, standing on the stream's banks.

Darby sifted through her thoughts, recalling the last thing she could remember. She recalled the old tree on Valderine, grabbing one of her shadowstone arrows as the darkness took them all. She remembered Hollowspace and fighting through the hordes of flying fiends only to be swallowed by the hellish chasm of . . .

"Razinoth," Sidaire said. "He brought us to the mindstream."

"The mindstream?" Dexius questioned. "What is that?"

"From what I have gathered," Malidora explained, "it is a construct that connects the five Gaith to each other."

"Using the minds of those they have taken from Solsellion and other worlds across the universe," added Kazial.

"The minds of their victims were used as conduits to process thoughts and store endless memories and knowledge," said Sidaire.

Darby watched as Malidora strode along the edge of the metallic water. As with the trees that lined the surreal riverbank, faces emerged from the depths, floating with the gentle current. The visages, victims lost in the tangled web of the mindstream, manifested in the reflective liquid. As the faces drifted, their expressions contorted and shifted with the current, mirroring numerous emotions. Some wore expressions of agony, frozen in perpetual torment, while others seemed to gasp for breath, their open mouths silent echoes of the struggles they faced.

"We're inside Ilganok's dream again," Kazial stated.

Ambrielle gazed at the dark sky gradually brightening on the horizon. "This is a dream?"

Darby surveyed the landscape, trying to discern the differences between this dreamworld and what she knew to be real. Though it should have been easy to see, something kept numbing her mind, blurring logic and reason, pulling her further into the illusion.

"How do we keep getting further away from escaping this place?" Dexius wondered.

"We're all in the same dream?" Darby asked.

"From my understanding, yes," Malidora confirmed.

"Where do our bodies lie if this is a dream?" Veridius questioned.

"Somewhere in the cavernous bowels of Razinoth," Malidora speculated. "Perhaps his mind, who knows?"

"In that case maybe we should stay in the dream," suggested Dexius. "I don't want to wake up to that."

"All these people here," Sidaire said, staring at the flowing stream. "We need to get them out."

"What people?" Ambrielle asked. "The faces in the water are real?"

The idea that these faces were all once people like them bothered Darby. She could not take her eyes off them as they flowed downstream. So many of them. The deep, unpleasant expressions on their faces, what thoughts must be running through their minds.

"Kazial and I were in this stream when we were taken from Solsellion," Sidaire explained. "And the trees too."

"We would all be there," Malidora stated, raising her shadowstone-covered hand. "If it weren't for this."

Darby peered over her shoulder to where her quiver normally stayed, eyeing the shadowstone covering her back and shoulder. The shadowstone in her arrows had spread out and hardened. Ambrielle, too, had her hands and feet coated with it, as well as her bladestaff made of shadowstone.

"Some of them are from Solsellion," Sidaire said. "We need to free them."

"We need to focus on getting out of this place," Dexius urged. "If we don't get out of here and figure something out, no one will be free."

"Can they even be freed?" Darby questioned. As much as she wished to see these beings escape this state of being, she did not wish to linger here. Silently scolding herself for her selfishness, Darby tried to muster the courage to face the creeping fears spreading in her mind.

"I managed to get Sidaire and Kazial out, but being in that water," Malidora admitted, a mixture of fear and disgust crossing her face, "it's not a good idea."

"There are too many to save," Dexius insisted. "We shouldn't stay much longer."

"If your people were here," said Sidaire, "would you be so willing to leave them behind?"

"We should at least get some of them out," Ambrielle suggested. "If the Gaith use them to power their thoughts, maybe some of them hold knowledge we can use."

"If the water needs to keep moving, perhaps we could disrupt it," Veridius proposed. "Stop the flow."

"How would we do that?" Sidaire asked.

"Trees," said Gavian. "There is plenty of wood in this forest. We could make a dam."

"There's four streams altogether," said Malidora. "Up ahead."

"So where does the stream go?" Veridius asked.

"The same place they all go," said Kazial. "They converge at the interface in the center of this place."

"When you were in the stream, did you flow into the middle? What happens after that?" Veridius asked.

"I don't have any tangible memories of it," said Kazial. "Only flashes here and there. Strange thoughts of everything being one mind. Images of Ilganok and the other Gaith."

"And then nothing?" Veridius said.

"And then it starts over," said Sidaire. "You grow in the forest. Inside the trees and eventually flow into the stream. It repeats over and over."

"The roots all run toward the water," said Dexius. "Couldn't we just cut through the roots?"

"Might be worth a try," said Malidora. "Gavian?"

Gavian drew his sword. He stared at the blade, now fully blackened with shadowstone, before swinging it at the clusters of roots that fed into the flowing water. As he cut through a group of them, glows of red turned on. Through the black thicket, hundreds of red eyes glared at them. Some were on the move, creeping slowly toward them.

"Crawlers," Malidora warned.

The group began backing away from the stream, and the dark crawlers ambled out of the woods. A few of them stopped at the damaged roots, spinning them as if weaving a web. They were somehow repairing the roots. Walking in a staggering motion, the four-legged creatures attacked. Darby grabbed one of her shadowstone arrows, but without a bow it was of little use as a weapon against these creatures. Gavian sliced through one of them, then lunged backward to stab one behind him. Twirling her bladestaff, Ambrielle whipped the front legs from underneath a crawler, then slashed two more on either side of her.

"Run!" shouted Veridius as he and the others sprinted into the grass, heading for the valley meadow ahead. Malidora reached for her crossbow before realizing it didn't transfer to this environment. Darby wanted to keep running but slowed as Gavian and Ambrielle continued to swing their weapons, cutting into the mass of crawlers until they began to get overwhelmed.

"Let's go!" Malidora called out to them. Gavian nudged Ambrielle and Darby on as he backed away from the crawlers, making sure they didn't close in behind them. The dark crawlers poured out of the forest. Veridius led the others into the valley while Malidora waited for Ambrielle and Gavian to catch up.

As they crossed the valley, they came to a wall of crystalized formations. With sharp, angular rocks and a sheer base, they looked formidable, but there was enough room to squeeze through.

"Down there." Dexius tapped on Malidora's shoulder as he pointed to the river. The flowing water carved a tunnel into the crystals. It wasn't as tight of a squeeze, but the path was close to the silver waters on either side.

Darby and the others followed Dexius until they reached the opening through the crystals. The dark interior shaded the direction of the light, but she could see a point at the end. Maybe they could make it through this way.

Darby eyed the others as they stood hesitant, facing the pitch dark of the tunnel. They had no silbraces to use for light to see their surroundings, but Ambrielle strode past them, heading into the darkness of the tunnel. Darby felt a bit braver as she followed Ambrielle into the dark. Gavian and the others moved in behind her.

"Keep out of the water," Malidora cautioned, her form leaning against the rocky side wall. The echoing sounds of water splashing and dripping within the confines of the two crystal walls created an eerie ambience. Malidora's side glowed around them, as the energized nyalith shard in her bag cast ample light, revealing their surroundings.

Movement stirred ahead, causing ripples in the water. The group's pace decelerated as caution took hold. They drew closer, and the presence ahead seemed perturbed by the shard's light. A peculiar goblin-like being emerged into view. The orange-skinned goblin's hands shielded his eyes as he addressed them. "You are not meant to be here." His voice held an otherworldly undertone, a whisper of command. "Return to the waters and reconnect."

Darby and the others exchanged uncertain glances, unsure of how to respond. Malidora urged them forward, gently guiding Ambrielle and maintaining their momentum. As they passed the enigmatic figure, the goblin worker's presence lingered like a riddle in the air. "Why are you unmelded?" he inquired, his wooden oar stirring the silver waters of the stream. Despite his presence, Darby continued on, resolute in her attempt to move forward, endeavoring to ignore his unsettling words.

Emerging from the cavern of crystals, they stepped into a glowing meadow where three other streams from the realms ahead converged into a calm, circular pool. The sky above held a hue of pale blue, while a bright radiance poured down without the presence of a discernible sun. The view was serene, a canvas of almost breathtaking beauty, yet there lingered an underlying quality, a strange disturbance that eluded Darby's grasp.

Amid the meadow's vividly illuminated grass, shadows were scarce, almost nonexistent, leaving the blades of grass undefined and appearing more like a blur. The roots of a huge tree tangled through the grass trailing like snakes into the pool where the streams converged. Faces knotted into its thick bark as red liquid ran through its veinlike roots into the silver stream. Above the gathering pool floated a colossal, shimmering orb. Its form pulsed rhythmically, akin to a beating heart, its hues shifting with rapid intensity, a mesmerizing display of color.

"What is that?" Ambrielle inquired, her gaze fixed on the orb.

"The interface," Kazial explained. "Where all connect through the mind of Ilganok."

"Even the other Gaith," added Sidaire.

Darby continued to keep her eyes on the orange-skinned goblin creatures, appearing as guardians, voicing their admonitions in unison as one of them stirred the pool's surface with an oar. "You should not be here."

"We must maintain the purity of this realm," another added, their collective statements like a harmonious chant.

"I don't remember this tree being here before," said Sidaire, as she gazed up at its branches, drooping as if under the weight of despair.

Malidora gazed up, her lips parting in dismay. "Hableides?" she called out.

The black leaves rustled through the tree's old, twisted branches. "Have you come to witness the ruins of my divinity?" said Hableides. "The darkness clings to me like a parasite, hungering for more than my mind. It craves the essence of existence itself."

"Is there anything we can do to get you out of here?" said Malidora.

The glowing red vines coiled around the tree's branches and trunk. "Do you sense it, young one? The chilling tendrils of despair that wrap around my very essence? They whisper of endings, of the futility of existence. For what purpose do I endure this endless twilight, this eternal void?"

"They mean to use you to destroy the universe," said Malidora. "We have to do something to stop it."

"I am the voice of the forgotten," said Hableides, "the embodiment of what was and what could have been. The very essence of my being is consumed by the voracious Shadows, and I am left to witness the unmaking of all that I held dear."

"You must focus, listen to me," said Malidora. "Tell us how we can help you."

"My existence is but a cycle of suffering, an endless loop of desolation," said Hableides. "If there ever was a purpose to my being, it has been eclipsed by the void that now consumes me. I beg of you, end this cycle, release me from the agony of existence."

"You want us to kill you?" said Malidora.

Something felt wrong about this. Darby had done her fair share of ending lives in the war on Isodonia. The Grundians ravaging through villages and towns made it easy to justify. But ending a life like this was unsettling.

"I offer you the choice, the privilege, to be the instrument of my liberation," said Hableides. "To sever the threads that tie me to this fractured reality. For there is nothing left for me in this endless void but torment."

"If they are going to use her to become even more powerful," said Dexius, "we should do it."

Even to save countless worlds, carrying out this execution was difficult for Darby to take in.

"Sadly, it may be the only way to stop them," said Veridius.

Darby closed her eyes as Gavian strode toward the old tree. He brandished his shadowstone blade, cutting through thick, gnarled roots that impeded his path to the base of the tree. He took a glance back at Ambrielle and the others, plunging the sword into the thick bark. The tree moaned, swaying in response as the ground rumbled beneath their feet.

"You must not do that!" shouted one of the goblin workers.

The horrid legs of the dark crawlers appeared from a large hollow in Hableides's trunk. They poured out, crawling down her limbs toward Gavian. Leaping over the twisted roots, Gavian dashed away from them.

"Will you heed my plea, brave souls?" said Hableides, as black sap oozed from the wound of Gavian's sword. "Will you step into the abyss that has become me and strike the final chord in this dirge of despair? I implore you, be the harbinger of my release, for there is naught but emptiness left for me to bear."

The dark crawlers ended their chase once Gavian was away from the tree. He sheathed his blade while he caught his breath. "I don't think I can get past all those things."

Malidora exhaled a breath of disappointment. "For a moment I thought there was hope."

Even though it would have helped their cause, Darby couldn't help but be somewhat relieved that Hableides had not succumbed to Gavian's sword.

"All of you, get back into the mindstream!" one of the workers reiterated, their tone insistent.

The goblin began to twist, morphing into one of the horrid four-legged crawlers. Gavian and Ambrielle quickly took action with their shadowstone weapons, killing the crawler before it could reach them.

Light flashed from the dead crawler and it vanished. Moments later, the same area flashed again, forming two crawlers where the one had died. Using her bladestaff, Ambrielle wounded one of the crawlers' legs as it tried to bring it down on top of her. Gavian sliced through its other front leg while he ran from the other crawler.

As the crawler bowed from its wounds, Ambrielle brought the pointed blade down on its head. With only one left, Gavian turned to fight the creature head-on. He went directly for its head but was met with its two front legs it used to defend itself. He cut into one of the legs, and Ambrielle skewered it with her staff. As it reeled in pain, Gavian plunged the sword into its small head.

"They're multiplying!" Ambrielle yelled.

Their situation seemed hopeless. Darby pulled Kazial clear of Gavian's and Ambrielle's swinging weapons until they were backed up to the edge of the waters as the crawlers crept forward. Fighting them was useless because it only made the situation worse. She drew one of her shadowstone arrows that transferred with her to this medium. Though it would be of little use since it required her to get inside the range of the crawlers' claws to attempt anything.

Darby realized that the universe would soon fall into shadow, and all their struggles, their fighting through impossible odds, none of it mattered in the end. Was there something they could have done differently that might have prevented this outcome? There didn't seem to be.

She huddled against Kazial and Veridius as the crawlers forced Ambrielle and Gavian back. Everything they had attempted, from finding Neristara, to sending Malidora and Ambrielle to Averess, to Gavian and everyone gathering amplifying crystals, to her and Kazial going to Elyravess to unravel the mysteries of the Gaith and finding which spring would take them to Valderine, was all for nothing.

As they were forced back to edge of the silver stream, Darby realized she had to make an impossible choice. Either step into the waters and become part of the mindstream or face a painful death at the claws of these dark creatures. If she chose the stream, she would live on in some horrid state, losing control of her mind to be used by the Gaith. At times she might have been so desperate to avoid the endless dark nothingness of death that surviving in the stream would have been an easy choice. Yet if there were ever a choice in which oblivion was not preferable to death, this was it. Darby readied herself to push past Gavian and Ambrielle and into the waiting arms of the dark crawlers, ensuring a swift demise. The only hope remaining was the possibility that what Ambrielle and Malidora had told them about the Afterglow was true, that she would leave this plane of existence through a doorway of pain to awaken in a glowing realm of near perfection.

"Wait . . . " Malidora uttered, retrieving the nyalith shard from the bag at her side. It glowed with a vibrant green hue in her hand. "This is it," she exclaimed. "Everything falls into place now."

"What does?" inquired Darby, as Gavian and Ambrielle relentlessly attacked the legs of the advancing crawlers.

"This is my purpose," Malidora stated confidently. "It's as if I've known it all along."

"What are you talking about?" queried Veridius.

"Gavian," Malidora said. He turned away from the crawlers for a moment and glanced at her. "I was wrong for stealing from you and for holding my knife to your throat. Don't make the same mistakes that I did."

A look of confusion crossed over his face as he stabbed at another encroaching crawler. "I guess it wasn't that big of a deal in hindsight. Why are you telling me this?"

Ambrielle and Gavian continued to stab, poke, and slash at the crawlers with their weapons, trying to hold them back or go down fighting. Darby and Dexius used their shadowstone arrows to stab at them and fight them off from the sides, and Veridius used his hands, covered in shadowstone, to swat and punch at them.

"And Dexius," Malidora continued, "I always did think you were kinda cute."

Dexius cleared his throat. "It's about time you admitted it," he quipped, as the crawlers' legs thrust at them.

"Darby, you are a beautiful soul and wise beyond your years," said Malidora. "I like to think I could have been a little bit like you if I had grown up a bit differently."

Darby wasn't sure what to say, but she needed to respond and quickly. "Why would you say that? I always admired your fearlessness, your quick mind. I've learned so much from you," she said shyly. Had Malidora given up too? Perhaps she was preparing to charge the crawlers to precipitate a swift end. Even though Darby had the same thought, it bothered her to hear this coming from Malidora. Her thoughts were a storm as they continued to fight.

"Ambrielle, if it weren't for your strength I could not have kept going. Everyone in this group knows that they would not have made it this far if it were not for the strength you've displayed," said Malidora. "I hope you never lose your curiosity and eagerness to explore."

Ambrielle turned back for a quick moment as she frantically used her bladestaff to make the crawlers back up. "Strength? Through all of this, I was never more afraid in my life. The only reason I haven't run back home yet is because I didn't want to let everyone down."

"If that is not strength, what is?" Malidora grabbed Ambrielle's right hand, sliding Niralys onto Ambrielle's wrist. "Hold on to this for me. I'm not taking no for an answer this time."

Darby didn't want it to end like this. Malidora should be the last one standing, fighting until the bitter end.

"And Sidaire and Kazial, you helped me more than you'll ever know," Malidora said. "When I arrived on Solsellion and saw you coming into the oasis . . . Knowing that you had made it here safe, made me think that maybe I did something right for once. That maybe I was not cursed."

"We could never thank you enough for saving us," said Sidaire, as she huddled behind Ambrielle and Gavian. "Even though it comes down to this."

Malidora turned to Veridius, kissing the side of his cheek. "Veridius, you've shown that you truly do care about others," said Malidora. "There are many ways to lead, and you keep us going. You will make a great thercon someday."

"Have you lost all hope?" said Veridius, as he continued to use his shadowstone-covered hand to impede the crawlers' claws from making it through.

Malidora's lips curled into a serene smile as the nyalith shard emitted a radiant glow in her palm. It shined with all the essence of the world of Kandom. "I've never had more."

"Then help us fight them off and find us a way out of here!" Veridius shouted. "Like you always do!"

"This is what I was meant to do," said Malidora, as she stepped into the thick, silver water. "Not for the universe, but for my friends."

"Malidora, what are you doing?" Darby's tone was laced with worry, as Malidora waded into the stream. Darby was shocked. Why would Malidora choose the stream? Why would she want to linger here as nothing more than a puppet of the Gaith?

The urgency in Veridius's voice rang out, "Malidora! Get out of there!"

Veridius's desperation stung Darby. She felt that she had to do something, anything to stop what was happening. Instead, she stood frozen, as if some force held her in place. Inside she was dying as Malidora sunk deeper and deeper into the silver water.

The goblin men poked their long oars into the water, bringing them down into the area where she flowed with the stream. "There is an unmelded substance in the mindstream!"

Malidora's body was covered with the silver waters of the stream, but she retained her human shape. She cradled the bright green light of the nyalith shard in her shadowstone hand as the current led her on. The dark crawlers stopped attacking and transformed back into goblins, frantically rushing toward the water. "Remove it from the waters!"

Even through the waters of the stream, Malidora's voice rang out. "I must complete the mission," she said. "I can't let anything happen to any of you."

CHAPTER 27

MALIDORA—THE HOLLOW

MALIDORA'S BODY BEGAN to go numb. She could see Legotian, her adoptive father, sending her to fetch water from the river. She thought it was foolish to have to walk all the way to the river while it was already raining, not realizing that he sent her away in hopes of saving her from the Blight Whidge that stalked them.

"Tell me you won't let the Shadows win," said the memory of Evala in her head. With resolve in her heart, Malidora clutched the bright nyalith shard in her shadowstone hand and allowed the rippling, silver waters to take her.

Her form seemed to merge seamlessly with the currents, and her mobility faded like a fleeting dream. Yet, Malidora's resolve remained unshaken. Her shadowstone hand clung to the energized shard, the vessel of Dabradan and Evala's essence, a repository of lives lost on Kandom. Her consciousness expanded, intermingling with the minds flowing down the silver river. Her body was a distant whisper, her shadowstone mekkadium hand that held the shard the sole connection to her singular existence, leaving her mind still in control.

As the stream carried her, Malidora's consciousness pooled into the convergence of a vast, luminescent basin—the reflection of the colossal orb that hung above, the interface of Ilganok's mind. The sensation was paradoxical—both weightless and immense. Every essence in the shard resonated with the energy that pulsed through the orb.

"I couldn't let anything happen to you." Malidora heard Dabradan's words in her mind as if he were standing beside her. "You're our best chance . . . to complete the mission . . ." he'd said with one of his last breaths.

Complex circuits ahead of her shimmered with surging energy, their pathways alight with elu as signals danced in a mesmerizing display. Was this intricate network the very manifestation of Ilganok's consciousness? The nyalith shard clutched in her hand throbbed with a brilliance that matched her anticipation. The flow of crystallized elu faltered. The once-unified currents fragmented like splintering glass. Amid this cascade of energies, the distinctive light of the Kandom nyalith shard pierced the maelstrom. The elu's integrity crumbled under its influence, a shattering effect spreading like ripples upon a pond.

"What is this intrusion?" thundered Ilganok. His very mind trembled with the force of his fear and anger. "Get out of our mind!"

The nyalith crystal shattered, its imprisoned energies bursting forth, surging through the expanse of Ilganok's consciousness. The very fabric of his being ripped asunder, a cosmic disintegration mirrored by Malidora's exhalation—an act that felt like both her first and final breath. This was her destiny, her purpose writ across the universe. In this moment, an unwavering certainty enveloped her, unlike any conviction she had ever known. If an Afterglow existed, as the Ureons spoke of, then perhaps its embrace awaited her just beyond the horizon of existence.

Amid the upheaval, a radiant burst erupted—a manifestation of Ilganok's end. A furious roar that had once shaken her to the core now heralded his dissolution. Yet, the blazing maw of that eruption transformed. The ferocious brilliance, once harsh and blinding, morphed into a tranquil illumination. It was a light that imbued Malidora with an unexpected serenity, a sense of peace she had yearned for since her journey began. In its soothing embrace, a fleeting assurance settled upon her—assurance that, in this universe or the next, all was harmonious, all was as it should be. A chorus of indescribable melodies voiced the cries of a new dawn. The woman who lived in darkness finally reached the light.

CHAPTER 28

AMBRIELLE—THE HOLLOW

AMBRIELLE'S HEART POUNDED. "Why did she go into the stream?"

Veridius kneeled in the grass, his fist pressing against his forehead as if trying to bear the weight of his shock. Ambrielle went to him to try and offer some measure of comfort.

Before Ambrielle could get to Veridius, the giant glowing orb floating over the pool splintered. Emitting a piercing squeal, followed by a resonating, guttural roar, the orb erupted. Shards of luminous material fragmented and scattered in all directions.

"Did you feel that?" said Kazial with delight. "She did it! Malidora destroyed Ilganok!"

A dreadful roar reverberated through the dream, triggering its rapid disintegration. Faster and faster, it fragmented into increasingly minute particles. The goblin workers, seemingly panicked and uncertain, agitatedly churned the water. A final blaze of luminance engulfed everything, and then an encompassing darkness enveloped them.

Ambrielle's consciousness gradually resurfaced, a sense of disorientation clinging to her. She felt herself descend gently, akin to a feather wafting to the ground. Then, in an instant, her perception ignited with a rush of sensations. Springing to her feet, she recognized that she had emerged from the dream. The expanse of a vast cave system surrounded her, and Ambrielle noticed her companions stirring nearby, each rousing from slumber.

She hugged Gavian as soon as he stood. He staggered, still groggy from the dream. Once everyone was on their feet, Ambrielle started to wander ahead.

Veridius lay crumpled on the cavern floor. "She did it to save us." He sobbed beside the body of Malidora, still enlarged from the elu she had absorbed earlier. As he moved around her, he seemed to be taking care not to touch her, as if doing so might make it all real. Ambrielle approached him, hoping to offer some sort of comfort. Gavian moved beside her.

"It was only a dream," Veridius said, sitting up and wiping his face. He looked at Ambrielle and then Gavian, as if seeking their affirmation. "She can't be really dead. It was only in the dream."

Ambrielle brushed back the hair from Malidora's eyes, but they remained closed. Not wanting to jar her awake, she started with a gentle caress of her cheek, hoping to stir her from this sleep.

"Why didn't anyone help her!" Veridius cried out. "You all just stood there letting her go!"

Ambrielle nudged Malidora, this time using more force. With no response from Malidora, Ambrielle grabbed ahold of her, shaking her, pounding her fists into her shoulders to make her wake up. Still no response. This couldn't be how it ended. They had faced the Savage Dark together and survived. Veridius took Malidora's hand in his as she continued to lie dormant on the stone. Ambrielle put more strength into it, shaking her harder. She was the awakener. Why couldn't she wake Malidora up?

The glimmer on Veridius's face turned to sadness again as he began to face the truth. "If she had only asked me, I would have done it."

Ambrielle's own realization cut into her, tearing open the wound of her mother's death. As Gavian lifted her from the ground, Ambrielle buried her head in his shoulder. Her tears in this place crystallized like stone. Why did this life have to be so unfair? The others stood nearby, their heads hung low.

"She followed her heart," said Darby as she let go of a pained breath. "She didn't believe she had anything to lose, but us."

The cavern rumbled as Ambrielle's head felt as though it would cave in. With a sudden shift, the world tilted, sending them all to the floor sliding to the wall on the other side. "Let's find a way out of here," said Gavian. "The time to properly mourn will come, but if we don't want to let her sacrifice be in vain, we have to make it out of here."

The sound of voices, screams, and cries approached from the vast dark tunnels behind them. Ambrielle held on to Gavian as the sounds grew louder, the speed of her heart rising. Veridius quickly stood, as if ready to run, but stood waiting to see what was coming toward them.

Several beings, some like them and some not, ran past them through the caverns. Ambrielle let go of Gavian, stepping against the cavern wall away from the rushing crowd.

"They made it out!" Sidairc shouted over the thunderous sounds. "Released from the mindstream!"

The crowd eventually began to thin out, and Ambrielle waved the others ahead. As the cave continued to vibrate, Darby found a small tunnel bathed in light coming from above.

She cautiously entered the space, her gaze directed upward. Attempting to ascend the tunnel, a rush of air surged through, lifting her and propelling her along the tunnel's trajectory. "Darby!" Ambrielle's voice echoed while she hastened toward the tunnel, her apprehension evident as she sought any trace of Darby's presence.

"I'm fine," said Darby, waving from above. "Come up here!"

Ambrielle eased her way into the crawlspace, and before long a gust of wind shot her through the pipe and out onto the surface. She looked down at the red scales and realized they were back on Razinoth. In the skies of Hollowspace were expanding clouds of blue and purple dust that surrounded a bright sphere of glowing energy. It was coming closer fast.

As Gavian climbed out of the vent, he came over to stand beside her as she watched. Grindak, Vazerinaz, and Zeragul were all racing toward the nearby clouds of elu spreading out from where Ilganok's body had exploded. Before they arrived, the ring of elu energy focused into a single beam, hurtling toward the world they stood on, which was Razinoth.

The people from the mindstream began pouring out of vents and other openings in the surface. Razinoth drained the remaining elu left over from Ilganok's shattered form. The ground beneath them vibrated. The pattern of scales began to stretch and grow larger. The horizon tilted as Razinoth closed in on Vazerinaz. With a powerful roar, Razinoth siphoned the elu from Vazerinaz, until nothing was left but a monstrous husk. With the connection to Ilganok severed and his elu stolen, the balance of power had shifted. With Razinoth growing in both size and power, he hunted down the other Gaith and took their elu for himself.

The shadow of Grindak enveloped them as he drew closer. Grindak's colossal form filled the entire sky when he collided with Razinoth, shaking the ground as far as they could see and sending a wave of red scales rising and falling, clicking back into place. The impact wave launched them all away from the surface and past Grindak into the dense thick liquid clouds of Hollowspace. The momentum carried them toward the dark sphere of the universe.

Ambrielle looked back as Razinoth fought off Zeragul while draining Grindak's energy. Using a swimming motion Darby guided herself ahead. Ambrielle and others tried to employ the same maneuver with their momentum as they plowed through Hollowspace. With the sounds of the battle behind her, Ambrielle pushed herself toward the dark sphere of the universe, slowly catching up to the others.

A blue cloud of swirling dust peeked out from behind the sphere, the vortex that led back to the universe. "There it is!" Ambrielle yelled out. "The vortex!"

Hundreds of others who had escaped the mindstream flew aimlessly through Hollowspace. Ambrielle slowed, allowing many of them to pass by her. "The blue tunnel is the way out!" she told them.

"We are all the power of the Gaith, united in one form!" said Razinoth, his voice tearing through Hollowspace itself, echoing all around her. "All will be under our control!"

Ambrielle felt like her aethrum body was breaking in half as a powerful force pulled her backward. She could see the others still heading toward the vortex, unaware that she was no longer with them.

"We see everything! The farthest reaches of space and the most minuscule of beings," said Razinoth, as he pulled Ambrielle toward him. His scale-covered form had grown so immense that her perception struggled to fathom it. Blotting out Hollowspace, all she could see were red scales radiating with shades of violet energy.

"You," he thundered. "The one who swims between worlds. You flit about like a pest, ceaselessly buzzing in our ear. Though your companions have forsaken you, we shall unravel your memories, unveiling everything about them. We shall unravel every ally that dared to stand by you. We will know the sanctuaries where they rest, the shadows where they seek refuge."

Panic surged through Ambrielle's veins, an urgent plea echoing in her mind. She couldn't become a pawn in Razinoth's game. If Gavian and the others were to escape the relentless pursuit, she couldn't reveal their potential hiding places.

Trapped within Razinoth's grasp, Ambrielle frantically searched for a solution. The weight of forgetting everyone and everything she held dear pressed upon her. As Razinoth pulled her ever closer to one of his many horrid red eyes, a spark of inspiration flickered in her mind.

Ambrielle peered into Niralys, locking eyes with the intricate model of the Everance it contained. If Solysta's theory held true, this immersive experience would shatter her mind, and hopefully her memories would be lost forever. Her vision began within the familiarity of her own universe, delving into the vast expanse of an interstellar void. A vast medium stretched before her, adorned with distant stars casting twinkling reflections across the cosmos. Swirling nebulae painted vibrant hues against the backdrop, giving birth to new suns and planets. Galaxies formed grand spirals and elliptical shapes, each containing billions of stars, with their own narratives of creation and destruction. Clusters of galaxies clung together in gravitational embrace, hinting at the intricate dance of celestial forces on a cosmic scale. As her sight extended, she glimpsed the intertwining filaments of cosmic web, where dark matter and energy exerted their invisible influence, shaping the very fabric of the universe.

"What is this object that beguiles you?" Razinoth said as energy focused around Niralys. Ambrielle's focus returned.

"The Everance," he said. "We must see it. We must understand its secrets."

In one of Razinoth's enormous red eyes, Ambrielle could see the images he perceived. The universe transformed into a minute point, a mere speck nestled among an infinite array of other points that dotted the expansive canvas of Hollowspace. The individual universes, each a distinct entity, now converged into an intricate mosaic of cosmic realms.

Beyond this intricate picture, the dark divisions of Erenis, the Savage Dark, emerged, flowing like black rivers demarcating the boundaries between Nulvare, Averess, and the other infinite realms. These divisions formed a lattice-like pattern, like the intricate structure of cells under a microscope. Ambrielle's perspective unveiled the profound relationship between the realms and the Savage Dark, a dynamic equilibrium that sustained the balance of existence. Some energies crossed the boundaries as the interwoven fabric of creation expanded, revealing a greater interconnectedness than Ambrielle had ever imagined.

"We believed that we'd grasped the concept of infinity," rumbled the ominous voice of Razinoth. "Yet, we stand corrected."

In Razinoth's great eye, she witnessed energy, radiance, light, darkness, life, death, and a multitude of inexplicable elements interchanging between the cells. The ceaseless flow powered the incomprehensible, propelling existence forward through endless time.

"We are but a fleeting spark," Razinoth murmured. "Adrift, devoid of significance in the boundless expanse. How can we fathom the depths of something so vast? Truly, this is an infinitude beyond comprehension."

The complexities of the Everance devolved from order to chaos as Ambrielle's mind could no longer make sense of what she was seeing. Her limited mind focused on the intricate exchange nurturing an extraordinary diversity of realms, spanning an array of mediums, universes, and an untold number of living beings within. The intricate symbiosis between all these elements was beyond human comprehension.

Without the context of harmony and symbiosis that the Ureons had impressed upon her in Averess, her mind might have drifted into insanity, losing all meaning of existence or any definition of self she had left. But she accepted her limitations. She didn't have to understand it all. She knew enough. Nothing was without importance. Every being held significance. From the tiniest to the grandest, every entity had its place in this complex, never-ending expanse.

"We thought we'd known what we were," said Razinoth, his once-mighty voice tinged with humility. "It is not the Everance, but we who embody chaos, unable to comprehend the intricate complexities that compose an ordered equilibrium. Amid vast diversity and stark differences, every element harmonizes. Each holds its distinct purpose within its immediate environment as well as within the vast expanse of the Everance. How naive were we to believe that we could govern such an infinite symbiotic harmony, or even that it relied on our intervention. Its radiant enigma is an exquisite beauty."

Ambrielle's mind reeled at what she saw in the reflections in Razinoth's eye. Truly the Everance was the grandest masterpiece of artwork that could ever be, and the replica in Niralys was only a fraction of its infinite glory.

"The memories of all those lives we have wasted," Razinoth said, with an eerie sadness to his tone. "Did they, too, serve a purpose beyond our comprehension?"

Ambrielle couldn't find the words to respond. Razinoth's humility was almost too stunning to be real, and she hesitated to speak, fearing that uttering anything might shatter the moment.

"Among the multitude of memories we have gathered, there is a recurring manifestation, a common thread that binds all living beings—a concept we mistook as a flaw because it eludes our understanding," spoke Razinoth. Thousands of visions of various beings confronted Ambrielle, her mind homing in on a few: a humanlike creature offering their fur wrappings to shield a shivering child from the cold, and another standing defiantly before a ferocious beast to protect their young. Millions of memories flashed by in seconds, and the final memory depicted Malidora entering the silver stream. She carried the nyalith full of the concentrated essence of Kandom into the mind of Ilganok and everything faded.

Ambrielle tried to hold in her sobs as she floated in Hollowspace in front of the giant eye of Razinoth. "Why do so many dismantle themselves for the sake of others?" he asked. "Countless sacrifice their own joy, they endure pain, even forfeit their own lives, all for the betterment of another."

Ambrielle now understood what Malidora must have felt in those last moments. She knew why her mother gave up her dream job traveling all over the county to capture extraordinary images. Wiping the crystallized tears from her cheeks, she tried to find her voice. "Love," said Ambrielle. "When you care about someone more than yourself, sacrifices become second nature. It doesn't feel like a sacrifice at all." Ambrielle realized that this was precisely how she felt about her family, Gavian, and the others.

And, at certain moments, he had demonstrated that he felt the same way about her. "It transcends space and time, life and death. It's like what they call eternium, a substance that persists across all realms of the Everance. Even if dawn never graced us again, love would endure in the darkness."

"And this is worth destroying yourself for?" Razinoth asked. "Is this love not destroyed too?"

"It endures in the hearts of anyone that remains," said Ambrielle, "maybe in some existence beyond this one. I guess deep down we realize there is something greater than ourselves, something worth living this life for. I don't think there is any greater purpose than to love and to be loved."

"The most potent force within the Everance," mused Razinoth, "lies in its symbiotic nature. Two distinct minds converging, not for power or dominance, but in mutual exchanges of . . . love?"

Ambrielle couldn't believe what she was hearing. "Yes, I think you are right," said Ambrielle, mustering a smile. She never had a greater appreciation of love than seeing it for the first time through this monster's eyes.

"We must understand this. We shall sacrifice our singular form and return to Erenis where we belong," said Razinoth. "We shall fulfill our purpose."

"You'll let me leave?" Ambrielle asked.

Using his vast power, Razinoth moved her across Hollowspace, placing her in front of the swirling vortex. "Return to those you love and fulfill your purpose."

Ambrielle's tears started again. "Thank you," she said, looking back once more as she rushed toward the vortex. "Wait." She turned back around. "Will your Shadows still go through the rift and try to destroy our universe?"

"Once we unite with Erenis, the vortex will stabilize," declared Razinoth. "Nothing will breach Nulvare into your universe."

It felt surreal, making Ambrielle worry she was dreaming. Without further hesitation, she plunged into the swirling clouds, into pockets of multiple tunnels. She followed the path of blue light.

Ambrielle found herself in the dark surrounded by an earthy smell and the sounds of trickling water. Several points of light aimed at her. "Amby! What happened?" Gavian hugged her before she could even see him.

"It's over," she said. "Razinoth returned to the Savage Dark, the connection between realms should stabilize now."

"Is that what he told you?" said Gavian as they moved through the cavern. They were all showing the way with their silbrace lights on. "Surely you don't believe that."

"I don't know, Gavian," said Ambrielle, as she noticed the huge pulsating crystal in the distance of the massive chamber, the apex nyalith. "I think he really meant it."

"Why would you think that?" Gavian started up a rocky incline.

"He . . . He started to understand," said Ambrielle as watery tears ran down her cheeks. "I don't even know how to explain what happened. You'll just have to believe me."

"It's okay," said Gavian. "I believe you." He moved ahead along the path as Ambrielle followed until they came to a small tunnel.

Ambrielle crawled into the tunnel. "It's going to take me a while to process all this," she said. "To fully understand everything that happened." She came out into an opening with a pool of water. Remembering this area from the last time she'd escaped The Hollow, she climbed into the pool and swam into the underground cavern that led to one of the springs. After emerging from the spring into the oasis where they last entered Valderine, hundreds of people, maybe thousands, all lay in the dry sand, resting from their ordeal in the mindstream. The sky had begun to dim as Solsellion entered twilight.

"What do we do now?" Sidaire asked. "If the Shadows are truly gone, what is left for us to do?"

"I plan on sleeping right here," said Dexius, groaning as he stretched. "I'm too tired to move."

Darby chuckled. "I may join you on that. It's been too long since I've had a good night's sleep."

"Sounds good to me," said Gavian with a yawn.

As they lay in the sand around the spring, Ambrielle stared up at the sparkling glitter of a thousand stars filling the night sky. Nebulous clouds stretched out among them. Before Ambrielle closed her eyes, she saw a shooting star flash across the sky. Its light was brilliant for a moment before it faded into the night.

CHAPTER 29

Ambrielle—Echo Solsellion

Upon waking, Ambrielle discovered Dexius and Sidaire perched on a rock by the water's edge, engaged in conversation. The darkness of Echo Solsellion enveloped everything, casting a sense of timelessness. Dexius idly tossed pebbles into the spring, the soft plinks breaking the silence. It warmed Ambrielle's heart to witness the camaraderie that had blossomed between them, a connection that seemed to hold more than just friendship.

She rose from her spot, dusting sand off her clothes with a rueful smile for choosing such an uncomfortable sleeping surface. The weight of uncertainty and possibility pressed upon her mind. What lay ahead in the uncharted territories of their futures? She considered her companions, the bonds forged through shared trials, and silently hoped that life would reward each of them with the happiness they deserved.

However, an itch for more, an unquenched thirst for one final adventure tugged at her thoughts. There was something yet to be discovered here, a final exploration that called out to her from the confines of the springs' mysteries. Yet, she hesitated, unsure if her fellow travelers would share her enthusiasm after the tumultuous events they had just endured.

She gave Gavian time to rouse from his slumber, allowing him to awaken naturally. Once he did, she joined him and settled beside him. "I want to go back to Valderine," she said.

"Why?" he inquired, rubbing his eyes with the back of his hand. "What's left there now?"

"Wegin may still be there," Ambrielle replied. "I'm not sure if he can get back on his own."

"Wegin?" Gavian questioned as he glanced past her over the endless dunes. "What about all the Ichtek and the whidges and the Nulthereals?"

"He's a part of our team," Ambrielle explained, "our family. We have to try."

"The Shadows are likely tearing apart that world by now," Gavian remarked, squinting his eyes.

"At least they haven't finished yet," said Ambrielle. "They haven't drained it all of life. The spring bed hasn't dried up like it did with Kandom. Maybe Razinoth remained true to his word."

"You're not going without me," Gavian declared, grabbing Stormwaker in its sheath as he stood.

She tilted her head playfully, allowing the breeze to catch her hair. "You're welcome to come if you would like."

Gavian smiled and shook his head. He collected his satchel, as Ambrielle went to the edge of the water where Dexius and Sidaire were talking. "Gavian and I are going back to find Wegin," she said. "We'll be back soon."

"Take some time to rest, and later we'll come with you," said Dexius as he threw another rock into the water.

"If it's too dangerous, we'll come back." She waded into the deep water and plunged in. As she surfaced, the familiar overgrown tangled mass of the Valderine forests welcomed her back. Gavian came up behind her as she used thick roots to climb out of the blue, milky water.

They made their way through the serpent path, Gavian taking her hand in his as they walked. They passed the empty camp of the Kalithor and continued to the sacred grove, surprised to find much of it still there. As they made their way up the stone steps, Ambrielle caught sight of the once-great tree, the celestial oracle, Hableides. She was now nothing more than a dried, dark husk. Her leaves blew like black smoke in the breeze. Ambrielle expected to see corpses of Ichtek and Kalithor from the battle, but none were anywhere to be found.

"Ambrielle," someone said nearby.

She and Gavian both turned to find Kalyx standing behind them.

"I wasn't sure what happened to you," Kalyx said. "I didn't see any of you among the dead."

"Are you the only one left?" Ambrielle said.

"A few of us remain," Kalyx said. "But Hableides . . ." Kalyx walked over to the tree, pressing her hand against its bark. "She is dead. All this time, I never realized that this great tree was Hableides herself."

"What happened to the Ichtek and the Nulvarians?" asked Ambrielle.

"There have been no signs of them," said Kalyx. "It's like they just vanished."

"I'm glad you and at least some of your people made it," Ambrielle said.

"I'm not sure what good it did," said Kalyx. "We've lost everything. All the knowledge of the Celestial Forest, all of the wisdom of Hableides died with the great tree."

"Not everything is lost," Ambrielle said, looking into her eyes. "Someone once said to me that you can't be told everything, some things you have to experience for yourself."

Kalyx waved her hand at Ambrielle dismissively. "This is not what I had in mind when I told you that."

"Maybe Hableides wasn't as wise as she led everyone to believe," said Ambrielle. "She thought she could control the forces of nature and everything around her. Not to your benefit, but to hers. Her pride was her undoing."

Kalyx looked up at the blackened tree. "Even if you are right that doesn't bring me any solace. I would have rather died than to have lived to see my life wasted. Hableides accumulated a wealth of knowledge over more than a thousand of our lifetimes," said Kalyx. "She had the power to travel to worlds beyond with her mind. It would be impossible for us to learn what she had learned."

"You should come back to Solsellion with us," said Ambrielle. "We can show you another way to travel to worlds across the universe. The Ureons spoke of The One, the source of all things. There is far greater wisdom to be discovered than what Hableides had to offer."

"Ambrielle!" said the distant voice of someone familiar. "I knew I would find you!"

"Wegin!" said Ambrielle. "How did you find me so quickly?"

"The tracking device you have," said Wegin.

Ambrielle rolled up her sleeve, and sure enough the small sticker she had put there on Isodonia was still on her arm. "I had forgotten that was still there."

Another one of the Kalithor pushed through the underbrush. "Ambrielle? It's good to see you. I'm sorry you came all this way for nothing. I'm afraid our destiny died with Hableides. All my life I thought this was what I was called for and now it's all gone."

"Ambrielle offered to take us with her," said Kalyx. "Perhaps we should go. The sun is dying. Without Hableides, there is nothing left for us here."

"It doesn't matter where we go," said the girl. "There is no reason for anything, no purpose to be found anywhere, I'm afraid."

"Who is to say this wasn't part of your purpose all along? I think destiny is too complex for us to ever fully understand," said Ambrielle. "Sometimes the right path is the one with the most obstacles. You should come to Solsellion. It's a place that has become a refuge for many of us who have felt lost like you do. We'll find our new path together."

❧

Ambrielle took Gavian's hand, their fingers intertwining, as they sat at a table inside the citadel built by the synthetics. One of the mech assistants replaced Wegin's cell with a fresh one. A sense of accomplishment and camaraderie tinged the atmosphere. Syra'Dosa stood near the doorway, overlooking their meeting.

"Kazial and I are going to help rebuild our village," said Sidaire as she turned to Dexius. "And I think . . ."

"I'm going to stay and help too," said Dexius, tapping his knuckles on the table. "I think Isodonia can manage for a little while without me."

Sidaire smiled at Dexius. "We can use all the help we can get."

"I should be able to get the drone factories working on my own soon," said Syra'Dosa. "Once we get a swarm of construction drones, we can build anything you want."

"I can't wait," said Sidaire. "I know you all came from different worlds, but I was hoping we could stay together and help make this your new home as well."

Ambrielle rubbed the blue jeweled necklace her mother had given her. It sounded exciting to help build new cities on Solsellion. Her imagination went wild with the possibilities of all those released from the mindstream, the former residents of Solsellion and those from other worlds, along with the Kalithor. She could see them all spreading out across this world, new cultures blossoming with them as they cultivated a new life. Some might choose to use the springs and find other worlds to live on. Ambrielle could even envision a day where those from other worlds came here, to visit, to trade, maybe even to hear the stories of what happened today. Solsellion as the new heart of the universe. Yet, Ambrielle's own heart wanted to be with her family. She needed them right now, as much as they needed her. "I'm sorry, Sidaire, but I need to get home, back to Earth," said Ambrielle, "to my family. It's time I figured out my own future."

"What kind of future are you hoping to have there?" Sidaire asked.

After his cell replacement was complete, Wegin zoomed over to Ambrielle, hovering nearby. "Well, I've always enjoyed seeing new things and exploring new places," Ambrielle said. "Maybe I will try photography like my mother did. Traveling around the world, and maybe eventually other worlds, taking pictures of landscapes and scenery, people, and animals."

"I'm sure that will be fun," Sidaire said with a smile, though a subtle shadow crossed her expression. "You should come back here and take some pictures of our new village once it's built."

"I definitely will," said Ambrielle. "I'll come and visit whenever I can."

"Is there room for anyone else in that future?" Gavian asked.

Ambrielle grinned. She had been fearful about asking him if he wanted to come with her to live on Earth for a while. His question was like a huge weight removed from her shoulders. "I might be able to squeeze in one more," she said. "As long as they can open up about their problems from the start so I can support them. And they would have to always be there to support me with mine."

Gavian glanced at his hands resting on the table. "I can do that."

"I'm going to be spending a lot of time with my family on Earth," said Ambrielle nervously as she looked at him. "The majority of the time in fact. Are you sure you can commit to something like that?" As much as she wanted him with her, she wanted to be sure it was by his own choice and not out of a feeling of obligation.

"Wherever you are," said Gavian, "is where I want to be."

Ambrielle leaned over and wrapped her arms around him. "I was hoping you would say that!" she said excitedly. "I think you are going to like it. There's so many things I want to show you, so many things I want to see myself, and we can do it all together. But . . . I'm not sure how much you would be willing to give up. For starters, a sword like Stormwaker probably wouldn't have a place in my world. Consider everything before you make a decision."

Sidaire looked at Ambrielle. "With all the new people here," she said, "we need to establish some kind of system, some rules. The refugees from the mindstream don't feel they are mentally ready to take on something like this. They want someone who freed them, one of us, to lead them into this new future. We were hoping, since you led us well before, you would do it again."

Ambrielle could hardly imagine all of these people taking her seriously as their leader, but it made her proud that anyone would ask. "Any one of us can be leaders," said Ambrielle. "Look at all we've accomplished."

"I've led people in battle," Dexius said to Ambrielle, "but I know nothing of managing cities or leading the planning of new buildings. Especially not to make rules."

"Neither do I. I'm honored that you thought of me, but I can't stay here forever." Ambrielle looked around at all of them—the Kalithor, those from the mindstream, and her friends. She felt that she was letting them down. Suddenly, she had an epiphany. An idea that made so much sense she could hardly believe no one else realized it. "But there is someone that I think would be far better suited for this," Ambrielle said. "He's been raised to lead his entire life and was a prominent leader in the capitol city of his world. At times, he has been the glue that held us together. Mediating our arguments, helping us keep our emotions in check, making sure everyone had what they need. I think he would be a great choice, if he would be willing to do it."

Everyone turned and looked at Veridius as he sat quietly by himself at the end of the table. "You mean me?" Veridius glanced up. "Thank you, Ambrielle. But I don't think they would want someone like me. I grew up in luxury all of my life. They need one among them, someone that understands what they have been through, and I would be honored to assist whoever is chosen."

"You would be perfect Veridius!" said Sidaire as she grabbed his shoulders. "You, of all of us, understand what we have gone through on Solsellion. Kazial and I lost our villages and everyone on it, and you lost your entire world. It was you who kept us all together despite our differences. With so many from Solsellion from different villages and so many from other worlds, that is exactly what we need. Please, if you would stay with us, show us how to rebuild for the sake of both Solsellion and Kandom."

Veridius's face beamed as he took a deep breath. "I gladly accept."

Ambrielle felt compelled to clap; her heart flowed with happiness for Veridius. The others joined her applause while Veridius pressed his lips together, as if trying to hold in his emotion.

"What about you, Darby?" said Sidaire.

Dexius leaned toward Darby. "You're going to stay here with us, right?"

Darby eyed the faces around the table, seeming unsure how to begin whatever she was about to say. Ambrielle could already tell she was going to say something unexpected. She could see in Darby's eyes that something had changed her through all of this.

Darby cleared her throat. "Ever since I discovered there are worlds above the clouds of Isodonia, worlds with people like us, with the same struggles and doubts that we have, other places that were destroyed by the Shadows or the Ichtek that we never heard of, I've wondered if maybe there are others out there who need help and maybe they too could come to learn about what you are building. It doesn't matter if they come here to stay. There are other vibrant worlds out here waiting. With Solsellion as a hub to worlds across the universe, I want to show them. I want to help them find a new beginning."

"That is an amazing idea, Darby," Sidaire said, "but one that would be extremely challenging."

"You're going to do this all by yourself?" said Dexius with a disbelieving look on his face.

"At first," said Darby. "But as time goes on, if I am able to help anyone, maybe they will join me."

"Will you still come back here from time to time?" Dexius asked.

"I definitely will," Darby said with a smile.

"You shouldn't go alone," said Ambrielle. "You need an assistant. If he is willing, you should take Wegin with you. I'm not sure if he would fit in on Earth. They're not quite ready for something like him yet."

"I'm not sure anyone is," Gavian quipped as Ambrielle playfully smacked his hand.

"I did enjoy Darby's company, just as much as yours Ambrielle," said Wegin. "If she needs my assistance, I would be glad to join her again."

Darby's cheeks gained a pink hue as she smiled. "I would be grateful for your assistance, Wegin."

Wegin's lights moved in a circular pattern around him. "Then we are off to save the universe! While everyone is here, let me bid you all, good—"

"Goodbye, Wegin, I will miss you," Ambrielle interrupted, making sure he used the right expression. "Take good care of yourself and Darby."

"Yes, goodbye everyone," said Wegin as he flashed his blue lights. "And good riddance!"

Ambrielle's hand met her forehead with an exasperated exhale, but a chuckle betrayed her amusement.

"Are you sure he doesn't do that on purpose?" said Gavian, shaking his head. "I think he does it on purpose."

"Before you go . . ." Gavian stood up from his chair and moved around the others to where Darby sat. He removed his sheath, handing both the sheath and Stormwaker to Darby. "Take this with you too."

Darby stood up, shaking her head. "No, the sword is yours. I'm not going to take it."

"It should be yours," said Gavian. "It belonged to your family. It was always meant for you. You can be a Stormwaker for the universe."

"I can't Gavian," said Darby, as she put her hand in front of her mouth. "I wouldn't want to see it in anyone else's hands but yours."

"Keep it safe for me then," he said, still holding the sheath as he wrapped his arms around her. "If I ever need it again you can pass it back to me."

Darby exhaled as she let him go, holding out her hand reluctantly. "You had better come to Solsellion and visit me when I am here, both of you."

"That's a promise," said Ambrielle as she stood and embraced Darby. She envied her in a way. Exploring unknown worlds all over the universe and helping others sounded amazing, but she was happy with her choice. Ambrielle imagined coming back one day and joining Darby on a new quest, but now wasn't the right time for that. She was glad that, in the meantime, Darby would fill this role.

Gavian made his way to Sidaire, tentatively reaching his hand to her shoulder, as if he expected her to draw away from him. "I regret not doing more when you were hurt. I hope I can make it up to you someday."

Sidaire warmly replied, "Gavian, you've done more than you know. We're a team, and I couldn't ask for better friends." She reached up, hugging him tightly.

Ambrielle moved over to Dexius, reaching over to hug him as he stood and drew her in. "We've been through so much together that I feel like I've known you my whole life," she said. "You, Sidaire, Kazial, Veridius, Darby, and Malidora will always be in my thoughts."

"Next time you come to Solsellion, it will be thriving," said Dexius. "We'll continue what you started."

Gavian came up behind her as she let go of Dexius. He stood there for a moment while both he and Dexius looked at each other with blank expressions. As if no longer able to hold it in, Gavian cracked a smile. "Can you believe Rethia called *us* the outcasts? If nothing else, we'll always be Descender brothers."

"How about just brothers?" Dexius retorted, giving Gavian a friendly pat on the shoulder. Gavian's hand twitched, ready to respond with a good-natured punch, but Dexius was quick to turn the motion into an unexpected embrace, pulling Gavian into a tight hug.

Ambrielle removed Niralys from her wrist. She handed it to Sidaire. "Put this in a safe place, somewhere that no one can look into the jewel."

"What is it?" Sidaire asked, mesmerized by the colorful reflections it cast around the room.

"Something to remember Malidora by," said Ambrielle. "She might have had the most difficult destiny of all of us. And still she chose to accept it and fulfill her purpose in the end."

Veridius nodded at her words, while the others saluted or bowed in respect to Malidora's sacrifice.

"We will display it high, and proudly," said Sidaire as she held it above her head.

After a moment of quiet reverence, Veridius made his way to Darby. "Your quest sounds like an extraordinary adventure, Darby," said Veridius. "I admire the courage it takes to embark on such a journey. Have you given any thought to where you are going?"

Darby glanced at the perfectly smoothed stone attached to her silbrace. "First I have to return something," she said, "to a friend."

CHAPTER 30

DARBY—ELYRAVESS

DARBY PULLED HER wet hair back as Wegin followed along across the ocean platform. The sun hung low in the sky, casting long shadows on the beach below. They reached the striped wisps of grass on the hill that led to the grand cityscape, voices nearby catching her attention.

"Nothing is going to happen," said a girl with a reassuring voice, as she and a young man walked along the beach. The girl reached her arms up toward the sky as if trying to touch the fading hues of the setting sun. "I'm telling you, it's finally over." Darby paused and watched from the platform while they stood on the shore.

"We shouldn't go too far," the boy said with uncertainty in his tone. He continued to survey their surroundings. "We have to be sure. If we let the whole world shake apart now, it would all have been for nothing."

"Do you think I would be here if I weren't sure?" the girl asked. Her voice carried a certain weight to it. "This breach connects to so many others. If this one destroys Elyravess, there's a chance it could do the same to every world it reaches."

They were both different species but neither quite human. The girl had long blonde hair and orange skin. Her face was nearly human, but from this distance Darby couldn't tell what made her different.

The boy anxiously wrung his hands. "You have a strange way of comforting someone," he remarked.

He had long ears that stood upright, and his hair was dark and fuzzy.

The girl stepped in front of him, her gaze unwavering as she faced him. "You know that I take this every bit as seriously as you do," she said firmly.

Darby put her finger over her mouth, hoping to convey to Wegin not to say anything. She knew she shouldn't listen in on their conversation, but something compelled her to understand what they were talking about.

The boy continued to voice his doubts. "What changed?" he wondered aloud. "After all this time?"

"I told you it would eventually happen," the girl responded with confidence. "I knew that she would be the one."

"You didn't know for sure," he countered.

She leaned in closer to him, their faces mere inches apart. "I carved her name in stone," the girl declared. The image of the white stone near the ocean cavern flashed into Darby's head.

His skepticism remained. "You carved a lot of names in that stone, and you've been wrong about all of the others." The names of Ambrielle, Gavian, and Malidora were carved into that stone tablet. Was that the one they were talking about?

"The names were only variables," she explained, "the ones I saw in the rift. I knew it would be her."

"You've said the same thing about others before her," the boy pointed out.

"This time was different," she insisted. "I know what I saw."

The boy nodded, conceding, "Maybe you are right. It should have started by now."

"I know I'm—" The girl looked up as she spoke. Darby turned around to see what she was looking at. A bright streak of light was coming toward them. It steadily grew until it landed in a patch of grass nearby. Avo'Doria stood, folding her wings made of light around her body.

"Darby," said Avo'Doria. "It is good to see you again. Did you come to return the silcron? Do we need to evaluate a different strategy?"

Darby pulled the silcron from her silbrace. "The Gaith are no more," she said. "Everything that I experienced should be recorded." She extended her hand, offering the silcron to Avo'Doria.

Avo'Doria glanced past Darby at the boy and girl, who had now walked closer to them. They appeared as curious about Darby and Avo'Doria as Darby had been about them. "Hello," said Avo'Doria with her slightly modulated voice.

The boy and girl looked at each other and then back to Darby, Avo'Doria, and Wegin.

"I was not expecting to see anyone else here," said Avo'Doria. "Welcome to Elyravess. You must be the new arrivals we have been waiting for."

"Arrivals?" said the girl. "What do you mean?"

"You just arrived on Elyravess didn't you?" said Avo'Doria. "Though your faces both appear very familiar."

"I've been on Elyravess my whole life," said the boy. "We've both been here so long. I don't even know how long it's been."

"Yet, you appear quite lost," said Avo'Doria.

"I think this must be a different time period." The girl glanced at the boy.

"Then you are our next arrivals," said Avo'Doria. "I am Avo'Doria. We have been preparing this world for you." Avo'Doria stared at them both for a moment. "I'm certain that I recognize your faces." Avo'Doria stepped closer, running a grid of light across the girl's face. "You're the ones from the cave! Hegane and Lyleth!"

Darby drew back in surprise as she now recognized them from the apparitions they had seen in the ocean caves. How were they here now in physical bodies?

"How do you know us?" asked Hegane as he and Lyleth looked at each other. They seemed to be as confused as Darby.

"I made daily visits to the sea caves," Avo'Doria explained. "I could hear your voices and catch glimpses of your images. It intrigued me, and I tried to piece together your story."

Lyleth's eyes widened. "I had no idea our voices reached anyone."

"You manifested as mere images, detectable only by my visual and aural sensors," Avo'Doria clarified. "I've been trying to make sense of it. Were you sending messages of your impending arrival?"

"We didn't intentionally send messages," Lyleth replied. "It might be some kind of temporal anomaly."

"You must come with me to the city," Avo'Doria said. "As our new arrivals, it is all yours to do with as you please, but first we must validate your status. I need to introduce you to the other sentinels."

As Avo'Doria led them over a small rise, the girl stopped in front of Darby. "I've seen you before," she said. "You defended the rifts against the Shadows."

Darby was stunned. How could they have seen her? "I played a part, along with others," Darby acknowledged.

"This is Darby," Avo'Doria introduced. "She has been instrumental in saving our universe."

"You're an arrival too, then," Hegane noted. "You should join us."

"I didn't intend to stay for long," Darby stated. As intriguing as this was, she was anxious to get started on her new journey.

"Why don't you come visit with us for awhile before you leave?" suggested Lyleth. "We have many questions."

As they moved up the hill, the enormous city unfolded before their eyes. Giant structures reached up into the sky, pathways made of red light crisscrossed over themselves in ordered rows and columns, and the air was filled with flying craft moving in all directions. Among the structures were perfectly trimmed trees, bushes, and grass, in various colors, shapes, and sizes. Darby saw the vast cityscape again for the first time through the eyes of Hegane and Lyleth. "This isn't the Elyravess I knew," said Hegane with an expression of wonder.

Lyleth turned to Avo'Doria. "It reminds me a bit of home." She put her arm around Hegane. "It's like Elyravess and Cerevesh combined!"

"Everything has left us behind," said Hegane, his excitement turning sour. "How can we start over in a world we have no place in?"

Lyleth leaned on his shoulder. "I know. It is quite overwhelming. I'm grateful that we have each other."

Darby followed them as they moved to one of the pathways made of red light. Even while the activity of the mektrons and drones buzzed around her, she barely noticed. Her thoughts soared with questions to ask Hegane and Lyleth. She wanted to understand what all they had gone through to arrive at this moment. She thought of her friends on Solsellion as they planned to rebuild Sidaire's village. Gavian and Ambrielle would be heading to Earth by now. It seemed everyone had begun their next adventure except for her.

She glanced at Wegin as the faint moon hung in the pale-yellow sky behind him, staring at a distant cloud. For a brief moment, she felt a connection, as if noticing another soul staring at the same cloud. Darby was anxious to start on her new journey, to explore all the springs of Echo Solsellion and discover unknown worlds. She wanted to make a difference for good in the universe, but sometimes it's important to recognize the current moment you are placed in, the biggest impact you can make might be right before your eyes.

Elyravess would make an invaluable resource for comprehending the intricacies of new worlds and diverse cultures that Darby might encounter. Avo'Doria seemed likely to offer assistance, and perhaps even Lyleth and Hegane would be interested in contributing. If they were feeling out of place, providing them with a sense of purpose could be the key. Without her realizing it, Darby's new journey had already begun.

CHAPTER 31

AMBRIELLE—ECHO SOLSELLION

OMINOUS SHADOWS DISSIPATED from the corners of Ambrielle's mind. Whispers of empowerment echoed through her soul. The last images of the warm blue glow, radiating from a swirling vortex, imprinted a sense of triumph on her consciousness. Ambrielle sat amidst vibrant blossoms; this lush haven mirrored the victory over the struggles they had faced. It was alive with the friends who had walked the journey with her.

In the midst of this vibrant sanctuary, majestic trees stood tall, their leaves a kaleidoscope of colors, dancing joyfully in the gentle breeze across the crystal-clear spring. Beyond the oasis, the horizon unfolded with endless promises of the future. A landscape transformed, barren deserts now blooming with hope, windswept dunes replaced by paths of growth, and cliffs of rock softened into a terrain of weathered wisdom.

For what felt like an eternity, she had navigated a path of self-discovery, overcoming the shadows that once clouded her spirit. The memories of her journey formed a shield of resilience, and the emptiness that once burdened her heart had been replaced by the warmth of connection.

Among this natural beauty, Ambrielle lifted her head confidently, surrounded by the laughter and camaraderie of those who had become her chosen family. The chains of loneliness and fear had been broken, replaced by a bond forged through shared experiences. Her heart, once heavy with doubt, now beat with the rhythm of courage.

Ambrielle knew she was not alone. Her friends, along with those freed from the mindstream, joined by the Kalithor, had all found a place they could call their own. Beings of all kinds inhabited the once desolate land, drawn to this world through shared understanding and compassion. Ambrielle's heart rejoiced, knowing that the world she had helped transform reflected the love that had been cultivated within her.

As she gazed toward the horizon, she saw not an end but an endless beginning. The future stretched before her like an open book, each page waiting to be written with tales of love, growth, and the possibilities that awaited. With a heart filled with gratitude and a spirit free from the shackles of the past, Ambrielle couldn't wait to share the light she had found with others on their journey.

After waving to Dexius, Sidaire, Veridius, Kazial, and Syra'Dosa, Ambrielle and Gavian made their way toward the waters of the spring. The large stone where she used to sit lay at the water's edge. Something peculiar sitting on top of the stone caught her attention. As Ambrielle moved closer, the realization of what the object was crept in, causing her to let out a loud gasp. A chill went through her fingertips as she touched it. She could barely take her eyes off it, afraid it would vanish if she even blinked. It was utterly impossible for it to be sitting here in this spot, and yet, there it sat, as though deliberately placed by someone who knew she would discover it.

Ambrielle gently picked up Malidora's crossbow from the stone. Underneath it, the familiar warning, "BEWARE THE HOLLOW" was scratched into the rock, its message no longer as ominous as it once was. A tender smile formed as her heart brimmed with both joy and relief. The crossbow held a promise, a promise that she would one day be reunited, not only with Malidora but with her mother as well.

Gavian held her hand as they stood at the edge of the spring connecting Solsellion to Earth. In the water's reflection, Ambrielle saw two people who had faced the storms of life, been engulfed by its tribulations, and emerged as something stronger, wiser. While the sword with the costly ability to save others from death had been destroyed, true immortality had not been lost. It would be found in a timeless legacy etched in the boundless echoes of their collective journeys and the profound impact they had on the lives of those they touched. Ambrielle and Gavian dove into the cold waters of the spring together as the future stretched out before them, a vast and uncharted expanse of possibilities.

THE END

THANKS FOR READING!

If you enjoyed reading Eternium, I would greatly appreciate it if you could take a moment to leave a review on Amazon. Your feedback helps other readers discover the book and is invaluable to me as an author. Thank you for your support!

ACKNOWLEDGEMENTS

I would like to begin by expressing my gratitude to God for providing me with the strength, guidance, and inspiration to complete this book. Without His blessings, this accomplishment would not have been possible.

To my family, who have always been my pillars of support and encouragement throughout my life, thank you for standing by me every step of the way. Your belief in me has been a constant source of motivation and inspiration.

To my friends, thank you for your unwavering support, your kind words, and your valuable feedback. Your presence in my life has enriched me in ways I cannot express.

I would like to extend my deepest gratitude to Emily Katzenberger for her unwavering support and encouragement throughout the creation of this book. Her invaluable insights and unwavering belief in my abilities pushed me to strive for excellence and make this book the best it could be. Thank you, Emily, for being a constant source of inspiration and motivation.

Once again, thank you to all those who have contributed to the creation of this book. Your support and encouragement have meant the world to me.

ABOUT THE AUTHOR

Author Kevin Cox has always been fascinated by the splendor of the universe and the mysteries it holds, using his imagination to fill in the vast unknown. Though he never planned to be a writer, he often had ideas for stories playing in his head. After deciding to write a single chapter to see if he could do it, he discovered a love for writing he never knew was there.

Much of his inspiration comes from growing up during the 80's, reading and watching all the fantasy and science fiction stories he could find. Ideas come to him during long drives or while listening to music. He often listens to music while writing, especially songs that match the mood he is trying to capture.

He believes that a good story needs great characters that each have struggles and desire to find ways to overcome them. Kevin hopes that his readers will see their own struggles in these characters and are inspired to find their own strengths and always be learning and improving to be the best version of themselves. Connection with friends and willingness to help others are central themes in his writing.

Kevin lives in southwest Georgia in a small town called Leesburg. When he isn't writing, he enjoys playing guitar and video games.

Please contact or follow me on social media.

for the latest news and info on the next book in the series.

Email: authorkevincox@gmail.com

Instagram: @kevincoxauthor

Twitter: @authorkevincox

OTHER BOOKS IN THE BEWILDERNESS SERIES

Bewilderness: Book One, Shadowsphere, Neverscape, and Stormwaker

Available on Amazon.com *https://www.amazon.com/dp/B09J3Z9J2F*

Named one of the BEST BOOKS OF 2022 by Kirkus Reviews

"This meticulously crafted YA journey will challenge readers' expectations until the last page."

— Kirkus Reviews (starred review)

When a young girl wakes up in an unknown world and encounters dark forces that threaten the universe, only she can change its destiny.

Accessing portals to other realms, Ambrielle journeys across multiple worlds as she searches for answers to find her way home.

Sixteen-year-old Ambrielle has no memory of her life. In fact, she doesn't even know if her name is Ambrielle, the name her new alien friend gave her when she woke up mysteriously stranded in a desolate world with no humans. As she slowly cobbles together bits and pieces of her life, Ambrielle tries to fit in with the many alien species she encounters and settle their divisive conflicts, all while eluding shadowy entities from a realm beyond the universe as she seeks a way to return to Earth.

www.ingramcontent.com/pod-product-compliance
Lightning Source LLC
Chambersburg PA
CBHW020609310726
48979CB00008B/1402/J

* 9 7 9 8 9 9 0 9 5 4 8 1 6 *